Aeneas Anderson

A Narrative of the British Embassy to China in the Years 1792, 1793 and 1794

containing the various circumstances of the embassy, with accounts of customs and manners of the Chinese and a description of the country, towns, cities

Aeneas Anderson

A Narrative of the British Embassy to China in the Years 1792, 1793 and 1794
*containing the various circumstances of the embassy, with accounts of customs and manners
of the Chinese and a description of the country, towns, cities*

ISBN/EAN: 9783337238346

Printed in Europe, USA, Canada, Australia, Japan

Cover: Foto ©Andreas Hilbeck / pixelio.de

More available books at **www.hansebooks.com**

A

NARRATIVE

OF THE

BRITISH EMBASSY

TO

CHINA,

IN THE YEARS 1792, 1793, AND 1794.

A NARRATIVE

OF THE

BRITISH EMBASSY

TO

CHINA,

IN THE YEARS 1792, 1793, AND 1794;

CONTAINING

THE VARIOUS CIRCUMSTANCES OF THE EMBASSY,

WITH ACCOUNTS OF

CUSTOMS AND MANNERS OF THE CHINESE;

AND A DESCRIPTION OF THE

COUNTRY, TOWNS, CITIES, &c. &c.

By ÆNEAS ANDERSON,

THEN IN THE SERVICE OF HIS EXCELLENCY EARL MACARTNEY, K. B. AMBASSADOR FROM THE KING OF GREAT BRITAIN TO THE EMPEROR OF CHINA.

LONDON:
PRINTED FOR J. DEBRETT, OPPOSITE BURLINGTON-HOUSE, PICCADILLY.

1795.

PREFACE.

AN embassy to China was a new event in the diplomatic history of this country, and very naturally excited a general curiosity concerning it : for, without considering the great commercial objects it had in view, the universal ignorance which prevailed respecting the interior parts of that empire, and the consequent novelty which must be produced by any authentic history of it, would irresistibly attract the attention of our enlightened country, to the only civilised nation in the world, whose jealous laws forbid the intrusion of any other people.

It is not my design to examine those writers who have preceded me on the subject of China : it is not for me to point out their contradictions, or display their fabulous interpo-

interpolations—my only bufinefs is to relate what I faw in the courfe of this embaffy, in every part of which I had the honour to attend Lord Macartney, who was appointed to be the reprefentative of his Britannic Majefty at the Court of Pekin.

The difadvantages which opprefs the trade of European countries with China are well known, and to remove them in behalf of our own, was an object well worthy the attentive wifdom of our government. It was not, however, a mere fpeculative project; as a fufficient intimation had been made to the Court of London, that an Ambaffador from thence would be gracioufly received by the Emperor of China: minifters, therefore, acted with a ftrict political attention to the commercial interefts of this country, by preparing an embaffy, fuited to the dignity of the Court of Great Britain, and fitted out in a manner to attract the attention of the Chinefe people, as well as to command the refpect, and fecure the regard of the Court of Pekin.

The Honourable Colonel Cathcart was, accordingly, invefted, in the year 1788, with the important character of minifter from this country to the Empire of China; a man whofe fuperior talents, amiable manners, fhrewd fagacity and active perfeverance qualified him, in a pre-eminent degree, to forward the important objects of his miffion: but

the

the premature death of that able, excellent, and accomplished man, which happened on his voyage, thwarted the progress of the embassy he was appointed to conduct; and as no person had been named in the King's commission, to succeed to his diplomatic office, if he should not reach the place of his destination, that embassy died with him; and may be said to have been buried on the distant shore where his ashes repose.

The wise attentions of government were not, however, to be turned aside from such an important, national object as a commercial alliance between the Courts of London and Pekin: the character of Ambassador to China was accordingly revived, with additional splendor, in the person of Earl Macartney; and an embassy was re-appointed in such a manner as became the empire it was to represent—and the empire before which it was to appear.

It is impossible to speak in higher terms of the anxious care and liberal attention of government to this diplomatic mission than it deserves. The superior talents which direct the board of controul, and the commercial spirit which animates the direction of the East India Company, combined to form those arrangements which certainly deserved success, if they did not obtain it. No narrow, or sordid views, mingled with the preparations of it: the means of exterior figure, and the allurements of

I

national

A Steward, and an under ditto,
2 Valets de Chambre,
A Cook,
2 Couriers,
A Footman,
A Baker,
A Band of 6 Muficians,
A Carpenter and Joiner,
A Saddler,
A Gardener,
A Taylor,
A Watchmaker,
A Mathematical Inftrument-maker.

Belonging to Sir G. Staunton:

2 Servants   1 Gardener.

Which, with Mr. Crewe's Valet de Chambre, formed the whole of the domeftic eftablifhment, except three natives of China, who went out with us from England.

The Military Eftablifhment, or Guards, confifted of

20 Men of the Royal Artillery;
10 Ditto 11th Light Dragoons;
20 Ditto drafted from the additional Companies of Infantry, at Chatham.

The Ships which were employed to take the Embaffy to China, were

The Lion, of 64 guns, Sir Erafmus Gower, Commander;
The Hindoftan Eaft Indiaman, Capt. William Mackintofh, Commander; and
The Jackall brig for a tender, manned by officers and men from the Lion.

Lift of the Officers on Board his Majefty's Ship Lion.

Sir Erafmus Gower, Knight, Commander;
Mr. Cambell, 1ft. Lieutenant;
Mr. Whitman, 2d. ditto;

Mr.

M. Atkins, 3d. ditto;
Mr. Cox, 4th. ditto——died at Chufan;
Mr. Ommaney, acting Lieutenant;
Mr. Jackfon, Mafter of the Lion;
Mr. Saunders, Mafter's-mate;
Mr. Tippett, ditto;
Mr. Simes, ditto (difmiffed from the fhip at Batavia);
Mr. Lowe, ditto;
Mr. Roper, ditto;
Mr. Warren, ditto (fon of Dr. Warren, Phyfician to his Majefty, and the Prince of Wales), promoted to be acting Lieutenant;
Mr. Kent;
Mr. Chapman, (appointed Gunner, vice Corke, deceafed).

Midfhipmen.

Right Hon. Lord Mark Kerr, (fon of the Marquis Lothian), promoted to be acting Lieutenant;
Hon. Wm. Stuart, (fon of the Earl Bute);
Mr. Bromely,
Mr. Swinbourne,
Mr. Kelly,
Mr. Dilkes,
Mr. Trollope,
Mr. Heywood,
Mr. Hickey,
Mr. Thompfon,
Mr. Waller, (died at Wampoa);
Mr. Beaumont, (returned home from Angara Point, for the recovery of his health);
Mr. Snipe,
Mr. Wools,
Mr. Montague,
Mr. Chambers,
Mr. Scott,
Mr. Bridgeman,

Mr. Perkins,
Mr. Sarradine.

Mr. Tothill, Purfer, (died at Cochin China) ;
Mr. Weft, Captain's Clerk ;
Mr. Nutt, Surgeon ;
Mr. Anderfon, Chief-mate ;
Mr. Cooper, 2d. ditto ;
Mr. Thomas, 3d. ditto ;
Mr. Humphries, Schoolmafter.

CONTENTS.

C 2

rangements

C H A P. XIV.

C H A P. XV.

C H A P. XVI.

C H A P.

C H A P. XX.

C H A P. XXI.

C H A P. XXII.

C H A P. XXIII.

C H A P.

C H A P. XXIV.

C H A P. XXV.

SUPPLEMENTARY CHAPTER.

NARRATIVE OF A VOYAGE

TO AND FROM

CHINA, &c. &c.

CHAP. I.

From England to Batavia.

EVERY neceſſary arrangement having been made, the Right Hon. Earl Macartney, with his whole ſuite, went, from the Point at Portſmouth, in ſeveral barges, on board the Lion man of war, then lying at Spithead.

Hoiſted in the launch—fired the ſignal gun for all the officers and men on ſhore to repair on board.

At eleven A. M. a ſignal was made for the Hindoſtan and the Jack-all to weigh : the Alfred and Orion of ſeventy-four guns weighed at the ſame time ; and, at five o'clock in the afternoon, we took our final departure from Spithead.

We got into Torbay, where we found the Hannibal and Niger men of war. Sir George and Mr. Staunton, with Dr. Gillan, went aſhore, and penetrated into the country as far as Exeter ; from whence they returned the next day.

1792.

Friday,
Sept. 21.

Sunday 23.

Tueſday 25.

Saturday 29.

B

A leak

A leak was repaired that had fprung in the fide of the Lion.

We made land at an early hour of this morning; and at eight faw the Deferter's Ifland at the diftance of about four leagues; and the ifland of Porto Santo at the diftance of about three leagues. Thefe iflands are fubject to the crown of Portugal, and form a part of the Madeiras: the latter of them is chiefly appropriated as a place of exile for thofe who commit any petty depredations on the ifland of Madeira. It is about fifteen miles in circumference, and very mountainous: it contains no harbours; but has a large bay wherein fhips may be tolerably fecure, except when the wind blows from the fouthweft; and is frequented by Indiamen outward and homeward bound. The ifland produces corn, but in no great quantity; it has alfo pafturage for cattle; and its thickets furnifh fhelter for wild boars. The inhabitants, who are few in number, are fubject to the government of Madeira. The Defart, or Deferter's Ifland, is an inconfiderable barren rock, and ferves alfo as a prifon for criminals, who are there obliged to pay the penance of their offences by various kinds of labour.

We arrived in Funchal Bay, in the ifland of Madeira, and anchored in forty-four fathom water; the town of Funchal being to the N. N. E. about a mile.

After breakfaft, Lieutenant Campbell was fent on fhore to the governor of the Madeiras, to notify the arrival of Lord Macartney; and, on the return of that officer, the Lion faluted the garrifon with thirteen guns, which was immediately returned. The Britifh Conful then came on board, attended by feveral Englifh gentlemen, among whom were the moft refpectable merchants of the place, to pay their refpects to the Ambaffador, and to invite him afhore.

His Lordfhip having accepted of the invitation, the fhip's company were ordered to get themfelves clean dreffed in white jackets and trowfers as preparatory for manning the yards: and, as I publifh this Narrative, not merely for the ufe of feamen, but for the entertainment,

ment, and, as I hope, for the information of thofe who know nothing 1792.
of maritime life, I fhall endeavour to explain what is underftood by Oct.
manning the yards; a ceremonial never obferved but on particular
occafions, as well as in honour of diftinguifhed characters, and has
not only a very peculiar, but, in fome degree, a very beautiful effect.
The fhip's company being all equipped in their beft cloathing, the
failors ftand upright on the yard-arms, as clofe to each other as the
fituation will admit, with their hands clafped together, and their arms
extended; ropes being drawn acrofs, to prevent them from falling.
In this curious manner the whole yards of the fhip are filled with men
up to the main-top-gallant royal. In this pofition the fhip's company
remained, till Lord Macartney had landed on the ifland.

On this occafion the matroffes were drawn up under arms on the
larboard fide of the quarter-deck, and the marines on the ftarboard
fide, lining both fides of the deck, as far as the accommodation ladder.
The troops faluted his Lordfhip as he paffed from the cabin, and the
band of mufic continued playing till he had left the fhip. Lord
Macartney and Sir Erafmus Gower proceeded in one barge, and the
gentlemen of the fuite followed in another. The Lion then fired a
falute of fifteen guns, which was anfwered by the fame number from
the fort on fhore. On this occafion every mark of mutual refpect was
paid, while the Governor of Madeira, with the Britifh Conful and the
principal inhabitants, were ready at the landing-place to welcome the
Ambaffador on his arrival at the ifland.

I went on fhore this morning after breakfaft, with feveral of the Saturday 13.
midfhipmen, and landed at Brazen-head rock. Oppofite to this
landing-place ftands a rock called the Loo, in which there is a pretty
ftrong fort, furrounded with a rampart, mounted with feveral pieces
of cannon, and garrifoned with foldiers. This rock is in the form of a
pillar, being very high, perpendicular on all fides, and commands the
bay: the only entrance to the fort is by a narrow flight of fteps hewn out
of the rock, and properly guarded. It is fituated about three quarters of

B 2 a mile

a mile from the fhore, and in water of near forty fathom, fo that there can be no communication with the land but by means of boats. The landing-place of the ifland is to the north-weft of the Loo rock, and from the depth of the fea, which, at the water's edge, is fifteen fathom, the violence of the furf and the rocky fhore, is extremely dangerous. Steps are formed in the rock to afcend to the top of it, which communicate with the road to Funchal, the principal town of the ifland.

This road is very rough and narrow, being no more than four feet and an half in breadth, with a low wall on either fide. It firft leads to an high afcent, on each fide of which are a few unenviable dwellings of the lower clafs of inhabitants. On the fuccceding declivity is a fmall church, in the front of which there is an altar and a crofs, which is fuppofed to poffefs fome healing powers of peculiar efficacy, as we faw feveral poor wretches afflicted with various difeafes, lying naked there, and expofing their bodies covered with fores and blotches. The church has fo little the appearance of any thing like a place dedicated to the worfhip of God, that, till I perceived the crofs, which was its diftinguifhing decoration, it appeared to me to be a barn or ftable; at the fame time I was informed, that the infide of it was very properly fitted up and furnifhed for the facred purpofe to which it was dedicated. Its fituation is beautiful beyond defcription : it ftands in a very elevated pofition, commands a very grand and extenfive view of the fea, with Porto Santo and the Deferter's Ifland ; overlooking, at the fame time, the charming vineyards in its own immediate vicinity. Many delightful gardens are feen on either fide of the road, abounding in delicious fruits; and, on the northern fide of it, the vineyards ftretch away to the extremity of the rock, which poffeffes a perpendicular height of feveral hundred feet above the fea.

About half a mile beyond the church is the entrance to the town of Funchal, through a gate, from whence a mean, dirty, narrow ftreet leads to a public walk difpofed in the form of a garden, which has a

principal

principal alley or avenue in the center, with orange and other trees on either fide of it, and lamps placed between them: the whole is terminated by the cathedral church, a large Gothic building, which is fitted up in a very fuitable manner for the purpofes of that religion to which it is confecrated.

I went after breakfaft to the houfe of the Britifh Conful, which is in the neighbourhood of the cathedral; and faw Lord Macartney, attended by his whole fuite, among whom was the Hon. Mr. Weft, brother to the Earl of De Lawarr, dreffed in the uniform of the embaffy, walk in proceflion to vifit the Governor of the ifland; who received the Ambaffador with every mark of attention and refpect, and requefted his company to dinner on the fucceeding day. His Lordfhip then returned to the Conful's in the fame order and formality.

As in the afternoon of this day I completed my view of this place, I fhall here finifh my account of it.

Madeira is extremely mountainous, and prefents a moft beautiful object from the bay. It lies between thirty-two and thirty-three degrees of north latitude, and between eighteen and nineteen degrees of weft longitude from London. Its length is feventy-five miles, and its breadth thirty. In the center of the fouthern fide of the ifland, at a fmall diftance from the fea, and on the firft rife of an amphitheatre of hills, is the town of Funchal: its population is very confiderable, and it contains feveral churches, as well as monafteries of both fexes, of the different orders of the church of Rome: the houfes are built of ftone, and the greater part of them are covered with white plafter, and generally roofed with tiles: the ftreets are very narrow, ill paved, and dirty, having no foot-path for paffengers, with all the inconvenience arifing from unequal ground and continual declivity. Except the refidence of the Governor, and of the Britifh Conful, and the houfes of fome principal merchants, glafs is an article of very rare ufe: the houfes are in general about three ftories high, with lattice windows, and balconies in the front, where the female inhabitants are continually feen to amufe themfelves in obferv-

1792.
October.

ing what happens in the ftreets, or converfing with thofe who are paffing along. There are neither courts, fquares, or principal ftreets in this town; the whole place compofing a fcene of architectural deformity. The cuftom-houfe, which is on the fea fide, is furrounded by a rampart mounted with cannon, and contains barracks for foldiers.

The town is about three miles in length, and one in breadth. Its inhabitants confift of Portuguefe, mulattoes, negroes, and a few Englifh, who refide there for the purpofes of commerce. The wine of this ifland, fo well known for its cordial and peculiar qualities, is the great object of its trade, and the principal fource of its riches. The drefs of the poorer fort of people is a kind of cap, made of cloth, which they wear inftead of an hat, a fhort jacket, and clumfy troufers, with a kind of boots of coarfe undreffed leather; though many of the lower clafs are feen almoft naked, and manifeft no common appearance of diftrefs and mifery. The religion is catholic, and the clergy poffefs the fame power as in the mother country. The natives are of a very courteous difpofition, and treat ftrangers with all the punctilio of refpect and politenefs.

No carriages are kept in this ifland, but by the Governor and the Britifh Conful: the fubftitute for them, among the higher order of the inhabitants, is a very fine filk net, of various colours, capable of containing a perfon to fit in it: it is borne by two men, by means of a long pole run through the four corners, which draws the net clofe on each fide like a purfe; a filk curtain is then thrown over the pole, that entirely obfcures the perfon who fits in this curious vehicle, which is the elegant mode of conveyance in vifits of ceremony, and to the occafional entertainments of the place. Thefe, however, are always in private houfes, as there are no theatres, or any places of public entertainment, except the public garden, where there are frequent exhibitions of the moft brilliant fire-works.

There are very few horfes in this ifland; mules and oxen being principally employed both for draught and burden: nor is it eafy to

conceive

conceive the fagacity and agility of thefe animals in adapting their powers to the inequalities of this very mountainous country.

The military eftablifhment of the Madeiras is very limited, and does not confift of more than three hundred men. The native militia, however, are numerous, but they are never embodied, except in time of danger and alarm. Thefe foldiers are moft wretchedly clothed; the regimental confifting of a very coarfe blue jacket, with a veft and breeches of the fame colour; the whole bound with a coarfe yellow worfted lace, and enlivened with red facing. They wear on their heads a kind of leathern helmet; but the artillery foldiers are diftinguifhed by hats: their arms and accoutrements are of the worft kind, and kept in the worft order: in fhort, fuch was their appearance, that when fome of our matroffes and light horfemen were permitted to go on fhore, the inhabitants, from the fuperiority of their appearance, could not be perfuaded but that they were all officers in the Britifh fervice.

The town is defended towards the fea, from eaft to weft, by a ftrong wall, mounted with cannon, and a fort at either end. The climate of Madeira is well known for its falubrious influence, as, excepting the month of January, when there are frequent rains, accompanied with violent thunder, it feldom undergoes any change of feafon. Thofe who have money may purchafe here, as in other places, all the luxuries of life; but they in general bear a very extravagant price, though the firft people live in a ftile of great plenty and elegance. Even the wine, which, as it is the produce of the fpot, might naturally be fuppofed to be purchafed at a reafonable rate, could not be obtained by us for lefs than four fhillings a bottle. This ifland, however, notwithftanding its mountainous ftate, muft be confidered, altogether, as a very fertile colony; and, as a picturefque object, nothing can exceed the romantic and beautiful views it contains, and the delightful fpots that are covered with gardens and vineyards.

Lord

1792.
Tuesday,
October 16.

Lord Macartney, with the principal people of the ifland, were very handfomely entertained by the Britifh Conful, at dinner; and, in the evening, Mr. Scot, an Englifh merchant, gave a ball and fupper, in honour of his Lordfhip, which wanted nothing, in point of elegant hofpitality, that our country can afford. The Englifh fervants alfo partook of the attention paid to their Lord, and were entertained with the greateft plenty, and in the moft agreeable manner, beneath the fame roof.

Wednef-
day 17.

We, this morning, paid a vifit to a convent of ladies, about three miles to the eaft of Funchal. It is a very handfome building, fituated near the fummit of an hill, and in the midft of vineyards, commanding a moft beautiful, various, and extenfive profpect; comprehending the adjacent country covered with gardens, the town of Funchal, and an expanfive view of the ocean.—Here the nuns are permitted to converfe very freely with ftrangers, whom they compliment with toys, and other articles of their own manufacture. I faw among them feveral very pretty women; who, as far as I could judge by their manners, feemed to regret the lofs of that fociety for which they were formed, and to figh after a communication with the world, which they were qualified to adorn.

Having taken a particular view of this charming fpot, we proceeded to the country refidence of the Governor, where Lord Macartney and his fuite had been invited to dinner. This entertainment confifted of three very fplendid courfes of fifty difhes; and at a certain part of it, Lord Macartney propofed to drink the health of the King and the Royal Family of England; which, being notified by a fignal, the Lion, at that inftant, fired a royal falute of twenty-one guns; and was immediately anfwered by the fame number of guns from the fort. The Governor then obferved the fame ceremony refpecting the Royal Family of Portugal, which was followed by the fame falutes from the Portuguefe battery and Englifh man of war. A very fine difplay of fire-works concluded the entertainment, which

was

was equally to the honour of the diſtinguiſhed perſons who gave and received it.

We returned on board, where we found ſeveral friars, whoſe curioſity had led them to take a view of the ſhip; where they were received with that kindneſs and hoſpitality as to call forth the moſt grateful expreſſions; and to obtain from them, all they had to give, their repeated benedictions.

The entire forenoon of this day was employed in making preparations for a breakfaſt in the ward-room, to which Lord Macartney had invited the Governor of the iſland, the Britiſh Conſul, and the principal inhabitants. This entertainment conſiſted of tea, coffee, and chocolate; cold meats of all kinds, with fruits, jellies, and variety of wines: the whole being decorated with ornamental confectionary. About noon Lord Macartney returned on board the Lion, with the uſual formalities; and was ſoon followed by the Governor, with his attendants, in very elegant barges. The biſhop of Funchal accompanied him on the occaſion. The Britiſh Conſul arrived ſoon after them. The company then partook of the repaſt, during which the healths of the royal families of England and Portugal were drank with becoming ceremony; and, having taken a view of the ſhip, they returned on ſhore. In the evening we weighed anchor, and quitted Madeira.

At five in the afternoon we ſaw the extreme points of Teneriffe; at midnight we ſaw the eaſt point of that iſland; and, early in the morning, ſtood in for land.

We anchored in twenty-two fathom water in Santa Cruz bay; where we found a French frigate, who had called here on her homeward bound paſſage from the Weſt Indies; but, in conſequence of the revolution in France, ſhe was detained till the pleaſure of his Catholic Majeſty ſhould be known, reſpecting the part he intended to take with the confederated powers, then at war with the national

assembly.

1792.
October.

affembly. The Governor being then at the Grand Canary ifland, and the Commandant informing Lieutenant Campbell, that there was not a fufficient quantity of powder in the magazine to admit of a falute, that ceremonial was waved on the prefent occafion.

The ifland of Teneriffe is one of the Canary iflands, and fubject to the King of Spain. It lies between twenty-eight and twenty-nine degrees north latitude, and between feventeen and eighteen degrees weft longitude. It is about fifty miles in length, twenty-five in breadth, and one hundred and fifty in circumference. Though it is the fecond in point of precedence, it is the moft confiderable with refpect to extent, riches, and commerce. The principal place in this ifland is the city of Laguna, and is the refidence of the Governor; but as we did not vifit it, I fhall confine myfelf to the defcription of Santa Cruz, before which we lay at anchor.

This town lies on the north-eaft fide of the ifland, and has an haven for fhipping; the beft anchorage not being more than half a mile from fhore, and very deep, with a rocky bottom. The fhore is bold and fteep, with the peak, which renders this ifland fo famous, rifing beyond it to the clouds.

Santa Cruz is about three quarters of a mile in length, and half a mile in breadth: the houfes are ftrongly built of ftone, and in the fame fafhion as thofe of Madeira. It has feveral neat churches, two of which being decorated with large, fquare, and lofty towers, add much to the effect of the town from the bay. There is one pretty good ftreet, and not inconveniently paved; but the reft anfwer to no other character than that of dirty lanes. There are two forts at the eaftern and weftern end of the town which command the bay. There are but few troops in this or any of its fifter iflands, and they are equally deficient in cloathing, equipment, and difcipline. The militia is numerous, but never embodied, or called forth, except on very particular emergencies. The town, though by no means large, is very populous: the inhabitants are chiefly Spanifh, and fuffer all the

difadvantages

difadvantages that arife from the proverbial pride and indolence of their character: for, notwithftanding the abundant fertility of this ifland, which yields the greateft plenty to the fmalleft exertions, the general appearance of the people moft evidently betray their poverty and wretchednefs. There is another fort to the weft of Santa Cruz, on a very elevated point, which appears to be built with great ftrength, and commands a part of the bay.

The climate of this ifland is warm, and, like that of Madeira, not fubject to change. During our ftay here, the thermometer ftood in the fhade, from feventy to eighty degrees, varying a little, on board the fhip. The Governor refides chiefly at the ifland diftinguifhed by the name of the Grand Canary, about twelve or fifteen leagues diftant from Teneriffe.

Sir George and Mr. Staunton, with the Doctors Gillan, Dinwiddie, and Not, Meffeurs Maxwell, Barrow, and Alexander, together with Colonel Benfon, having formed a plan to vifit the peak; they fet out at eight o'clock in the morning of this day, from the hotel at Santa Cruz, with every proper aid and provifion to carry the defign into execution. The thermometer then ftood at feventy-feven degrees. They proceeded on mules, and under the direction of guides hired for the purpofe, with little or no interruption, till they had advanced about eight miles up the mountain, when the air became fo cold, that every one was glad to make fome addition to his cloathing; at the fame time the thermometer had fallen upwards of twenty degrees. Here the party added fome very neceffary refrefhment to the change in their drefs, and then proceeded on their journey till they arrived at the foot of the peak, which was entirely covered with fnow, fix feet in depth: but difficulties every moment occurred to impede their progrefs; Sir George Staunton had been thrown from his mule at a moment of great danger; the animal on which Doctor Gillan rode, had fallen with him, and it was at length determined, from the awful appearance of the journey before them, the exhaufted condition of the party, and the late hour of the evening, to pafs the night

on

on the mountain. A kind of rude pavilion, therefore, was formed by a fail, which, being lined with cloaks, and great coats, soon produced a comfortable apartment. A fire was then kindled near the tent; and after taking an hafty fupper, every one laid himfelf down to repofe.

At fix o'clock in the morning, the arduous journey was renewed; the thermometer being at that time confiderably below the freezing point—which, after infinite fatigue and confiderable hazard, proved fruitlefs as to its principal object; and about three o'clock in the afternoon, the different gentlemen of the party, who had taken different ways to afcend the peak, were, at length, happily re-affembled at the place where the mules had been ftationed. It was, however, neceffary, as the diftance from Santa Cruz was at leaft eleven or twelve miles, to pafs the night of this day, as we had paffed the preceding one; and, on the following morning, the party returned to Santa Cruz, after a moft fatiguing expedition of two days and two nights, in which curiofity, at leaft, had received confiderable gratification.

The peak of Teneriffe is one of the higheft mountains in the world, and may be feen at the diftance of an hundred miles. It rifes in the center of the ifland, and takes its afcent from Santa Cruz and Oratavia, another principal town of this ifland, in an oblique direction for near twenty miles; being furrounded by a great number of inferior mountains. The lower parts towards Santa Cruz, are covered with woods and vineyards; its middle is clad in fnow, and the top difembogues flames from a volcano, which the natives call the Devil's Cauldron. In travelling to the peak, the beft way is on the fide of Oratavia, both as to the convenience of afcent, and the confequent diminution of danger. In fome parts of the mountain there are hot, burning fands; in other places there is fnow; and to that fucceeds a ftrong fulphurous vapour. Though the top of the peak, from its great height, appears to finifh in a point, it contains a flat furface of at leaft an acre of ground. We experienced three diftinct changes of climate in the courfe of our journey. In the firft ftage of it the air is warm,

warm, to that fucceeds intenfe cold, which is followed by a volcanic heat. The bottom is continual fertility, the middle is fnow and froft, and the top is fmoke and flames; giving the fucceffive effects of a garden, an ice-houfe, and a furnace.

Soon after our return to Santa Cruz, a fignal was given for our going on board, which was obeyed with all poffible expedition. On our return to the fhip, we found feveral young ladies, inhabitants of the ifland, who, having been educated in England, were naturally induced to vifit a fhip belonging to a country to which they apparently owed the fincereft acknowlegements. They were received with the greateft politenefs by Lord Macartney; and the band of mufic was ordered to play during the whole of their very agreeable vifit.

The French frigate, which we have already mentioned as detained here, was, this day, releafed from its embargo, and fet fail from the ifland.

About eleven o'clock at night the wind blew a very frefh gale, and the Indoftan drifted fo faft towards the fhore, that it was thought prudent to let go her fheet anchor. But this precaution was not fufficient to prevent the danger from becoming fo imminent, that Captain Mackintofh fired a gun for affiftance from the Lion; when Sir Erafmus Gower immediately ordered off three boats, by whofe exertions the Indoftan was difengaged from her unpleafant fituation, when fhe put to fea; after having loft her anchors, from the rubbing of the cables againft the rocky bottom.

At one in the morning we weighed anchor, and took our leave of Santa Cruz.

At three in the afternoon we faw Mayo, one of the Cape de Verd iflands, bearing W. S. W. at the diftance of four or five leagues. Hove too, and hoifted out the launch. At feven, we fpoke to a fhip from

1792.
November.

from Topſham, in Devonſhire, which had been out thirty-two days. At eight in the evening, the town of Saint Jago, a town of the iſland of that name, bore north, half weſt, ſeven miles; and, at three quarters after eleven, we came too in Port Praya bay. The thermometer at noon ſtood at 82 degrees.

Saturday 3.

After the uſual ſalutes, ſeveral boats were employed in watering. The Seine was alſo hauled, and freſh fiſh ſerved to the ſhip's company.

Monday 5.

Lord Macartney went on ſhore in a private manner; and, after a ſhort ſtay, returned to the Lion.

Tueſday 6.

This day arrived three French and one American South-ſea whale fiſhermen.—A canoe came along-ſide the Lion, with grapes, cocoa-nuts, and other fruits, for ſale. This is the only kind of boat uſed in theſe iſlands, and nothing could exceed, in the exterior appearances of wretchedneſs, the owner of it. The thermometer ſtood, this day, on ſhore, at 90.

Wedneſday 7.

Several of the men belonging to the corps of artillery went on ſhore to waſh and dry their linen; when they returned extremely ſcorched, and their legs covered with blotches, from ſtanding in the burning ſands. Having given my linen to be waſhed by a man of Praya, and having reaſon to apprehend, that I might ſhare the fate of others, who had not found the natives of the country perfectly correct in their returns, I went in queſt of my waſherman, and was obliged to be content, not only with paying an exorbitant price for what he had done very ill, but with the loſs of ſeveral articles which he could not be perſuaded to reſtore. I, however, took this opportunity of view-ing the town of Praya; in which there is very little to excite curi-oſity, or encourage deſcription.

Saint Jago is the largeſt of the Cape de Verd iſlands, which lie be-tween twenty-three and twenty-ſix degrees of weſt longitude, and be-

tween

tween fourteen and eighteen north latitude. It is very mountainous, and has much barren land on it; neverthelefs, it is the moft fruitful and beft inhabited of them all—and is the refidence of the Viceroy, or Governor.

1792.
November.

Praya is fituated on the eaft fide of the ifland, and is built on the top of a flat hill, about an hundred yards above the furface of the bay; having a miferable fort on the weftern fide, which, however, fuch as it is, commands the entrance into it. The only landing place is oppofite the Governor's houfe, which is fituated in a confiderable valley, formed by two large mountains. A very rugged and afcending path, of about a quarter of a mile, and taking an eafterly direction, leads to an arched gate-way, which forms the entrance to the town; a mean and miferable place, confifting of nothing more than one wide ftreet, about half a mile in length, formed of low houfes, built of ftone and mud, and covered with trees; and, except two, reach not beyond the firft ftory. The furniture of fuch as we could look into, was perfectly fuited to the exterior appearance; confifting of nothing more than planks, which anfwered the double purpofe of feats and tables, while the beds were as humble as folitary ftraw could make them. There is but one fhop, and one public houfe in the town; and the former is as deficient in point of commodities, as the other is incapable of convenient accommodation. The church, and the governor's houfe partake of the general appearance of the place. The natives are all negroes, who fpeak the Portuguefe language, with an intermixture of exiles, banifhed from the Brazils and the Madeiras for capital offences. There is one convent in the ifland, and the whole is fubject to the fpiritual jurifdiction of a Popifh bifhop.

There appears to be great plenty of goats here, but the fcorching heat of the climate, and the confequent fcarcity of every kind of herbage, is not calculated to give them a very thriving appearance.

Praya

Praya has a good port, and is feldom without fhips; thofe outward bound to Guinea or the Eaft-Indies, from England, Holland, and France, frequently touching here for water and refrefhments.

While we were rambling about this miferable place, we heard the fignal to repair on board, and, haftening to the fhore, found a boat waiting to receive us, and a crowd of the naked inhabitants ftanding there with their fruits for fale.—At noon we left Port Praya.

At eleven o'clock in the forenoon, we found ourfelves under the Equator, where the burlefque and ridiculous ceremonies frequently allowed by the commanding officers of fhips were completely obferved, by permiflion of Sir Erafmus Gower, to the great entertainment of the fhip's company.

At five o'clock in the afternoon, we came to anchor in the Rio Janeiro harbour, in fifteen fathom water. Paffed by this afternoon into the harbour the Hero of London, a South-fea whaler, from the South-feas, bound for London. A great many fhips were at this time at anchor in the river, and, among the reft, was a Portuguefe Eaft-Indiaman homeward bound; by whom it was intended to have fent letters to England, by way of Lifbon, had not the arrival of the Hero afforded a more ready, as well as more fecure conveyance.

The country offers from the river a moft delightful profpect, confifting of a fine range of hills covered with wood, whofe intervening vallies are adorned with ftately villas, affording at once a fcene of elegance, richnefs, and beauty.

The cutter was hoifted out, and the firft lieutenant difpatched on fhore, to acquaint the Viceroy with the arrival of the Ambaffador, and to demand the falute; but, as that officer was at his country refidence, the ufual formalities were neceffarily fufpended,

In

In the morning of this day, the deputy viceroy came, accompanied with guards and attendants, in elegant barges, to wait on Lord Macartney, to know his intentions, and to acquaint him with the regulations to which all foreigners muſt ſubmit on landing at Rio Janeiro. But, his Lordſhip having been for ſome time afflicted with the gout, and ſtill remaining very much indiſpoſed, Sir George Staunton and Sir Eraſmus Gower received the deputy viceroy, who, after an introductory conference, partook of a cold collation, and returned on ſhore.

The deputy viceroy, with his attendants, paid a ſecond viſit to the ſhip, and accompanied the general meſſage of congratulation from the Viceroy to the Ambaſſador, on his arrival at the Brazils, with an invitation to accept of an houſe for his reſidence, during the time he might find it neceſſary to ſtay there. This obliging propoſition was accepted by Lord Macartney; and Sir George Staunton went on ſhore to make the neceſſary preparations for his reception, as ſoon as he ſhould be ſufficiently recovered to quit the ſhip.

The Viceroy's ſecretary, attended by ſeveral gentlemen, came on board the Lion to inquire when the Ambaſſador would come on ſhore; who was pleaſed to appoint the following day at one o'clock, to make his entrance into the city of Rio Janeiro.

At noon, Sir Eraſmus Gower having been on ſhore to notify to the Viceroy that Lord Macartney was ready to land, he returned to the Lion in order to conduct him; and they ſoon arrived with all the ceremonials ſuited to the occaſion. The landing-place, which is immediately oppoſite to the Viceroy's palace, was lined on each ſide by a regiment of horſe, and the Viceroy's body-guards. The Viceroy himſelf was alſo there with his official attendants, and he moſt diſtinguiſhed perſons of the city, to receive the Ambaſſador, who was conducted along the line, and diſtinguiſhed by every military honour. The ceremony had altogether a very grand appearance, and a

D

prodigious

prodigious crowd of people had affembled to be fpectators of it. They then proceeded to the palace of the Viceroy, and paffed through a large hall lined with foldiers under arms, and enlivened by the found of martial mufic, to the ftate apartments. Here the company remained for fome time, when Lord Macartney and Sir George Staunton were conducted to the Viceroy's ftate coach; Sir Erafmus Gower and Capt. Mackintofh were placed in a fecond; and the whole Britifh fuite being accommodated with carriages, the cavalcade fet off, efcorted by a troop of light cavalry, to the houfe appointed for Lord Macartney's reception, which is about two miles from the city: the Ambaffador receiving, as he paffed, every honour due to the high character with which he was invefted. A captain's guard, appointed by the Viceroy, was alfo drawn up in the front of the houfe, who received the Britifh vifitors with colours flying and mufic playing, and every military diftinction. Thus concluded the ceremony of the Ambaffador's reception at Rio Janeiro.

It would not only be tedious, but altogether unneceffary, to mention the common daily occurrences during our ftay at the Brazils; I fhall, therefore, confine myfelf altogether to fuch circumftances, as from their novelty and importance may intereft the mind, and reward, in fome degree, the attention, of the reader.

Lord Macartney, with his whole fuite, paid a vifit of ceremony to the Viceroy, and was received with every mark of attention and refpect. The gentlemen who attended on the occafion, afterwards dined with his Lordfhip; and, in the evening, vifited the public garden of the place: this garden is about half a mile in length, and half that fpace in breadth; it is furrounded by a ftrong high wall, and guarded at the entrance by a party of foldiers. The interior difpofition confifts of large grafs-plots and gravel walks, agreeably fhaded with trees, and perfumed with flowers. In the center is a large bafon of water, and a great number of lamps are placed between the trees, on each fide of the walks, for the purpofe of illumination. At one end

of

of the garden is a large building for balls and mufic; but, as the 1792.
feafon of amufement at this place was paffed when we were there, December.
we muft be content with giving a defcription of the fpot, without
fpeaking of the diverfions to which, at certain feafons of the year,
it is applied, as we doubt not, to the recreation of the inhabitants.

All poffible preparation was made in the long gallery and great Tuefday 11.
room of Lord Macartney's houfe to receive the Viceroy, who had given
notice of his intention to return the Ambaffador's vifit in the morning
of this day. At ten o'clock, Sir Erafmus Gower, with the officers
from the Lion, dreffed in their beft uniforms, as well as Capt.
Mackintofh, with the officers of the Hindoftan, came on fhore to
attend the ceremony.

At eleven, the Viceroy's departure from his palace was announced
by a difcharge of artillery from the garrifon; when the guard, appointed by the Viceroy to attend the Britifh Ambaffador, immediately
paraded in front of the houfe; and, in about half an hour, the Viceroy
arrived in grand proceffion, preceded and followed by a fquadron
of horfe, and attended by all the principal officers and perfons of diftinction in the city. His Excellency was received at the door of the
houfe by Lord Macartney, and conducted to a fofa at the upper end
of the beft apartment. Sir George Staunton then prefented all the
gentlemen attached to the embaffy, according to their refpective rank,
to the Viceroy; who, after partaking of a very elegant repaft prepared
for him and his company, returned in the fame form, and with the
fame ceremonies, as diftinguifhed his arrival.

The drefs of the Viceroy was fcarlet cloth, very much enriched
with gold, embroidery, and precious ftones; his attendants wore a
fplendid livery of green and gold, and he had feveral black running
footmen, who were dreffed in fancy uniforms, with large turbans on
their heads, and long fabres by their fides.

D 2

This

This morning, at an early hour, Sir George and Mr. Staunton, accompanied by Mr. Barrow and a Portuguese gentleman, fet off on a fhort excurfion into the country. At the fame time, I took an opportunity of vifiting the place, of which I fhall now proceed to give fuch a defcription, as my capacity for obfervation will enable me.

This city, which is by fome called Saint Sebaftian, and by others, Rio Janeiro, ftands on the weft fide of the harbour of the latter name, in a low fituation, and almoft furrounded by hills, which, by retarding the circulation of the air, renders the place very unfalutary to European conftitutions. Its extent is very confiderable, being from eaft to weft about four miles in length, and from north to fouth about two miles in breadth. The ftreets, for there are no fquares, are very regular and uniform, interfecting each other at right angles: they are well paved, abound in fhops of every kind, and are compofed of houfes equally well built, and adapted to the climate. In the center of the city, and oppofite to the beach, ftands the palace of the Viceroy: it is a large, long, and narrow building, without any attraction from its exterior appearance, but contains within a fucceffion of fpacious and noble apartments. It confifts only of two ftories; the lower one being appropriated to the domeftics and menial officers, and the upper range of building containing the apartments of the Viceroy: it is built of rough ftone, plaiftered with lime, and covered with pantiles. The Viceroy's chapel is a neat edifice, near the palace, but detached from it. The ftreets are not only fpacious and convenient, but remarkable for their cleanlinefs; many of them containing ranges of fhops and warehoufes that would do credit to the cities of Europe. There is a cuftom here, which appears to be worthy of imitation in all places of confiderable trade and commerce, that all perfons of the fame profeffion occupy the fame ftreet or diftrict; and a deviation from this rule is very rarely known in this city. Of the population of this place, I could not procure any accurate information, but from its extent, and the general obfervations I was enabled to make, it may, I think, be confidered, without exaggeration, as amounting to two

hundred

hundred thoufand fouls. The people, who are Roman Catholics, are very much attached to the ceremonials of their religion, which they obferve with extreme fuperftition. The churches are very numerous, and fitted up with oftentatious finery. On the feftivals of their patrons thefe edifices are richly adorned, and beautifully illuminated. Some of them, indeed, during our ftay, were lighted up with fo much fplendor, as to offer a very ftriking fpectacle, and to bear the appearance rather of a public rejoicing, than a partial act of parochial devotion. Near the middle of the city, and on a commanding eminence, there is a public obfervatory furnifhed with an aftronomical apparatus.

The inhabitants are very oftentatious in their drefs; and every rank of people are in the habit of confidering fwords as effential to their public appearance; even children are not confidered as exempt from this ornamental weapon. The drefs of the ladies bears a near refemblance to that of European women, except in the decoration of the head. Their hair is fmoothed back in the front, and adorned with artificial flowers, beads, and feathers, fantaftically arranged; behind, it falls down in a variety of plaited treffes, intermixed with ribbons of various colours, each trefs terminating in a rofe made of ribbon. They alfo wear a large mantle of filk, hanging loofely behind in the form of a train, which is borne by one fervant, while another holds an umbrella to fhade the face of his miftrefs from the fun. The females of Brazil are generally of a pale complexion, but have a certain delicacy of feature which renders them very pleafing objects; and the affability of their manners heightens the agreeablenefs of their perfonal attractions.

The trade of this place is very confiderable, and the fource of great wealth to the inhabitants, as well as to the mother country. The various articles which are exported from hence, are the fame as thofe produced in other parts of the Portuguefe fettlements in Brazil. The wharfs are very large and peculiarly commodious; and we were

very

1792.
December.

very much amufed on obferving the dexterity with which the flaves loaded and unloaded the barges that lay along fide them. The rice, of which great quantities appeared to be exported from this fettlement, was all contained in undrefied bullock's hides.

At a fmall diftance from the city, on the weft fide of it, is a large convent, but more remarkable for ftrength than elegance. It is built round feveral quadrangular courts, paved with large flat ftones, furrounded by piazzas, and kept in a ftate of perfect cleanlinefs. It is divided into two parts, each containing a great number of apartments, each part being refpectively appropriated to a religious community of either fex.

The perfons who compofed Lord Macartney's fuite were indulged with the permiffion to vifit this convent, and the nuns took opportunities to throw out to them a variety of little elegant toys of their own fabric. Nor had even their confined and devoted fituation prevented them from knowing the art of manufacturing another kind of article, called *billets doux*, which they contrived to have conveyed to fome of the Englifh vifitors. They even applied to Lord Macartney, by the director of the convent, for the ufe of his band of mufic, which accordingly performed at feveral morning concerts, within thefe facred walls. There is alfo a very fpacious garden, where the religious ladies are allowed to enjoy fuch recreation as they can find in a place, furrounded with walls of at leaft forty feet in height; which, as if they did not form a fufficient fecurity, are conftantly guarded on the outfide by a party of foldiers.

On the north-weft fide of the town there is a ftupendous aqueduct, which is an object of uncommon curiofity. It is in the form of a bridge, contains eighty arches, and in fome parts is, at leaft, one hundred and fifty feet in height; and is feen, in fome points of view, with peculiar effect, rifing gradually above the loftieft buildings of the city. This immenfe chain of arches ftretches acrofs a valley, and unites the hills that form it. The object for which it was erected is completely anfwered, as it conveys water from perennial fprings, at

the

the diftance of five miles, into the town, where, by means of leaden pipes, it is conducted to a large and elegant refervoir at the beach, oppofite to the Viceroy's palace. This water is of the beft quality, and is withal fo very abundant, as not only to afford an adequate fupply for all the wants of the inhabitants, but to furnifh the fhips that come into the harbour with this neceffary element.

The military eftablifhment at Rio Janeiro is on a very refpectable footing. The foldiers are not only well cloathed and difciplined, but are allowed to enjoy all the privileges of citizens. It feems to be a policy of the Portuguefe government, and a very wife one it is, to render the fituation of the foldiery in their American fettlements, not only comfortable in itfelf, and refpectable in its character, but, in fome degree, as I fhould imagine, the fource of pecuniary advantage. Thus the loyalty and zeal of the foldiers are happily fecured in a fituation fo important from its value, and where vigilance and fidelity in thofe who guard it become more neceffary in proportion to its remotenefs from the mother country. Whether it is that their pay is proportionably advanced in the fervice of thefe fettlements, or that they are allowed any diftinct advantages, I cannot tell, but they certainly appear to be in a ftate of comparative affluence, which no other foldiery that I have ever feen or heard of can be fuppofed to poffefs. The number of troops in Rio Janeiro, including cavalry and infantry, amount to twenty thoufand men; and the militia are, at leaft, double that number. At the fame time the place is admirably fortified, both by art and nature. It is fituated about two miles from the mouth of the bay, and is defended by nine ftrong forts, well fupplied with artillery, and fufficient garrifons. There are alfo two fmall iflands in the middle of the bay, one at the entrance, called Santa Cruz Fort, and another at a fmall diftance, which ftill add to the ftrength of the fituation, and the difficulty of attacking it with advantage.

Sir George Staunton fet off with a party on an excurfion to the Sugar Loaf Hill, a very high rock fituated on the left fide of the entrance to the harbour; and at five o'clock in the afternoon, Lord Macart-

ney,

ney, who was still very much indifposed, accompanied by Sir Erafmus Gower, returned, in a private manner, on board the Lion.

Sunday 16.   All the baggage being put into carts to be carried to the beach, the officers who commanded the guard at the houfe where Lord Macartney had refided, ordered a party of foldiers to attend each cart, till the whole of their cargoes was depofited on board the boats which were in waiting to receive them.   While I was attending on this duty, I had an opportunity of feeing the Viceroy return in great ftate from the church, where he had been to attend fome particular ceremonial of his religion.

Monday 17.   At half paft ten in the morning we weighed anchor, and worked down to Santa Cruz Fort, and came too, foon after, in fifteen fathom water.   The next day we foon ran out of the harbour, and took our leave of Rio Janeiro.

Nothing now occurred for fome time, in the courfe of the voyage, which requires particular notice; nor even that change of weather which would juftify a circumftantial account of it.   The weather was, in general, moderate; light airs, frefh breezes, with occafional hazinefs and drizly rain, would include every defcription of it during the remainder of the year 1792. It may not, however, be thought altogether improper in me to mention, that, though fo far removed from our friends and native clime, with fuch a wafte of water around us, and fo long a track Tuefday 25.   of ocean before us, the feftival of Chriftmas-day was not forgotten, and that its focial diftinctions were practifed and enjoyed in the little world that bore us along.

Monday 31.   About ten in the morning we faw the ifland of Triftan de Cunha. It is a barren, uninhabited, and almoft inacceffible ifland, fituated in the heart of the fouthern ocean, in thirty-feven deg. feven min. and thirty fec. fouth latitude, and about forty-five deg. eaft longitude.   When we firft obferved this mountain rifing above the clouds, it appeared to be

as high as the peak of Teneriff. It is a natural place of refort to prodigious numbers of wild birds; while the furrounding fea is the
habitation of whales, fea-lions, and other monfters of the deep. Lieutenant Whitman, who was fent on fhore in the cutter, to found for
anchorage, gave a very favourable report of the beach, as well as of a
run of water which iffued from a cliff, and, flowing acrofs the fhore,
difcharged itfelf into the fea.

Mr. Whitman, on this occafion, fhot a fea-lion and an albatrofs;
the latter of which he brought on board. It meafured nine feet from
the bill to the extremity of the tail, but weighed no more than three
pounds and an half.

In confequence of this information, Sir Erafmus Gower propofed
to fend a watering party on fhore the next morning; while Sir George
Staunton fuggefted an excurfion thither at the fame time, to fee what
this ifland offered to his obfervation in any branch of natural hiftory:
for this purpofe, a certain number of artillery men were ordered to
be in readinefs by three o'clock in the morning, and to be properly
equipped for the expedition againft the amphibious monfters of the
fhore. At midnight, however, a very heavy gale came on, which
caufed the fhip to ftart her anchor, and our fituation became very
alarming; for if the wind, which blew directly on the rock, had not
changed, we muft inevitably have perifhed. This unexpected alteration in the weather fruftrated the defigns which had been formed of
obtaining further information relative to this curious place.

The weather continued to be moderate, with light airs, and frefh
breezes, till this day; when there came on an heavy gale of wind,
which occafioned fuch a rolling of the fhip, as to interfere with thofe
enjoyments which make feamen forget the inconveniencies of their
fituation.

The moderate weather returned, with all the comforts that ufually
attend it.

1793.
January.

Tuefday 1.

Sunday 20.

Tuefday 22.

E   About

1793.
February.
Friday 1.

About four o'clock in the morning faw land, bearing E. N. E. fuppofed to be ten leagues diftant; which, in about four hours, was difcovered to be the ifland of Amfterdam, fituate in the Indian ocean, and lying in latitude thirty deg. forty-three min. fouth, and feventy-feven deg. twenty min. eaft longitude. As we approached the ifland, we could plainly difcover three men on the fhore; in confequence of which the enfign was immediately hoifted. We here faw great numbers of water fnakes, and a prodigious quantity of fifh refembling cod, and weighing, in general, about three to eight pounds. At noon the yawl was hoifted out, and the mafter fent to found for anchorage. In confequence of his information we hove too, and anchored with the beft bower, in twenty-eight fathom water, on the eaft fide of the ifland. The mafter alfo gave an account that there were five men on the ifland, who had come from the Ifle de France, for the purpofe of killing feals, with which this place abounds.

Wednefday 6.

Sir George and Mr. Staunton, with feveral other gentlemen, accompanied by a party of artillery foldiers, properly armed, went on fhore, and made great deftruction among the natives of the place: fuch as feals, penguins, albatroffes, &c. Great quantities of fifh were alfo caught here, and falted, for the fervice of the fhip.

On the north-eaft end of the ifland, nearly oppofite to where the Lion lay at anchor, there is a very commodious bafon, about a mile in diameter, and furrounded by inacceffible and perpendicular rocks; at the entrance of which, on the north-weft corner, ftands a lofty infulated rock, which bears the form of a fugar-loaf. This bafon might, at a fmall expenfe, be made a place of fafe retreat for fhips of any burthen; as it contains, in many parts, thirteen fathom water, and poffeffes an excellent landing place. We here caught great quantities of fifh which refemble our lobfter, both in fhape and fize, but of a very fuperior flavour. We alfo obferved great numbers of fharks all round the ifland; which is the more extraordinary, as the fhark is feldom feen in thefe latitudes.

On

On our landing, we were met by the five feal-hunters, whom we have already mentioned ; who, with great civility, conducted us to an hut at a fmall diftance from the beach. They were natives of France and America, who had made a commercial engagement to come and refide in this ifland for the fpace of eighteen months, in order to kill feals, whofe fkins are fold to very great advantage to fhips which touch at the ifle of France. At this time they had only been fix months in their prefent fituation, when, according to their account, they had already killed eight thoufand feals.

At a fmall diftance from their hut, thefe men had, with much labour, and no fmall hazard, formed a path, by which they contrived to get over a mountain to kill feals on the other fide of the ifland. On afcending this path, we came to a fmall fpring, whofe water is equal to boiling heat; and fome fifh which we put into it, were as perfectly dreffed in fix minutes, as if they had been cooked on board the fhip. It fhould be alfo obferved, that while we were attending to this procefs, we diftinctly heard the fame kind of bubbling founds as proceeds from water boiling in a veffel over the fire. On the top of the mountain there is a volcano, from whence a fubftance iffues, which thefe men reprefented as bearing the appearance, and poffeffing the qualities, of falt-petre.

This ifland is about eight miles in length, and fix in breadth ; in fome parts it is altogether flat, particularly to the weft, and gradually rifes to the very high land in the center of it. It is a very barren fpot, bearing neither tree nor fhrub, and whofe only produce is a kind of coarfe, tufted grafs, with very thick ftalks. Every thing in this ifland bears the mark of having undergone the action of fire. The earth, and even the rocks and ftones, on approaching the volcano, were fo hot as to fcorch our fkin, to burn our fhoes, and blifter our feet. We were conducted about this defolate place by the five feal-hunters ; whofe care and kind attentions preferved us not only from inconvenience, but danger, which it would have been impoffible for us to have avoided, if we had not been fubject to their direction.

The

1792.
February.

The volcanic mountain is about three miles in its afcent, which is very fteep and rugged; and in its afcent, as well as defcent, attended with continual difficulties. In fhort, we had met with fo many obftacles both in going up and coming down it, that two fignal guns had been fired from the Lion, which, with the Hindoftan, were both under weigh, when we reached the fhore; where, after an interval of no common alarm and apprehenfion, we found a boat that conveyed us on board. The night being dark, we faw the flames of the volcano burfting forth in fix different places, at a confiderable diftance from each other, which formed a grand and affecting fpectacle.

It may here be proper to remark, that the thermometer, which, on board, ftood at fifty-five degrees, rofe on the ifland to feventy-four; and, towards the top of the mountain, to feventy-feven degrees and an half: a circumftance which muft be attributed to the heat of the volcano.

Friday 15.

This morning, at three o'clock, a very large meteor, or fire-ball, rofe from the north-north-weft, and continued in view for fome minutes, paffing off, without any explofion, to the fouth-fouth-eaft. It threw a kind of blue light over the fails and decks; but the illumination was fo ftrong, that the moft trifling object could be diftinguifhed.

Monday 18.

At eight o'clock in the morning difcovered the Trial rocks, about a league to the windward; the fea beating over them to an immenfe height. Thefe rocks are not vifible, as they do not rife above the furface of the water, nor are they much beneath it. They are fituated in the Indian ocean, in about one hundred and fix degrees of eaft longitude, and twenty-five, or twenty-fix degrees of fouth latitude.

Thurfday 28.

In proceeding up the ftraits of Sunda, we faw the Hindoftan lying at anchor, near the north ifland. In the afternoon a Dutch prow came along-fide the Lion, laden with turtle, poultry, and fruit, for fale. The owner of the prow was a Dutchman; but thofe who rowed it were Malays, and fome of them females.

At

At three o'clock in the afternoon we came too in Batavia road, in five fathom water: the careening island bearing weft-north-weft. We were faluted by all the Englifh fhips in the road, and one French veffel. At fun-rife we faluted the Dutch garrifon with thirteen guns, which were returned : at feven we returned the falutes of all the fhips ; and at eight received the members of the Dutch council with the fame honours. Thofe gentlemen compofed a deputation from the Governor-General of Batavia, to invite Lord Macartney on fhore, and to know on what day and hour he would be pleafed to land. His Lordfhip, accordingly, fixed on Friday, the 8th inft. at nine o'clock in the morning, that being the anniverfary of the birth-day of his Serene Highnefs the Prince of Orange.

At fix o'clock in the morning, a falute of twenty-one lower-deck guns was fired, in honour of his Serene Highnefs : and, at the time appointed, the Ambaffador, attended by his whole fuite, went on fhore with the ufual formalities.

In a fhort time after Lord Macartney had quitted the fhip, a Dutch officer of diftinction, with feveral ladies and gentlemen, came on board the Lion, from Batavia, to take a view of her. They were received with all poffible politenefs by Lieutenant Campbell, and appeared to be much fatisfied with their reception. A very fine young Englifh lady was one of the party, and enhanced the honour of the vifit.

In the afternoon I went on fhore in the launch, having charge of the baggage belonging to the fuite, which was, with fome difficulty, rowed up the canal, and fafely landed before the door of the royal Batavian hotel, where the packages were diftributed in the apartments of the gentlemen to whom they refpectively belonged. The Ambaffador, with Sir George and Mr. Staunton, were received at the houfe of Mr. Wiggerman, one of the members of the fupreme council.

At

1793.
March.
Wednefday 6.

Friday 8.

At fix o'clock Lord Macartney went in form to an entertainment at the Governor-General's country refidence, at which the principal perfons of both fexes in Batavia were prefent. The whole concluded with a magnificent fupper and ball, which lafted to a very late hour of the following morning.

Sunday 10.

While I was at breakfaft this morning, my cars were affailed by the moft dreadful fhrieks I ever heard; and, on making the inquiry which humanity fuggefted, I difcovered that thefe horrid founds proceeded from a Malay flave, whom the mafter of the hotel had ordered to be punifhed for fome omiffion of his duty. This poor wretch, who was upwards of feventy years of age, was ftanding in a back court, while two other flaves were fcourging him in the moft unrelenting manner with fmall canes. This horrid punifhment they continued for thirty-five minutes, till the back and hips of this victim to feverity exhibited one lacerated furface, from whence the blood trickled down on the pavement. The mafter then commanded the correcting flaves to give over their tormenting office, and fent the fmarting culprit, as he was, and without any application whatever to his wounds, to continue the laborious duties of his ftation. On remonftrating with the mafter of the hotel, for this cruel and barbarous treatment of his fervant—he anfwered, that the Malays were fo extremely wicked, that neither the houfe, nor any one in it, would be fafe for a moment, if they were not kept in a ftate of continual terror, by the moft rigid and exemplary punifhment. But this was not all; for another act of neceffary feverity, as it was reprefented to me, though of a different kind, immediately fucceeded. Two flaves, in carrying off the breakfaft equipage from our table, contrived between them to break a plate; for which offence, as it could not be precifely fixed upon either, they were both ordered to fuffer. They were, accordingly, each of them, furnifhed with canes, and compelled to beat each other; which they did with reciprocal feverity; as two other flaves ftood with bamboos, to correct any appearance of lenity in them.

Notwithftanding

Notwithstanding the extreme heat of the weather, I was impatient to take a view of the city; and the result of my observations I now present to the reader.

1793.
March.

The city of Batavia is situate in the island of Java, and is the capital of all the Dutch settlements and colonies in the East Indies. It lies in one hundred and four degrees of east longitude, and six degrees of south latitude; and from its situation between the Equator and the Tropic of Capricorn, the climate is insupportably hot.

The city is built in a square form, and surrounded with a strong wall, about thirty feet high. There are four gates, one in each angle, with a fort, battery, and barracks for soldiers at each gate. The forts are mounted with artillery, garrisoned with troops, and surrounded with ditches, over which draw-bridges are let down during the day; but after nine o'clock at night there is no passage over them without a signed order from the Governor-General.

The streets of the city are broad, handsomely built, and well paved; and in the center of every principal street there is a canal of about sixty feet broad; so that there is no communication between the two sides of the same street but by bridges, of which there are great numbers thrown over the water at no great distance from each other. The houses are, in general, three stories high; and each story very lofty, on account of the excessive heat of the climate. They are all built according to one general design, and possess a certain degree of grandeur, both in their external and interior appearance. The lower story of the houses is built of stone, covered with marble; and the upper part is composed of a fine red brick : the windows, which are very large, are coped with marble, and the wooden frame-work richly gilt and ornamented. The inhabitants appear to have a very great pride in preserving the exterior beauty of their houses, and use a sort of red paint for that purpose, with which they wash, or colour the fronts of them at least once a week.

On

On each fide of the canal there are two rows of evergreen trees, which add very much to the beauty of the ftreets. There are alfo in different parts of each ftreet, fmall fquare buildings, with feats in them for the accommodation of paffengers, as fhelter or fhade may be neceffary, from the violence of the rain or the heat of the fun.

The only public buildings which merit particular attention, are the palace of the Governor-General, the arfenal, the ftadthoufe, and the high church.

The firft of them forms a termination to the principal ftreet of the place, its fore-court is handfomely railed, and the front gate is guarded by centinels. This edifice is of ftone, and of an impofing appearance: it confifts of four ftories, with a central dome crowned with a turret: there are alfo large wings projecting on either fide from the main body, with furrounding piazzas. There is a battalion of foldiers conftantly on duty here, which confifts chiefly of Malays commanded by European officers. I faw alfo a few European foldiers, who, though they were much better clothed and accoutred than the native troops, have fuch a meagre, pale, and ghaftly appearance, as to be but ill-qualified for the duties of their own, or any other profeffion. I was informed by fome of them, that not one in twenty of the military who came from Europe, ever returned there; and that even thofe who efcape from hence, and furvive all the dangers and diforders of the climate, generally go back to their own country with emaciated forms and debilitated conftitutions.

This palace appears to have been built at feveral diftinct periods, from the dates which are engraved in different parts of it. The dates 1630, 1636, and 1660, mark, as I fuppofe, the particular periods when certain principal parts of it were erected. Before the court there is a kind of lawn, with a walk in the middle, fhaded with rows of trees; and to the left of this lawn, at a fmall diftance from the palace, ftands the arfenal, before which lay a great number of new brafs guns, gun-

carriages,

carriages, fhot of all kinds piled up, and fifty large cannon completely mounted. This building, as may be fuppofed, is more remarkable for its ftrength, than the beauty of its external appearance,
and contains an immenfe quantity of all kinds of ordnance and
military ftores, both in its chambers, and in the deep vaults beneath
the building.

Beyond this lawn or walk is a canal, over which a drawbridge
communicates with one of the forts ; and near it is a very elegant ftone
building, with correfponding wings, built in a very pleafing ftile of
architecture: it is called the fmall armory, and, as I was informed on
the fpot, contains two hundred thoufand ftand of arms. Around this
edifice, there are feveral large courts, which contain refidences for the
principal officers, as well as barracks for twenty-thoufand men; but
this vaft range of buildings is no longer inhabited, on account of the
contagious diforders that are fo frequent in this city. The officers
have all of them places of refidence at fome diftance from the town ;
and all the European regiments are quartered in the country ; the guard
on the city duty being regularly relieved every morning. The regiment appointed for duty marches every day into town, at fix o'clock
in the morning, to the grand parade oppofite the Governor's palace ;
one battalion of which attends the Governor's duty, and the other is
diftributed among the feveral guards round the city.

Near the fort, which has been already mentioned, ftands the cuftom-houfe, belonging to the Dutch Eaft-India Company, with their
ftore-houfes, and other commercial erections. There is alfo a fmall
dock-yard, where boats and a few inconfiderable veffels were building. There is a chain thrown acrofs the canal, every night, to prevent
all communication with boats after a certain hour, and a fort has been
erected near the cuftom-houfe, with a view, as it appears, to protect it ;
but, without pretending to any knowlege in the fcience of defence, or
military tactics, I could difcover that this place was in no condition to

F

refift

1793.
March.

refift a well-appointed enemy; nor could I reconcile the defencelefs ftate of this valuable fettlement to the wealth and importance of it.

At the end of the ftreet leading from the Governor's houfe, and in a handfome fquare, ftands the ftadthoufe, where the courts of juftice are held, and the fupreme council meet to proceed in their deliberations: it is a very fine building, with an interior court furrounded by a piazza. At a fmall diftance from the ftadthoufe is the principal church of the city, which is furrounded by a cemetery. It is a large, plain, fquare building, with a dome in the center, and a lofty turret fpringing from it; the infide is fitted up in a very beautiful manner: the tribune belonging to the Governor General is very much enriched; the pews are very commodioufly arranged; and, indeed, every part is admirably adapted to the purpofes of that religion to which it is devoted. The walls of the church are entirely covered with efcutcheons. and painted infcriptions, facred to the memory of the dead: thefe infcriptions are of different fizes, but being painted in the fame form, enclofed in gilt frames, and difpofed with judgment, produce a very beautiful effect.

The civil government of Batavia and the ifland of Java is perfectly arbitrary, and vefted in the Governor and Supreme Council in all matters, excepting thofe of trade and commerce, which are fubject to an officer called a Director General, from whofe decifions there is no appeal.

The feverity of the laws, and the rigour with which they are executed, could find no juftification in a fettlement belonging to an European government; were it not for the favage and ferocious difpofition of the natives of the country, whom no punifhments, however frequent or fevere, are able to maintain in that ftate of difcipline and good order, which is fo neceffary to the well-being and comfort of civilifed life.

The

The number of regular troops quartered in the neighbourhood of Batavia, including both the European and Malay regiments, amounts to about twelve thousand men: there are also upwards of twenty-thousand native militia, who are regularly cloathed and paid; but though they are frequently muftered, by order of the Governor, they are never actually embodied, but in time of war, or in confequence of fome civil commotion. The European troops are cloathed in a manner fuitable to the climate, are allowed to carry on any trade or profeflion for which they are qualified, and otherwife remunerated by particular privileges; if any thing can remunerate them for the dangers and in-conveniencies that refult from this ungenial clime. The Malay troops, on the contrary, are deftitute of any decent clothing; none of them at leaft being allowed fhoes or ftockings; and in this miferable ftate of equipment they do their duty.

Batavia is extremely populous; and among its inhabitants may be found the natives of every European country: the larger proportion of them, however, are Chinefe, who appear to be a quiet and induftrious people. It feemed to be a general opinion among thofe, of whom I had an opportunity to make the inquiry, that this city contains two hundred thoufand fouls; one half of which are fuppofed to be Chi-nefe, and the other, Europeans and native Malays: nor when I con-fider the extent of the city and its fuburbs, do I conceive it to be an exaggerated calculation.

On my return to the hotel after the morning's excurfion, of which I have given the information it produced, I found, with great concern, that Lord Macartney had been feized with a violent fit of the gout, and was returned on board the Lion; fo that all the various entertain-ments which were preparing to have enlivened the time of our ftay at Batavia, were fruftrated by this very unpleafant change in the health of the diftinguifhed perfon who was the object of them.

F 2

I fupped

I fupped this evening at the Batavian hotel, in company with two French gentlemen, who had been fo fortunate as to efcape from a band of Malays. The villains had attacked them in the ftreet: a circum-ftance which often happens, and particularly to ftrangers who pafs the ftreets after it is dark.

I repeated my excurfions through the city.

Several gentlemen of the Ambaffador's fuite being taken ill, they were ordered to go on board their refpective fhips, and large quan-tities of fruit were purchafed for their ufe and refrefhment.

In the evening I went to fee the tragedy of Mahomet, and paid a rix-dollar for admiffion. The theatre is fituated in the middle of a large garden, which is a place of public refort for the Batavians of every rank and denomination, It is a fpacious brick building, decorated with great elegance, and fitted up with front and fide boxes, and gal-leries; its orcheftra alfo contained a tolerable band of mufic.

The play, as far as I could judge from the attitudes of the actors, and the expreffion of their countenances, for the whole was in the Dutch language, was very well performed. The entertainment was Barnaby Brittle, and afforded a great deal of amufement. The au-dience was very brilliant, but the more fplendid part of it arofe from the fuperior figure, appearance, and beauty of fome Englifh ladies who graced the boxes on the occafion.

At noon there was an auction, or, as it is here termed, an outcry, of certain lands and eftates, belonging to fome of thofe fortunate indi-viduals, who, having efcaped the dangers of the climate, return with the large fortunes they have acquired here, to enjoy the comforts and luxurious eafe of Europe.

Thefe

These sales cannot take place, but under the inspection of the Commissary General, or his deputies, who must always be present on the occasion. Notice is given of these auctions throughout the city and suburbs by a certain number of men, who beat gongs to collect the people together in the different streets, when a person authorised by the Commissary General reads over the articles to be sold, and the conditions of sale: in every other respect, these sales are conducted in the same manner as those in England.

Capt. Mackintosh came on shore, and purchased a French brig, to answer the purpose of the Jackall, from whom we had been so long separated, that we despaired of seeing her again.

This evening I have reason to consider as one of the most fortunate of my life, having escaped from a gang of the Malays, who certainly formed a design, as they had an almost irresistible temptation, to destroy me.

The principal part of the baggage belonging to the Ambassador's suite having been already sent on board the respective ships, I was charged by Mr. Maxwell to see that the rest of the packages, and a chest of dollars, were put on board a proa hired for that purpose, and ordered to go down with the proa to the boom, and remain there till Mr. Maxwell arrived, which he promised to do in half an hour. I accordingly set off, and arrived at the boom about eight o'clock, when I fastened the boat to the custom-house quay, and anxiously waited the arrival of Mr. Maxwell. In this unpleasant situation I remained till nine o'clock, when the boom was thrown across the water, and the bridge drawn up. My uneasiness now became of a very serious nature, as I well knew that Mr. Maxwell could not reach me but by a special order from the Governor; while I was not only in danger of losing the property under my care, from the Malays, who were continually running backwards and forwards in the proa, and examining the articles on board, but of being myself sacrificed to make

the

1793.
March.

Friday 15.

Saturday 16.

the booty more fecure to them. In this fituation, I formed the refolution of making the beft of my way to the Lion; and, accordingly, ordered the Malays to row off for the fhip, which they at firft refufed; but after fhewing them fome money, they took the oars, as I expected, to comply with my wifhes; but, inftead of making towards the fhip, they rowed the proa clofe to the fhore, about a gun-fhot from the mouth of the canal, and at leaft half a mile from any houfe. They then all run afhore, and, in fpite of threats or entreaties, left me to myfelf in a much worfe fituation than I was before, as I was now more remote from any affiftance, in cafe I fhould be in a fituation to require it.

In about twenty minutes thefe wretches returned in greater numbers, which increafed my apprehenfions, as they all entered into the proa, and, putting off from the fhore, attempted to row into the bay: in fhort, a violent fcuffle enfued between us, in which I at length fucceeded, by means of a drawn fword that I ufed with fome effect, in driving them all on fhore, except one man, whom I compelled, by terror of the fame inftrument, to row the veffel to the cuftom-houfe, where I waited till paft eleven; and, defpairing of feeing Mr. Maxwell till the next day, I took all the articles out of the boat, and lodged them in a public-houfe for further fecurity. I had, however, fcarce finifhed this neceffary arrangement, when I faw Mr. Maxwell, attended by feveral flaves with flambeaus, arrive on the oppofite fide of the water. I inftantly hailed him; when he came over to me, and, all the packages being again put into the proa, we fet fail for the Lion, and fome time after midnight arrived on board.

The hotel in which the Ambaffador's fuite refided, during our ftay at Batavia, is a very fuperb building of its kind, and was erected at the expenfe of government for the accommodation of foreigners and mercantile ftrangers: it is under the fole management and controul of the Governor General and Council, by whofe regulations the bufinefs of the houfe is conducted.

It

It is called the Royal Batavian and Foreign Hotel, and this title appears in large golden letters in the front of the houſe, with the date of 1729, the year in which it was built. It contains three regular ſtories; and, as each floor is very lofty, for the benefit of the air, the building riſes to a very conſiderable height. It is conſtructed, like the other edifices of the place, with brick painted of a red colour, while the ſeams of mortar between are proportionably whitened; the windows are alſo very large and broad, the frames of which are gilt or curiouſly painted; the whole forming a very large and handſome ſtructure.

There are three doors in the front, and a kind of terrace raiſed above the pavement before them, which is covered by a portico; where the company reſident in the houſe uſually ſit after dinner and ſmoke their pipes: each of theſe doors forms an entrance into an hall about two hundred feet in length, and about ſixty in breadth; at the further end of which there is a large ſtair-caſe that leads to the bed-chamber apartments, and the flat roof above them.

In the center hall there are at leaſt thirty elegant lamps and chandeliers, which are lighted up every night, and, oppoſite to them, on the wall, is a range of looking-glaſſes, which reflect, and, of courſe, heighten the brilliance of the illumination: the piers between them are adorned with paintings. In the center of the middle hall is a large arch, from which a ſilver chandelier is ſuſpended: the other halls have each a door of the ſame dimenſions exactly oppoſite, and theſe reſpectively lead to an apartment with an alcove roof, neatly ornamented with ſtucco, which contains a billiard table ſurrounded with lamps. From the center of the principal hall the coup d'œil at night is perfectly enchanting, from the great number of lights, and the regular order in which they are placed: the billiard rooms alſo. with their lamps, correſponding exactly with each other.

Behind.

1793.
March.

1793.
March.

Behind the houfe there is a fpacious gallery with piazzas, from whence a large fhade of filk, fancifully painted with figures and grotefque characters, is occafionally lowered in the day, as the heat of the fun may require, and in the evening it is entirely dropped, when the gallery is lighted up in the fame manner as the apartments already defcribed. Beyond this gallery, there is a court paved with large flat ftones, and furrounded with a variety of offices for poulterers, butchers, and other domeftic ufes, with a fpacious kitchen, and every neceffary accommodation. The upper ftory of this range of building is divided into granaries and chambers for the principal and other flaves, of which there are altogether at leaft ninety, of both fexes, who belong to the mafter of the hotel. Thefe menial perfons are promoted according to their merits ; and, if they are induftrious and attentive to the duties of their feveral departments, they may, from the emoluments of their fituation, which are very confiderable, be foon in a condition to purchafe their freedom.

In the great hall on the firft floor, which ferves as a veftibule to the fleeping apartments that furround it, there is a chryftal lamp replenifhed with cocoa-nut oil, always burning on a table at the door of each room, which is ready for the perfon who occupies it, at whatever time he may chufe to retire to his repofe; as it is the cuftom of the hotel that every one fhould keep the key of his own room, as a fecurity againft the Malays, who are of fuch an incorrigible nature, that no punifhment can ultimately deter them from indulging their difpofition to pilfer.

The public regulations of the houfe refemble thofe of European hotels, and the table which was kept for the Ambaffador's fuite was very fuperb. The breakfaft always confifted of tea, coffee, chocolate, and cocoa, with every kind of cold meat, broiled fifh, and eggs; to which were added, jellies, fweetmeats, and honey, with various kinds of wines and confectionary, all furnifhed in great abundance, and arranged in the handfomeft manner. Both the dinner and fupper confifted

of

of the moſt delicate diſhes, and dreſſed in a ſuperior ſtile of cookery. The ſervants table was alſo ſupplied with equal propriety and
plenty.

1793.
March.

The rate of living here, however, is very expenſive, and the prices
of liquors very exorbitant : ſmall beer and porter were charged half a
crown Engliſh per bottle. But when the prodigious rent of this
hotel, amounting, as the landlord himſelf aſſured me, to ſixty thouſand rix-dollars per annum, and the expenſe of importing liquors and
other commodities from Europe, with the duties on them, is confidered, the high price of living, in ſuch a ſituation, could no longer be
regarded either with ſurpriſe or diſcontent.

The dreſs of the inhabitants of Batavia takes its riſe from the cuſtom
of their reſpective countries. The European ladies, indeed, ſeem
not to be altogether governed by this principle, but ſuit their dreſſes
to their own peculiar fancy, and the circumſtances of the climate ;
while the Dutch and the Malay women, in ſome degree, imitate their
faſhions. The head-dreſs of the latter, however, is altogether different, and of a very curious appearance.—The hair is combed back-
ward from the forehead, and ſmoothed with oil and eſſences in ſuch
a manner as to wear the appearance of being japanned : it is then
twiſted hard, and, being laid in a circular form round the crown of the
head, is faſtened by a large comb with a number of gold and ſilver
pins, the heads of which are formed of precious ſtones, according to
the rank of the wearer. Hair powder is very little uſed in Batavia,
and by the Europeans alone. It was, however, with no ſmall degree
of exultation that I ſaw the decided ſuperiority which the few Engliſh
ladies who reſide here, poſſeſs over every other denomination of females, not only as to the gracefulneſs of their perſons, and the ſweet-
neſs of their countenances, but, alſo, in the ſimplicity of their dreſs and
the elegance of their manners.

G

The

The fuburbs of Batavia, or, as it is generally calleo, the Chinefe town, being moftly inhabited by thofe people, lie on the fouth and weft fides of the ditch that furrounds the city wall, and are fcattered about the country for feveral miles. The houfes are, in general, of wood, and have no pretenfions to elegance or beauty; though their warehoufes are fitted up with a certain degree of glare and gaudinefs. A great variety of manufactures are carried on here by the induftrious Chinamen: indeed, all the artificers and mechanics in Batavia are from China; the Europeans, through a foolifh and unpardonable pride, confidering it as beneath them to perform any mechanical operations; and the Malays appear to be curfed with a natural incapacity to be inftructed in any thing above the drudgery of manual labour.

The whole of thefe fuburbs forms a fcattered mafs of deformity and confufion; and the horrid ftenches which arife from ftagnant water and various filthy caufes, cannot be defcribed. In the furrounding country there are a great many beautiful feats and villas, with fine gardens; but the ground being every where fwampy, the number of drains, with which it is neceffarily interfected, renders it more or lefs unwholefome in every part.

In paffing through the fifh market, I was under the neceffity of retiring into a tavern, to get fome Madeira and water, in order to recover myfelf from the overcoming effects of the putrid fmells that affailed me. There appeared, however, to be a great abundance of fifh in this obnoxious place; but, except turtle, they bore a very exorbitant price.

The city and fuburbs of Batavia certainly form one of the moft unwholefome fpots in the world, and may be juftly termed the grave of Europeans: but the unfalutary and infectious nature of the place

might

might be very much alleviated by an attention to cleanliness, which seems to be not, in the least, considered by the government or police of the city. A company of scavengers would be of infinite use to the comfort and health of the inhabitants of Batavia; but there is no such establishment.

The heat of the sun is so great, that the canals are frequently dried up, or their waters rendered putrid: but this is not so malignant a source of pestilential disease, as the nastiness that prevails among the lower classes of the people, and the inattention to remove the receptacles of putrefaction among the higher orders of them. Nor is it easily to be reconciled, that the spirit of cleanliness, so prevalent in Holland, should so totally evaporate in a voyage to the most important of its Asiatic possessions. Nay, it has been considered by political writers, that the inattention to remedy the evils which have been described, is to be attributed to the commercial policy of the Dutch, in order to discourage foreigners from settling among them, and sharing the great, but hazardous advantages to be derived from participating in any branch of commerce in this oriental emporium: or, in case of a foreign war, to deter any enemy from invading a place, the very airs of which are more hostile to human life, than the weapons of battle. I shall only add, that, within the last twenty years, no less than ninety-eight thousand deaths appear on the records of the public hospital in Batavia.

At six o'clock in the morning we weighed anchor and made sail, running between the island of Onroost and the main.

This island is situated in the middle of the bay, and about four miles from Batavia. Its length does not exceed three quarters of a mile, and it is no more than half a mile in breadth. It contains, nevertheless, an handsome populous town, with a strong fort. In

1793.
March.

Sunday 17.

G 2 this

this little ſpot there are ſeveral founderies and manufactures, and the whole is a ſcene of induſtry and landſcape beauty. It is alſo ſurrounded with ſeveral iſlands of the ſame deſcription, moſt of which are inhabited; great numbers of people wiſely preferring theſe ſituations; which, though immoderately hot, are free from thoſe contagious diſeaſes that infect the city and ſuburbs of Batavia.

CHAP. II.

C H A P. II.

*The Jackall brig rejoins the Lion. Leighton, the carpenter, murdered
by the Malays. Lord Macartney views the spot where Colonel
Cathcart was buried. Came to Pulo Condore; some account of its
inhabitants; their alarm. Passed various islands. Arrived at
Turon bay, in Cochin China. Several mandarins came on board
the Lion; an account of them. The chief minister of the King of
Cochin China visits Lord Macartney. Presents received. Lord
Macartney returns the visit on shore in form. The master of the
Lion seized by the natives, but released in a few days. The inter-
ment of Mr. Tothill, purser of the Lion.*

THE owner of the French brig came on board, and was paid for
her in dollars.

1793.
March.
Monday 18.

The weather insupportably hot: Lord Macartney was still so much
indisposed as not to see company.

Tuesday 19.

The new brig joined us, which Lord Macartney was pleased to
name the Clarence, in honour of his Royal Highness the Duke of
Clarence.

Wednes-
day 20.

Boarded the Achilles, from Ostend to Batavia, who gave some
account of the Jackall brig, with whom we parted company in a gale
of wind, in the Bay of Biscay.

Thursday 21.

This morning, at six, we discovered a sail at a great distance, which,
from the account given by the Ostend vessel, was supposed to be the
Jackall. After a long series of doubts, conjectures, and solicitudes on

Saturday 23.

the

1793.
March.

the subject, Sir Erasmus Gower dispatched Lieutenant Cox, in the pinnace, to ascertain the truth. At noon, the pinnace returned with the agreeable intelligence, that the ship we had seen was the Jackall brig, whom we had long ago supposed to have been lost.

Sunday 24.

Mr. Saunders, from the Jackall, came on board to deliver his log-book to Sir Erasmus Gower. At four o'clock, we saw a sail, which proved to be the Concord, from China to Bengal.

Friday 29.
Good Friday.

William Leighton, Lord Macartney's joiner, who went ashore, in order to wash his linen at the watering-place at Sumatra beach, was murdered by the Malays. His body being found covered with wounds, was brought on board the Lion, and afterwards interred, with all becoming ceremony and respect, on North Island. He was a very ingenious artisan, and an honest, intelligent, and amiable man. But the melancholy which pervaded every countenance throughout the ship's company, on his death, is a more honourable and decided testimony of his merit and character, than any expressions of regard which I might employ on the occasion.

April.
Monday 1.

At half past six, A. M. we weighed and came to sail; at eight, Mortnay Island, south by east; Stroome Rock, south-east, half a mile: at eleven, came too, in seventeen fathom water. Angara Point, flag-staff, south by east. The cap, north-north-east, and button, north by east. The accommodation ladder was hoisted out after dinner, and soon after Lord Macartney, accompanied by Sir Erasmus Gower, went ashore, and viewed the spot where the Honourable Colonel Cathcart, brother to Lord Cathcart, a former Minister from the King of Great Britain to the court of China, was interred; and whose death put an end to that diplomatic expedition.

The weather continued moderate, with occasional fresh breezes and light airs, for the succeeding fortnight, which was employed in wooding, watering, receiving buffaloes on board, and making the

necessary

neceffary arrangements for the remaining part of the voyage. We
paffed, and, occafionally, anchored at Ninah Ifland, and the Polar,
Hound, and Tamarind iflands.

1793.
April.

At four in the afternoon the body of Tharbuny Ifland bore north-
north-weft; at five came into fifteen fathom water. Found here the
Sullivan homeward bound Indiaman, the Jackall, and the Clarence,
with an Imperial fhip. Arrived the Royal Admiral Indiaman.

Sunday 14.

The Sullivan and the Royal Admiral, Indiamen, failed for England.

Tuefday 16.

We continued coafting along, and paffed by numerous iflands, with
moderate weather; which was only once interrupted by a fquall, accompanied by rain, and followed by thunder and lightning, till we
came to anchor in the fouth-weftern extremity of Pulo Condore bay.

A party, foon after our arrival, went on fhore, after having called
at the Hindoftan, for Sir George and Mr. Staunton, and Mr.
Niaung, one of the Chinefe interpreters. We reached the fhore in
about an hour and a half; and, on our landing, fome of the natives
came out to meet us on the beach, with whom we proceeded towards
a wood, with fix men from the boats, properly armed with mufquets and ammunition. We had not, however, proceeded more than
an hundred yards, when we came to a few miferable huts, built of
bamboo, and fcattered about the place where they are fituated. One
of them was inhabited by a perfon ftyled the chief, or mandarin, in
whom was vefted the government of the ifland. This hut, like the
reft, was raifed about three feet from the ground, with a roof of
bamboo, and fupported by four pofts fixed in the earth. Such is
the only miferable fhelter which the inhabitants poffefs.

May.
Thurfday 16,

In this houfe, if it may be thought to deferve that name, there
were feveral people, all natives of Cochin China, but who fpoke
the Tartar language. None of them, except the chief, had any
covering

covering but a ftrip of linen round their waifts, and a kind of black turban on their heads. The chief, to whom the reft paid great obedience, was diftinguifhed by wearing a loofe black gown, made of a ftuff like crape; under which he wore a wide pair of black filk trowfers. Over his fhoulder was thrown a filver cord, to which was fufpended behind a fmall embroidered bag of very exquifite workmanfhip. His head was alfo covered with a black turban; but he was, in common with the reft, without fhoes.

At the diftance of a few yards from the hut ftood their temple, whofe exterior form was the fame as the other buildings. The infide was furnifhed, or, as it muft have been confidered by them, ornamented with fome old fire-arms, a few cutlaffes, and three daggers. One fwivel, and fome long fpontoons, were laid acrofs the roof: there were alfo feveral lances, and creafes (a kind of poifonous dagger, ufed by the Afiatic favages) piled up againft a bamboo poft, in the middle of the building. It was evident, from the conduct of thefe people, that they were not accuftomed to the ufe of fire-arms, as they appeared to confider thefe warlike inftruments as objects of adoration. This opinion was confirmed by the alarm and aftonifhment they expreffed on my difcharging a mufquet at the trunk of a tree; and the eagernefs with which they examined the place where the ball had entered. But this did not content them; for they contrived to extract the ball, which they fhewed to each other with marks of extreme amazement.

We remained near two hours on fhore, and entered into a treaty with the chief, to procure us as many buffaloes, with as much poultry, fruit, &c. as could be fpared from the ifland, and for which he was to be paid his own price: to this propofition he readily agreed, and promifed that the commiffion fhould be immediately executed, and the different articles be ready for delivery on the next day. After the agreement was thus amicably fettled, the chief offered us a regale of rice and fifh, of which we all tafted. He then pointed to fome cocoa-nut

trees,

trees, as if to know if we fhould chufe to have any of them; and no
fooner was it fignified to him that a prefent of that fruit would be
very acceptable, than a number of his people were inftantly ordered
to gather them. It was furprifing to fee with what agility they
climbed up thofe very lofty trees; and as they threw down the
nuts, others below immediately fkinned and handed them round to
the company. We then took our leave of the mandarin, and on
our way to the beach faw feveral canoes which were building, and
one of them appeared to be of a very ingenious conftruction.

The ifland of Pulo Condore has but few inhabitants, and thofe it poffeffes are not collected together in any town, but live in bamboo huts,
fcattered up and down the country. It produces no fruit but cocoa-nuts
and water-melons, and no grain but fome coarfe rice. It has, however,
plenty of buffaloes, with a kind of wild-duck, and the common
fowls, fome of which are domefticated with them. This ifland,
however, has a noble bay, which produces a fifh that refembles our
whiting, in great abundance, and has a fafe anchorage, except along
the fhore, where for about three quarters of a mile it is full of
fhoals. The ifland is fubject to the King of Cochin China, and lies
in the Chinefe ocean. Long. one hundred and feven deg. twenty-fix
min. eaft. Lat. two deg. forty min. north.

On returning to the fhips we met with a very heavy fquall, attended with violent rain.

This morning I went afhore with a party, accompanied by Mr.
Niaung, in order to receive the feveral articles for which a bargain had
been made with the mandarin on the preceding day.

On our landing, and going to the hut belonging to the Chief, we
found, to our utter aftonifhment, that the people had deferted their
habitations, and carried off every article with them: even the temple

H   was

1793.
May.

was ftripped of all its warlike treafure. This extraordinary and unexpected circumftance was, however, explained in a letter, which we found in the Chief's hut. It was written in Chinefe characters, and expreffed the apprehenfions of the iflanders at feeing our fhips in their bay; a fight they had never beheld before. In fhort, this appearance was fo formidable to them, that they concluded our defigns muft be hoftile; and in order to avoid the deftruction which they imagined us to have meditated againft them, they had, during the night, conveyed away their effects, and retired to the mountains. The letter alfo reprefented their extreme poverty, and implored us with the moft humble expreflions, not to burn or deftroy their huts, as they propofed to re-inhabit them as foon as the fquadron had failed. We, therefore, returned to the fhips as we left them, without fruits, or fowls, or buffaloes.

Saturday 18.   Heavy gales. At four in the afternoon, fqually; at eight, weighed anchor, and came to fail.

Thurfday 23.   Having paffed in the intermediate time feveral iflands of different forms, we, this day, faw the extremes of Pulo Canton, an ifland off the coaft of Cochin China, bearing north by weft, to northweft by weft.

Sunday 26.   At nine in the evening anchored in Turon Bay, in Cochin China. Found here a Portuguefe brig, who faluted us with eleven guns.

Monday 27.   The fhip's company employed in watering. The water here is of a reddifh colour. Several proas came along-fide the Lion with ducks, cocoa-nuts, and joghry, for fale. Several mandarins alfo came on board to fee the fhip.

Tuefday 28.   Men were fent on fhore to raife tents for the fick.

4

The

The Ambaffador was vifited by feveral mandarins, with a great train of attendants. They were entertained with wines and liquors of various kinds, which, however, they were very cautious in tafting, till Lord Macartney banifhed all apprehenfion by fetting them the example: they then drank, without referve, whatever was offered to them; but they appeared to prefer cherry and rafberry brandy, above all the other liquors with which they were regaled.

The drefs of thefe perfons confifted chiefly of a black loofe gown, of a kind of crape, with filk trowfers, flippers, and a black turban: a girdle, of filver cordage, was alfo tied round their waifts. Some of them, but whether it arofe from accident, or was a badge of diftinction, I cannot tell, wore dark blue gowns of the fame ftuff. The domeftics were clad in a plaid, or Tartan drefs; their trowfers were tucked up to the knee, and they wore no fhoes or flippers; their legs were entirely naked; and their turban was of plaid, like the reft of their very curious drefs.

In the evening, the Prime Minifter of the King of Cochin China, came on board the Lion, accompanied by feveral mandarins, and a confiderable train of attendants, to requeft the Ambaffador's company to dinner, in the name of the King, who had given his minifter a fpecial commiffion to make this invitation. It was, accordingly, fignified to this diftinguifhed perfonage, that his Excellency received the meffage with the utmoft refpect, and would, in confequence of it, go on fhore on Tuefday morning, at ten o'clock.

After this conference, the Chinefe minifter, and his fuite, returned in their barges, which were decorated in a very gaudy manner. They were faluted on their departure from the fhip with five guns.

H 2

In

In the forenoon the Ambaſſador received a viſit from two mandarins, who brought from the King of Cochin China a preſent, conſiſting of

10 Buffaloes
50 Hogs
160 Fowls
150 Ducks
200 Bags of rice, and
6 Large jars of ſamptſoo.

The laſt is a liquor made in China, and imported from thence.

I went aſhore in the forenoon and ſaw the town, the name of which is Fic-Foo. It conſiſts of nothing more than a crowd of wretched bamboo huts, though it contains a ſpacious market-place, well ſupplied with ducks, fowls, eggs, cocoa-nuts, and fruits. The ſurrounding country is flat, and very fertile : but the natives ſeem to have little or no idea of cultivation, which would make it the ſcene of extreme abundance. Their principal traffic ſeems to be with their women, by conſigning them, for a certain conſideration, to the ſociety of Europeans who touch here. They have no coin, but a ſort of ſmall caxee ; and all their ſilver is in the form of long bars, or wedges. The reſidence of the principal mandarin conſiſts of a large open range of bamboo huts, of a better form, and more elegant appearance than the reſt ; containing ſeveral rooms of a tolerable ſize and proportions, which are fitted up and furniſhed in a neat and ornamental manner.

In the afternoon the Ambaſſador's guards, with ſome of the marines, went on ſhore to practiſe the ceremonial duties that had been aſſigned them for the following day.

This morning the Ambaſſador, attended by his whole ſuite, in full uniform, with Sir Eraſmus Gower, Captain Mackintoſh, and ſeveral

of

of the officers of the Lion and the Hindoftan, went on fhore with great
ceremony; when, in honour of the birth-day of our moft excellent
Sovereign, George the Third, he was faluted with twenty-one guns
by the Lion, the Hindoftan, and Portuguefe brig. The Britifh
troops, with their officers and band of mufic, had been previoufly
fent afhore to wait his Excellency's arrival.

On this day the royal ftandard of Great Britain was difplayed at the
main-top-gallant-royal maft; the St. George's enfign at the fore-top-
gallant ditto; and the union at the mizen.

The Ambaffador was received, on his landing, by feveral mandarins with every mark of attention and refpect; when he proceeded,
under an efcort of his own troops, to the houfe of the Prime Minifter,
where a collation in the beft manner of the country was prepared for
him. Here his Excellency remained for fome time; and, after an
exchange of mutual civilities, returned to the Lion, when he was
faluted by fifteen guns from all the fhips lying at anchor.

I went afhore in the afternoon, and purchafed fome fruit and fugar
of a very good quality: it is made in large cakes, and refembles fine
bread, for which, at fome fmall diftance, it may be actually miftaken. I alfo faw fix large elephants, which had been brought for
the amufement of the mandarins: they appeared to be perfectly inno-
cent, were obedient to every command, and performed many feats of
unwieldy agility. Thefe huge animals moved at the rate of eight
miles an hour.

On this morning the fick were received on board the fhips from the
ftation on fhore.

Mr. Jackfon, mafter of the Lion, went in the cutter to take foundings
in the bay; but having gone up the mouth of the river Campvella, which
rifes about eighty miles up the country, and forms a confluence with
the

1793.
June.

Wednefday 5.

Friday 7.

1793.
June.

the river that difcharges itfelf into Turon Bay, he inconfiderately began to furvey, and take plans of, the coaft; but, in attempting to execute this defign, he, with the feven men who accompanied him, were made prifoners by the natives, who feized the boat, and carried them to the capital city of the kingdom.

This very difagreeable intelligence was communicated from the fhore by the mandarins, whofe good offices were earneftly folicited by Lord Macartney, and Sir Erafmus Gower, to obtain the return of thefe men to the fhip. Indeed, this unreflecting conduct of the mafter might, as it was apprehended, be attended with confequences that would have interrupted the courfe of the embaffy; as the country of Cochin China is tributary to the Chinefe empire, and fends an annual Ambaffador to the court of Pekin; fo that all this bufinefs might have been mifreprefented in fuch a manner to the Chinefe go-vernment, as to have leffened the good difpofitions we were difpofed to believe that they entertained towards the Britifh embaffy. In fhort, it appeared, that very ferious apprehenfions were entertained on that fubject, by thofe who were the beft qualified to form a right judgment of the policy and temper of the court which was the object of our deftination.

Tuefday 11.

Mr. Niaung, one of the interpreters, went on fhore with fome of the Ambaffador's fuite, to inquire concerning the Britifh prifoners, and he was informed by the mandarins, that they had been releafed, and were on their return.

Wednef-
day 12.

William Tothill, Efq. purfer of the Lion, died this morning, after an illnefs of a few days.

The King of Cochin China fent another large prefent of rice to the Ambaffador.

The

The body of Mr. Tothill was interred on fhore with every poffible mark of refpect and regard: Sir Erafmus Gower alfo ordered an infcription to be cut in wood, which was afterwards placed on his grave.

At four o'clock in the afternoon Mr. Jackfon returned with the cutter and his men, from their imprifonment; during which period they had undergone the fevereft fufferings both in body and mind; and no circumftance, but their belonging to the Britifh embaffy, could have preferved them from being put to death.

1793.
June.
Thurfday 13.

C H A P.

C H A P. III.

Leave Turon Bay. Sir George Staunton, &c. sail in the Jackall for Macao. Enter the Yellow Sea. Lieut. Campbell goes to Mettow. Present from the mandarin of Chusan. Number of sick on board the Lion. Messrs. Huttner and Plumb go to Mettow to arrange the landing of the embassy. A mandarin arrives on board. The soldiers, mechanics, and suite go on board the junks, with the presents, baggage, &c. The Ambassador lands at Mettow. Description of that place.

1793.

June,
Sunday 16.
Thursday 20.

AT four in the afternoon weighed and set sail from Turon Bay.

The weather was moderate and fair. At six P. M. saw the land north-north-east; at eight the body of the Grand Ladrone bore north-north-east.

Sir George and Mr. Staunton, with one of Lord Macartney's secretaries, were charged with letters and business to the commissioners, Messrs. Brown, Irvine, and Jackson, who were sent from England to notify in China the expected embassy, and who were then at Macao. They accordingly set sail in the Jackall brig, accompanied by the Clarence, for that place, to execute their commission. Mr. Coa and Mr. Niaung, the Chinese interpreters, accompanied them on the occasion, with the design to proceed over land to the place of their nativity.

These worthy and amiable men took a very affectionate leave of their friends on board the Lion, with whom they had made so long a

voyage;

voyage; but with all the impatience natural to thofe who had been removed at fuch a diftance, and for fo great a length of time, from their relations, friends, and native land.

1793.
Jun.

At half paft eight in the morning we came to anchor in eleven fathom water, on the north point of the Grand Ladrone ifland.

The Jackall and Clarence returned from Macao. Sir George Staun-Sunday 23. ton foon after came on board; and, from the intelligence communicated to him by the Commiffioners, the moft fanguine hopes were entertained that this extraordinary and important embaffy would be crowned with fuccefs.

We now entered the Yellow Sea, when nothing material happened, that can juftify particular defcription, till we arrived at the end of this branch of our voyage. In our paffage, we faw many iflands, and occafionally met with Chinefe junks, fifhing-boats, and other circumftances, which denoted our approach to that part of the continent to which we were deftined.

There being feveral rocks on the Chinefe coaft, in the Yellow Sea, that had no denomination in any chart, Sir Erafmus Gower thought proper to name them after the three principal characters of the embaffy. Thus we find our journals contain, in this part of the voyage, the names of Cape Macartney; Cape Gower, and Staunton's Ifland.

At fix o'clock in the afternoon, the Lion came to an anchor in July,
Sunday 21. Jangangfoe Bay; Mettow Iflands bearing from north, to north-weft by weft, two miles off fhore.

Lieut. Campbell, with Mr. Huttner, Mr. Plumb, and Lieut. Ommaney, went in the cutter to Mettow, to be informed if there was any track by which the Lion could enter the river, or if there was any river on that coaft, which was navigable for fhips of her burthen, and

I

by

1793.
July.

by whofe navigation fhe could make a nearer approach to the capital. If the anfwers to thefe inquiries did not prove fatisfactory, thofe gentlemen were then to concert meafures with the mandarin of the place for the difembarkation of the fuite there.

Monday 22.　The brig Endeavour arrived from Macao and Canton with difpatches from the Commiffioners.

Tuefday 23.　This morning a mandarin of Chufan fent a prefent of twelve fine fmall bullocks, a number of hogs, with a large quantity of fruit, garden ftuff, and rice.

Thurfday 25.　The cutter returned with Lieut. Campbell and his company, who gave a very favourable account of the hofpitality of the Chinefe at Mettow; where they were not only received with the greateft civility, but furnifhed with every poffible accommodation, and fupplied with the greateft plenty and abundance. At the fame time Mr. Campbell reported the abfolute impracticability of proceeding further, as the whole way to the mouth of the river forms a chain of fhoals, while a bar runs acrofs the entrance of it, which is not more than fix feet deep, even at high water. In confequence of this report, Sir Erafmus Gower refolved to proceed no further.

Saturday 27.　The report of the furgeon amounted to ninety-three men fick on board the Lion.

The Jackall and Clarence failed with Mr. Huttner and Mr. Plumb to Mettow, to make arrangements with the mandarins for the landing of the embaffy, and to fix the time when the Ambaffador fhould go on fhore: the refult of whofe commiffion was, that large junks would be fent for the reception of the fuite and baggage, as foon as the wind ferved.

A pre-

A prefent of fixteen bullocks, thirty-two fine large fheep, fome hogs, with vegetables, tea, fugar, &c. was fent on board the Lion. A principal mandarin alfo came on board from one of the junks, and dined with Lord Macartney; where he appeared in a very aukward fituation, as the Chinefe do not know the ufe of knives and forks. This officer finally fettled with his Excellency that the fucceeding Monday fhould be the day of his difembarkation; but that the heavy baggage, &c. fhould be previoufly tranfhipped into the junks. The mandarin expreffed great furprife at our wooden palace, and could fcarce believe the various arrangements and wonderful conveniencies of it. He was hoifted into one of our boats in the accommodation chair; a ceremony with which he appeared to be infinitely delighted.

A mandarin came on board to dinner. The prefents, baggage, &c. were all fhipped into the junks; on board which veffels the foldiers, mechanics, and great part of his Excellency's fervants, were alfo fent.

This morning at four o'clock feveral junks came along fide the Lion to receive the remainder of the Ambaffador's baggage. His Excellency then took his breakfaft on board, and was joined by the remainder of his fuite from the Hindoftan.

At eight o'clock Sir Erafmus Gower gave orders for the fhip's company to man fhip, previous to his Excellency's difembarkation, which took place almoft immediately; when he was faluted with three cheers from the feamen, and the difcharge of nineteen guns from the Lion and Hindoftan.

At nine o'clock the remainder of the fuite took their ftations on different junks; the Ambaffador, Sir George Staunton and fon, having gone on board the Clarence brig, the accommodations of the junks being not only very inconvenient, but extremely dirty, and otherwife very unfit to receive them.

1793.

August.
Friday 2.

Sunday 4.

Monday 5.

I 2

The

1793.
Auguſt.

The number of junks employed on this occaſion for the reception of the ſuite and baggage, amounted to twenty ſail, of about an hundred tuns burthen.

At two o'clock in the afternoon we ſaw the town and fort of Met-tow; at three the junks came to anchor at the mouth of the river, where we found the Jackall, Clarence, and Endeavour arrived before us. From the ſeveral ſhort windings at this part of the river, we were obliged frequently to anchor and weigh, in order to avoid the ſhoals.

At four the whole fleet came to anchor oppoſite the palace of the principal mandarin.

The town, though extenſive, has not the charm of elegance or the merit of uniformity; indeed, its ſituation is ſuch as to exclude any encouragement to beautify and adorn it, as it is ſituated on a ſwamp, occaſioned by the frequent overflowing of the ſea, notwithſtanding the precaution of the inhabitants to make an embankment on the ſhore.

The houſes, or huts, for they rather deſerve the latter name, are built altogether of mud, with bamboo roofs: they are very low, and without either floors or pavements. At a ſmall diſtance from the town there are ſeveral buildings of a very ſuperior form and appearance, which belong to the mandarins of the place: they are conſtructed of ſtone and wood; the body of the houſe being of the former, and the wings and galleries, which are very pretty, and painted of va-rious colours, of the latter material: they are of a ſquare form, and three ſtories in height; each ſtory having a ſurrounding range of pa-liſadoes, which are richly gilt and fancifully painted. The lower ſtory, or ground floor, is fronted with piazzas, which are ornamented in the ſame manner. The wings project on each ſide the body of the houſe, and appear to contain a conſiderable range of apartments.

Each

Each mandarin is attended by a great number of guards, confifting both of infantry and cavalry, who live in tents pitched round the refidence of the perfonage whom they ferve.

1793.
Auguft.

Notwithftanding its unfavourable fituation, the immenfe crowd of fpectators who affembled to fee the Ambaffador come on fhore, proves Mettow to be a place of prodigious population. Many of thefe curious people were on horfeback and in carriages; fo that the banks of the river where our junks lay at anchor were entirely covered with them.

The only fort in this place confifts fimply of a fquare tower, and feems to have been conftructed for ornament rather than public utility; for, though it ftands on the very margin of the fea, and commands the entrance of the river, not a fingle piece of ordnance appears on the walls.

The breadth of this part of the river is about a furlong, and the colour of the water is muddy, refembling that of the Yellow Ocean with which it mingles: its depth is very unequal, being in fome parts nine, and in others fix feet deep; but in no part lefs than two. At the entrance, as has been already mentioned, there is a bar or bank of fand, which ftretches acrofs it, and at full tide has not more depth than fix or feven feet; though on the fide towards the fea, and at a few yards only from the bar, there is upwards of fix fathoms water.

The environs of the town prefent, on both fides the river, an expanfe of flat country. The foil is rich, and can boaft extraordinary fertility.

In the evening we received from the mandarin a very refrefhing and acceptable prefent of dreffed meats and fruits.

CHAP.

C H A P. IV.

An account of the mandarin appointed to conduct the accommodations for the embassy. Various presents of provisions. Gross habits of the Chinese respecting their food. Description of the junks. Order of those vessels fitted up for the accommodation of the British Ambassador and his suite.

1793.

August.
Tuesday 6.

THE whole of this morning was employed in transhipping the baggage to the accommodation junks, hired for the embassy by *Van Tadge-In*, a mandarin of the first class, who had been appointed by the Emperor to conduct the business of the embassy, in every thing that related to the residence, provisions, and journey of the suite.

This person became interesting to us, as he was appointed to attend the embassy during the whole time we should remain in China. He was about five feet nine inches in height, stout, well made, and of a dark complexion, but of a remarkable pleasing and open countenance: his manners and deportment were polite and unaffected; and the appointment of such a man, so admirably qualified to fulfil the peculiar duties to which he was nominated, gave us a very favourable opinion of the good sense of the Chinese government, and served to encourage our hopes of success in the important objects of this distinguished embassy.

We received at noon, from the mandarin's boat, which was accompanied by Mr. Plumb, Lord Macartney's interpreter, a quantity of raw beef, with bread and fruit: the beef, though not fat, is of a very good quality; but the bread, though made of excellent flour, was by no means pleasant to our palate: as the Chinese do not make use of

yeast,

yeaft, or bake it in an oven, it is, in fact, little better than common dough.
The fhape and fize of the loaves are thofe of an ordinary wafh-ball
cut in two.   They are compofed of nothing more than flour and water,
and ranged on bars which are laid acrofs an iron hollow pan, containing a certain quantity of water, which is then placed on an earthen
ftove : when the water boils, the veffel, or pan, is covered over with
fomething like a fhallow tub, and the fteam of the water, for a few
minutes, is all the baking, if it may be fo called, which the bread
receives.   In this ftate we found it neceffary to cut it in flices and
toaft it, before we could reconcile it to our appetites.   The fruits,
which made a part of this prefent, confifted of apples, pears, fhad-
docks, and oranges of a fuperior flavour.

In the afternon we received another very large fupply of provifions
ready dreffed, confifting of beef, mutton, pork, whole pigs, and poultry of all forts, both roaft and boiled.

The roaft meat had a very fingular appearance, as they ufe fome
preparation of oil, that gives it a glofs like that of varnifh ; nor was its
flavour fo agreeable to our palates, as the difhes produced by the clean
and fimple cookery of our European kitchens.   Their boiled meat,
being free from the oily tafte of that which is roafted or baked, was
far preferable.

We were, however, in fome degree, affected by the accounts we
had heard of the indifference of the Chinefe, concerning their food ;
and that they not only eat all animal food without diftinction, but do
not difcard even fuch as die of difeafes, from their meals.   This circumftance made feveral of our party very cautious of what they eat ;
and as to their hafhes and ftews, many refufed their allowance of thefe
difhes, from the apprehenfion of their being compofed of unwholefome
flefh.

But

1793.
August.

But it was not merely from the information of others that we felt a difguft at Chinefe cookery, as we had ocular demonftration of the grofs appetites of the Chinefe people. The pigs on board the Lion being affected with a diforder, which is always fatal to thefe animals, feveral of them were thrown overboard;—which circumftance being obferved by the Chinefe belonging to the junks, they inftantly got out their boats and picked up thefe difeafed carcafes, which they immediately cut up, and having dreffed a part of them, appeared to make a very comfortable meal, that was accompanied with frequent marks of derifion at the Englifh for their foolifh extravagance.

We were at firft difpofed to believe that this grofsnefs of appetite was confined to the lower claffes of the people, who were generally in fuch a ftate of indigence, as to be glad to obtain meat in the accidental way which we have juft mentioned: but we afterwards learned, that the more independent claffes of people, and even the mandarins themfelves, are not exempt from a cuftom, in domeftic œconomy, at which the eager appetite of the ftarving European would revolt.

In the warm feafon, this part of the country fwarms with mofquitos, that tormenting infect which is fo diftreffing to the inhabitants of the warmer climates.

Wednefday 7.

This morning I went on board the accommodation junk, occupied by Captain Mackintofh, of the Hindoftan, who was required to accompany the embaffy to Pekin. The fquadron, in the mean time, received inftructions to return to Chufan harbour, and to wait there till further orders.

The junks, or Chinefe veffels, are formed on a conftruction I never remember to have feen in any other part of the world. They are built of beach wood and bamboo, with a flat bottom: they are of different fizes, from thirty to an hundred feet in length; the breadth
of

1793.
August.

of the largeſt are from twenty to thirty feet, and the ſmaller ones in proportion.

In this junk there was on the firſt deck a range of very neat and commodious apartments, which were clean, and decorated with paintings. They conſiſted of three ſleeping apartments, a dining parlour, with a kitchen, and two rooms for ſervants. The floor is made to lift up, by hatches all along the junk, to each of which there is a braſs ring: beneath is an hold, or vacant ſpace for containing lumber; and the quantity of goods that can be ſtowed away in theſe places is almoſt incredible.

On the upper or main deck, there is a range of fourteen or fifteen ſmall chambers, allotted for the uſe of the men belonging to the junk, and an apartment for the captain or owner of the veſſel.

In the lower deck, the windows are made of wood, with very ſmall ſquare holes, covered with a ſort of glazed, tranſparent paper; the ſaſhes are divided into four parts, and made to take out occaſionally, either to admit the air for coolneſs, or to ſweeten the apartments. On the outſide there is a coloured curtain, that extends from one end of the junk to the other, which, in very hot weather, is unfurled and fixed up to ſhade the apartments from the heat of the ſun. There are alſo ſhutters, which ſlide before the windows on the outſide, to prevent the effects of cold weather, or any inclemency of the ſeaſon.

There is a gang-way on both ſides of the veſſel, about thirty inches broad, by way of paſſage, without entering into any of the apartments; and though many of theſe veſſels carry from two to three hundred tons, they only draw three feet water, ſo that they can be worked with eaſe and ſafety in the moſt ſhoaly rivers. Some of theſe junks have two maſts, though, in general, they have but one, with a very aukward kind of rudder; and the more elegant veſſels of this kind, which I have juſt deſcribed, are only calculated for the navigation of a river;

K

1793.
August.

as they are not constructed with sufficient strength to resist the violent. effects of wind and weather.

It is usual for all vessels which navigate the rivers in China, to have a lamp, with a lighted candle in it, hoisted to the mast head, as soon as it is dark, to prevent those accidents which would otherwise very frequently happen from vessels running foul of each other. These lamps are made of transparent paper, with characters printed on it, to notify what junk it is, or the rank of any passengers on board it: if they are persons of distinction, three of these lanterns are usually suspended. The vessel is also illuminated in other parts of it, particularly round the deck; and the number of lights are generally proportioned to the rank of the persons who occupy the junk. The same service which the lamps perform by night, as far as relates to notification, is performed in the day-time by silken ensigns, whose printed characters specify in the same manner, the existing circumstances of the vessel. It may be easily conceived, that, from the prodigious number of junks which navigate this river, a very pleasing, and sometimes, indeed, a grand effect is produced, by such an assemblage of lights moving along the water.

I am not qualified to determine whether it proceeds from the domestic policy of the Chinese, from prejudice, in favour of long-established habits, or an ignorance of mechanics, but they have not made any advancement in the science of naval architecture: the junks of the last century, and those of the present day, are invariably the same.

The order in which the vessels, appropriated for the purpose of conveying the British embassy to Pekin, proceeded, was as follows:.

The grand Mandarin, and his suite, in five junks.
Junk, No. 1.   His Excellency the Earl Macartney.
Ditto,   — 2.   Sir George and Mr. Staunton.
———   — 3.   Mr. Plumb, the Chinese interpreter.

3

Junk, No. 4.   Lieutenant-Colonel Benfon, Lieutenant Parifh, and 1793.
              Lieutenant Crewe.   Auguſt.

Ditto, — 5.   Captain Mackintofh, of the Hindoſtan, Mr. Max-
              well, Doctor Gillan, and Mr. Huttner.

—— — 6.   Mr. Barrow, Mr. Winder, and Mr. Baring, (fon of
              Sir Francis Baring).

—— — 7.   Doctor Scott, Doctor Dinwiddie, Mr. Hickey, and
              Mr. Alexander.

Thefe, with the junks which contained the foldiers, mechanics, and feryants, completed the naval proceſſion.

CHAP. V.

Lord Macartney leaves Mettow, and sets sail for Pekin. Beauty and fertility of the country. Various circumstances of the voyage. The soldiers of China described. The navigation of the river. Some account of the tea-tree, with the manner of making tea as a beverage. Prodigious population of the country. Arrive at the city of Tyen-sing. Some account of it. A Chinese play. Description of the mandarin's palace, &c.

1793.
August.
Thursday 8.

THIS morning the Ambassador paid a visit to the principal mandarin of Mettow, to take leave, on his departure for Pekin : and at eleven o'clock, the fleet of junks, with his Excellency and the whole suite on board, proceeded on their voyage.

We received a large supply of provisions, ready dressed, together with tea, sugar, bread, vegetables of all sorts, and a large quantity of fruit, consisting of apples, pears, grapes, and oranges, which never failed to make a part of those supplies for the table with which the embassy was at all times furnished, in the greatest abundance. We also received, at this time, a provision of wood and charcoal, for culinary uses. I made some inquiries after mineral coal, but it was not known at Mettow, nor could I learn whether it is found or used in any part of China.

We had proceeded but a very few miles up the river, when the country displayed prospects of such peculiar novelty and beauty as would baffle any attempts of mine to describe them. The view on all sides presents fields rich in various cultivation, with extensive meadows covered with sheep and the finest cattle. Their gardens appeared to be equally disposed for domestic use and pleasure ;

producing

producing at the fame time abundance of vegetables, and the fineft fruits; while the eye was charmed with the beauty of their fcenery, and the gaiety of their decorations. On the firft glimpfe of their grounds, whether applied to the more folid ufes of agriculture, or the more elegant arrangement of their gardens, in raifing grain and efculent plants, or cultivating fruits and flowers, I was convinced that the Chinefe were no mean proficients in botanical knowledge, as well as the fcience of farming, and the art of ornamental gardening. I alfo obferved, that the fields were as well guarded by fences, both in the form of hedges and ftone walls, as any I had feen in the enclofed parts of my own country.

During the day, the guards belonging to the mandarin marched along the banks of the river; and at night pitched their tents oppofite to the ftation where the junks lay at anchor; when they kept a regular watch till the hour of the morning when the fleet proceeded on its voyage. The front of each tent was adorned with lamps, fo that the camp on fhore, and the junks on the water, formed together a confiderable illumination, and produced a very uncommon and pleafing effect.

The centinels on fhore have, each of them, a piece of hollow bamboo, which they ftrike at regular intervals, with a mallet, to announce that they are awake and vigilant in their refpective ftations. This cuftom, as I was informed by the peyings, or foldiers themfelves, is univerfal throughout the Chinefe army.

We were awakened at a very early hour by the found of the gongs, which was the fignal for failing.

The gong is an inftrument of a circular form, made of brafs; it refembles, in fome degree, the cover of a large ftewpan, and is ufed as bells or trumpets are in Europe, to convey notice, or make fignals from one place to another: when they are ftruck with a large wooden mallet, which is covered with leather, a found is produced that may be diftinctly heard at the diftance of a league.

W

We received the ufual fupply of provifions, with the addition, for the firft time, of fome wine of the country in a ftone jar: its colour is nearly that of what is called Lifbon wine in England, and is equally clear: it is rather ftrong, but is of an unpleafant flavour, being harfh and fharp, and, in fhort, has more the tafte of vinegar than wine. The jar which contained it was equal, in meafure, to three Englifh gallons; and the mouth of it was covered with a large plantane leaf, clofed in with a cap of clay; on which was fixed a red label, marked with certain Chinefe characters, to denote, as I fuppofe, the contents of the veffel.

We paffed feveral very populous towns on both fides of the river, but fituated at fome diftance from it. The Ambaffador, however, received military honours from the foldiers belonging to them, who were drawn up on the bank, on either fide, contiguous to their refpective cantonments; and furrounded by an immenfe crowd of fpectators.

The uniform of the foldiers confifts of a large pair of loofe, black nankeen trowfers, which they ftuff into a kind of quilted cotton ftockings, made in the form of boots. They always wrap their feet in a cotton rag before they draw thefe boots over their trowfers; they add alfo a pair of very clumfy fhoes, made of cotton, the foles of which are, at leaft, an inch thick, and very broad at the points. Thefe trowfers have no waiftband, fo that they lap over, and are tied with a piece of common tape, to which is generally fufpended a fmall leathern bag, or purfe, to contain money. Thefe foldiers do not ufe either fhirts, waiftcoats, or neckcloths; but wear a large mantle of black nankeen, with loofe fleeves, which is edged with nankeen of a red colour. Round their middle there is a broad girdle, ornamented in the center with what appears to be a pebble of about the fize of half-a-crown, though, as I was informed, it is an hard fubftance or pafte made of rice. From this girdle is fufpended a pipe and bag to hold tobacco, on one fide, and a fan on the other; which are

annually

annually allowed them by the Emperor, as well as a daily portion of tobacco, a plant that grows in the utmoft abundance in every part of China.

1793.
Auguft.

The Chinefe troops were always, when I faw them, drawn up in fingle ranks, with a great number of colours or ftandards, which are chiefly made of green filk, with a red border, and enriched with golden characters. They wear their fwords on the left fide, but the handle or hilt is backwards, and the point forwards, fo that, when they draw thefe weapons, they put their hands behind their backs, and unfheath them without being immediately perceived; a manœuvre which they execute with great dexterity, and is well adapted for the purpofes of attack, as a foreign antagonift, who is not accuftomed to this mode of affault, would be probably wounded, at leaft, before he was prepared to defend himfelf againft it. Under their left arm is flung a bow; and a quiver, generally containing twelve arrows, hangs on their backs; others are armed with match-locks of a very rufty appearance..

Their heads are fhaved round the crown, ears, and neck, except a fmall part on the back of the head, where the hair, which is encouraged to grow to a great length, hangs down their backs in a plait, and is tied at the end with a riband. They wear a fhallow ftraw hat very neatly made, which is neceffarily tied under the chin with a ftring, and is decorated with a bunch of camel's hair, dyed of a red colour.

On all occafions, fimilar to that which brought thefe troops to the banks of the river to do military honour to the Britifh Ambaffador, a temporary arch covered with filk is placed at each end of the line, in which the mandarins fit till the proceffion, or perfon to be faluted, appears, when they come forward and make their appearance. Near thefe arches are three fmall fwivels about thirty inches in length, which are fixed in the ground with the muzzle pointing to the air: thefe are difcharged as the perfon to be honoured with the falute paffes the

mandarin.

1793.
Auguſt.

mandarin at the end of the line. This mode of firing ſalutes the Chineſe very ſenſibly adopt to prevent accidents, obſerving, at the ſame time in their account of it, that a loaded gun ſhould never be levelled, but at their enemies. In the management of artillery and fire-arms, it is not to be ſuppoſed that Europeans can derive any one improvement from the inhabitants of the eaſt ; but we well know, neverthelefs, that very melancholy, and ſometimes fatal accidents are occaſioned from the want of ſimilar regulations, by the diſcharge both of great guns and ſmall arms on our days of public rejoicing.

The houſes, ſcattered on the banks of the river, were chiefly built of mud, rarely intermixed with ſome of a better form, which were conſtructed of ſtone, and finiſhed with great neatneſs ; producing a very pretty effect, as we paſſed them, from the water.

The women at theſe places, of whom we ſaw great numbers, have their feet and ancles univerſally bound with red tape, to prevent, as it is ſaid, their feet from growing of the natural ſize: ſo very tight is this bandage drawn round them, that they walk with great diffi-culty; and when we conſider that this extraordinary practice com-mences with their infancy, it is rather a matter of ſurprize that they ſhould be able to walk at all. If we except this ſtrange management, or rather miſmanagement, of their feet, and their head-dreſs, there is very little diſtinction between the dreſs of the males and females.

The women wear their hair combed back on the crown of the head, and ſmoothed with ointment : it is then neatly rolled into a ſort of club, and ornamented with artificial flowers and large ſilver pins : the hair on the back part of the head is done up as tight as poſſible and inſerted beneath the club. In every other reſpect their dreſs correſponds with that of the men : they differ, indeed, in nothing from that of the ſoldiers, which has been already deſcribed, but that they bear no arms, have no red border on their clothes, or tuft of hair on their hats.

As

As far as I could judge of the length of this day's voyage, it could not have exceeded twenty-four miles; in the course of which we reckoned upwards of fix hundred junks that paffed us, and I may fay, without the leaft fear of exaggeration, that we faw twice that number lying at anchor; nor fhall I hefitate to add, that, on the moft moderate computation, we beheld at leaft half a million of people.

The river, befides the variety and extent of its navigation, is in itfelf a grand and beautiful object, and enriched with an equal diftribution of rich and picturefque fcenery: its courfe waves in the fineft meanders; its banks on either fide are adorned with elegant villas and delightful gardens; while the more diftant country offers the intermingled profpect of fplendid cultivation and landfcape beauty.

The fleet came to anchor clofe into the fhore at eight o'clock in the evening.

The gongs, as ufual, gave the fignal for weighing anchor, and proceeding on our voyage. The weather was extremely hot and fultry, and the country continued to wear that appearance of fertility, which had hitherto diftinguifhed it.

We for the firft time faw fome plantations of the tea tree, an object which was rather interefting to the natives of a country, where, though the climate will not admit of its growth, it has defcended, from being a luxury, into a neceffary of life.

The tea tree is of a dwarf fize, with a narrow leaf refembling myrtle. It was the feafon when thefe trees were in bloffom, which the Chinefe pluck and dry; and the younger the bloffom is, when plucked, the higher the flavour of the tea is confidered with which it is mixed.

1793.
Auguft.

Saturday 10.

L

It

1793.
August.

It is a curious circumftance that, although this province is fo abundant in its produce of tea, it appears to be a very fcarce commodity among the lower clafs of people ; as the men belonging to our junk never failed, after we had finifhed our breakfaft, to requeft the boon of our tea-leaves, which they drained and fpread in the fun until they were dry; they then boiled them for a certain time, and poured them with the liquor into a ftone jar, and this formed their ordinary beverage. When the water is nearly drawn off, they add more boiling water; and in this manner thefe leaves are drawn and re-boiled for feveral weeks. On fome particular occafions, they put a few grains of frefh tea into a cup, and, after having poured boiling water upon it, cover it up: when it has remained in this ftate for a few minutes, they drink it without fugar, an article which the Chinefe never mix with their tea.

We this day paffed feveral populous villages, compofed of very neat houfes of one ftory, and built of brick ; and from every one of them the Ambaffador received thofe honours which have been already defcribed. The crowds of people which affembled to fee a parade of fo much novelty as the fleet that conveyed the Britifh embaffy, were beyond all calculation, and almoft beyond belief, and gave us a complete idea of the immenfe population attributed to the Chinefe empire. Nor was the ftate of the navigation that appeared on the river lefs aftonifhing ; the junks which we continued to fee at every moment of our paffage, were fometimes fo numerous, that the water was covered with them.

The fleet came to an anchor at the ufual hour of eight o'clock in the evening.

Sunday 11.

At four o'clock in the morning we renewed our voyage; the country ftill appearing in its ufual ftate of fertility and beauty ; and as far as the delighted eye could reach, an uncultivated fpot was no where to be feen.

The

The banks of the river were now varied with fields of millet and rice. The stalks of the former are very tall, with branching leaves, and the points of them bear the feed, which is a very principal article of food in this country. The rice grows very much like our corn, and thrives best in a marshy foil: I observed, indeed, that some of the rice fields were entirely covered with water.

About six o'clock we approached the city of Tyen-sing, where we were met by crowds of spectators, both in junks and on the shore, that exceeded all calculation.

As we proceeded, we saw a long range of heaps, or ricks, of salt, in ranks, or columns of fifty each, from front to rear: these heaps are about eighteen or twenty feet square, and twenty-four feet in height, and are covered with matting to preserve them from the effects of the weather; each of them containing, as I was informed, about five hundred tons of salt. In this order, and without variation, or interruption, the range continued for two miles along the banks of the river. For what purpose this immense quantity of salt was deposited there I could not learn; nor was there any appearance of a manufactory to justify the idea of its being made there.

At nine o'clock we entered the city, amidst the noise and shoutings of, I doubt not, some hundred thousands of spectators. The houses of this place are built of brick, and, in general, are carried to the height of two stories, with roofs of tiles: they were all of a lead colour, and had a very neat and pretty appearance. The place, however, is not formed on any regular plan: the streets, or rather alleys, are so narrow, as to admit, with difficulty, two persons to walk abreast; and have no pavement. It is, however, of great extent, and populous beyond all description.

Before the palace of the mandarin, a larger body of troops was drawn up than we had yet seen, who carried, at least, one hundred and fifty standards.

L 2

At

1793.
Auguſt.

At half paſt ten, the Ambaſſador, attended by all his ſuite, guards, &c. in full formality, went on ſhore to pay a viſit to the chief mandarin of the city, whoſe palace is at a ſmall diſtance from the river, and placed in the center of a very fine garden: it is a lofty edifice, built of brick, with a range of paliſadoes in the front, fancifully gilt and painted. The center building has three, and the wings two ſtories. The outſide wall is decorated with paintings, and the roof is coloured with a yellow varniſh that produces a very ſplendid effect. This building contains ſeveral interior courts, handſomely paved with broad flat ſtones.

The Ambaſſador, and his ſuite, were entertained with a cold collation, conſiſting of diſhes dreſſed in the faſhion of the country, with tea, fruit, and a great variety of confectionary; a branch of table luxury, which is well underſtood by the Chineſe.

A play was alſo performed on the occaſion, as a particular mark of reſpect and attention to the diſtinguiſhed viſitor. The theatre is a ſquare building, built principally of wood, and is erected in the front of the mandarin's palace. The ſtage, or platform, is ſurrounded with galleries; and the whole was, on this occaſion, decorated with a profuſion of ribbons, and ſilken ſtreamers of various colours. The theatrical exhibitions conſiſted chiefly of warlike repreſentations; ſuch as imaginary battles, with ſwords, ſpears, and lances; which weapons the performers managed with an aſtoniſhing activity. The ſcenes were beautifully gilt and painted, and the dreſſes of the actors were ornamented in conformity to the enrichments of the ſcenery. The exhibition was varied alſo, by ſeveral very curious deceptions by ſlight of hand, and theatrical machinery. There was alſo a diſplay of that ſpecies of agility which conſiſts in tumbling, wherein the performers executed their parts with ſuperior addreſs and activity. Some of the actors were dreſſed in female characters; but I was informed at the time, that they were eunuchs, as the Chineſe never ſuffer their women to appear in ſuch a ſtate of public exhibition as the ſtage. The performance

formance was alfo enlivened by a band of mufic, which confifted entirely of wind inftruments : fome of them were very long, and refembled a trumpet; others had the appearance of French-horns, and clarinets : the founds of the latter brought to my recollection that of a Scotch bag-pipe; and their mufic, being deftitute both of melody and harmony, was of courfe, very difagreeable to our ears, which are accuftomed to fuch perfection in thofe effential points of mufic. But we had every reafon to be fatisfied with the entertainment, the circumftances of which were replete with novelty and curious amufement.

1793.

Auguft.

The drefs of the foldiers was, with their arms and accoutrements, the fame as thofe which we have already defcribed, except in the colour, which was both white and blue, though equally bound with the fame broad red binding : fome of them, on the prefent occafion, were employed, with long whips, to keep off the crowd from prefling on the proceffion of the Ambaffador and his fuite.

His Excellency was faluted, both on his arrival and at his departure, with three pieces of fmall ordnance : and, foon after his return to the veffel the fleet fet fail, amidft the greateft concourfe of boats and people I ever beheld :—indeed, fo great was the crowd of both, that I confidered it to be impoffible for us to pafs on without being the witneffes of confiderable mifchief. One very old junk that lay at anchor had fuch a number of people on board it, to fee the extraordinary fight of the day, that the fternmoft part of the deck yielded to the enormous preffure, and fuddenly gave way, when about forty of thefe curious people fell into the river, and feveral of them were unfortunately drowned. Some were, indeed, faved by clinging to the ropes which were thrown out to them; though it was very evident to thofe who witneffed the accident, that curiofity rather than humanity prevailed on the occafion; and that the people were more anxious to get a fight of the foreigners, than to fave the lives of their countrymen.

We

We received the ufual fupply of provifions of all kinds, and a large jar of wine, from the mandarin, which contained about ten Englifh gallons : it was found to be of a much fuperior quality to that which had been received on a former occafion, and had not only the flavour, but the colour, of mountain.

A confiderable proportion of thefe provifions was diftributed among the crews of the junks, who received fuch an accceptable mark of kindnefs with the utmoft gratitude and delight. The fuperfluous hofpitality of their country proved, as it ought to do, a fource of occafional plenty to thefe poor people, during the courfe of that voyage in which we were conducted by their fkill and labour.

It may here be mentioned that, as the quota of provifions allotted by the Chinefe government for the maintenance of the embaffy, was on the calculation that every individual kept a feparate table, it muft have been, as it really was, infinitely beyond the poffibility of being confumed by thofe alone for whofe ufe it was prefented.

CHAP. VI.

C H A P. VI.

Violent storm of thunder and lightning. Presents distributed among the suite of the embassy. The manner of towing the junks. The ordinary meals of the Chinese, and their mode of preparing them. The increasing appearance of the navigation. Strange habit of the lower classes of the natives. Passed the town of Cho-tang-poa. Circumstances of the river. A visit from the mandarin of Tyen-sing to the Ambassador. His procession described. The neatness, fertility, and various productions. of the fields on each side of the river.

ABOUT four o'clock in the morning there was a most tremendous storm of thunder, lightning, and rain, which lasted about two hours.

1793.
August.
Monday 12.

The Mandarin of Tyen-sing having sent three parcels of coloured silk, as a present, to be distributed among the embassy, Mr. Maxwell, by Lord Macartney's order, delivered two pieces of it to each gentleman in his suite: but as the remainder did not allow of a similar division, the lots were all separated and numbered ; when the mechanics, servants, and musicians, took their chance in drawing them, and, except three persons, they all obtained two pieces of the manufacture. The soldiers received, each of them, half a piece : these pieces were only half a yard wide, and about seven yards and an half in length ; the colours were green, mulberry, and pink ; but the silk was of a very indifferent quality, and would not, in England, be worth more than eighteen-pence a yard. It may, therefore, be very easily imagined that, on the spot, the present was of little or no value. to those who received it..

During

1793.
Auguſt.

During the great part of this day the junks were towed along by men particularly hired for that purpoſe : and the mode of drawing theſe veſſels, as may be ſuppoſed, is very different from that employed on ſimilar occaſions in any of the European rivers.

On all the rivers of China there are large bodies of men, whoſe buſineſs it is to drag, or tow the junks, when the wind or tide fails. The method of proceeding in this buſineſs is by faſtening one rope to the maſt, and another to the head of the junk, which, being properly ſecured, the draughtſmen take the rope on ſhore along with them ; the length of which muſt depend, in a great meaſure, on the breadth of the river. Theſe men have, each of them, a piece of wood, about two feet and an half in length, with a piece of ſtout cord at each end, by which it is faſtened to the ropes attached to the junk : theſe pieces of wood being thrown over their heads, reſt upon their breaſts, and by leaning againſt them the towers increaſe the power of their exertions : they are thus har-neſſed, if I may uſe the expreſſion, in a ſtrait line, at the diſtance of about a pace and an half from each other, and when they are all ready, the leader of them gives the ſignal : they then begin a particular kind of march, the regularity of whoſe ſtep is eſſential to the draft of the veſſel, and can only be maintained by a ſort of chime which they chant on the occaſion : this chime, or cry, is a kind of brief ſong ; but the words, as far as I could learn, have no more meaning an-nexed to them, than the bawling tones employed by our ſeamen, as notices to pull at the ſame moment : they appeared, however, to give the following diſtinct, articulate ſounds, not altogether unlike ſome of thoſe which we might hear on the Thames, or the Severn.—Hoy-alla-hoya ;—which word, for it is delivered as one, was regularly ſucceeded by the following ones—hoya, hoya, hoy—waudi-hoya. Theſe words are ſung in a regular tune ; and ſo univerſal is this cuſtom among the claſs of labouring Chineſe, that they cannot per-form the moſt ordinary work, where numbers are employed together, without the aid of this vocal accompaniment ; which I was diſpoſed to think, had ſome agreeable notes in it.

4

It

It feemed, indeed, to be neceffary that thefe poor men fhould have confolation to fupport, or fome aid to affift, them in the prodigious labour of dragging thefe large junks, both night and day, which is frequently increafed by muddy banks, and marfhy fhores, where I have fometimes feen them wading up to their very fhoulders, and dragging one another, as well as the veffel, after them.

This morning, at feven o'clock, we received our ufual fupply of provifions, which we were obliged to drefs ourfelves, as the Chinefe are fo very dirty in their mode of cookery, that it was impoffible for the inhabitants of a country where cleanlinefs is fo prevailing a circumftance of the kitchen, unlefs impelled by fevere hunger, to fubmit to it. Their manner of drefling meat is by cutting it in very fmall pieces, which they fry in oil, with roots and herbs. They have plenty of foy and vinegar, which they add by way of fauce.

The diet which the common people provide for themfelves is always the fame, and they take their meals, with the utmoft regularity, every four hours: it confifts of boiled rice, and fometimes of millet, with a few vegetables or turnips chopped fmall, and fried amongft oil: this they put into a bafon, and, when they mean to make a regale, they pour fome foy upon it.

Their manner of boiling rice is the only circumftance of cleanlinefs which I have obferved among them: they take a certain quantity of rice, and wafh it well in cold water; after which it is drained off through a fieve: they then put the rice into boiling water, and when it is quite foft, they take it out with a ladle, and drain it again through a fieve: they then put it into a clean veffel, and cover it up; there it remains till it is blanched as white as fnow, and as dry as a cruft, when the rice becomes a moft excellent fubftitute for bread.

The table on which they eat their meals is no more than a foot from the ground, and they fit around it on the floor: the veffel of rice is

M

they

1793.

Auguft.

Tuefday 13.

1793.
Auguſt.

then placed near it, with which each perſon fills a ſmall baſon; he then with a couple of chop-ſticks picks up his fried vegetables, which he eats with his rice; and this food they glut down in a moſt voracious manner. Except on days of ſacrifice or rejoicing, the common people of China ſeldom have a better diet. Their drink, which has already been deſcribed, is an infuſion of tea-leaves.

We this day paſſed ſeveral very populous villages, though, as far as our experience qualified us to determine, there is no ſuch thing as a village which is not populous; and perhaps, after all, among the wonders of this country the population is the greateſt.

The ſhores of the river was this day lined with ſuch crowds of people to ſee us paſs, as to baffle all deſcription; and the number of junks which we paſſed in this day's voyage, I ſolemnly believe, without the leaſt exaggeration, amounted to at leaſt four thouſand: and if I calculate the people we ſaw in the different villages at twenty times that number, the account, I believe, is very much below the reality. At each of theſe places the Ambaſſador was ſaluted in the manner which has been already deſcribed.

Although it is not a very delicate picture to preſent to the attention of my readers, yet, as I profeſs to give a relation of every thing which I ſaw, I ſhall not omit to mention, that, this evening, two of the Chineſe belonging to our junk ſtripped themſelves naked, and, picking off the vermine, which were found in great plenty on their clothes, proceeded to eat them with as much eagerneſs and apparent ſatisfaction, as if they were a gratifying and delicate food.

Wedneſ-
day 14.

The weather was extremely hot and ſultry, and the muſquitos ſo troubleſome during the night, as to prove a very painful interruption to our repoſe.

2

We

We continued to pafs very extenfive fields of millet and rice, and the country, as we proceeded, maintained its character for fertility, cultivation, and abundance; though in feveral parts it aflumed a more varied and regular appearance than we had yet feen.

1793.
Auguft.

In the forenoon we paffed a large town, whofe name is Cho-tung-poa. It is pleafantly fituated on the banks of the river, and is a place of confiderable extent. The houfes are of brick, and in general do not afcend beyond one ftory: they were here remarkable for the walls which were erected in the front of them, over which a great number of ladies were feen taking a view of the junks as they paffed before the town; while the fpectators, whom curiofity had led to the banks of the river, were, as ufual, in fuch numbers as to renew our aftonifhment.

We now came to a fork of the river, and over the lateral branch of it there were two bridges of two arches, built of ftone on a pleafing form, and conftructed with the appearance of no common architectural knowledge. At a fmall diftance from them were the ruins of another bridge of one arch: it had been built of hewn ftone, and the part which remained bore the appearance of a regular defign and European mafonry. At a fmall diftance from this ruin, and on a gentle eminence, was the feat or villa of the mandarin. It is a new ftone building of two ftories, in a pleafing ftile of architecture, with a flight of fteps rifing to the door. The approach to it was through a neat gateway, which was not quite finifhed; the mafons were then employed in completing it; and I was rather furprifed on obferving that their fcaffolding was erected on the fame principle, and their work conducted very much in the fame manner, as is employed and practifed by the builders of our own country.

The junks were towed during the greateft part of this day; and at fix o'clock in the evening they came to an anchor near the fhore.

In

in a ſhort time after the fleet came to its moorings, the grand mandarin of Tyen-ſing, eſcorted by a numerous train of attendants, came
to pay a viſit to the Britiſh Ambaſſador.

The proceſſion commenced with an advanced troop of men, who
were employed in ſhouting aloud as they came on, in order to notify
the approach of the mandarin, that the way might be cleared from
paſſengers, and any accidental obſtacle removed which might impede
his progreſs. This party was followed at ſome diſtance by two men
carrying large umbrellas of red ſilk, with a broad pendent curtain of
the ſame materials: they are uſed to ſhelter the palankin from the
burning rays of the ſun. A large band of ſtandard-bearers then ſuc-
ceed; the foot ſoldiers follow; the palankin next appears which bears
the mandarin, and a large eſcort of cavalry cloſes the proceſſion.

Such is the manner in which perſons of diſtinction travel in China;
and their particular rank and quality is marked by the number of their
attendants.

The mandarin of Tyen-ſing remained with Lord Macartney about
an hour; and, on his return, the proceſſion was illuminated by a great
number of people bearing lamps and torches, which produced a very
ſplendid appearance.

The heat ſtill continued to be extreme: the country varies not in
the fertility of its appearance, and the large fields of corn which we
paſſed to-day, appeared to be as fine, both as to crop and cultivation,
as thoſe which are the boaſt of England. We alſo paſſed a large
plantation of tea, and a very great number of boxes ranged in order,
for the purpoſe of packing the tea, and ſending it to Canton.

In this day's voyage, the banks of the river appeared in ſuch
various clothing of art and nature, as to diſtract the attention; and the
alternate view of extenſive meadows, luxuriant fields, and the moſt

beautiful

beautiful gardens, did not fuffer the gratification of the eye, or the mind, to be for a moment fufpended.

In the evening I went on fhore, and walked along the banks of the river for a couple of miles; and, on a nearer examination of the corn-fields, I found that the grain, which was now almoft ripe, was of a fuperior quality, and the hufbandry equal to that of the Englifh farmer.

C H A P. VII.

Arrive at the city of Tong-tchew, where the voyage ends. The embassy disembarks; ceremonies on the occasion. The place appointed for the reception of the presents and baggage described. Description of the building appropriated for the residence of the Ambassador and his suite. The domestic worship of the Chinese. The entertainment of the embassy. An account of the city of Tong-tchew. Circumstances relative to its civil government. The presents for the Emperor examined. The artillery exercised. Visit from the mandarin. The death of Mr. Eades, and his funeral. The Ambassador receives notice of the time appointed for his departure for Pekin.

1793.
August.
Friday 16.

As we proceeded on our voyage, the villages became more frequent, and the people more numerous. We continued to receive our usual supply of meat, fowls, vegetables, and fruit; and about five o'clock in the afternoon of this day, we arrived at the city of Tong-tchew, which is situated at the distance of twelve miles from Pekin, and where our voyage up this fine river found its termination. It may appear to be a continual repetition of the same subject, but the circumstance appeared to be so extraordinary, that I cannot fail to repeat it, by observing that, at this place, the people who covered the banks of the river far exceeded in number any thing that we had yet seen.

Soon after the arrival of the fleet at this place, Lord Macartney and Sir George Staunton, accompanied by the conducting mandarin, Van Tadge-In, went on shore to inspect the place allotted for the landing the presents and baggage, which the Chinese had previously erected for that purpose. It contained about the space of an acre, fenced in with matting, and furnished with long sheds made of uprights of wood and
matting,

matting, with a roof of the latter, in order to prevent the packages from being injured by the rain or dew The ground was entirely covered with mats, and the place well guarded on all fides by petty mandarins and foldiers.

1793.
August.

The grand mandarin of the place fent to inform the Ambaffador that a public breakfaft would be prepared at the temple allotted for the refidence of the embaffy, during its ftay at Tong-tchew, on the following morning at feven o'clock; to which Lord Macartney and his whole fuite, including mechanics, foldiers, and fervants, were invited. Notice of this general meffage was confequently given to each junk, and orders were at the fame time iffued to prepare for difembarkation.

At fix o'clock this morning two palanquins were fent for Lord Macartney and Sir George Staunton, who, in about an hour after their arrival, left the junks, and were carried to the temple already mentioned, as the place appointed for their refidence, efcorted by a party of Chinefe foldiers and an immenfe concourfe of fpectators.

Saturday 17.

The breakfaft confifted of a profufion of ftews and made difhes, meat of all kinds, tea, wines, boiled eggs, with a great variety of fruits, and elegant confectionary.

A certain number of coolies, in fmall boats, were ordered to each junk, to remove all the articles belonging to the embaffy to the place already mentioned as prepared for their reception. During the greater part of the forenoon I was employed in taking care that the proportion of baggage committed to my charge, was conveyed in fafety to the fheds.

At the gate of this inclofure there were two Chinefe officers, who infpected all cafes and packages which were brought from the junks: they firft took their dimenfions, of which they appeared to take a

written

1793.
Auguſt.

written account, and then paſted, as it ſeemed to me, a counterpart of their minute on every ſeparate article ; nor was a ſingle box, package, or parcel, ſuffered to paſs, till it had undergone this previous cere-mony ; which was ſpecially ordered, as I was informed, to aſcertain to the Emperor the quantity of preſents and baggage in poſſeſſion of the embaſſy.

Every exertion was made both by us and the natives to complete the landing of our cargoes from the junks ; and ſo much expedition was uſed on the occaſion, that the whole of the private baggage, and a great part of the preſents, were ſafely brought on ſhore, and placed in the depot, in the courſe of this day.

The temple, which had been appropriated by the Chineſe govern-ment for the reſidence of the Britiſh Ambaſſador to Tong-tchew, is ſituated about three quarters of a mile from the river, and about one mile from the city, and ſtands on a riſing ground ; the building has a neat appearance, but is ſo very low, as to have no claim to that diſ-tinction, which it might be expected to poſſeſs, when we conſider the purpoſes to which it was applied.—It riſes no higher in any part of it than one ſtory.

The entrance to this building is a common ſquare gateway, that opens into a neat, clean court, which was occupied by the ſoldiers belonging to the embaſſy, as a kind of barracks : another court beyond it, and to which there was an aſcent of three ſteps, contained ſeveral ſmall buildings, occupied by the Chineſe who belonged to the houſe : immediately adjoining to it, Lord Macartney's ſervants occupied a ſimilar ſituation. Oppoſite to the ſervants quarter was a ſmall ſquare building, which is uſed as a place of worſhip, and contains only one room of common dimenſions : in the middle of this chamber there was an altar, with three porcelane figures as large as life placed upon it ; there were alſo candleſticks on each ſide of it, which are lighted regularly every morning and evening, and at ſuch other times as per-

ſons

fons come there to pay their devotions. Before thefe images there is a
fmall pot of duft, in which are inferted a number of long matches, that are alfo lighted during the times of worfhip. When the period of devotion is paft, the candles are extinguifhed, and the flame of the matches blown out, but the matches are left too moulder away. When this ceremony is over, an attendant on the altar takes a foft mallet, with which he ftrikes a bell, that is fufpended to it, three times: the perfons prefent then kneel before the images, and bow down their heads three times to the ground, with their hands clafped in each other, which they extend over their heads as they rife: a low bow is then feen to conclude the ceremony of the daily worfhip of the Chinefe, which is termed by them, chin-chin-jofh, or worfhip of God.

Such is the domeftic mode of worfhip that prevails throughout the whole empire of China, as every inhabitant of it, from the meaneft peafant to the Emperor himfelf, has an altar and a deity: the moft wretched habitation is equally furnifhed in regard to its idols, though, as may be fuppofed, in proportionate degrees of form and figure, with the Imperial palace. Nor are thofe who are confined to the occupations of the water without them; every kind of veffel that navigates the fea, or the river, being provided with its deity and its altar.

The court adjoining to this domeftic chapel is occupied by the Chinefe, and employed as a kitchen: from thence there is a circular entrance to that part of the building which was particularly affigned to the Ambaffador and his fuite.

It furrounds a very handfome and fpacious court, which was ufed as a dining apartment on the occafion: on one fide of it there was an elegant platform, raifed on two fteps, with a beautiful roof, fupported by four gilt pillars; and an awning was ftretched over the whole court to protect it from the heat of the fun. This place was furnifhed alfo with beautiful lamps, regularly difperfed all around it: they confift of frames made of box-wood, lined with tranfparent filk and flowered

N   gauze

1793.
August.

gauze of various colours, which, when the lamps are lighted, add very much to the pleafing effect of the illumination. The two principal fides of the court were occupied by the gentlemen of the fuite, who flept in two equal divifions in thefe feparate apartments. Lord Macartney and Sir George Staunton were each accommodated with a diftinct and feparate wing of the building.

At two o'clock dinner was ferved up for the Ambaffador and his company: it confifted of about one hundred various difhes, dreffed according to the cookery of the country; they confifted principally of ftews, and were ferved in fmall bafons: there were neither table-cloths or knives and forks; and the only method thefe people have of conveying their meat to the mouth is by fmall pointed lengths of wood, or ivory, in the form of pencils. It is abfolutely neceffary, therefore, that their folid food fhould be cut in fmall pieces.

During the time of dinner, a great number of Chinefe, who belonged, as I fuppofe, to the mandarin, whofe office it was to fuperintend the arrangements for accommodation of the embaffy, crowded round the table; when they not only expreffed their furprife by peculiar actions and geftures, but frequently burft into fhouts of laughter.

Sunday 18.

In order to give all poffible dignity and importance to the embaffy, a guard of Britifh foldiers was ordered to attend on the Ambaffador's apartments; but as they were removed from public view, thefe centinels were placed at the outer gate, and the entrance of the inner court, that they might attract the notice of the Chinefe, and elevate the confequence of the diplomatic miffion, in the general opinion of the people of the country; a circumftance on which the fuccefs of it was fuppofed, in a great meafure, to depend.

In the feveral apartments of the building appropriated to the refidence and ufes of the embaffy, Chinefe fervants were diftributed, to fupply thofe who were difpofed to call for drink, with the beverage

of

of the country: such as kie tigau, hot tea; liang tigau, cold tea; with liang fwee, cold water; kie fwee, hot water; pyng fwee, ice water; and any of these liquors were ready to be brought whenever they should be demanded, from an early hour of the day, till night.

This morning I took the opportunity to visit the city of Tong-tchew, with its suburbs; and with no small fatigue, and some trouble, I traverfed the greateſt part of it.

It appears to be built in a ſquare form, and is defended by a very ſtrong lofty wall, with a deep ditch on the outſide of it in the moſt acceſſible parts: the wall makes a circuit of about ſix miles, is thirty feet high, and ſix broad: it has three gates, which are well fortified; each being defended by ramparts mounted with cannon: there is alſo a ſtrong guard within them towards the city, in a ſtate of regular duty. Theſe gates are always ſhut at ten at night, and opened at four in the morning; the keys of which are always lodged with the mandarin of the city at night, and returned to the officer of the guard in the morning; on which occaſion a report is made of whatever may have occurred, and ſuch orders are iſſued as circumſtances may require.

The houſes of this city are like the greater part of thoſe I have ſeen in China, and riſe no higher than one ſtory: they differ, however, in ſome degree, from the common habitations of other places which we have paſſed, that they are here almoſt univerſally built of wood; as there is very rarely a ſtone or brick houſe to be ſeen, but ſuch as are inhabited by the mandarins of the place.

The exterior appearance of the houſes is very pleaſing from the prettineſs of their decorations; but they are moſt wretchedly furniſhed within, if that term can be applied where there is very little or no furniture at all. They have only one apartment behind their ſhops, which is without floor or pavement, and muſt ſerve them for every

domeſtic

1793.

Auguſt.

domeſtic uſe and employment. Before the doors of the ſhops, wooden pillars are erected, from which an awning is ſuſpended during the day, to protect not only the paſſengers, but the ſhopkeepers themſelves, from the rays of the ſun : ſome of theſe pillars are conſiderably higher than the houſes before which they ſtand ; and are not only gilt and painted, but decorated with ſtreamers, which ſerve as ſigns to denote the commodities of the particular ſhops : the tops of them alſo are frequently mounted with a wooden figure, which ſerves as a direction to the ſpot.

As to variety, either in the form and dimenſions of the houſes or ſhops, there is none ; for an almoſt univerſal ſameneſs prevails in the ſtreets of this extenſive city : they differ, indeed, in breadth ; and the inhabitants of thoſe which are narrow, ſpread matting from the tops of the houſes quite acroſs the ſtreet, which is a very agreeable circumſtance in the hot ſeaſons : there is alſo, for the convenience of foot paſſengers, a pavement of four feet in breadth on each ſide of every ſtreet.

Glaſs is not any where uſed in China for windows, and the common ſubſtitute for it is a thin glazed paper, which is paſted on the inſide of a wooden lattice : ſilk, however, is employed for this purpoſe in the houſes of the higher claſſes of the people.

Tong-tchew is a place of great trade, as appears from the vaſt number of junks which we ſaw lying in the river before it ; and the aſtoniſhing number of its inhabitants ; which is very generally believed, as I was informed by ſome of the reſident merchants, to amount, at leaſt, to half a million of people.

During the ſummer and the autumn months the heat here is very ſultry and oppreſſive : the winter, however, brings inclemency along with it, as ice of thirty inches thick is preſerved here, in ſubterranean

caverns,

caverns, till the fummer. It is confidered as an article of great luxury among the people, who mix it with their drink, to give it a refrefhing coolnefs in the hot feafons of the year.

1792.
Auguft.

In the courfe of my excurfions through the city, I endeavoured to make myfelf acquainted with the nature of its municipal government. Of this important fubject it is not to be fuppofed that I could learn much : I was, however, in one way or other, made to underftand, that all civil caufes are determined by a certain number of inferior mandarins ex- prefsly appointed to the judicial office; but that their decifions are fubject to the review of the chief mandarin of the place or diftrict, who may confirm or reverfe them at pleafure : this officer, and his decrees, are alfo fubject to the Viceroy of the province, from whom, in all civil caufes, there is no appeal.

In capital offences, the final determination refts with the Emperor alone ; though it is very rare indeed, that a criminal is fentenced to die : but if fuch a circumftance fhould happen in the moft remote corner of the empire, application muft be made to the Emperor him- felf to annul, to mitigate, or enforce the fentence. Executions, how- ever, are very feldom feen in China. I was very particular and curious in my inquiries on this fubject, wherever I had an opportunity to make them, and not one perfon that was queftioned on the occa- fion, and fome of them were, at leaft, feventy years of age, had ever feen or known of a capital execution. Nor are the leffer crimes fo frequent as might be expected in fuch a populous and commercial coun- try ; as the more obnoxious claffes of them, at leaft, are kept down by the vigour of the police, and the promptitude of punifhment, which follows conviction without the delay of a moment :—a regu- lation which might, in many cafes, be adopted with the beft effects by the boafted judicature of Great Britain. Nor fhall I hefitate to obferve, that whatever may be the defects or excellencies of the Chinefe govern- ment, of which I am not altogether qualified to judge, the people of

China

1791.

August.

China feem to be happy and contented under it, and to enjoy as much liberty as is confiftent with the beft arrangements of civilifed fociety.

The palaces of the mandarins are the only public buildings which I could difcover, or was informed of, in this extenfive city : they are built of brick, and appeared to be very fpacious ; but were more remarkable for extent, than elegance or grandeur.

I finifhed this curious excurfion in the evening, when I was not only very much fatigued by my walk, but very much haraffed by the curiofity of the people. I was fometimes furrounded by twenty or thirty of them, who preffed fo much upon me, that I was frequently under the neceffity of taking fhelter in fhops, till the crowd that perfecuted me was difperfed ; and, in return for the protection afforded me, I made fome purchafes of fans and tobacco-pipes, which were formed with curious neatnefs and ingenuity.

Monday 19. This morning Mr. Barrow, the comptroller, received the whole of the remaining part of the prefents, which were lodged in the depot already defcribed. Lieut. Parifh of the royal artillery, with a party of his men, attended there to examine the ordnance ftores : they alfo uncafed the guns, and got them mounted on their carriages : they confifted of fix new brafs field pieces, two mortars, and one wall piece, with complete artillery apparatus. On the report of the ftate of the ordnance, &c. being made to the Ambaffador, he was pleafed to come to the fheds, attended by Col. Benfon, the officers, and other gentlemen, to fee the guns exercifed ; when feveral rounds were fired with great quicknefs, activity, and exactnefs. His Excellency remained there about two hours, when he returned to his refidence, where the gentlemen of the embaffy dined in the fame manner as on the preceding day.

In the evening the Ambaffador received a vifit from the attendant mandarin, accompanied by the chief mandarin of the city. The band

was

was ordered on the occafion to play on the platform, and the Chi- 1793.
nefe vifitors appeared to be infinitely delighted with the European Auguft.
mufic.

This evening, at eight o'clock Mr. Harry Eades, one of the mechanics attached to the embaffy, died in confequence of a violent flux,
with which he had been for fome time afflicted. Mr. Plumb, the
interpreter, was requefted to order a coffin on the occafion; and, as
thefe fad receptacles are always ready made in China, our departed
companion was foon placed, with all poffible decency, in a fituation to
receive the laft act of refpect which we can pay to each other.

The coffins of this country are all of the fame fize, and bear a
ftronger refemblance to a flat-bottomed boat, than to thofe of Europe:
they are very ftrong and heavy, and the lid is not nailed down, as
with us, but faftened with a cord.

About eleven o'clock there began a moft. tremendous ftorm of
thunder, lightning, and rain, which continued without any inter-
miffion till four o'clock.

This morning the Ambaffador gave orders for the funeral of Mr. Tuefday 20.
Harry Eades,. which, in order to give the Chinefe a favourable impreffion even of our funeral folemnities, was directed to be performed
with military honours.

All the fervants, mechanics, and muficians, attached to the embaffy, were ordered to be in readinefs on the occafion: Col. Benfon
alfo iffued orders to the troops to appear with their fide arms, except
a ferjeant and fix privates of the royal artillery, who were ordered to
be armed and accoutered for firing over the grave. As no clergyman
accompanied the embaffy, I was appointed to read the funeral fervice
of the Church of England on this melancholy occafion.

At

At nine o'clock the proceſſion began in the following order:

> Detatchment of the royal artillery, with arms reverſed.
> The coffin ſupported on men's ſhoulders.
> Two fifes playing a funeral dirge.
> The perſon appointed to officiate at the grave.
> The mechanics, ſervants, &c. two and two.
> The troops then followed, and cloſed the whole.

This proceſſion was alſo accompanied by ſeveral of the gentlemen ·belonging to the embaſſy.

Thus we proceeded, with all due ſolemnity, to the burying-ground, which is ſituated about a quarter of a mile from the Ambaſſador's reſidence; and where permiſſion had been granted for the interment of our countryman, with a liberality that would not have been prac-tiſed in ſome of the countries of enlightened Europe. Such a cere-monial, as may well be imagined, had excited the curioſity of the city, and we were attended by a concourſe of ſpectators that the moſt intereſting, and ſplendid ſpectacles would not aſſemble in the cities of Europe.

On our arrival at the place of interment, the ſoldiery formed a circle round the grave, with the firing party ſtanding on the ſide of it. The coffin being placed on two planks of wood, the funeral ſervice was then read, when the body was committed with the uſual ceremonies to the earth, and the party diſcharged three vollies over the grave,—which, according to a cuſtom of the country that we cannot recon-cile with the general good ſenſe of the people, had no greater depth than was juſt neceſſary to cover the coffin.

In this burying-ground there was a great number of marble and ſtone monuments with inſcriptions on them. Some of theſe memorials were gilt, and enriched with various devices of no ordinary ſculpture: this

funeral

funeral spot is very extensive, but without any enclosure. There are, indeed, no public places of burial, but near large towns and cities; as, in the country, every one is buried on the premises where he had lived.

When the grave was closed, and this last act of duty performed to the dead, the procession returned in the same order that has been already described.

The Ambassador was visited by several mandarins, a mark of respect which we were disposed to consider as a favourable prognostication of success in the great objects of this extraordinary mission. His Excellency also received notice that the following day was appointed for the departure of the embassy to Pekin, and that every necessary preparation was made for that purpose.

It is a curious circumstance that the place of residence appointed for the embassy, proved, after all, to be the house of a timber merchant, whose yard was adjoining to it : but the communication between them was, on this occasion, closed up by a temporary fixture of deals that were nailed acrofs it. On making inquiry concerning the truth of what had been suggested to me, a Chinese soldier pointed to the timber yard; and, at the same time, made me understand, that the owner of the place sold that kind of wood which was employed in the building of junks.

CHAP.

C H A P. VIII.

Leave the city of Tong-tchew. The road to Pekin defcribed. Arrive at a large town called Kiyeng-Foo. Halt there to breakfaft. Prodigious crowds of people to fee the embaffy pafs. Arrive at Pekin. Some account of that city. Cuftoms and manners of the Chinefe. Leave Pekin. Arrive at the imperial palace named Yeuman-man-yeumen.

1793.
Auguft.
Wednef-
day 21.

THIS morning at two o'clock the general was beat through all the courts of the houfe, as a fignal for the fuite to prepare for their departure. After an hafty breakfaft, the whole of the embaffy was ready to proceed on their journey. The foldiers were firft marched off to covered waggons provided for them; the fervants then followed, and were received into fimilar machines; the gentlemen of the fuite next proceeded in light carts drawn by a fingle horfe. Lord Macartney, Sir George Staunton, and Mr. Plumb, the interpreter, were conveyed in palanquins, which were each of them borne by four men.

The vehicles which carried the foldiers and fervants were common hired carts, drawn by four horfes, unequally coupled together, and covered with ftraw matting. The harnefs, if it may deferve that name, was made of rope and cordage. The fingle-horfe carts were covered with blue nankeen, and had doors of lattice work lined with the fame ftuff: the drivers walked by the fide of them.

At four o'clock this proceffion was in motion, which confifted of fixty carts for the foldiers and fervants, and twenty for the conveyance of the gentlemen belonging to the fuite, exclufive of carts for the

I

private baggage, and the coolies, or porters, employed to carry the
prefents and heavy baggage, which were conveyed on their fhoulders;
four hundred of whom were employed on this extraordinary occafion.

1791.
Auguft.

About five o'clock we had quitted the city of Tong-tchew, and
entered immediately into a fine level country of the moft luxuriant
fertility, which, as far as the eye could reach, appeared to be one
immenfe garden.

The road along which we travelled, is not only broad but elegant;
and is a proof of the labour employed by the Chinefe government to
facilitate the communications between the capital, and the principal
parts of the kingdom. The middle of this road confifts of a pavement of broad flag ftones about twenty feet wide, and on each fide of
it there is fufficient fpace to admit of fix carriages to run abreaft. The
lateral parts are laid with gravel ftones, and kept in continual repair
by troops of labourers, who are ftationed on different parts of the road
for that purpofe.

At feven o'clock the cavalcade ftopped at a large town, whofe name
is Kiyeng-Foo. To call it populous, would be to employ a fuperfluous expreffion, that is equally appropriate to the whole kingdom, as
every village, town, and city; nay, every river, and all the banks of
it, teems with people. In the country through which we have paffed
the population is immenfe and univerfal: every mile brought us to a
village, whofe inhabitants would have crowded our largeft towns;
and the number of villas fcattered over the country, on each fide of
the road, while they added to its beauty, were proofs of its wealth.
Thofe which we approached near enough to examine as we paffed,
were built of wood, and the fronts of many of them were painted
black, and enriched with gilded ornaments.

The

1793.
August.

The day of our journey from Tong-tchew to Pekin was, I doubt not, a matter of general notification, from the prodigious concourse of people who abfolutely covered the road; and, notwithftanding the utmoft exertions of the mandarins to keep it clear, the preffure of the crowd was fometimes fo great, that we were obliged to halt, for at leaft a quarter of an hour, to prevent the accidents which might otherwife have happened from the paffage of the carts amidft this continual and innumerable throng. I cannot but add to the obftacles which we received from the curiofity of the Chinefe people, fome fmall degree of mortification at the kind of impreffion our appearance feemed to make on them: for they no fooner obtained a fight of any of us, than they univerfally burft out into loud fhouts of laughter: and I muft acknowledge, that we did not, at this time, wear the appearance of people, who were arrived in this country, in order to obtain, by every means of addrefs and prepoffeffion, thofe commercial privileges, and political diftinctions, which no other nation has had the art or power to accomplifh.

At Kiyeng-Foo, which is about nine miles from Tong-tchew, the whole embaffy of all ranks alighted from their refpective carriages: here the inferior department found tables fpread for their refrefhment in an open yard, but covered at the fame time, with great plenty of cold meats, tea, fruits, &c. while the upper departments were ferved with their regale in fome adjoining rooms of a very miferable appearance.

Before the proceffion re-commenced its progrefs, the conducting mandarin, with his ufual attention, ordered fome Joau, an harfh four white wine, to be offered to the attendants of the embaffy, to fortify their ftomachs, as a confiderable time might probably elapfe before they would obtain any further refrefhment: we were then fummoned to prepare for our departure, when a fcene of confufion and difturbance took place among ourfelves, which, whatever its real effects might have been, was not calculated at leaft to give any very

favourable

favourable impreſſion of the manners and diſpoſition of the Engliſh na-
tion. In ſhort, from the crowd of people aſſembled to ſee us, the neglect
of a previous arrangement, and diſtribution, of the carts, together with
the inconſiderate eagerneſs to ſet off among ourſelves, it was a matter
of no inconſiderable difficulty for the mandarins to aſſign the people to
their reſpective vehicles.

At eight o'clock we took our leave of the town of Kiyeng-Foo,
which is a very conſiderable and extenſive place: the ſtreets are broad
and unpaved, and the houſes are built altogether of wood; at leaſt in
the part which we traverſed there were none conſtructed of any other
materials. The ſhops made a very pleaſing appearance, and ſeemed
to be well furniſhed with their reſpective commodities.

Of the country, which occupies the few miles from this place to
Pekin, I have little to ſay, as the crowds of people that ſurrounded us,
either intercepted the view, or diſtracted our attention.

At noon we approached the ſuburbs of the capital of China, and I
cannot but feel ſome degree of regret, that no alteration was made in
the ordinary travelling, and ſhabby appearance, of the embaſſy, on ſuch
an important occaſion. Whatever reaſons there might be to prevent
that diſplay, which it poſſeſſed ſuch ample proviſions to make, I cannot pretend to determine, but our cavalcade had nothing like the appearance of an embaſſy, from the firſt nation in Europe, paſſing
through the moſt populous city in the world.

On entering the ſuburbs, we paſſed beneath ſeveral very beautiful
triumphal arches, elegantly painted, and enriched with various fanciful ornaments: the upper part of them was ſquare, with a kind of
pent-houſe, painted of a green colour, and heightened with varniſh:
from the inſide of this roof was ſuſpended the model of an accommodation junk, admirably executed, and adorned with ribbons and
ſilken ſtreamers.

4

Theſe

1793.
August.

These suburbs are very extensive; the houses are of wood, the greater part of them two stories in height, and their fronts painted in various colours. The shops are not only commodious for their respective purposes, but have a certain grandeur in their appearance, that is enlivened by the very pretty manner in which the articles of the respective magazines are displayed to the view of the public, either to distinguish the trade, or to tempt the purchaser.

We proceeded gradually through spacious streets, which are paved on either side for the convenience of foot passengers. The whole way was lined with soldiers, and, indeed, without such a regulation, it would have been impossible for the carriages to have proceeded from the crowd that attended us.

At two o'clock we arrived at the gates of the grand imperial city of Pekin, with very little semblance of diplomatic figure or importance: in short, for I cannot help repeating the sentiment, the appearance of the Ambassador's attendants, both with respect to the shabbiness of their dress, and the vehicles which conveyed them, bore a greater resemblance to the removal of paupers to their parishes in England, than the expected dignity of the representative of a great and powerful monarch.

Pekin, or as the natives pronounce it, Pitchin, the metropolis of the Chinese empire, is situated in one hundred and sixteen degrees of east longitude, and between forty and forty-one degrees of north latitude. It is defended by a wall that incloses a square space of about twelve leagues in circumference: there is a grand gate in the center of each angle, and as many lesser ones at each corner, of the wall: they are strongly arched, and fortified by a square building, or tower, of seven stories, that springs from the top of the gateway; the sides of which are strengthened by a parapet wall, with port-holes for ordnance. The windows of this building are of wood, and painted to imitate the muzzle of a great gun, which is so exactly represented, that the deception is not discoverable but on a very near approach:

there

there are nine of thefe windows to each ftory on the front towards the fuburbs. Thefe gates are double; the firft arch of which is very ftrongly built of a kind of free-ftone, and not of marble, as has been related by fome writers: the depth of it is about thirty feet, and in the middle of the entrance is a very ftrong door of fix inches thick, and fortified with iron bolts: this archway leads to a large fquare which contains the barracks for foldiers, confifting of mean wooden houfes of two ftories: on turning to the left, the fecond gateway is feen, whofe arch is of the fame dimenfions and appearance as that already defcribed, but without the tower.

1793.
Auguft.

At each of the principal gates there is a ftrong guard of foldiers, with feveral pieces of ordnance placed on each fide of the inner entrance. Thefe gates are opened at the dawn of day, and fhut at ten o'clock at night, after which hour all communication with the city from the fuburbs is impracticable; nor will they be opened on any pretence, or occafion whatever, without a fpecial order from the principal mandarin of the city.

The four leffer gates are defended by a fmall fort built on the wall; which is always guarded by a body of troops.

The wall is about thirty feet high, and ten feet in breadth on the top: the foundation is of ftone, and appears about two feet from the furface of the earth: the upper part is of brick, and gradually diminifhes from the bottom to the top. Whether it is a folid ftructure, or only filled up with mortar or rubbifh, is a circumftance concerning which I could not procure any authentic information.

This wall is defended by outworks and batteries, at fhort diftances from each other; each of them being ftrengthened by a fmall fort, though none of the fortifications are garrifoned but thofe which are attached to the gates; and though there is a breaft-work of three feet high, with port-holes for cannon, which crowns the whole length of

1793.
Auguſt.

the wall, there is not a ſingle gun mounted upon it. On the ſide towards the city, it is, in ſome places, quite perpendicular ; and in others, forms a gentle declivity from the top to the ground. It is cuſtomary for bodies of ſoldiers to patrole the wall every night during the time that the Emperor reſides in the city, which is from October to April, when his Imperial Majeſty uſually goes to a favourite palace in Tartary. From its perfect ſtate of repair and general appearance, I ſhould rather ſuppoſe it to be of modern erection, and that many years cannot have paſſed away ſince it underwent a complete repair, or was entirely rebuilt.

The diſtance from the ſouth gate, where we entered, to the eaſtgate, through which we paſſed out of the city, comprehends, on the moſt moderate computation, a courſe of ten miles. The principal ſtreets are equally ſpacious and convenient, being one hundred and forty feet in breadth, and of great length, but are only paved on each ſide for foot paſſengers. The police of the city, however, ſpares no pains to keep the middle part clean, and free from all kind of nuiſance ; there being large bodies of ſcavengers continually employed for that purpoſe, who are aſſiſted, as well as controlled, in their duty by ſoldiers ſtationed in every diſtrict, to enforce a due obſervance of the laws that have been enacted, and the regulations which have been framed, for preſerving civil order among the people, and the municipal œconomics of this immenſe city. I obſerved, as we paſſed along, a great number of men who were ſprinkling the ſtreets with water, in order to lay the duſt, which, in dry weather, would not only be troubleſome to paſſengers, but very obnoxious alſo to the ſhops ; whoſe commodities muſt be more or leſs injured, were it not for this beneficial and neceſſary precaution.

Though the houſes at Pekin are low and mean, when conſidered with reſpect to ſize and domeſtic accommodation, their exterior appearance is very handſome and elegant, as the Chineſe take a great pride in beautifying the fronts of their ſhops and

dwellings ;

dwellings; the upper part of the former is ornamented with a profusion of golden characters; and on the roofs of the latter are frequent galleries, rich in painting and other decoration; where numerous parties of women are seen to amuse themselves according to the fashion of the country. The pillars, which are erected before the doors of the shops, are gilded and painted, having a flag fixed at the top, whose characters specify the name and business of the owner: tables are also spread with commodities, and lines attached to these pillars are hung with them.

I observed a great number of butchers shops whose mode of cutting up their meat resembles our own; nor can the markets of London boast a better supply of flesh than is to be found in Pekin. My curiosity induced me to inquire the prices of their meat, and on my entering the shop, I saw on a stall before it an earthen stove, with a gridiron placed upon it; and on my employing a variety of signs to obtain the information I wanted, the butcher instantly began to cut off small thin slices of meat, about the size of a crown piece, and broiled as fast as I could eat them. I took about a dozen of these slices, which might altogether weigh seven or eight ounces; and when I paid him, which I did by giving him a string of caxee, or small coin, he pulled off, as I suppose, the amount of his demand, which was one conderon, or ten caxee, the only current money in the empire. I saw numbers of people in other butchers shops, as I passed along, regaling themselves with beef and mutton in the same manner.

The houses for Porcelain utensils and ornaments are peculiarly attractive, having a row of broad shelves, ranged above each other, on the front of their shops, on which they dispose the most beautiful specimens of their trade in a manner full of fancy and effect.

Besides the variety of trades which are stationary in this great city, there are many thousands of its inhabitants who cry their goods about, as we see in our own metropolis. They generally have a bamboo placed

acrofs

acrofs their fhoulders, and a bafket at each end of it, in which they carry fifh, vegetables, eggs, and other fimilar articles. There are alfo great numbers of hawkers and pedlars, who go about with bags ftrapped on their fhoulders like a knapfack, which contain various kinds of ftuff goods, the folds of which are expofed to view. In felling thefe ftuffs, they ufe the cubit meafure of fixteen inches. Barbers alfo are feen running about the ftreets in great plenty, with every inftrument known in this country for fhaving the head and cleanfing the ears: they carry with them for this purpofe a portable chair, a portable ftove, and a fmall veffel of water, and whoever wifhes to undergo either of thefe operations, fits down in the ftreet, while the operator performs his office, for which he receives a mace. To diftinguifh their profeffion, they carry a pair of large fteel tweezers, which they open with their fingers, and let them clofe again with fome degree of violence, which produces a fhrill found that is heard at a confiderable diftance; and fuch is their mode of feeking employment. That this trade in China is a very profitable one may be pronounced, becaufe every man muft be fhaved on a part of the head where it is impoffible to fhave himfelf.

In feveral of the ftreets I faw perfons engaged in felling off goods by auction: the auctioneer ftood on a platform furrounded with the various articles he had to fell; he delivered himfelf in a loud and bawling manner, but the fmiling countenances of the audience, which was the only language I could interpret, feemed to exprefs the entertainment they received from his harangue.

At each end of the principal ftreets, for there are no fquares in Pekin, there is a large gateway fancifully painted, with an handfome roof coloured and varnifhed; beneath which the name of the ftreet is written in golden characters: thefe arches terminate the nominal ftreet, or otherwife there would be ftreets in fome parts of the city of at leaft five miles in length, which are formed into feveral divifions

by

by thefe gateways. They are very handfome, as well as central objects, and are railed in on each fide from the foot pavement.

The narrow ftreets are enclofed at each end with fmall lattice gates,
which are always fhut during the night; but all the confiderable ftreets
are guarded both night and day by foldiers, who wear fwords by their
fides, and carry long whips in their hands, to clear the ftreets of any
inconvenient throng of people, and to chaftife fuch as are refractory
in ordinary decorum or good behaviour.

Notwithftanding the vaft extent of this place, there is little or no
variety in their houfes, as I have before obferved, but in the colours
with which they are painted; they are in reality nothing better than
temporary booths, erected entirely for exterior fhew, and without any
view to ftrength or durability. It is very rare, indeed, to fee an houfe
of more than one ftory, except fuch as belong to mandarins, and even
thofe are covered, as it were, by the walls which rife above every
houfe or building in Pekin, except a lofty pagoda, and the imperial
palace.

There are no carriages ftanding in the ftreets for the convenience of
the inhabitants, like our hackney coaches in London: the higher
claffes of people keep palanquins, and others of lefs diftinction have
covered carts drawn by an horfe or mule.

The opinion, that the Chinefe women are excluded from the view
of ftrangers, has very little, if any, foundation, as among the immenfe crowd affembled to fee the cavalcade of the Englifh embaffy,
one fourth of the whole at leaft were women; a far greater proportion
of that fex than is to be feen in any concourfe of people whom curiofity affembles in our own country: and if the idea is founded in truth,
that curiofity is a peculiar characteriftic of the female difpofition in
Europe, I fhall prefume to fay that, from the eagernefs which we
obferved in the looks of the Chinefe women as we paffed by them,

that

1793.
August.

that the quality which has juft been mentioned is equally prevalent among the fair ones of Afia.

The women we faw on our paffage through Pekin poffeffed, in general, great delicacy of feature, and fair fkins by nature, with which, however, they are not content, and therefore whiten them with cofmetics; they likewife employ vermilion, but in a manner wholly different from the application of rouge among our European ladies, for they mark the middle of their lips with it by a ftripe of its deepeft colour, which, without pretending to reafon upon it, certainly heightened the effect of their features. Their eyes are very fmall, but powerfully brilliant, and their arms extremely long and flender. The only difference between the women of Pekin, and thofe we had already feen, as it appeared to us, was that the former wear a fharp peak of black velvet or filk, which is ornamented with ftones, and defcends from the forehead almoft between their eyes; and that their feet, free from the bandages which have already been mentioned, were fuffered to attain their natural growth.

When we had paffed through the eaftern gate of the city, fome confufion having arifen among the baggage carts, the whole proceffion was obliged to halt. I, therefore, took the opportunity of eafing my limbs, which were very much cramped by the inconvenience of the machine, and perceiving a number of women in the crowd that furrounded us, I ventured to approach them; and, addreffing them with the Chinefe word *Chou-nu,* (or beautiful) they appeared to be extremely diverted, and gathering round me, but with an air of great modefty and politenefs, they examined the make and form of my clothes, as well as the texture of the materials of which they were compofed. When the carts began to move off, I took leave of thefe obliging females by a gentle fhake of the hand, which they tendered to me with the moft graceful affability; nor did the men, who were prefent, appear to be at all diffatisfied with my conduct, but, on the contrary, expreffed, as far as I could judge, very great fatisfaction at

2

this

this public attention I paid to their ladies. It appears, therefore, that in this city, the women are not divested of a reasonable portion of their liberty, and, consequently, that the jealousy attributed so universally to the Chinese men, is not a predominant quality, at least, in the capital of the empire.

1793.
August.

Among other objects which we saw in our way, and did not fail to attract our notice, we met a funeral procession, which proved to be a very striking and solemn spectacle: the coffin is covered by a canopy decorated with curtains of satin, enriched with gold and flowers, and hung with escutcheons: it is placed on a large bier or platform, and carried by at least fifty or sixty men, who support it on their shoulders with long bamboos crossing each other, and march eight abreast with slow and solemn step. A band of music immediately follows, playing a kind of dirge, which was not without a mixture of pleasing tunes: the relations and friends of the deceased person then followed, arrayed in black and white dresses.

Having passed through the eastern suburbs of the city, we entered into a rich and beautiful country, when a short stage of about four miles brought us to one of the Emperor's palaces named Yeumen-manyeumen, where we arrived about five o'clock in the afternoon, op-pressed with fatigue from the extreme heat of the day, and the various impediments which obstructed our passage, arising from the immense crowds of people that may be said to have filled up the whole way from Tong-tchew to this place, a journey of thirty miles.

In a short time after our arrival, we received a very scanty and in-different refreshment, when the whole suite retired to sleep off the fatigue of the day.

CHAP.

CHAP. IX.

*Description of the palace of Yeumen-manyeumen. Disagreeable circum-
stances belonging to it. Disputes with the natives who guarded it.
Lord Macartney applies for a change of situation. The embassy re-
moves to Pekin. Description of a pagoda. Arrive at the palace
appointed for the residence of the embassy. Description of it. The
arrangements made in it. Several mandarins visit the Ambassador.*

1793.
Auguft.
Thurfday 23. THE whole of this morning was employed in removing the baggage, &c. belonging to the embaffy, from the outer gateway, where
it had been depofited, to the different apartments appointed for the
gentlemen who compofed it.

The palace of Yeumen-manyeumen is in a very low fituation, about
a quarter of a mile from a village of the fame name, and is a very
mean, inconvenient building of no more than one ftory.

The entrance to this palace, if it may be faid to deferve that name,
confifted of a very ordinary ftone gateway, guarded by foldiers, and
beyond it was a kind of parade, where the baggage was placed on its
being taken out of the carts that had brought it hither. In the center
of this parade there is a fmall lodge, where feveral mandarins of an
inferior order were in waiting; and through it is the paffage that leads
to the body of the palace, which being no more than four feet wide,
the carriages could make no nearer approach than to this lodge.

The pofition of this palace is not only low, but in a fwampy
hollow, and between two ponds of ftagnant water, whofe putrid ex-
halations cannot add to the comfort of this unwholefome fituation;

4

and

and fome apartments which were on the banks of one of thefe ponds, were occupied as barracks by the Britifh foldiers. To the weft of thefe buildings there is another gate, but conftructed of wood, which leads to another building, where I obferved a confiderable number of Chinefe foldiers; but, on my approach to take a view of them, they fuddenly retired, and locked the door againft me. Indeed, the native jealoufy of thefe people refpecting ftrangers feemed to be awakened in a very great degree, when they thought it neceffary to watch all our actions with fuch a minute and fcrutinifing attention.

The palace, for I muft by way of diftinction continue to give it that name, though unworthy the refidence of the reprefentative of a great monarch, is divided into two fquare courts, with a range of apartments all round them, which were not only deftitute of elegance, but in a wretched ftate of repair: there is a paved footway around them, with a wooden roof painted and varnifhed. Before the principal doors of the building, and in the midft of a large court, there are a few trees of no very peculiar figure or beauty; but the ground itfelf is covered with a kind of gravel. There are fome fmall fields of grafs that belong to the place, which wear an appearance of neglect we fhould not have expected to find in a country where we had not hitherto feen an uncultivated fpot.

The windows of the apartments confifted of lattice work covered with a glazed and painted paper. In the hot feafons the doors are opened during the day, and their place fupplied by cooling blinds made of bamboo, fancifully coloured, and wrought as fine and clofe as a weaver's reed; they certainly ferved to refrefh the rooms where they were placed, and afforded fome degree of coolnefs to alleviate the heat of the day; but at night the doors were reftored to their office, and thefe blinds were rolled up and faftened to the wall over them.

The whole range of apartments contained no other furniture than a few very common tables and chairs; not a bed or bedftead was to be

be feen in the whole place; it was, therefore, a fortunate circumftance for us that we providently brought our cots and hammocks
from on board the fhips, or we fhould not have flept in a bed, at leaft
during our refidence in China. The natives have no fuch comfortable article of furniture in their houfes, but fleep on a kind of mattrefs,
and cover themfelves with a cufhion ftuffed and quilted with cotton.
They pull off a very fmall part of their drefs when they go to reft, and
when the weather proves cold, they increafe the number of thefe
cufhions as the circumftances of the feafon may require. In the place
of bedfteads they ufe a large wooden bench, which is raifed about two
feet from the ground, and covered with a kind of elaftic bafket work
made of bamboos, on which feven or eight perfons may fpread their
bedding. I have alfo feen fome of them formed of planks, and covered
with carpets.

This habitation had a moft ungracious and deferted appearance;
and, from the ftate in which we found it, a long time muft have
elapfed fince it was inhabited by any thing but centipes, fcorpions,
and mufquetos, which infefted it in every part. It is furrounded by a
very high and ftrong wall of ftone, which excluded every external
object; nor was any perfon belonging to the embaffy permitted, on
any pretence whatever, to pafs its boundaries, mandarins and foldiers
being ftationed at every avenue to keep us within the precincts of this
miferable abode; fo that we were in reality in a ftate of honourable
imprifonment, without any other confolation for the lofs of our liberty,
but that we were fupplied with our daily provifions at the expenfe of
the Emperor.

The Ambaffador's apartments were guarded both night and day by
Britifh centinels; and, to fupport the dignity of his great diplomatic
character, his Excellency required that a table fhould be, in future,
furnifhed for himfelf and Sir George and Mr. Staunton, diftinct from
the gentlemen of his fuite. This requifition found a ready compliance, and this day he dined in his own apartment, while the upper

ranks

ranks of thofe who attended on the embaffy, had a table prepared for them in one of the courts, and beneath the fhade of a tree.

The place where the prefents were depofited, was fo expofed to the fun, that it was apprehended fome of them would receive confiderable injury from their unfavourable fituation; a temporary fhed was therefore immediately erected, to which they were fpeedily removed.

Lord Macartney being very much diffatisfied with his fituation, made a ferious requifition for the appointment of a refidence more fuited to the character with which he was invefted, as well as to the convenience and proper accommodation of the embaffy. To obtain this object, Mr. Plumb, his Excellency's interpreter, made feveral vifits to Pekin: little, therefore, occurred worthy of a recital during the remainder of our ftay in this uncomfortable abode. It continued, however, till the twenty-feventh day of this month, which was appointed for the Ambaffador's departure for Pekin; a more commodious refidence having been allotted for the embaffy, in confequence of Mr. Plumb's negotiation with the Chinefe government on the occafion.

This interval was not paffed by any of the gentlemen of the fuite, or the inferior attendants, with fatisfaction or patience; and Col. Benfon was fo hurt and mortified at being denied the liberty of paffing the walls of the palace, that he made an attempt to gratify his inclinations, which produced a very unpleafant affray, when he was not only forced back from his defign, but threatened with very illiberal treatment from the Chinefe who were on duty at the gates.

Several other difputes of a fimilar nature took place between the fuite and the natives who guarded the palace. It was, without doubt, a very humiliating circumftance for Englifhmen, attending alfo as they were upon a miffion, that by the law of nations poffeffes the moft enlarged and univerfal privileges, to be treated in a manner

Q

fo

so ill-fuited to their individual, as well as political, character : at the same time, it would, perhaps, have been more difcreet to have fpared thofe menaces which were continually expreffed againft perfons charged with an official duty, and acting under the direction of their fuperiors ; and to have fubmitted with patience to thofe regulations, which, however unpleafant, were fuch as were adopted by, and might be the ufage of, that government, whofe partial favour and friend-fhip it was the intereft, and, therefore, the duty of the Britifh em-baffy, by infinuating addrefs and political manœuvre, to obtain and eftablifh.

Saturday 24.   The pleafure that was this day felt by the whole of the fuite of every denomination, is not easily defcribed, when orders were received to prepare for quitting this horrid place on the Monday following.

Sunday 25.   This and the fucceeding day were employed in removing the greater part of the baggage and prefents, which was accomplifhed, as it had hitherto been, by the coolies, or porters.

The chandeliers, mathematical apparatus, together with the clocks and time-pieces, were left at the palace of Yeumen-manyeumen, as fuch frequent removals might materially injure, if not altogether fpoil thofe pieces of mechanifm, the wonders of whofe operations muft depend upon the delicacy of their movements.

Monday 26.   At ten o'clock in the morning fingle horfe carts were provided for the whole train of the embaffy. The foldiers, mechanics, and fervants, were lodged two in a cart ; and each of the gentlemen had a cart to himfelf; but the Ambaffador, with his fecretary and interpreter, were, as before, accommodated with palanquins.

The bufinefs of our fetting off was, as it had hitherto been, a fcene of confufion and diforder; but by eleven o'clock, we had, to our extreme fatisfaction, bid adieu to our late uncomfortable refidence.

fidence. We foon paffed through the village from whence the palace appears to derive its name, amidft a vaft crowd of fpectators; and, at one o'clock, arrived at the north gate of the city of Pekin; which is the counterpart of that we have already defcribed. In our progrefs through the ftreets we paffed a pagoda, which is the firft we had feen in China. In our voyage up the river, or in our journey from Tong-tchew to Pekin, we had not feen one of thefe buildings, which are, in a great meafure, peculiar to this part of the eaft, till we arrived in this city: it is fituated in the center of a very pretty garden adjoining to a mandarin's palace.

1794. August.

This pagoda is a fquare ftructure, built of ftone, and diminifhes gradually from the bottom, till it terminates in a fpire. It had only one gallery, which encircled it near the top, and was guarded by a rail: a curtain of red filk at this time, hung from a projecting canopy, and gave this part of the building, when feen at a dif-tance, the appearance of an umbrella. It was feven ftories in height, and was without any kind of exterior ornament, but that which I have already defcribed.

As our return to Pekin was not only fudden but unexpected, our re-entry was not particularly interrupted by the public curiofity, and, at half paft two in the afternoon, we arrived, without having met with any material impediments at the princely palace, which had been ap-pointed for the future refidence of the embaffy. It is the property of John Tuck, a name generally given by Englifhmen, but why, or wherefore, I cannot tell, to the Viceroy of Canton, who was now here as a ftate prifoner, for fome embezzlement of the public treafures, or other mifdemeanors refpecting his government there.

This palace is built of a grey brick, and is extremely fpacious, con-taining twelve large and fix fmall courts. The bricks are cemented with fuch curious care, that the feams of mortar between them are as fmall as a thread, and placed with fuch peculiar uniformity, that a mi-

Q 2

nute

1793.
August.

nute examination is neceffary to convince the fpectator that it is not the work of a painter, rather than that of a bricklayer, and that the pencil has not been employed to produce the effect inftead of the trowel. Thefe bricks have the fmoothnefs of marble, are fixteen inches in length, eight inches broad, and two and an half in thicknefs.

The whole range of buildings, except two diftinct parts, which were inhabited by the Ambaffador and Sir George Staunton, occupy but one, though a very lofty ftory. The courts are fpacious and regular fquares, and paved with large flat ftones. Before the building, in each of thefe fquares, there is a raifed terrace of about three feet, to which there are regular flights of fteps in the center of each angle, and, of courfe, correfponding with each other. Over thefe terraces there is a projecting roof, which extends the breadth of them, and is fupported by light pillars of wood, ranged at equal diftances, and connected by a railing of fanciful contrivance. The whole is gilt and painted with much prettinefs, as to pattern and colour; and forms a moft elegant piazza, that not only adds to the grandeur, but, which is a better thing, to the convenience of this fuperb manfion.

Here I firft obferved the fuperiority of the Chinefe in the art of houfe painting, to which they give a glofs equal to japan, that not only preferves the colours from fading, but never fuffers any injury itfelf from the expofition of air, or fun, or rain. I at firft confidered this effect to have been produced by varnifh; but I afterwards difcovered that it proceeded from certain ingredients with which the colours are originally mixed, and not from any fecond operation.

The apartments are very commodious and of large dimenfions; fome of them were hung with a gliftening paper of a pattern, both as to colour and beauty, far fuperior to any I had ever feen in Europe: others were curioufly painted and enriched with gilding. Thofe occupied by Lord Macartney were numerous and elegant, and contained a private theatre. The latter is of a fquare form, with a paint-

ed

ed gallery which runs entirely round it for the audience: the ftage is raifed from the floor about three feet, and has the appearance of a large platform: it is furrounded by a wooden railing, and has a paffage of eight feet wide all round it: behind the ftage is a fuite of rooms for the convenience of the actors, who drefs in them, or retire thither to make any neceffary transformation in their characters during the performance. The building is very lofty, and the roof elegantly painted. The apartments of Sir George Staunton were alfo very handfome and convenient. The whole fuite were likewife accommodated in a manner that gave them the moft entire fatisfaction.

The windows are covered with glazed paper, and the doors of the principal rooms confift of gilded frame-work, which is fitted up with fine filk gauze, inftead of glafs. The frames, both of the doors and windows, are richly gilt; and, in the warm feafons, the former being always kept open, a curtain, if it may be fo called, of painted fret-work, made of bamboo, fupplies their place, as I have already obferved in former defcriptions.

In feveral courts of the palace there are artificial rocks and ruins of no mean contrivance, which, though not very congenial to their fitua-tion, were formed with confiderable fkill, and were, in themfelves, very happy imitations of thofe objects they were defigned to repre-fent. To thefe may be added, the triumphal arches, which arife, with all their fanciful devices, in various parts of the building.

This noble manfion is of great extent, and calculated to afford every kind of princely accommodation; but, with all its magnificence, as to the number of the apartments, and the general difplay of the whole, its only furniture was fome chairs and tables, and a few fmall plat-forms covered with carpets and bamboo matting.

Beneath the floor, in each of the principal apartments, is a ftove, or furnace of brick-work, with a circular tube that is conducted round

the

1793.
Auguft

the room where it ſtands, which is ſufficient alſo to warm the apartment above it. They are, in cold weather, conſtantly ſupplied with charcoal, and communicate their heat in the manner of our hot-houſes in England. The houſes here have no chimnies that I could diſcover, and, of courſe, no other means of adminiſtering heat can be employed but thoſe which have juſt been mentioned.

At four o'clock in the afternoon, the whole ſuite ſat down to dinner, which conſiſted, as uſual, of a great variety of ſtews and haſhes. Indeed, a joint of meat is ſeldom or ever ſeen, but on feſtival days; of which I ſhall ſpeak more hereafter. His Excellency and Sir George Staunton dined together. But with all the ſuperiority of accommodation we enjoyed here, we continued to be guarded with the ſame ſuſpicious vigilance as in our late reſidence. On no pretence whatever was any one permitted to paſs the gates, and every acceſſible part of the place was under the active care of military power.

This palace, according to the reports of the country, was erected by the Viceroy of Canton, from the fruits of his exertions during his government there, and particularly on the ſhipping of the Engliſh nation at that port; for which acts of injuſtice and oppreſſion he was, as I have before mentioned, at this time, a priſoner at Pekin. The money expended on this immenſe building amounted to ninety-ſeven thouſand pounds ſterling. A moſt enormous ſum in a country where the materials for building, and the labour which puts them together, are to be obtained at ſo cheap a rate.

This day was principally occupied in arranging the various apartments for the convenience of the gentlemen, &c. to whom they were allotted, as well as in providing ſuitable places for the reception of the heavy baggage.

The cloths and bale goods, with that part of the more valuable preſents which were of the ſmalleſt compaſs, were diſtributed between

the

the apartments of Lord Macartney and Sir George Staunton : the remainder was removed to feveral large chambers, which formed a large and commodious magazine for their reception. The fix pieces of fmall ordnance and two mortars were placed in the inner court, with all their appendages, and mounted on their carriages, in front of the Ambaffador's apartments.

Thefe arrangements being made in the moft proper and convenient manner which our fituation would admit, it remained for us to wait with patience, till his Imperial Majefty's pleafure fhould be known, whether the embaffy was to proceed to Tartary, or to be cooped up in its prefent abode till the ufual feafon of his Majefty's return to the capital of his empire. To obtain this intelligence fo important to us, a mandarin had been difpatched, on our arrival at Tong-tchew, to the Emperor's fummer refidence in Tartary, and we were in continual expectation of the return of this meffenger.

In the courfe of this day, the Britifh Ambaffador was vifited by a company of mandarins, among whom were feveral perfons, natives of France, who had been of the order of jefuits; but being prohibited from promulgating their doctrines in this country, had affumed its drefs and manners ; and, on account of their learning, had been elevated to the dignity of mandarins. Thefe French gentlemen, who were, as may be very readily conceived, well acquainted with the interefts of the country in which they were now naturalized, encouraged Lord Macartney to hope for the moft fatisfactory and beneficial iffue of the embaffy which he conducted.

CHAP.

C H A P. X.

*Lord Macartney receives notice, that it is the Emperor's pleasure to re-
ceive the embassy at the Imperial residence in Tartary. The persons
selected to attend the Ambassador in his progress thither. The particular occupations assigned to those who were left at Pekin. Arrangements for the journey into Tartary. Leave Pekin; circumstances of
the journey.*

1793.
August.
Wednes-
day 28.

THE Ambassador received a visit this morning from the mandarin
Van-Tadge-In, who informed his Excellency, that the messenger who
had been sent to know his Imperial Majesty's pleasure respecting the
British embassy, was returned, and that the Emperor desired the Ambassador to proceed to Tartary, where he wished to see him, and to
receive his credentials.

Thursday 29.

This morning the final arrangements were made respecting that part
of the suite who were to accompany the embassy into Tartary. They
consisted of

 Sir George Staunton,
 Mr. Staunton,
 Lieutenant-Colonel Benson,
 Captain Mackintosh, of the Hindostan,
 Lieutenant Parish,
 Lieutenant Crewe,
 Mr. Winder,
 Doctor Gillan,
 Mr. Plumb, the interpreter,
 Mr. Baring, and,
 Mr. Huttner.

Mr.

Mr. Maxwell remained at Pekin, with three fervants, in order to fettle the houfehold of the Ambaffador, as, on his return from Tartary, it was intended that his eftablifhment and appearance fhould be, in every refpect, fuited to the character and dignity of the fovereign whofe reprefentative he is.

Doctor Scott was alfo to be left, in order to take care of feveral of the foldiers and fervants, who were, at this time, very much afflicted with the bloody flux.

Mr. Hickey and Mr. Alexander were to be employed in preparing the portraits of their Britannic Majeflies, which, with the flate canopy, were to be the appropriate furniture of the prefence chamber of the Ambaffador.

Doctor Dinwiddie and Mr. Barrow were to regulate the prefents that had been left at the palace of Yeumen-manyeumen, and to put them in a ftate to be prefented to the Emperor, on the Ambaffador's return to Pekin.

The guards, muficians, and fervants received orders to hold themfelves in readinefs, to fet out on Monday morning, with no other baggage but their bedding, and fuch neceffaries as were abfolutely indifpenfable on the occafion.

The gentlemen of the fuite were likewife requefted to content themfelves with the uniform of the embaffy, a common fuit of clothes, and fuch other articles as they might judge to be abfolutely neceffary for their own comfort, and the formality of the occafion.

Mr. Maxwell received orders to diftribute to each of the muficians and fervants, a fuit of the ftate liveries, in order that the attendants might appear in that uniform drefs, which would add to the dignity and fplendor of the Ambaffador's entrance into Jehol.

The

R

1793.
August.
Friday 30.

The carpenters were employed this morning in unpacking an old travelling chaife belonging to Sir George Staunton, in which Lord Macartney propofed to travel to Jehol. This carriage greatly attracted the notice of the Chinefe, who flocked about it to fee the nature of its conftruction, and the materials of which it was formed, which they examined with a very fingular curiofity; and fome of them were fo anxious to underftand all its parts, that they made various drawings of it. But fo familiar are the eyes of thefe people to the glare and glitter of colours and gilding, that, however they might admire the mechanifm and contrivance of the carriage, they did not hefitate to exprefs their difapprobation of its exterior appearance; which, I muft own, did not poffefs any very uncommon degree of attraction.

At noon Mr. Plumb came to inform the fuite, on the part of Van-Tadge-In, the attendant mandarin, that fuch as preferred to travel on horfeback, were to give in their names, that horfes might be prepared for them; and thofe who chofe the conveyance by carts, fhould be provided accordingly.

After thefe travelling arrangements were fettled, the muficians, fervants, &c. attended at Mr. Maxwell's apartment, to receive the clothes in which they were to make their public appearance at Jehol. A large cheft was produced on the occafion full of clothes: they were of green cloth, laced with gold; but their appearance awakened a fufpicion that they had already been frequently worn, and on tickets, fewed to the linings, were written the names of their former wearers; and as many of thefe tickets appeared, on examining them, to be the vifiting cards of Monfieur de la Luzerne, the late French Ambaffador, it is more than probable, that they had been made up for fome gala, or fete, given by that minifter. But whether they were of diplomatic origin, or had belonged to the theatres, is of no confequence, they were never intended for actual fervice, being made only for a few temporary occafions, whatever they

might

might be. With these habiliments, however, such as they were, every man fitted himself, as well as he could, with coats and waist-coats, as there was a great dearth of small-clothes, of which there were not more in the whole package than were sufficient for the accommodation of six persons. The Chinese may not be supposed to be capable of distinguishing on the propriety of our figure, in these ill-suited uniforms; but we certainly appeared in a very strong point of ridicule to each other. The two couriers were furnished with beaver helmets, but not an hat was distributed to accompany these curious liveries; which, after all, the servants were ordered not to put on till the day when they were to add so much to the entry of the embassy into Jehol.

1793.
August.

. When the chaise was put in complete order for the journey, a difficulty arose, against which, as it was not foreseen, no provision could be made; and this was no less than to get a couple of postillions: at length, however, a corporal of infantry, who had once been a post-boy, offered his service, and a light-horseman was ordered to assist him in conducting the carriage.

This morning such of the presents and baggage as were intended to be forwarded to Tartary, were sent off: some of them were carried by mules, others in carts; but the more valuable articles, and those of delicate fabric and curious construction, were borne by men.

Saturday 31.

This important business being dispatched, a great number of horses were brought to the palace, when each of the gentlemen and the other persons of the suite who proposed to ride, made choice of his horse; and the animals which were thus selected for the service of the approaching journey, were then delivered to those persons whose office it was to take proper care of them till the time of our departure.

The postillions were permitted to exercise the horses in the chaise for an hour, through the streets of Pekin. They were guarded both

by

by mandarins and foldiers; and, indeed, fuch were the crowds which affembled to fee this extraordinary fpectacle, that fome kind of authority and exertion was neceffary to give the drivers an opportunity of fhewing their fkill, and exhibiting the equipage and its apparatus to advantage. The corporal being alfo furnifhed on the occafion with the jacket, helmet, &c. of the light horfe, the poftillions not only made an uniform, but a very pretty, appearance.

The Ambaffador received a vifit from feveral mandarins; when the band played on the ftage of the theatre for their entertainment.

Lieut. Parifh exercifed his men in the ordnance evolutions, to keep them in practice, as it was thought very probable that, on prefenting the artillery to the emperor, he might defire to fee an exhibition of European tactics.

September.
Sunday 1.

As it was ordered that the embaffy fhould fet out to-morrow morning at two o'clock, fome of the baggage, to prevent as much as poffible the confufion which had been hitherto experienced, was fent forward this evening.

Monday 2.

Soon after one o'clock this morning, the drums were beat through all the courts of the palace, and in half an hour the whole fuite was in motion. The bedding was then fent on in carts; and the Ambaffador, with his attendants, having made a flight breakfaft, quitted the palace at half an hour paft three o'clock, under a ftrong efcort of Chinefe cavalry. But, even at this early hour, the crowd of fpectators was fo great to fee our departure, that the progrefs of the cavalcade was very much impeded, efpecially the carriage of the Ambaffador, which, from the concourfe of people, and the aukwardnefs of the horfes that had not been properly broke into their new geer, was for fome time very much delayed.

5

At

At feven o'clock we paffed through the city gate, and in about half an hour had exchanged the fuburbs for a very rich and finely-cultivated country. The road, though very broad, had no pavement in the center, like that which leads from Tong-tchew to Pekin. At the end of fix miles we ftopped at a confiderable village called Chin-giho, where we ftayed to take the ufual refrefhments of the morning, which have been fo often mentioned. Our route was then continued through a great number of villages, and near two o'clock arrived at one of the Emperor's palaces named Nanfhifhee, where we were appointed to remain during the firft night of our journey.

The mandarin Van-Tadge-In, whom I have had fuch frequent occafion to mention, rather increafed than diminifhed his activity on the prefent journey; which might arife, perhaps, from our being more particularly under the Imperial care and protection. We were here provided with every requifite accommodation, and in a very comfortable manner. To our dinner each day was added a regale of Jooaw and famtfhoo: the former is a bitter wine of the country; and the latter, a very ftrong fpirit diftilled from rice and millet, whofe appearance refembles that of Britifh gin.

In the evening the foldiers were exercifed by Lieutenant Col. Benfon.

We computed the journey of this day to be about twenty-five miles; and, though it may appear but dull travelling to perfons accuftomed to the expedition of Englifh roads, it will be confidered as no very tardy progrefs, when the obftacles are known which tended to impede it.

The fame horfes were to take us the whole journey, and the fame men to carry the baggage; befides, the whole of our provifions was ordered and dreffed at the feveral places through which we paffed on the road, and conveyed in bowls, carefully covered up

in

1794.
September.

1793.
September.

in trays, on men's shoulders, to every stage of our journey, for our refreshment there.

The distance from Pekin to Jehol is one hundred and sixty miles, which was divided into pretty nearly equal journies of seven days. This arrangement was made that the embassy might be accommodated each day beneath an Imperial roof; as the Emperor, for his own convenience and dignity, has a certain number of palaces built at equal distances on the road from Pekin to his summer residence in Tartary. This privilege was considered to be a most flattering mark of distinction, as it is never granted to the first mandarins of the empire.

Of this palace we can say but little, as no parts of it were open to us but those which we inhabited. It did not rise higher than one story; nor, from what we had an opportunity of seeing, did it appear that the interior apartments were superior to the external form; which had nothing either of elegance or figure to attract attention. The central part of the courts was planted with trees and flowers of various kinds, which had a very pleasing effect. An extensive garden surrounded the palace, but we could not, to our very great disappointment, obtain access to it.

Tuesday 3.

We continued our journey at four o'clock this morning, with the same guard of Chinese cavalry; and, after having passed the village of Cantim, which possesses the usual characteristic of every Chinese village we have yet seen, an overflowing population, we arrived at the town of Wheazou, a place of some consideration; and, after the usual refreshments, proceeded beneath a burning sun along dusty roads, but through a very fertile country, to the palace of Chanchin, where we arrived at one o'clock. It is a very extensive building of one story throughout, and contains ten or twelve spacious courts, surrounded with piazzas, and adorned with a garden, in the center, planted with

trees

trees and fhrubberies that were interfected by walks. The country around it boafts a continuation of that fertility which has been already mentioned. It was enclofed, and fed innumerable herds of cattle and flocks of fheep: the former are fmall but very fat, but the fheep are both large and fat, with white faces, and a fhort thick tail, which is a lump of fat, and weighs feveral pounds.

We fet off this morning at five o'clock. The diftant country appeared to be mountainous, and rofe boldly in the horizon. That fertility of which fo much has been faid, began fenfibly to diminifh, and the richnefs of the foil was proportionably decreafing. At half paft feven o'clock we arrived at a fmall village, called Cuaboocow, where we breakfafted, and, from fome accidental circumftance, not in the ufual ftile of plenty, in a place like a farm yard.

The road, as we proceeded on our journey, became extremely rugged and difagreeable, and the heat of the weather continued without any alleviation.

At noon we faw a very large walled city, called Caungchumfoa; the walls of which were built of ftone, and, though not fo lofty, in the fame form as thofe of Pekin.

We paffed at leaft two hundred dromedaries and camels carrying very heavy loads of wood and charcoal, as it appeared, to the city which has been juft mentioned. This large drove was under the direction of one man, who feemed to manage them all without the leaft difficulty. Thefe animals are among the moft docile of the brute creation; befides, the length of time they can faft, and the burthens they can bear, render them invaluable in the commerce of the eaft.

The palace where the embaffy was received at the end of this day's journey, derives its name from the city of Caungchumfoa, near which it
ftands:

1793.
September.

stands : it is surrounded with gardens, but has little to distinguish it from those which we have already inhabited.

This was the most fatiguing and unpleasant day of our whole route, both from the heat of the weather and the badness of the road, which was so rugged and narrow in many places, that some of the carts were overturned; but, happily, without any accident to those whom they conveyed.

C H A P. XI.

*Arrive at the town of Waung-chauyeng. Description of Chinese fol-
diers, &c. Pass the great wall. Description of it. The different
appearance of Tartary and China. Pass an extraordinary mountain.
Arrive at the palace of Chaung-shanuve; the circumstances of it.
Example of the industry of the peasants, and the cultivation of the
country. Some account of the tenure by which lands are held in
China. Arrive at the palace of Callachottueng. Description of it.
Arrangements settled for the manner in which the embassy was to
make its entrance into Jehol.*

As the country was now become very irregular and mountainous,
the roads were proportionably fatiguing. At nine we arrived at the
town of Waung-chauyeng. At a small distance from it, we passed
an arch of great strength, which stretched across a valley to unite the
opposite hills, and is guarded by a broad wall on either side of it.
A little further, the road proceeds up a very steep hill, on the top
of which there is a fort, with a strong wall or rampart stretching on
either side of it, to the distance of two or three miles. From the elevated situations which the inequality of the road frequently offered,
this wall was a very visible object in its whole extent, and appeared to
be in a state of decay.

Beneath the fort is a strong, thick, stone archway, through which
the road conducted us down a hill, whose declivity was such, as to
oblige the drivers to have but one horse in each carriage, and to secure
a wheel with ropes, to prevent a too rapid descent. At the bottom of
this hill, and in a most romantic valley, stands the town of Waung-
chauyeng, which resembles those places of the same kind that have
been already described, except in the uniformity of them ; this being

1793.
September.
Thursday 5.

S

built

built with greater irregularity than any we have yet feen. It is about a mile in length, as well as I could judge from our paffage through it, but I had no opportunity of afcertaining its breadth: populous it was, of courfe, and appeared to be a very bufy place.

After breakfaft we proceeded towards a fpot on our journey, of which we had all heard or read with wonder and aftonifhment; which fo few Europeans had ever feen, and which no one of our own country would probably ever fee but ourfelves: this was the great wall, the ancient boundary of China and Tartary, through whofe portals our paffage lay.

At the end of the town which has been juft mentioned, there was a temporary triumphal arch erected in honour of the embaffy, finely decorated with ftreamers and filks of various colours; at the entrance of which the Ambaffador was faluted with three guns. There we paffed between a double line of foldiers, which extended on either fide of the road, from the triumphal gateway towards the great wall.

Thefe were the only foldiers we had yet feen in China, who pof-feffed a martial appearance; and, according to my notion of fuch things, I never faw a finer difplay of military parade. They were drawn up in a very regular manner, each regiment being diftinguifhed by a different drefs, and divided into companies: thefe were ranked in clofe columns, and in their front ftood the officers with two ftands of colours. They were all arrayed in a kind of armour, which confifted of a loofe coat or robe, in imitation of a coat of mail, with fteel hel-mets that covered their heads and fhoulders. Their implements of war were various, comprifing matchlocks, fabres, daggers, fpears, halberts, lances, bows and arrows, with fome other weapons, of which I knew not the name, and cannot particularly defcribe. Thofe companies of foldiers who wore no warlike inftrument but the fword, had a fhield to accompany it. In fhort, every one of thefe

military

military divisions was distinguished by their dress and arms, and arranged with the utmost propriety, not merely as to regularity of position in their general distribution, but as to the effect of contrast in the variety of external appearance. On each side of the road there were seventeen of these divisions, each consisting, as I should think, of about eighty men; and a band of musicians, placed in a building, erected, as it appeared, for the occasion, continued to play, as the cavalcade of the English embassy passed between the lines.

On approaching the wall, there were cantonments for a considerable army, at the extremity of which there is a very strong gateway, built of stone, and still strengthened with the addition of three vast iron doors; on passing them, you enter at once into Chinese Tartary. On the outside of another gateway is a strong redoubt, from whence I ascended the hill, and contrived to get on the top of the great wall which formerly separated the two empires.

This wall is, perhaps, the most stupendous work ever produced by man: the length of it is supposed to be upwards of twelve hundred miles, and its height in the place where I stood upon it, for it varies in its circumstances, according to the nature of the surface, is upwards of thirty feet, and it is about twenty-four feet broad. The foundation is formed of large square stones, and the rest is brick: the middle is of tempered earth, covered with broad stones: there is also a parapet wall or breast-work of stone, three feet thick, on each side of an embattled wall.

When it is considered that this immense structure is not merely carried along level ground, but passes over immense rivers, where it assumes the form of bridges, some of which contain double rows of immense arches; or stretches, in the same expansive shape across deep vallies, to connect the mountains that form them; and that it not only descends, but also ascends, the steepest declivities; the idea of its gran-

deur,

deur, and the active labour employed in conftructing it, in the fhort fpace of a few years, is not eafily grafped by the ftrongeft imagination.

Where it climbs the heights, the afcent is aided by large flights of fteps, fo that the paffage along it is at once eafy, fecure, and uninterrupted. In fhort, it formed a fine military way, by which the armies of China, employed to defend its frontier againft the Tartars, could march from one end of the kingdom to the other. There are alfo, at proper diftances, ftrong towers, from whence, by certain fignals, an alarm could be communicated, in a very fhort fpace of time, acrofs the whole empire; and wherever the wall attains the fummit of an hill, or mountain, there is a ftrong fort defigned to watch the excurfions and movements of the enemy.

The part of this wall, on which I ftood, commanded a very extenfive view of it, with all the romantic fcenery connected with it. From hence I faw the amazing fabric take its courfe for many miles over a beautiful plain, watered by a large river, which it croffed in the form of a bridge. A little to the weftward it afcends a very lofty mountain, which, on that fide, completes the profpect.

But the moft ftupendous works of man muft at length moulder away; and fince Tartary and China are become one nation, and, confequently, fubject to the fame government, the wall has loft its importance: it being no longer neceffary for defence or fecurity, no attention is now paid to its prefervation; fo that the time is approaching when this ftupendous monument of perfevering labour; when this unparalleled effort of national policy, will become an enormous length of ruins, and an awful example of decay: many parts of it are already fallen down, and others threaten to encumber the plain that they were reared to defend.

One

One of the mandarins informed me, as we were walking together on the wall, that, according to the hiftories of his country, it had been finifhed upwards of two thoufand years ago; and, confequently, two hundred years before the Chriftian æra.

1793.
September.

I muft, however, acknowledge that, after all, this renowned barrier of China did not, altogether, fatisfy my expectations. The wonder of it confifts in its extent, of which a fmall part is to be feen, and the fhort time in which it was erected, may equally aftonifh by reading an account of it. When I ftood on the top of it, I was ftill obliged to exercife my imagination as to the aftonifhing circumftances connected with it, and faw it alfo in a comparative view with natural objects infinitely fuperior, at leaft, to any partial appearance of it.

When we had paffed the wall, there was an immediate change in the appearance of the country, as well as the temperature of the feafon. Inftead of a level range of various and unceafing cultivation, of the habitations of wealth, the crowd of population, and the exertion of induftry; we beheld a wide and barren wafte, finking into vallies, and rifing into mountains; where no harveft waved, no villages poured forth its inhabitants, or fplendid manfions enriched the fcene. The traveller, however, is amply compenfated by the variety of natural objects which prefent themfelves to him; and the lover of picturefque beauty finds, amidft all the increafing inconveniencies of his journey, a fource of enchantment which makes him forget them all.

At the diftance of about feven miles from the great wall, we came to the foot of a very high mountain, which the carts could not afcend without an additional number of horfes. The paffage through this mountain is another proof of the genius and indefatigable fpirit of the Chinefe people in all works that relate to public utility. It is thirty feet in breadth, cut through a folid rock; and, which is the more extraordinary part of this undertaking, the incifion made from the top of the mountain to the furface of the road, is, at leaft, one

hundred

hundred feet:—a ſtupendous labour. But with this aid in eaſing the paſſage, the beginning of the aſcent has a very fearful appearance; but on the other ſide the way ſlopes down with a gentle declivity between two large mountains towards a beautiful valley.

At two o'clock, we arrived at the palace of Chaung-ſhanuve, which is ſituated on a ſmall elevation, at the diſtance of a mile and a half from the bottom of the hill which has been juſt deſcribed. It is of large dimenſions, and ſurrounded by an high wall, being the reſidence of a conſiderable number of the Emperor's women; many of whom I ſaw peeping over the partition which ſeparated their apartments from the part of the palace aſſigned to the accommodation of the embaſſy. Though it was not permitted for any of the Ambaſſador's ſuite, as may well be ſuppoſed, to viſit theſe ladies; the guardians of them, who were all eunuchs, came to viſit us. There were, indeed, ſeveral mandarins among them, to whom was conſigned the care and conduct of the female community. This palace was ſurrounded with very extenſive gardens, but, from the particular ſervice to which it was applied, it would have been a ſtrong mark of folly, as well as an idle riſk of danger, to have made any attempt to ſee them.

Friday 6. We left Chaung-ſhanuve this morning, at half paſt ſix, and found the weather extremely cold and piercing. The road continued to take the form of the country, which was very mountainous and irregular, as well as naked, and without any other marks of cultivation but ſuch as denoted the poverty of it. But this barren appearance does not proceed from the inactivity of the inhabitants, who ſeize on every ſpot capable of being tilled, and in ſituations which are acceſſible only to the adventurous peaſant, whom neceſſity impels to gather a ſcanty and dangerous harveſt. One example of this hazardous induſtry, which I obſerved this morning, will ſufficiently illuſtrate the barrenneſs of the country, and the ſpirit of its ſcattered inhabitants.

On

On a very high mountain I difcovered feveral diftinct patches of
cultivated ground, in fuch a ftate of declivity, as to be altogether inacceffible; and while I was confidering the means which the owner
of them muft employ to plant and gather his vegetables on thefe
alarming precipices, I beheld him actually employed in digging a fmall
fpot near the top of the hill, and in a fituation where it appeared to me to
be impoffible, without fome extraordinary contrivance, for any one to
ftand, much lefs to be following the bufinefs of a gardener. A more
minute examination informed me, that this poor peafant had a rope
faftened round his middle, which was fecured at the top of the mountain, and by which this hardy cultivator lets himfelf down to any part
of the precipice where a few fquare yards of ground gave him encouragement to plant his vegetables, or his corn: and in this manner he
had decorated the mountain with thofe little cultivated fpots that hung
about it. Near the bottom, on an hillock, this induftrious peafant had
erected a wooden hut, furrounded with a fmall piece of ground, planted
with cabbages, where he fupported, by this hazardous induftry, a wife
and family. The whole of thefe cultivated fpots do not amount to more
than half an acre; and fituated, as they are, at confiderable diftances
from each other; and, abftracted from the continual danger he en-
counters, the daily fatigue of this poor man's life, they offer a very
curious example of the natural induftry of the Chinefe people.

1793.
September.

It is, certainly, a wife policy in the government of China to receive the greater part of the taxes in the produce of the country; and
is a confiderable fpur to improvement and induftry in every clafs of
the people, who are to get their bread by the exertions of genius, or the
fweat of their brow. The landlord, alfo, receives the greater part of
his rents in the produce of his farms; and the farmer pays his fervants, in a great meafure, by giving them pieces of wafte uncultivated
land, where there are any, with occafional encouragement to excite
their induftry. Such are the cuftoms which prevail throughout China,
and tend fo much to preferve the profperity, and promote cultivation
of every part of that extenfive empire.

I

By

By ten o'clock this morning we arrived at the palace of Calla-chottueng, near a fmall village of the fame name, where we remained the whole of this day, on account of the length of the next ftage; and in order to make a more equal divifion of the reft of our journey.

This palace is fituated in a plain, between two very large and lofty mountains: in form and external appearance it refembles thofe we have already defcribed; but appears to be of modern erection; and its apartments are fitted up in a better ftyle than any we had yet feen. In fome of the courts there were artificial ruins, a favourite object in the ornamental gardening of this country, furrounded with plots of verdure.

As the embaffy now approached the termination of its journey, and was foon to appear before the fovereign, to obtain whofe favour and friendfhip it had traverfed fo large a part of the globe, the Ambaffador gave orders for rehearfing the proceffion, with which we were to make our appearance at the imperial court. This evening, therefore, the ceremonial was arranged, and performed, under the direction of Lieutenant-Colonel Benfon, and approved by the Ambaffador. The band played the Duke of York's march during the time of our rehearfal.

CHAP.

C H A P. XII.

*Arrive at the palace of Callachotreshangfu. Stop at one of the Em-
peror's pagodas. The public entry into Jehol; and circumstances of it.
Description of the palace provided for the British embassy. A principal
mandarin pays a visit of ceremony to the Ambassador. Singular conduct respecting the provisions supplied for the suite. The presents unpacked and displayed. An account of them.*

WE set off this morning at six o'clock, when the air was cold and
piercing, and passed through a very hilly and mountainous country.
After having breakfasted at a village of the name of Quanshanglin, the
route was continued.

1793.
September.
Saturday 7.

The villages we now passed were well peopled, but the difference is
very great indeed between the population, as well as cultivated
state, of China and Tartary. On this side of the wall, the picture is
extremely varied, the face and productions of the country are no
longer the same; nor were there any towns of confideration in the
latter part of our journey.

At two o'clock in the afternoon we arrived, very much fatigued by
the badness of the roads, and the jolting faculties of our carriages, at
the palace of Callachotreshangfu. It is a spacious and noble edifice,
but has not been lately inhabited; as might well be supposed, from the
great number of squirrels running about the courts, and haunting the
apartments.

The embassy continued its route at six o'clock, and, in about two
hours, arrived at one of the Emperor's pagodas, about three miles from

Sunday 8.

T

the

1793.

September.

the Imperial refidence. There a more abundant difplay of refrefhments was prepared than we had feen for fome time, from the difficulty of procuring them in the country through which we paffed.
Some time was alfo neceffary for every part of the fuite to arrange
their drefs, and fettle their appearance. At half paft nine, however,
we arrived at a fmall village, called Quoangcho, at about the diftance
of a mile from Jehol. Here the fuite alighted from their horfes and
carriages, and put themfelves in a ftate of preparation for the entry ;
which proceeded in the following manner, amidft a prodigious concourfe of people, whom curiofity had led to fee fuch a fpectacle as
they had never feen before, and will never, I believe, behold again.

The foldiers of the royal artillery, commanded by Lieutenant Parifh ;
The light-horfe and infantry, commanded by Lieutenant Crewe ;
The fervants of the Ambaffador, two and two ;
The couriers ;
The mechanics, two and two ;
The muficians, two and two ;
The gentlemen of the fuite, two and two ;
Sir George Staunton in a palanquin ;
The Ambaffador and Mr. Staunton in the poft-chaife, with a black-
boy, dreffed in a turban, behind it, clofed the proceffion.

There was, indeed, fomewhat of parade in all this bufinefs,
but it was by no means calculated to imprefs a favourable idea
of the greatnefs of the Britifh nation, on the minds of thofe who
beheld it : they might be pleafed with its novelty ; but it did not,
in any degree, poffefs that characteriftic appearance which was fo
neceffary on the prefent occafion. The military departments made a refpectable figure, and the gentlemen of the fuite cannot be fuppofed
for a moment to derogate from the diplomatic character in which
they were involved ; but the reft of the company exhibited a very
aukward appearance : fome wore round hats, fome cocked hats, and
others ftraw hats : fome were in whole boots, fome in half boots, and

others

others in fhoes with coloured flockings. In fhort, unlefs it was in fecond-hand coats and waiftcoats, which did not fit them, the inferior part of the fuite did not enjoy even the appearance of fhabby uniformity.

In this ftate and order the proceffion moved on with a flow pace to the city of Jehol, and foon after ten o'clock arrived at the palace provided for the accommodation of the Britifh embaffy in this city. Here the military part of the cavalcade formed a line to receive the Ambaffador with the ufual honours.

Thus the embaffy arrived at the end of its tedious and troublefome journey: but the manner of its reception did not fill us with any extravagant expectation as to the iffue of it: for not a mandarin appeared to congratulate the Ambaffador on his arrival, or to ufher him, with that form which his dignity demanded, to the apartments provided for him. In fhort, we came to this palace with more than ufual ceremony; but we entered into it with as little, as any of thofe where we had been accommodated during our journey. This appeared to be the more extraordinary, as it was the avowed expectation of the principal perfons of the fuite, that the Ambaffador would be met, on his entry at Jehol, by the Grand Choulaa, the Imperial Minifter of ftate: but on what grounds this expectation was formed, or for what reafon it received fuch a difappointment, it is not for me to offer a conjecture.

On our arrival, Lieut. Col. Benfon ordered the troops to hold themfelves in readinefs to fall into a line at a moment's warning; and defired the fervants, mechanics, &c. to range themfelves in order before the door of the Ambaffador's apartments, in order to receive the Grand Choulaa, who was expected every moment to pay his vifit of falutation and welcome.

In

In this ſtate of ſuſpenſe we remained from our arrival till paſt four o'clock; in the courſe of which time we had paraded at leaſt a dozen times, as ſeveral mandarins came to take a curious view of us, and every one of them was ſuppoſed, in his turn, to be the Grand Chou-laa. The arrival of dinner, however, put an end to all expectations of ſeeing him on this day.

The palace, which was now become the reſidence of the embaſſy, is built on the declivity of a hill; the entrance to it is by eight large broad ſteps which lead to a wooden gateway, through which there is a paſſage to a large court, paved in the center with large flat ſtones. On each ſide of this court there is a long and broad gallery roofed with black ſhining tiles, and ſupported in front by ſtrong wooden pillars. That on the left was employed at this time as a kitchen, and encloſed by mats nailed along the pillars to the height of ſeven or eight feet: the other, on the oppoſite ſide, was quite open, and uſed as a place of parade and exerciſe for the ſoldiers. At the upper end of this court there is another neat gallery or plat-form laid with ſtones, and roofed in the ſame manner as the others. To this there is an aſcent of three ſteps, and a door opens from it into another court, the wings of which afforded chambers for the military part of the embaſſy; and the center part, fronting the gallery, to which there is an aſcent of three ſteps, contained the apartments of the Ambaſſador and Sir George Staunton: beyond this is another court of the ſame dimenſions, the wings of which were occupied by the mechanics, muſicians and ſervants, and the center of it by the gen-tlemen of the ſuite: but it conſiſted only of two large rooms, where they ſlept in two diviſions, and a lobby of communication, which was uſed as an eating ſaloon.

This building cannot be deſcribed as poſſeſſing either grandeur or elegance: it does not riſe beyond a ground floor, but is of unequal height, as the ground on which it is built is on a gradual aſcent. It

is

is furrounded by a wall, but is overlooked, from the upper parts of the hill, on whofe declivity it is erected.

But though we were as yet rather difappointed in the reception of honours, we had no reafon to be diffatisfied with the attention paid to our more urgent neceffities; and we dined in comfort and abundance.

This morning, at fo early an hour as feven o'clock, was received a large quantity of boiled eggs, with tea and bread, for breakfaft. At noon his Excellency was vifited by feveral mandarins. Nothing, however, as yet tranfpired that could lead us to form a judgment as to the final iffue of the bufinefs: as far as any opinion could be formed from the general afpect of things, it did not bear the promife of that fuccefs, which had been originally expected from it.

The Grand Choulaa ftill delayed his expected vifit.

In this palace, as in our former places of refidence, we experienced the jealous precaution of the Chinefe government: we were kept here alfo in a ftate of abfolute confinement; and, on no pretext, was it permitted to any perfon, attached to the embaffy, to pafs the gates.

This morning his Excellency was vifited by a mandarin, accompanied by a numerous train of attendants. He remained with the Ambaffador and Sir George Staunton about an hour, in which fome neceffary formalities were interchanged; and then returned with the fame form in which he came. During the vifit of the mandarin, his attendants were very bufily employed in examining the drefs of the Englifh fervants; the lace of which they rubbed with a ftone to certify its quality, and then looking at each other with an air of furprize, they fhook their heads and fmiled; a fufficient proof that the Tartars are not unacquainted with the value of metals; at leaft, they clearly comprehended the inferior value of the trimmings that decorated

the

the liveries of the embaſſy. They appeared to be a polite and pleaſant people, and of an agreeable appearance.

Though it cannot be ſuppoſed that ſuch a conference as was this morning held between the Britiſh Ambaſſador and the mandarin would be communicated to the general attendants on the embaſſy, yet we could not reſiſt the ſpirit of conjecture on the occaſion: the following circumſtance, which took place this morning, did not ſerve to diſſipate that diſpoſition to forebode ill, which prevailed among us.

The Ambaſſador ordered Mr. Winder, one of his ſecretaries, to intimate to the ſervants that, in caſe they ſhould find, in the courſe of the day, any deficiency in their proviſions, either in quality or quantity, they ſhould not reflect or complain to the people who ſupplied them, but leave them untouched, and intimate the grievance to his Ex-cellency; who requeſted, for very particular and weighty reaſons, that this order might be punctually obſerved.

It became thoſe to whom this intimation was made, to pay the moſt willing obedience to it; at the ſame time, it excited no ſmall degree of aſtoniſhment that we ſhould thus be ordered to prepare our-ſelves for ill-treatment in the article of proviſions, of which we had, hitherto, ſo little reaſon to complain. Our treatment in this reſpect had been not only hoſpitable, but bounteous in the extreme. To ſuggeſt cauſes of complaint to thoſe who never yet had reaſon to com-plain, was a conduct perfectly unintelligible in itſelf; and was, there-fore, very naturally referred to the interview of the morning between the mandarin and the Ambaſſador.

When, however, dinner came, we were ſenſible that the precau-tions communicated to us were, as we expected to find them, the reſult of ſome well-grounded ſuſpicion; for, inſtead of that abun-dance with which our tables had hitherto been ſerved, there was not

now

now a fufficient quantity of provifions for half the perfons who were ready to partake of them.

1793.
September.

The emotions of every one attached to the embaffy were, I believe, very unpleafant upon the occafion. We not only felt the probability that we might be ftarved as well as imprifoned; but that the embaffy itfelf was treated with difrefpect; and, of courfe, we felt fome alarm, left the important objects of it would quickly vanifh into nothing. We had alfo our feelings as Britons, and felt the infult, as it appeared to us, which was offered to the crown and dignity of the firft nation in the world.

This meagre meal, therefore, was left untouched; and, in conformity to the orders which had been received, complaints were preferred to his Excellency on the occafion; and, on a report being made to him that the reprefentations which had been made were founded in reality, Mr. Plumb, the interpreter, was requefted to communicate the caufe of difcontent to the mandarin, and to infift on more hofpitable ufage: nor was the remonftrance without an immediate effect; for, within five minutes after it was made, each table was ferved with a variety of hot difhes, not only in plenty, but profufion.

Why this entertainment, when it muft have been in actual ftate of preparation to be ferved, was thus withheld from us, could not be reconciled to any principle of juftice or policy. To fuppofe that it proceeded from caprice, or an humorous fpirit of tantalifing, cannot be readily imagined; and, as for any faving of expenfe in the bufinefs, that could be no object to the treafury to the Chinefe Emperor. It was confidered, therefore, as an enigma, which, as the evil was removed, foon ceafed to be a fubject of curiofity or inquiry.

The Ambaffador was this morning pleafed to order the prefents which were brought from Pekin, to be unpacked in the great platform, or portico, facing his Excellency's apartments; where feve-

Wednef-
day 11.

ral

ral ranges of tables were placed to receive them. They were as follows :

Two hundred pieces of narrow coarfe cloth, chiefly black and blue.

Two large telefcopes.

Two air guns.

Two beautiful fowling pieces; one inlaid with gold, and the other with filver.

Two pair of faddle piftols, enriched and ornamented in the fame manner.

Two boxes, each containing feven pieces of Irifh tabinets.

Two elegant faddles, with complete furniture; the feats of thefe were of fine doe fkin, ftitched with filver thread; the flaps were of a bright yellow fuperfine cloth, embroidered with filver, and enriched with filver fpangles and taffels; the reins and ftirrup-ftraps were of bright yellow leather, ftitched with filver; the ftirrups, buckles, &c. were of fteel double plaited; and,

Two large boxes, containing the fineft carpets of the Britifh manu-factory.

Thefe were all the prefents which were brought from Pekin: the reft, confifting of various pieces of clock-work and machinery, with carriages, and pieces of artillery, were either too cumberfome or too delicate to venture on fo long a journey; and were, therefore, intended to be prefented to his Imperial Majefty, on his return, for the winter feafon, to the capital of his empire.

The prefents were ordered to remain in their prefent fituation till the Imperial pleafure fhould be known concerning them. Centinels were appointed to do duty on the platform where they were placed.

CHAP.

C H A P. XIII.

The prefents removed from the palace. A notification received that the Emperor would give audience to the Britifh Ambaffador. Orders iffued to the fuite on the occafion. The proceffion to the Imperial palace defcribed. The Ambaffador's firft audience of the Emperor. Prefents received on the occafion. The Ambaffador's fecond vifit to the Emperor. Additional prefents. Favourable opinions entertained of the fuccefs of the embaffy.

THIS morning, the conducting mandarin Van-Tadge-In, accompanied by feveral of his mandarin brethren, and a troop of attendants, removed the prefents, as was prefumed, to the palace of the Emperor.

His Excellency, at the fame time, received a vifit from a mandarin of the firft order, who came to notify that the Emperor would, on Saturday morning, give audience to the Ambaffador of the King of Great Britain at the Imperial palace. This intelligence enlivened the fpirits, as it animated the hopes, of the whole embaffy: and, though the Grand Choulaa had not vifited the Ambaffador, and other circumftances of an unfavourable afpect had taken place, the news of the day not only diffipated our gloom, but renewed the tide of expectation, and made it flow with an accelerated current.

His Excellency received the vifits of feveral mandarins of diftinction, who continued with him upwards of an hour.

Orders were iffued, that the whole fuite fhould be ready on the following morning, at three o'clock, to accompany the Ambaffador to

U

the

1793.
September.

the Imperial palace. The fervants were ordered to drefs in their green and gold liveries, and to wear white filk, or cotton ftockings, with fhoes; boots of any kind being abfolutely prohibited on this occafion. It was, at the fame time, intimated, that neither the foldiers, or the fervants, were to remain at the palace for the return of the Ambaffador; but when they had attended him there, they were requefted to return immediately to Jehol, without prefuming to halt at any place whatever for a fingle moment; as his Excellency had every reafon to expect that, in a few days, the prefent reftrictions, which were fo irkfome to the retinue of the embaffy, would be removed, and every indulgence granted them which they could reafonably defire: and as any deviation from this order would tend to rifque the lofs of that meditated favour. His Excellency ferioufly expected it to meet with a general and willing obedience.

Saturday 14.

This morning, at fo early an hour as three o'clock, the Ambaffador and his fuite proceeded, in full uniform, to the Emperor's court.

His Excellency was dreffed in a fuit of fpotted mulberry velvet, with a diamond ftar, and his ribbon; over which he wore the full habit of the order of the Bath, with the hat, and plume of feathers, which form a part of it. Sir George Staunton was alfo in a full court drefs, over which he wore the robe of a doctor of laws in the Englifh univerfities, with the black velvet cap belonging to that degree.

Though the morning was fo dark that we could not diftinguifh each other, Lieutenant-Colonel Benfon made an attempt to form a proceffion, to proceed the palanquin of the Ambaffador. But this manœuvre was of very fhort duration, as the bearers of it moved rather too faft for the folemnity of a flow march; and, inftead of proceeding it with a grave pace, we were glad to follow it with a quick one. Indeed, whether it was the attraction of our mufic, or any accidental circumftance, I know not, we found ourfelves intermingled

with

with a cohort of pigs, affes, and dogs, which broke our ranks, fuch
as they were, and put us into irrecoverable confufion. All formality
of proceffion, therefore, was at an end; and the Ambaffador's palanquin was fo far advanced before us, as to make a little fmart running
neceffary to overtake it.

After a confufed cavalcade, if it can deferve that name, we arrived
at the palace of the Emperor, in the fame ftate of confufion in which
we had proceeded—the pedeftrian part of the fuite being a little out
of breath with running; and the gentlemen on horfeback, not altogether infenfible to the rifk of accidents from the dark hour of the
morning. In fhort, it appeared, to the greater part of thofe who were
concerned in it, to be rather ridiculous to attempt to make a parade
that no one could fee.

At about five o'clock the Ambaffador alighted from his palanquin,
amidft an immenfe concourfe of people; Sir George and Mr. Staunton bearing his train, and followed by the gentlemen attached to the
embaffy.

The fervants, &c. returned according to order, and the foldiers
marched back with fife and drum. As our return was by day-light,
we had fome opportunity of examining the appearance of the city
where we refided.

It is a large and populous place, built without any attention whatever to regularity of defign, and lies in an hollow, formed by two
large mountains. The houfes are low, of a mean appearance, and
built chiefly of wood: the ftreets are not paved in any part of the
city, but in that quarter of it which is moft contiguous to the Emperor's palace; the road to which is laid with large flat ftones.

As this place is not watered by any river, it cannot be fuppofed to
enjoy a large portion of commerce. Its trade, however, is not al-

together

1793.
September.

together inconfiderable, from the confumption occafioned by the refidence of the Emperor in the immediate neighbourhood; a circumftance which not only occafions a great increafe of inhabitants, but
brings with it the wealth, the luxury, and the expences of a court.

The furrounding country wears a greater appearance of fertility,
than any I have feen in thofe parts of Tartary through which the
embaffy had paffed; but, in its beft ftate, it is by no means comparable
to that of China.

At eleven o'clock in the forenoon, the Ambaffador and his fuite
returned from the Imperial palace. It was a vifit of mere form and
prefentation; and his Excellency, Sir George Staunton, and Mr.
Staunton, with Mr. Plumb, the interpeter, were alone admitted into
the prefence of the Emperor.

The Emperor, it was faid, received the credentials of the embaffy,
with a moft ceremonious formality. All, however, that we could
learn, as a matter of indubitable occurrence, was the notice his Imperial Majefty was pleafed to take of Mafter Staunton, the fon of Sir
George Staunton. He appeared to be very much ftruck with the
boy's vivacity and deportment; and expreffed his admiration of the
faculty which the young gentleman poffeffed of fpeaking fix different
languages. The Emperor, to manifeft the approbation he felt on the
occafion, not only prefented him, with his own hand, a very beautiful
fan, and feveral fmall embroidered bags and purfes, but commanded
the interpreter to fignify, that he thought very highly of his talents
and appearance.

In a very fhort time after the Ambaffador had returned from court,
a large quantity of prefents were received from his Imperial Majefty.

They confifted of the richeft velvets, fatins, filks, and purfes beautifully embroidered. To thefe were added large parcels of the beft

tea

tea of the country, made up in folid cakes, in the fize and form of a Dutch cheefe. It is thus, in fome way, baked together, by which means it will never be affected by air or climate, nor ever lofe its flavour, though kept without any covering whatever. Each of thefe balls weigh about five pounds.

His Excellency diftributed to every gentleman of the fuite his proportion of the prefents. Thofe which were peculiarly addreffed to their Britannic Majefties, were depofited in the lobby, in the boxes wherein they arrived.

This morning, at one o'clock, the Ambaffador, accompanied by his fuite, but unattended by any of his guards or fervants, proceeded to pay a fecond vifit to the Emperor. The object of this interview was, as we underftood, to make an attempt to open the negotiation, for the purpofe of obtaining that extenfion of commerce fo anxioufly defired by our Eaft India Company.

His Excellency did not return till near three o'clock ; and, on his arrival, appeared to be very much exhaufted. Mr. Plumb, the interpreter, gave, however, fuch a favourable account of the general afpect of the negotiation, as to elevate the hopes of every one concerned in the iffue of it. He mentioned, that the Emperor had, through the medium of the Grand Choulaa, entered upon the bufinefs of the embaffy with Lord Macartney ; which, as far as it went, had altogether fucceeded. This favourable information appeared to be confirmed by a fecond cargo of prefents from his Imperial Majefty. They confifted of large quantities of rich velvets, filks, and fatins, with fome beautiful Chinefe lamps, and rare Porcelain. To thefe were added a number of callibafh boxes of exquifite workmanfhip, beautifully carved on the outfide, and ftained with a fcarlet colour, of the utmoft foftnefs and delicacy : the infide of them was black, and fhone like japan.

His

His Excellency made the fame diftribution as he had before done to the gentlemen of the fuite; while the prefents, addreffed to their Britannic Majefties, were affigned to the fame apartment which contained thofe of the preceding day.

The evening of this day was paffed in great mirth and feftivity by the whole fuite, from the very favourable forebodings which they now entertained of the final fuccefs of their important miffion.

CHAP.

C H A P. XIV.

*The Ambassador visited by mandarins on the part of the Emperor, to in-
vite him to court on the anniversary of his Imperial Majesty's birth-
day. The whole suite attended on the occasion. The Imperial palace
described. Some account of the Emperor. A succession of presents.
Business transacted with the Imperial court. Particular present of
the Emperor of China to the King of Great Britain. Description
of theatrical amusements. A British soldier tried by a court-martial,
and punished. Leave Jehol.*

THE Ambassador received the visits of several mandarins, who
came to inform him, that as the following day was the anniversary of the Emperor's birth-day, his presence, and that of the whole
embassy, would be expected at court.

This morning, at two o'clock, his Excellency, with the whole of
the British suite, set out for his Imperial Majesty's palace, where we
arrived, with much interruption, in about two hours, amidst an immense crowd of spectators without, and a great concourse of people
within the palace; the latter consisting of mandarins of all classes and
distinctions.

This palace is built on an elevated situation, and commands an extensive view of the mountainous country that surrounds it. The
edifice itself is neither lofty or elegant, but very extensive; and contains a very numerous range of courts, surrounded with porticos,
ornamented with gilding and colours. · The gardens extend for several miles, and are surrounded by a strong wall, about thirty feet in
height.

1793.
September.
Monday 16.

Tuesday 17.

1793.
September.

height. In front of the palace there is a large plain, with a confiderable lake in the center of it.

Here we waited feveral hours, till, at length, the approach of the Emperor was announced, by the proftration of the mandarins, as he advanced.
This great perfonage was in a very plain palanquin, borne by twenty
mandarins of the firft order ; and were it not for that circumftance, he
could not have been diftinguifhed from a common mandarin, as he
wore no mark or badge of diftinction, nor any article of drefs fuperior to the higher claffes of his fubjects. The fimplicity of his appearance, it feems, proceeds from that wife policy which diftinguifhes
his reign ; as it is a favourite principle of his government to check,
as much as poffible, all ufelefs luxury, and to encourage œconomy
among his people. It is from the fame paternal regard for the fituation and circumftances of his fubjects, that he has fuppreffed all public
rejoicings on account of his birth-day, in this lefs flourifhing part of
his dominions; from the apprehenfion that the loyal and affectionate
fpirit of the poorer claffes of the people would diftrefs themfelves, in
promoting the feftive celebration of the day. This prohibition, however, as we underftood, reached no further than the immediate
vicinity of the Imperial refidence; the birth-day of the fovereign
being obferved with great joy and folemnity through every other
part of a grateful empire.

The Emperor on this day completed the eighty-fifth year of his
age, as he was in the fifty-feventh of his reign. Though he had dark,
piercing eyes, the whole of his countenance difcovered the mild traits
of benignant virtue, mixed with that eafy dignity of exalted ftation,
which refults rather from internal confcioufnefs, than exterior
grandeur.

The appearance of the fuite was exactly the fame as on the firft day
of audience ; and we returned, in an equal ftate of embarraffment and
fatigue, at one o'clock. A very large quantity of prefents foon followed

lowed us, confifting of the fame kind of articles as had been already
fent, but of different colours and patterns. There were, however,
added, on the prefent occafion, a profufion of fruits and confectionary, fufficient to have furnifhed a fucceffion of fine deferts, if our
ftay had been prolonged to twice the period which was deftined for
our abode at Jehol.

1793.
September.

The Chinefe poffefs the art of confectionary in a very fuperior degree, both as to its tafte, and the variety of its forms and colours.
Their cakes of every kind are admirably made, and more agreeable to
the palate than any I remember to have tafted in England, or any other
country. Their paftry is alfo as light as any I have eaten in Europe,
and in fuch a prodigious variety, as the combined efforts of the European confectioners, I believe, would not be able to produce.

This morning the Ambaffador went to the Imperial palace, but not
in the former ftyle of parade, to have his audience of leave, as the
period of our ftay in Tartary was verging to a period.

Wednef-
day 18.

His Excellency, at the fame time, tranfacted certain official bufinefs at court, which was faid without referve at the time, by the
gentlemen of the fuite, to be as follows:

The Emperor of China refufed, in the firft inftance, to fign, and of
courfe, to enter into any engagement by a written treaty with the
Crown of Great Britain, or any other nation; as fuch a conduct, on his
part, would be contrary to the ancient ufage, and, indeed, an infringement of the ancient conftitutions, of the empire. At the fame
time he was pleafed to fignify his high refpect for his Britannic
Majefty and the Britifh nation; and that he felt a ftrong difpofition to
grant them greater indulgencies than any other European power trading
to his dominions; nor was he unwilling to make fuch a new arrangement of the duties payable by Britifh fhips arriving at Canton, as ap-

peared

1793.
September.

peared to be a leading object of the negotiation. At the same time, however, he should be ever attentive to the real interests of his own subjects, an atom of which he would never sacrifice; and should, therefore, withdraw his favours to any foreign nation whenever it might appear to be incompatible with the interests of his own; or that the English should, by their conduct in trade, forfeit their pretensions to any advantages which might be granted them in preference to other nations trading to China. These were the declarations of the Emperor on the occasion, which did not, in his opinion, require any written instrument or signature to induce him to realise and fulfil.

At the same time, to prove the high regard and esteem the Emperor of China entertained for the King of Great Britain, his Imperial Majesty delivered, from his own hand, into that of the Ambassador, a very valuable box, containing the miniature pictures of all the preceding emperors; to which is annexed, a description in verse by each emperor, descriptive of himself, and the principal features of his government, as well as a line of conduct recommended to their several successors.

The Emperor, on presenting this gift to the Ambassador, spoke to the following purport:

" Deliver this casket to the King your master, with your own hand, and tell him, though the present may appear to be small, it is, in my estimation, the most valuable that I can give, or my empire can furnish; for it has been transmitted to me through a long line of my predecessors, and is the last token of affection which I had reserved to bequeath to my son and successor; as a tablet of the virtues of his ancestors, which he had only to peruse, as I should hope, to inspire him with the noble resolution to follow such bright examples; and, as they had done, to make it the grand object of his life to exalt the honour of the Imperial throne, and advance the happiness and prosperity of his people."

Such

Such were the words delivered by the Emperor on the occasion, as communicated by Mr. Plumb, the interpreter, and which occasioned, as may be imagined, no small degree of speculation among the gentlemen of the retinue.

1793.
September.

The Ambassador returned to dinner, and soon after repaired again to the Imperial palace, with his whole suite and attendants, to see a play which was expressly performed as a particular mark of respect to the embassy.

This dramatic entertainment was represented in one of the inner courts of the palace, on a temporary stage erected for the purpose. It was decorated with a profusion of silk, ribbons, and streamers, and illuminated with great splendour and elegance.

The performance consisted of a great variety of mock battles and military engagements; lofty tumbling, as it is expressed with us, and dancing both on the tight and slack ropes; and in all these exercises that agility was displayed, which would have done no discredit to the gymnastic amusements of Sadler's Wells or Astley's amphitheatre; but the skill of the performers was more particularly astonishing in the art of balancing, in which they excelled any thing of the kind I had ever seen. By an imperceptible motion, as it appeared, of the joints of their arms and legs, they gave to basons, jugs, glasses, &c. an apparent power of loco-motion, and produced a progressive equilibrium, by which these vessels changed their positions from one part to another of the bodies of the balancers, in a manner so extraordinary, that I almost suspected the correctness of my own senses.

The succession of entertainments was concluded by a variety of curious deceptions by slight of hand, which the almost magical activity of Breslaw or Comus has never exceeded: and, as a proof of my assertion, I shall mention one of them, which, I must own, astonished me, and seemed to have an equal effect on the rest of the spectators.

The

1791.
September.

The performer began by exhibiting a large bason in every possible position, when he suddenly placed it on the stage with the hollow part downwards, and instantly taking it up again, discovered a large rabbit, which escaped from the performer, who attempted to catch it, by taking refuge among the spectators. This deception was perfectly unaccountable to me, as there were no visible means whatever of communication, by which it was possible to convey so large an animal to the spot: the stage was also covered with matting, so that it could not be conveyed through the floor, which, if that had been the case, must have been discovered by those, and there were many of them, who were within three yards of the spot; besides, the whole display of the trick occupied but a few seconds. Several other deceptions of a similar kind prolonged our amusement. The whole of the entertainment was accompanied by a band of musicians, placed on the stage.

The theatre was filled with persons of distinction, and formed a very splendid appearance. The Ambassador and his suite returned about nine o'clock, having been very much gratified by the entertainment of the evening.

Thursday 19.

At noon several mandarins came to visit his Excellency; when every individual belonging to the embassy received a pipe and tobacco-bag containing a quantity of that herb for smoaking.

In the several visits which the mandarins of different classes paid to the Ambassador, they never varied in their exterior appearance, and changes of raiment do not seem to be an object of attention in China, as it is, more or less, in every part of Europe. Even the court dress of the mandarins differs very little from their ordinary habiliments. It consists of a robe that falls down to the middle of the leg, and is drawn round the lower part of the neck with ribbons. On the part which covers the stomach, is a piece of embroidery worked on the garment about six inches square; and is finished in gold or silk of different co-

lours,

lours, according to the rank of the wearer: this badge of diftinction has its counterpart on a parallel part of the back, minutely correfponding in pattern and dimenfions. In winter, it is generally made of velvet, and its prevailing colour is blue. The fafh, which, on all other occafions is worn round the waift, is difpenfed with at court, and the drefs is left to its own eafe and natural flow.

As I am now come to a period when a certain degree of authority was attempted to be affumed, altogether inconfiftent with the character and privileges of Englifhmen, and which, I fear, conveyed no favourable impreffion to the Chinefe of our national character and cuftoms; I fhall previoufly ftate the orders iffued by Lord Macartney, and read to the fhip's companies, and all perfons of every rank attached to the fuite, about five o'clock in the evening of the 20th day of July 1793.

Sealed and figned MACARTNEY.

" As the fhips and brigs attendant on the embaffy to China are now likely to arrive in port a few days hence, his Excellency the Ambaffador thinks it his duty to make the following obfervations and arrangements:

" It is impoffible that the various important objects of the embaffy can be obtained, but through the good will of the Chinefe: that good will may much depend on the ideas which they fhall be induced to entertain of the difpofition and conduct of the Englifh nation, and they can judge only from the behaviour of the majority of thofe who come amongft them. It muft be confeffed, that the impreffions hitherto made upon their minds, in confequence of the irregularities committed by Englifhmen at Canton, are unfavourable even to the degree of confidering them as the worft among Europeans; thefe impreffions are communicated to that tribunal in the capital, which reports to, and advifes the Emperor upon all concerns with foreign countries. It is

therefore

therefore effential, by a conduct particularly regular and circumfpect, to imprefs them with *new, more juft, and more favourable* ideas of Englifhmen; and to fhew that, even to the loweft officer in the fea or land fervice, or in the civil line, they are capable of maintaining, by example and by difcipline, due order, fobriety, and fubordination, among their refpective inferiors. Though the people in China have not the fmalleft fhare in the government, yet it is a maxim invariably purfued by their fuperiors, to fupport the meaneft Chinefe in any difference with a ftranger, and if the occafion fhould happen, to avenge his blood; of which, indeed, there was a fatal inftance not long fince at Canton, where the gunner of an Englifh veffel, who had been very innocently the caufe of the death of a native peafant, was executed for it, notwithftanding the utmoft united efforts on the part of the feveral European factories at Canton to fave him; peculiar caution and mildnefs muft confequently be obferved in every fort of intercourfe or accidental meeting with any the pooreft individual of the country.

" His Excellency, who well knows that he need not recommend to Sir Erafmus Gower to make whatever regulations prudence may dictate on the occafion, for the perfons under his immediate command, as he hopes Capt. Mackintofh will do for the officers and crew of the Hindoftan, trufts alfo that the propriety and neceffity of fuch regulations, calculated to preferve the credit of the Englifh name, and the intereft of the mother country in thefe remote parts, will infure a fteady and cheerful obedience.

" The fame motives, he flatters himfelf, will operate likewife upon all the perfons immediately connected with, or in the fervice of, the embaffy.

" His Excellency declares that he fhall be ready to encourage and to report favourably hereupon the good conduct of thofe who fhall be found to deferve it; fo he will think it his duty, in cafe of mifconduct or difobedience of orders, to report the fame with equal exactnefs,

and

(159)

and to suspend or dismiss transgressors, as the occasion may require. Nor, if offence should be offered to a Chinese, or a misdemeanor of any kind be committed, which may be punishable by their laws, will he deem himself bound to interfere for the purpose of endeavouring to ward off or mitigate their severity.

" His Excellency relies on Lieutenant-Colonel Benson, commandant of his guard, that he will have a strict and watchful eye over them; vigilance, as to their personal demeanor, is as requisite in the present circumstances, as it is, though from other motives, in regard to the conduct of an enemy in time of war. The guard are to be kept constantly together, and regularly exercised in all military evolutions; nor are any of them to absent themselves from on board ship, or from whatever place may be allotted them for their dwelling on shore, without leave from his Excellency, or commanding officer. None of the mechanics, or servants, are to leave the ship, or usual dwelling on shore, without leave from himself, or from Mr. Maxwell; and his Excellency expects, that the gentlemen in his train will shew the example of subordination, by communicating their wishes to him before they go, on any occasion, from the ship, or usual dwelling place on shore.

" No boxes or packages, of any kind, are to be removed from the ship, or, afterwards, from the place where they shall be brought on shore, without the Ambassador's leave, or a written order from Mr. Barrow, the comptroller; such order describing the nature, number, and dimensions of such packages.

" His Excellency, in the most earnest manner, requests that no person whatever belonging to the ships be suffered, and he desires that none of his suite, guard, mechanics, or servants, presume to offer for sale, or propose to purchase, in the way of traffic, the smallest article of merchandize of any kind, or under any pretence whatever, without leave from him previously obtained. The necessity of avoiding the least appearance of traffic accompanying an embassy to Pekin was

such,

fuch, as to induce the Eaft India Company to forego the profits of a new market, and deterred them from fhipping any goods for fale in the Hindoftan, as being deftined to attend upon the embaffy, the dignity and importance of which, in the prejudiced eyes of the Chinefe, would be utterly loft, and the good confequences expected from it, even on commercial points, totally prevented, if any actual tranfactions, though for trifles, for the purpofe of gain, fhould be difcovered amongft any of the perfons concerned in conveying, or attending an Ambaffador; of which the report would foon infallibly fwell into a general fyftem of trading. From this ftrictnefs his Excellency will willingly relax whenever fuch advances fhall have been made by him in negotiation as will fecure the object of his miffion; and when a permiffion from him to an European, to difpofe of any particular article of merchandize, fhall be confidered as a favour granted to the Chinefe purchafer. His Excellency is bound to punifh, as far as in him lies, any the flighteft deviation from this regulation; he will eafily have it in his power to do fo, in regard to the perfons immediately in his train, or fervice. The difcipline of the navy will render it equally eafy to Sir Erafmus Gower, in refpect to thofe under his immediate command; and the Eaft India Company have, by their order of the 5th of September, 1792, and by their letter of the 8th of the fame month and year, fully authorized his Excellency to enforce compliance, with the fame regulation, among the officers of the Hindoftan. A copy of the faid order, and an extract from the faid letter, here follow, in order that Captain Mackintofh may communicate the fame to his officers. His Excellency depends upon him to prevent any breach or evafion of the fame among any of his crew.

At a Court of Directors held on Wednefday, the 5th of September, 1792,

" Refolved,

" That the Right Honourable Lord Vifcount Macartney be au-
" thorized to fufpend, or difmifs the commander, or any officer of
" the Hindoftan, who fhall be guilty of a breach of covenants, or
" difobedience

" difobedience of orders from the Secret Committee, or from his
" Excellency, during the continuation of the embaffy to China.

1792.
September.

(Signed)   " W. RAMSEY, Secretary."

*Extract from the Chairman and Deputy Chairman's Letter to Lord Ma-
cartney, dated the 8th of September,* 1792.

" The Secret Committee having given orders to Captain Mackintofh,
" of the Hindoftan, to put himfelf entirely under your Excellency's
" direction, as long as may be neceffary for the purpofe of the em-
" baffy, we have inclofed a copy of his inftructions, and of the
" covenants which he has entered into, together with an account of
" his private trade, and that of his officers : there is no intention
" whatever, on the part of the court, to permit private trade in any
" other port, or place, than Canton, to which the fhip is ultimately
" deftined, unlefs your Excellency is fatisfied that fuch private trade
" will not prove of detriment to the dignity and importance annexed
" to the embaffy, or to the confequences expected therefrom, in which
" cafe your confent in writing becomes neceffary to authorize any
" commercial tranfaction by Captain Mackintofh, or any of his
" officers, as explained in the inftructions from the Secret Committee.
" But as we cannot be too guarded with refpect to trade, and the con-
" fequences which may refult from any attempt for that purpofe, we
" hereby authorize your Excellency to fufpend, or difmifs the com-
" mander, or any officer of the Hindoftan, who fhall be guilty of a
" breach of covenants, or difobedience of orders from the Secret
" Committee, or from your Excellency, during the continuance of
" the prefent embaffy."

" His Excellency takes this opportunity of declaring alfo, that however determined his fenfe of duty makes him to forward the objects of
his miffion, and to watch, detect, and punifh, as far as in his power,
any crime, difobedience of orders, or other behaviour tending to en-

Y

danger,

danger, or delay the fuccefs of the prefent undertaking, or to bring difcredit on the Englifh character, or occafion any difficulty, or embarraffment to the embaffy: fo in the like manner fhall he feel himfelf happy in being able at all times to report and reward the merit, as well as to promote the intereft, and indulge the wifhes, of any perfon who has accompanied him on this occafion, as much as may be confiftent with the honour and welfare of the public.

" In cafe of the abfence or engagements of his Excellency, at any particular moment, application may be made in his room to Sir George Staunton, whom his Majefty was pleafed to honour with a commiffion of minifter plenipotentiary, to act on fuch occafions."

*Given on board his Majefty's fhip the Lion,
the 16th day of July, 1793.*

By his Excellency's Command.

(Signed)   **ACHESON MAXWELL,** }Secretaries.
                EDWARD WINDER,

Having thus given at large, and from the firft authority, the whole of thofe regulations which were framed, and with great good fenfe and true policy, to forward the objects of the embaffy, I fhall now proceed to ftate certain circumftances, which do not altogether appear to be confiftent with, if they may not be confidered by fome, as violations of, them.

It was now hinted to all the fervants of the Ambaffador, that they were hereafter to confider themfelves as fubject to military law, and that the corporeal punifhment ufual in the army would be applied to them, if they fhould refufe to obey the commands of any of their fuperiors in the fuite. Such an idea, as may be fuppofed, occafioned no fmall alarm, as well as abhorrence in the minds of thofe who would be affected by a regulation fo contrary to every principle of right or
justice:

juſtice : and when they were at ſuch a diſtance from their own happy country, that any one injured by ſuch an act of tyranny, might never again return to the protection of that power which would avenge it.

To the honour of Sir George Staunton, I have the ſatisfaction to ſay, from the general report in the palace, that he reprobated, in very ſevere terms, the propoſition of a meaſure ſo ſubverſive of thoſe privileges, which, as Engliſhmen, we carried with us into the heart of Tartary ; and which no power of the embaſſy had a legal right to invade.

This ſtrange extenſion of military diſcipline was certainly propoſed to Lord Macartney by ſome officious perſons in the ſuite ; but the experiment, very happily for all parties, was never attempted to be made.

When Lieutenant Colonel Benſon ordered a court-martial to be held on one of his ſoldiers, and ſaw the ſentence of it carried into execution, he did that which he had a legal power to do, however indifferct the exerciſe of it might be : but in the verge of an embaſſy, which, within its own circle, carries the liberties of Engliſh ſubjects to the remoteſt regions of the globe, any attempt to infringe them, deſerves the ſevereſt reprobation.

This morning, James Cootie, a private in the infantry, who compoſed a part of the Ambaſſador's guards, was reported to the commanding officer, for having procured, by the aſſiſtance of a Chineſe ſoldier, a ſmall quantity of ſamtchoo, a ſpirituous liquor already deſcribed : for which offence he was immediately confined, and ſoon after tried by a court-martial, conſiſting of a certain number of his comrades, and a corporal as preſident ; and the ſentence pronounced on this unfortunate man was approved by Lieutenant-Colonel Benſon.

In

1793.
September.

In confequence of this fentence, all the Britifh foldiery were drawn up in the outer court of the palace; and, after obferving all the forms ufual on fuch occafions, the culprit was tied up to one of the pillars of the great portico, and, in the prefence of a great number of the Chinefe, he received the punifhment of fixty lafhes, adminiftered with no common feverity.

The mandarins, as well as thofe of the inferior claffes who were prefent, expreffed their abhorrence at this proceeding, while fome of them declared, that they could not reconcile this conduct in a people, who profeffed a religion, which they reprefented to be fuperior to all others, in enforcing fentiments of benevolence, and blending the duties of juftice and of mercy. One of the principal mandarins, who knew a little of the Englifh language, expreffed his own fentiments, and thofe of his brethren, by faying, " Englifhman too much cruel, too much bad."

Of the nature of the foldier's offence, I do not pretend to determine; nor fhall I obferve on the neceffity of applying the feverity of military difcipline on the occafion; thefe things are not within the fcope of my information or experience: but a little common-fenfe alone is neceffary to determine on the impolicy of exhibiting a kind of punifh-ment which is unknown in China, and abhorrent to the nature of the people, in the prefence of fo many of them; as from their numbers, and our general ignorance of the language, it was impoffible to ex-plain or juftify it to them, by the policy of our laws. Whether this punifhment was neceffary to the difcipline or good order of the troops, I do not, as I before obferved, propofe to confider; but of this I am fure, that it was by no means neceffary to make it a public fpectacle, and to rifque the unfavourable impreffions which it might, and, in-deed, did make in the minds of the Chinefe, before whom it was purpofely exhibited.

This

This meafure, as I have reafon to believe, was very much canvaffed at
the time when it was carried into execution, and juftified on the policy
of convincing the Chinefe of our love of order, and the rigour we
employed in punifhing any infringement of it. That it had, as I fuf-
pected it would have, the contrary effect, the looks, geftures, and
expreffions of the Chinefe prefent on the occafion, are unanfwerable
teftimonies.

Sir Erafmus Gower, however, as I was informed on my return to
the Lion, went a ftep further at Chufan, when fhe lay at anchor
off that ifland, in the Yellow Sea. The fact, to which I allude, is
known to every one at that time on board the fhip.

A Chinefe had come on board the Englifh man of war, from
Chufan, and brought with him a fmall bottle of famtchoo, a kind of
dram, in expectation of exchanging it with the failors for fome European article. A difcovery, however, being made of his defign, Sir
Erafmus Gower ordered him to be feized and punifhed by the boat-
fwain's mate, with twelve lafhes; and to add to the bad effects of
fuch a conduct, in the prefence of a great many of the Chinefe, who
were then on board.

This is one of thofe irreconcileable circumftances which occafionally
happened in the progrefs and completion of this embaffy: becaufe an
application to the mandarins would have had all the effects, which
could be defired, in redreffing the grievance, and affumed the form
of a proper and regular proceeding.

C H A P.

C H A P. XV.

Leave the city of Jehol. Description of two rocks in its neighbourhood. Circumstances of the journey. Arrive at Pekin. Arrangements made there. The remainder of the presents prepared to be sent to the Emperor. Sickness prevails among the soldiers. The Ambassador attends his Imperial Majesty. Brief account of his palace. Further arrangements respecting the household of the embassy. Presents to the Emperor and the Grand Choulaa. The Emperor goes to Yeumen-man-yeumen to see the presents. His person and dress particularly described. Presents received from court for their Britannic Majesties. Circumstances concerning those which had been sent to the Emperor. Report prevails that the embassy is to leave Pekin.

1793.
September.
Tuesday 20.

IT was notified by orders, issued this morning, that the embassy was to quit Jehol on the morrow, to proceed to Pekin, where the final issue of it would be known and settled.

In the evening, the whole of the heavy baggage was sent off for Pekin. At nine there was a very heavy storm of thunder, lightning, and rain, which continued, without any intermission, till four o'clock of the following morning.

Wednes-
day 21.

This morning, at eight o'clock, the British embassy took their leave of the city of Jehol, after a strict confinement of fourteen days; as the liberty, with which we had been flattered soon after our arrival, had never been granted.

We passed the Emperor's pagoda at nine o'clock, where we saw an Ambassador and his suite, from the King of Cochin China, refreshing

I   themselves.

themfelves. It is an annual vifit to pay tribute from that Prince to the Emperor of China.

The confufion and folicitude which attended the entry into Jehol, prevented me from giving a defcription of the two rocks, which are among the moft extraordinary objects I have ever feen or read of; and muft not be paffed by without fuch a particular defcription, as it is in my power to give of them.

The firft is an immenfe pillar, or column of folid rock, which is feen from the palace, occupied by the embaffy at Jehol, at the dif-tance, as it appeared to me, of about four miles. It is fituated on the pinnacle of a large mountain, and near the verge of it: from which it rifes, in an irregular manner, to the height of one hundred feet. Its bafe is fmall, but it gradually thickens towards the top; and from feveral of its projecting parts iffues ftreams of the fineft water.

The upper part of this enormous rock, which is rather flat, appears to be covered with fhrubs and verdure; but as it is abfolutely inacceffi-ble, there is no poffibility of knowing the kind of plants which crown it. When its own individual height is confidered, and added to the eminence where nature, or, perhaps, fome convulfion of the elements, has placed it, the paffenger in the valley below cannot look up to it without an equal degree of horror and amazement. It is efteemed, and with great propriety by the Chinefe, as among the firft natural curiofities of their country; and is known by the name of Panfuiathaung.

The other rock, or rather clufter of rocks, is alfo a very ftupendous object, and ftands on the fummit of a very grand, though not a fertile, mountain. They are alfo in the form of pillars, and appear, except in one particular point of view, to be a folid rock; though they are actually feparated from each other, by an interval of feveral feet. Their height rifes to near two hundred feet, as I underftand from a correct mathematical admeafurement.

Oppofite

Oppofite to the mountain which forms the bafe, rifes another of a fimilar form, which flopes with a more gentle declivity, down to a charming valley, that is formed by them, and is itfelf watered by a pretty rivulet, abounding in fine trout.

In the courfe of this afternoon we arrived at the Imperial palace of Callachottueng, where we had the misfortune to lofe Jeremiah Reid, one of the royal artillery, who died of the bloody flux, with which he had been afflicted but a very few days. Several men belonging to the military detachments were attacked with the fame complaint.

Thurfday 22. This morning, at one o'clock, the body of the deceafed foldier was removed to the next village, to remain there till our arrival, to receive the interment which was due to him. This meafure was fuggefted by the mandarin, who expreffed great apprehenfion left the circumftance fhould reach the Emperor, and awaken his alarm refpecting any contagious diforder.

At fix o'clock the embaffy continued its route, and at the fmall village of Quangchim, where it ftopped to breakfaft, the body of our deceafed companion was interred with military honours.

In the courfe of this morning intelligence was received by the mandarin, Van-Tadge-In, that his Imperial Majefty had left Jehol, on his return to Pekin: he, therefore, requefted the Ambaffador and his train to exert themfelves in making two ftages without halting, that the palaces might be left to receive the attendants of the Emperor.

In confequence of this unexpected requifition, we arrived, after a very fatiguing journey, at the town of Waungchauyeng, in the vicinity of the great wall, of which ftupendous object I took another and a laft view; but without any novelty of impreffion, or the acquifition of an additional circumftance concerning it.

At

At a very early hour we continued our route ; the air was cold and
piercing, and we breakfaſted at a place called Caungchumſau ; after
which we paſſed a prodigious number of carts, containing the Emperor's baggage. Arrived at three o'clock at Cubacouoo, as the ſtation
of the day.

We proceeded on our journey at four in the morning, by the aſſiſt-
ance of a very bright moon, and took our firſt meal at the town of
Chanchin ; our ſecond regale was taken at Mecucang, and we then
proceeded to Whiazow, the laſt ſtage of the day.

Breakfaſt was this morning provided for the embaſſy in the barn-
yard of a ſmall village ; and the journey of the day was finiſhed at
Nanſhiſhee. There I was ſurprized by the ſight of ſeveral fields of
turnips of an excellent quality.

This day finiſhed our returning journey from Tartary, which, as
it was by the ſame route that conducted us thither, and offered no
novelty that deſerved attention, I have diſpatched, with little more
than the names of thoſe places where we ſtopped for refreſhment, or
repoſe. After a breakfaſt at Chingcho, which we found leſs plentiful
than on former occaſions, we arrived early in the afternoon at Pekin,
and proceeded to the palace of the Britiſh Ambaſſador.

His Excellency employed a great part of this morning in examining
the ſeveral arrangements which had been made in the palace during
his abſence ; the whole of which was favoured with his approbation.
The gentlemen of the ſuite alſo received their particular baggage in
their reſpective apartments, and the final adjuſtment and diſtribution
of the different parts of the palace was ſettled.

In the principal room of the Ambaſſador's apartments, the ſtate
canopy, brought from England, was immediately put up. It was
made of flowered crimſon ſatin, with feſtoons and curtains, enriched
Z

with

1793.
Septembe r.

with fringes of gold. On the back part of it the arms of Great Bri-tain appeared in the richeſt embroidery; the floor beneath it was ſpread with a beautiful carpet, on which were placed five chairs of ſtate, of the ſame materials as the canopy, and fringed with gold. The center chair immediately under the coat of arms was elevated on a platform above the reſt, to which there was an aſcent of two ſteps. The whole had been arranged with great taſte in England, and, in its preſent ſituation, made a very ſuperb appearance, in every reſpect ſuited to the occaſion for which it was erected. At the other extremity of the apartment, oppoſite to the canopy, were hung the whole length portraits of their Britannic Majeſties; ſo that this chamber wanted no decoration appropriate to the exterior of diplomatic dignity.

Theſe diſpoſitions being compleated, and in a manner equally ſuited to the ſplendor of the embaſſy, as to the individual convenience of thoſe who compoſed it, nothing remained to perfect the domeſtic eſtabliſhment, but the regulation of the different tables to be provided for the ſeveral departments of the houſehold; which it was thought proper to delay till the arrival of the Emperor in Pekin.

Captain Mackintoſh propoſed to ſet off on the Monday to join his ſhip, the Hindoſtan, now lying at Chuſan, and to proceed to Canton, there to take in his cargo for England, having ſeen, as he conceived, a favourable commencement of this important embaſſy, in which his maſters, the Eaſt India Company, had ſuch a predominant intereſt.

Saturday 28.

This day the Emperor of China returned to the Imperial palace in Pekin; and his arrival was announced by a grand diſcharge of artil-lery.

The occupations of this day in the palace of the Ambaſſador were entirely confined to writing letters for England, of which Capt. Mackintoſh was to take the charge; it then being conſidered by Lord Macartney as a ſettled arrangement with the court of Pekin,

that

that the Englifh embaffy fhould remain in that city during the winter, to carry on the important negotiations with which it was entrufted.

His Excellency received the vifits of feveral mandarins. Certain packages defigned for the Emperor were prepared to be prefented to his Majefty: they confifted of fuperfine broad and other cloths of various kinds of Britifh manufacture.

In confequence of the ficknefs that prevailed among the foldiers belonging to the embaffy, it was thought expedient to eftablifh an hofpital for their more fpeedy cure, as well as to feparate the invalids from thofe who were in health and capable of duty. Dr. Gillan and Dr. Scott were accordingly defired to examine a range of buildings behind the Ambaffador's apartments, with an open area beyond it, and on the report of thofe gentlemen, it was determined that they fhould be formed into an hofpital. Accordingly feveral arrangements took place, to render it comfortable to thofe who were under the neceffity of taking up an occafional abode in it. At this time, of the fifty men which compofed the guards of the embaffy, eighteen were in fuch a ftate as to require the attentive care and fkill of the phyfician.

A mandarin came from the Emperor to requeft that the ordnance prefents might be immediately fent to the palace of Yeumen-manyeumen, where they were to be proved and examined: but the Chinefe thought themfelves equal to the tafk of proof and examination; for the Britifh artillery foldiers were never employed, as was expected, to difplay their fuperior fkill in the fcience of engineering and gunnery.

The chariots, &c. were alfo removed to the fame place, and the fadler and carpenters belonging to the embaffy, with fome affiftant mechanics, were fent thither to unpack and hang them on their carriages: this was done, but the workmen were not permitted to adjuft them fully for prefentation; and came back in the evening to Pekin without receiving orders to return to complete their work, and explain

the

the mode of applying the different machines, under their direction, to the respective uses for which they were designed.

The Ambaffador received a formal intimation to wait on the Emperor as to-morrow; when it was hoped and anxiously expected that the final ratifications would take place between the minifters of the two courts, and prepare the way for entering upon the projected negotiation, from which fo many advantages were expected to be derived to the commerce of Great Britain.

The fick were this day removed to that part of the palace which had been fitted up as an hofpital.

Another package of prefents was opened and examined preparatory to their being fent to his Imperial Majefty.

The Ambaffador, in obedience to the requifition of yefterday, went in a private manner to the Emperor's palace; where bufinefs was tranfacted between his Excellency and the officers of ftate; and it was a report among the Englifh fuite, but on what foundation I cannot tell, that the requifitions of the Britifh Minifter were fubmitted to the confideration of the Imperial Council. This conference lafted two hours, but the refult of it was not, as may be fuppofed, a matter of general communication; but there were no apparent reafons to fuppofe that it was not favourable to the fuccefs of the embaffy.

As I had this day attended the Ambaffador, I fhall juft mention what I faw of the Imperial palace, which will be comprifed in a very few lines.

It is fituated in the center of the city, and furrounded by a wall about twenty feet in height, which is covered with plaifter painted of a red colour, and the whole crowned or capped with green varnifhed tiles. It is faid to occupy a fpace that may be
about

about feven Englifh miles in circumference, and is furrounded by a kind of gravel walk: it contains a vaft range of gardens, full, as I was informed, of all thofe artificial beauties, which decorate the gardens of China. I can only fay, that the entrance to the palace is by a very ftrong ftone gateway, which fupports a building of two ftories: the interior court is fpacious, and the range of building that fronts the gateway rifes to the height of three ftories, and each of them is ornamented with a balcony or projecting gallery, whofe railing, palifadoes, and pillars, are enriched with gilding: the roof is covered with yellow fhining tiles, and the body of the edifice is plaiftered and painted with various colours. This outer court is the only part of this palace which I had an opportunity of feeing, and is a fine example of Chinefe architecture. The gate is guarded by a large body of foldiers, and a certain number of mandarins of the firft clafs are always in attendance about it.

Of the magnificent and fplendid apartments this palace contains for private ufe or public fervice; of its gardens appropriated to pleafure, or for the fole production of fruit and flowers, of which report faid fo much, I am not authorifed to fay any thing, as my view of the whole was very confined; but, though I am ready to acknowledge that the palace had fomething impofing in its appearance, when compared with the diminutive buildings of the city that furround it, I could fee nothing that difpofed me to believe the extraordinary accounts which I had heard and read of the wonders of the Imperial refidence of Pekin.

It cannot be fuppofed for a moment, that thofe who had no other concern in the embaffy, than as a part of the retinue neceffary. for its exterior conduct and appearance, fhould be informed of any of the official circumftances of it; they could, therefore, only judge of its progrefs from the general arrangements which were made concerning its domeftic eftablifhment. It was, however, with particular fatisfaction that the following directions were this day received from the

Ambaffador,

5

1793.
October.

Ambaſſador, relative to the future order and diſpoſition of the tables for the different departments of the houſehold; as an attention to domeſtic buſineſs ſeemed to announce his Excellency's opinion concerning the permanency of our reſidence at Pekin; and, of courſe, an entire diſpoſition in the court of China to give the negotiation every advantage that might be derived from frequent conference and deliberate conſultation.

The order of the tables was as follows:

The table of the Ambaſſador was ordered for himſelf alone; with two covers for gentlemen of the ſuite, who were to be invited in daily ſucceſſion to dine with him.

The next in precedence was that of Sir George Staunton, at which he was to be accompanied by Mr. Maxwell, one of the ſecretaries, Doctor Gillan, Captain Mackintoſh, while he remained at Pekin, Mr. Barrow, and Maſter Staunton. The table of Lieut. Col. Benſon was to be attended by the Lieutenants Pariſh and Crewe, Dr. Scott, Meſſrs. Hickey, Baring, Winder, Alexander, and Dr. Dinwiddie.

The foregoing diſpoſition of the houſehold commenced on this day; but it was thought proper to continue the Chineſe diſhes till the kitchen in the palace was completed, when a certain proportion of Engliſh cookery was to be blended with that of the country. To complete the table arrangements, the cheſts containing the ſervice of plate were removed to the apartments of the Ambaſſador, in order to be prepared for general uſe.

The cabinets of Britiſh manufacture were removed by Chineſe porters to the Imperial palace.

Saturday 5.

A large quantity of plated goods, hardware, and cutlery, were unpacked at Sir George Staunton's apartments, a conſiderable quantity

of

of which was damaged. There were alfo feveral of Argand's lamps, with a great variety of watches, trinkets, jewellery, &c. &c. The whole of this cargo was equally divided between the Emperor and the Grand Choulaa.

The carpenters with feveral affiftants were fent to Yeumen-manycu-men, to clean and complete the carriages, and alfo to fet up the model of the Royal Sovereign, an Englifh firft-rate man of war.

The Emperor himfelf came to the palace; and, after he had taken a view of the prefents, his Majefty was pleafed to order eight ingots of filver to be given to each perfon; which were inftantly received.

The account I have given of the perfon of the Emperor was from a partial view as he was feated in a palanquin; I fhall, there-fore, repeat the more particular defcription of him, which was given by the fix Englifh artificers who were employed in fitting up and arranging the prefents, when he came to view them, and who were the immediate objects of the Imperial generofity which has juft been mentioned.

The Emperor is about five feet ten inches in height, and of a flen-der but elegant form; his complexion is comparatively fair, though his eyes are dark; his nofe is rather aquiline, and the whole of his coun-tenance prefents a perfect regularity of features, which, by no means, announce the great age he is faid to have attained: his perfon is at-tracting, and his deportment accompanied by an affability, which, without leffening the dignity of the prince, evinces the amiable cha-racter of the man.

His drefs confifted of a loofe robe of yellow filk, a cap of black velvet with a red ball on the top, and adorned with a peacock's feather, which is the peculiar diftinction of mandarins of the firft clafs. He wore filk boots embroidered with gold, and a fafh of blue filk girded his waift.

As

As to the opinion which his Imperial Majesty formed of the prefents, we could not learn, as he never communicated it, at leaft, to
any of thofe mandarins, by whom it would have been conveyed to the
palace of the British embaffy. We only knew, at this time, that the
two camera obfcuras were returned, foolifhly enough, as more fuited
to the amufement of children, than the information of men of fcience.

A large number of bales, containing various kinds of broad and
narrow cloths of Englifh manufacture, together with a confiderable
quantity of camlets, two barrel organs, with the remainder of fuch
prefents as were not damaged, were removed from the palace by the
Chinefe employed on thefe occafions. Mr. Plumb, the interpreter,
fometimes accompanied the prefents to explain the nature and application of them, or performed that office to the mandarins, previous to
their departure.

As it now was become a matter of certainty that the embaffy would
remain for fome time at Pekin, the fuperb faddles which had been
brought over for his Excellency, and Sir George Staunton, were unpacked and got ready, with all the elegant furniture, for immediate
ufe.

A very large quantity of prefents were fent from the Emperor to
their Britannic Majefties, accompanied with others for the Ambaffador
and his fuite; which were, as ufual, diftributed among them,

At noon his Excellency went, with no other attendants than two
gentlemen of his retinue, and one fervant, to vifit the Emperor; but,
on his arrival at court, he very much alarmed the gentlemen with him
by fainting away: he was immediately conveyed home, and continued
to be very ill during the remainder of the day. The intended interview,
therefore, was not effected in confequence of his fudden indifpo-
fition.

In

In the forenoon of this day the fervants of the embaffy were fummoned to the apartments of Sir George Staunton, and the foldiers to thofe
of Lieut. Col. Benfon; when each perfon received four pieces of filk,
four pieces of dongaree, (a fort of coarfe nankeen) and a junk of filver, being a fquare folid piece of that metal, weighing fixteen ounces,
as a prefent from his Imperial Majefty.

The gentlemen and mechanics were difmiffed from their attendance
at the palace of Yeumen-manyeumen; for, as all the optical, mechanical, and mathematical inftruments were removed from thence, their
prefence was no longer neceffary. Befides, feveral of thefe prefents,
when a trial of them was made before the mandarins, were found to
fail in the operations and powers attributed to them; and others
of them did not excite that furprife and admiration in the breafts of the
Chinefe philofophers, which Dr. Dinwiddie and Mr. Barrow expected, who immediately determined upon the ignorance that prevailed
in China, and the grofs obftinacy of the people.

A report was in circulation this day throughout the palace, that the
embaffy was to quit Pekin in the beginning of the week: a circumftance which was fo contrary to the general expectation, that it did not
at firft meet with the credit, which it was afterwards found to deferve.

A a   C H A P.

CHAP. XVI.

*Orders iffued for the fuite to prepare for an immediate departure from
Pekin. The Emperor refufes to allow of any delay. Great confu-
fion occafioned by this fudden departure. The embaffy leaves Pekin.
Returns to Tong-tchew. Order of the junks which are to take
the embaffy to Canton. Difficulties refpecting the baggage. The
junks enter a canal. Defcription of it. Circumftances of the voyage.
View and cultivation of the country. The Chinefe poft defcribed.
Pafs through feveral large cities. A general account of them.*

1793.
October.
Monday 7.

THE carpenters were employed in ftrengthening the cafes that contained the prefents from the Emperor of China to their Britannic
Majefties.

In the afternoon the report of yefterday was confirmed by an order,
iffued by the Ambaffador, to the whole fuite to prepare for departure
from Pekin, on Wednefday. Our furprize at fuch unexpected intelligence may be readily conceived, but the mortification which
appeared throughout the palace, on the occafion, was at leaft equal to
the aftonifhment: for, in one moment, as it were, all the domeftic
arrangements, which had been formed with every attention to individual comfort and repofe, were overthrown—our fatiguing pilgrimage
was to be renewed, and with all the humiliation that accompanies a
forced fubmiffion to peremptory power, and the painful defpondency
which arifes from the fudden annihilation of fanguine and well-
grounded hope. But, though we might, in the firft moments of
furprize, be difpofed to feel fomething for ourfelves, fuperior con-
fiderations foon fucceeded, and we forgot the trifle of perfonal
inconvenience, in the failure of a political meafure, which had been

purfued

purfued with fo much labour, hazard, and perfeverance; had been
fupported with fuch enormous expence, and to which our country
looked with eager expectation, for the aggrandizement of its commercial interefts. There was, however, no remedy; and nothing now could
be done but to ufe every endeavour to prolong the period affigned to
the departure of the embaffy, that there might be fufficient time to
make the neceffary preparations for leaving Pekin with convenience,
and that the Ambaffador might not appear to be turned out of the
metropolis of a country, where he had reprefented the crown of Great
Britain.

For thefe reafons, and they were, it muft be acknowledged, of very
great importance, the attendant mandarin was requefted to ftate to the
prime minifter the impoffibility of our departure at fo fhort a notice,
not only without very great inconvenience, but abfolute injury; as
it would be impoffible to pack up and arrange the baggage, &c. of the
Ambaffador and his fuite, in a manner to tranfport it with fafety, in fo
fhort a time as was then allotted for that purpofe.

This commiffion he readily undertook to execute; and, in the evening, he returned with the permiffion of the Grand Choulaa, to delay
the departure of the Britifh embaffy till Friday, which would have
given time fufficient to have made every neceffary preparation.

The mandarin came with a counter-order of the permiffion of yefterday, from the Emperor himfelf, who exprefsly commanded the Ambaffador, and all his retinue, to quit Pekin on the next day. They
were again thrown into a renewed ftate of confufion, which I fhall
not attempt to defcribe.

It was reported in the palace, by the Chinefe, that the Emperor
having confidered the bufinefs as completed between the two courts,
expreffed his furprize that the Englifh minifter fhould wifh to make an
unneceffary ftay at Pekin, and not be eager to return to his own country. His Imperial Majefty was alfo faid to be alarmed at the num-

A a 2

ber

1793.
October.

ber of fick perfons in the retinue of the embaffy, and to apprehend the communication of a contagious diforder among his fubjects. It was alfo reported, that when the brafs mortars were tried in the prefence of the Emperor, his Majefty admired the fkill and ingenuity of thefe engines of deftruction, but deprecated the fpirit of a people who employed them ; nor could he reconcile their improvements in the fyftem of deftruction to the benign fpirit which they reprefented as the foul and operating principle of their religion.

Many other reports of a fimilar nature were propagated ; but the reafon affigned by the Chinefe government, for thus urging the departure of the Ambaffador, was the near approach of winter, when the rivers would be frozen, and the journey to Canton, through the northern provinces, be crowded with inconvenience and impediment.

Whatever policy governed the councils of China on this occafion ; whether it was an enlarged view of national intereft, which it was fuppofed the propofitions of Great Britain would not tend to advance, or any difguft or prejudice proceeding from mifconduct, and mifmanagement in the embaffy itfelf, the manner in which the Ambaffador was difmiffed from Pekin, was ungracious, and mortifying in the extreme. For even if it is fuppofed to be a policy of the Chinefe government, that no foreign minifter fhall be received, but on particular occafions, and that he is not fuffered to remain in the country when he has finifhed his particular miffion ; it does not appear that the bufinefs was at all advanced which Lord Macartney was employed to negotiate ; and he certainly would not have entered into any domeftic arrangements, if he had not confidered himfelf as fecure of remaining at Pekin throughout the winter. He muft have been encouraged to believe that his refidence would not only be permitted, but acceptable to his Imperial Majefty ; and that there was a very friendly difpofition in the councils of China, towards the entering into a treaty with Great Britain, refpecting a more enlarged fyftem of commercial intercourfe between the two countries.

The

The jealousy of the Chinese government had so far subsided as to express a wish for an embassy from this country, and afterwards to receive it. The power of Great Britain, its possessions in the East Indies, with the manner in which they have been acquired, and the general state of Europe, are subjects, by no means, unknown at the court of Pekin; nor was the English settlement at Chusan, or the manner in which it was destroyed, altogether forgotten. The Emperor himself had not only manifested a respect for the British embassy, by the great attentions which had accompanied its progress, but discovered an impatient desire to receive it by inviting it to his residence in Tartary, when he was so soon to return to Pekin. In short, there was no apparent public reason, when the Ambassador was once received, why he should not be permitted to proceed in his negotiation: But, even, if any change had taken place in the mind of the Emperor, or any prejudice arisen against the embassy, from any indiscretion or misconduct in the management of it, which might induce the court of China to put an immediate termination to it ; it is wholly irreconcileable to the common rules of political decorum and civility, as well as the principles of justice and humanity, that an Ambassador, of so much consequence as Lord Macartney, should be dismissed, under his peculiar circumstances, without the least ceremony ; and be not only ordered to depart without allowing the time necessary to make the common arrangements for his journey, but also refused a respite only of two days to his urgent solicitations. In short, we entered Pekin like paupers ; we remained in it like prisoners ; and we quitted it like vagrants.

This day, —— Newman, a marine, who, with three of his comrades, had been taken from on board the Lion, to fill the vacancies occasioned by the death of some of the soldiers belonging to the embassy, died of the flux ; and to prevent this circumstance from being known, his corpse was conveyed away in the night.

Lord

Lord Macartney sent his own state carriage as a present to the Grand Choulaa, who refused to accept it. It was then re-demanded to be unflung and packed up; but no answer whatever was returned; and so short was the period allotted us to stay, and so much was to be done in it, that there was no time to make farther inquiries concerning the fate of this chariot, or the reasons of such an ungracious behaviour on the part of the minister by whom it was refused.

The hurry and confusion of this day is beyond description; and if the soldiers had not been called in to have assisted in packing the baggage and stores, a much greater part must have been left behind, that actually became a prey to the Chinese.

The portraits of their Majesties were taken down, but as the cases in which they had come from England, had been broke up for fixtures in the apartments, a few deals, hastily nailed together, were now their only protection. As for the state canopy, it was not taken down, but absolutely torn from the wall; as the original case that contained it, had been also employed in various convenient uses, and there was not time to make a new one. The state chairs were presented to some of the mandarins; and the canopy was given to some of Lord Macartney's servants. Though, in the scramble, the Chinese contrived to come in for a share. They also contrived to purloin a very large quantity of wine; nor was it possible, in such a scene of hurry and confusion, to prevent those opportunities which they were on the watch to seize. In one way or other, however, the public baggage, stores, furniture, &c. were jumbled together as well as circumstances would admit; and no pains or activity were wanting in those employed to perform that sudden and unexpected duty.

The whole of the suite were occupied, at a very early hour of this morning, in getting their packages in readiness, which were taken away by the Chinese appointed to convey them on the road. The whole of the embassy soon followed. Newman, the marine, was buried on the

(183)

the road to Tong-tchew, and at that town we arrived in the evening, where we found a great change in the article of our accommodations. The apartments which were now allotted to us, were nothing more than temporary sheds, hung with straw matting.

On going to the river side we found the junks ready to receive us; and when the circumstances of the embarkation were settled, the junks were arranged in following order:

No. 1. The Ambassador.
2. Sir George and Master Staunton.
3. Captain Mackintosh, Mr. Maxwell, Mr. Barrow, and Dr. Gillan.
4. Lieutenant-Colonel Benson, with the Lieutenants Parish and Crewe.
5. Messrs. Winder, Barring, Huttner, and Plumb.
6. The Doctors Dinwiddie and Scott, with Messrs. Hickey and Alexander.
7. The Musicians, Mechanics.

The mandarin, Van-Tadge-In, and his attendants, were in separate junks.

All these matters being finally adjusted, his Excellency, with Sir George Staunton, &c. went on board their junks: while the gentlemen were employed in getting their baggage into their respective vessels, which exhibited a new and superior scene of confusion to any we had yet experienced. There was, in the first place, no small difficulty in assorting the junks, with the persons who belonged to them. Nor were there a sufficient number of coolies to transport the different effects on board the vessels. In short, those attentions which were shewn to the Ambassador on his former abode in this city, seemed to have been forgotten; and the place which was now appropriated to re-

ceive

ceive the baggage, was a small spot, on the side of the river, and protected only by a screen of matting.

I have already mentioned the strange conduct of the Grand Choulaa, respecting the chariot which he refused to accept from Lord Macartney, and then refused to return it. On our arrival, however, at Tong-tchew, the chariot appeared to have found its way thither before us; and though we were rather in the habit of being surprized, we could not help feeling a confiderable degree of aftonishment at feeing the carriage oppofite the houfe appointed for the reception of the embaffy, furrounded by crowds of Chinefe, and many of its ornaments defaced. It was, accordingly, drawn down to the river fide, and a cafe being made for it on the fpot, to fecure it from any further injury, it was re-configned to the hold of a junk; and after having rolled a few ports in China, was hereafter fent to figure at Madras.

About four o'clock the whole fuite were embarked, when dinner was immediately ferved; nor was it long before they retired to reft, after the moft fatiguing day they had experienced fince their arrival in China.

Friday 11.

At a very early hour the junks were unmoored, and the fleet proceeded down the river: but as I have already given the beft defcription in my power of the country through which it flows, and the local circumftances of it, I fhall pafs on to the day when we changed the natural for the artificial water, with one folitary obfervation; that though we ftill attracted the notice of the inhabitants who lived near the river, the refpectful attentions of our former voyage were not repeated.

Wednefday 16.

This morning the fleet entered a very noble canal, which communicates with the river near Tyen-fing. It is a work of great labour, and prodigious expence; and its fides are faced with mafonry throughout its courfe. At certain diftances locks are erected to give a current

to

to the water: they are in the form of an half-moon, and confine the
water to a narrow paſſage in the middle of the canal, which occaſions
a fall of about three feet.   The junks acquired an accelerated motion
in paſſing theſe locks, which continued for a conſiderable diſtance;
and, in order to prevent their receiving any injury from ſtriking againſt
the walls of the lock, which, on account of the ſudden ferment of the
water, it is not often poſſible to avoid, men are always ſtationed there
to let down large leathern pads, which effectually break the ſhock that
would otherwiſe be felt from ſuch an accident.

We paſſed through at leaſt thirty of theſe locks in the courſe of this
day's voyage, without being able to diſcover any variation in them,
as to their conſtruction, or the effects produced by them.

On each ſide of the canal, the country, as far as the eye can reach,
is one entire flat, but ſmiling with fertility.   Several villages, with
their crowds of inhabitants, varied the ſcene; and, at each of them
the ſoldiers of the diſtrict appeared in military array, and ſaluted the
fleet as it paſſed with three guns.

We paſſed by ſeveral towns and villages, and at every one of them
the Ambaſſador and mandarins were received with military honours.

It may be proper to obſerve in this place, that a mandarin of the
ſecond claſs, named Chootadzin, was on board the fleet, and was to
continue with us till our arrival at Hoang-tchew, of which province
he is appointed the viceroy. Van-Tadge-In, although a mandarin of the
firſt claſs, was inferior to him in authority, as the appointment of
viceroy gives precedence to the higheſt order of mandarins.

I obſerved a conſiderable number of rice fields, in which there were
ſtone gutters or channels, finiſhed with great neatneſs, and admirably
contrived to convey water to every part of the plantations.

B b

For

For some days the provisions with which we had been supplied, were not only deficient in quantity, but were sent ready dressed and cold; so that we found it necessary to dress them again, or rather heat them up as well as we could. Mr. Plumb, the vehicle of all complaints, and who, in general, contrived to procure redress, was employed on the present occasion to represent the dissatisfaction which was felt by the different departments of the embassy, respecting the deficiency and quality of the daily provisions.

The same flat and fertile country appeared on either side of the canal, though the view was this day varied by several gardens, in which there were plantations of that shrub which bears what is called the Imperial and gunpowder teas: it grows to the size of a goosberry bush, with leaves of the same size. The former of those teas is collected from the first, and the other from the successive, blossoms of that plant.

We continued to pass through a succession of locks, and to excite the curiosity of various towns and villages which poured forth their inhabitants to see the extraordinary spectacle of an European embassy.

Towns and villages alternately presented themselves on either side of the canal, with their prodigious population, but possessed no peculiarity, and offered no circumstances of novelty which would justify a particular description.

The representation which had been made concerning the provisions produced an immediate change in the supply of them: we this day received a large quantity of mutton and beef, with fowls and ducks; to these were added bread, flour, tea, sugar, rice, vegetables of all kinds, with soy, oil, candles, charcoal, and wood; and, while the solid part of the meal, with the means of preparing it, were amply

administered,

administered, the elegant addition of fruits of various kinds, and the
liquors of the country, were not forgotten.

In the very unexpected situation of the embassy, it was very natural
for those who composed the retinue of it to be continually forming
conjectures, and eagerly inquiring after any information that might
tend to elucidate the extraordinary circumstances of it. Thus we
became acquainted with various reports on the subject, some of which
we were disposed to credit, while we rejected others, as they seemed
to concur with, or contradict, the events of the moment.

Thus we were not unwilling to believe, as it was propagated among
us by some of the Chinese, that a Tartar mandarin had been able to
prejudice the Emperor against the English people, by representing
them as barbarous, inhuman, and destitute of all those amiable qualities which they pretended to possess: nor were many of the suite
indisposed to believe that to such an unpropitious circumstance the
embassy had been treated, to use no worse expression, with such
strange disrespect and peremptory dismission. It was also added, that
Van-Tadge-In, the attendant mandarin, had since represented the conduct and character of the embassy in a very different point of view, in
a written memorial addressed to the Emperor; which had induced his
Imperial Majesty to give orders that the British Ambassador and his
suite, should be abundantly supplied with every thing necessary for
their convenience and comfort, and that they might at all times enjoy
the liberty of going on shore, and amusing themselves at their own
discretion.

We passed a great number of tobacco plantations. The Chinese
cultivate and manufacture this plant in a very superior degree, and are
supposed to possess greater varieties of it, than any other country in
the world.

The quantity of tobacco consumed, and, of course, grown in
China, must be beyond all calculation, as smoaking is universally

B b 2

practised,

practised, and by all ranks and ages. Children, as soon as they have sufficient strength or dexterity to hold a pipe in their hands, are taught by their parents to smoke, which they feel not only as an habitual amusement, but is considered as a preservative against all contagious diseases.

Several walled cities appeared at some distance from the canal, whose guards and garrisons were marched to the banks, in order to give the usual salute; and one in particular of very great extent and amazing population, called Tohiamsyn. The crowds of people of both sexes which came to see the junks pass, were beyond all belief.

We this day passed several stone bridges, some of them were of one, and others of two arches, which appeared to be constructed with great strength and excellent masonry. The number of locks appeared rather to increase than diminish in the course of this day's voyage.

The country offers a very fruitful scene, and, in some places, rose into hills and uplands. The water-mills, of which we saw several at work, appear to be in a great measure the same as those used in Europe: they were corn-mills, as we were informed; and were situated in the midst of very extensive fields of that grain, which was almost ready for the sickle.

Several gentlemen of the suite went on shore to enjoy the exercise and variety of walking on the banks of the canal; but the junks were carried on with such rapidity from the quick succession of locks, that they were left behind, and the whole fleet was obliged to come to anchor till they rejoined it.

We this morning saw a very lofty pagoda situated on an eminence: it appeared to be a stone building, consisting of eight stories, each of which was encircled with a balcony, and the whole terminated in an ornamented roof that runs up to a very slender point.

We

We this day faw the Chinefe poft pafs along the road, on the fide of the canal, with great expedition. The letters and packets are carried in a large fquare bamboo bafket, girt with cane hoops and lined: it is locked, and the key is given to the cuftody of one of the attendant foldiers, whofe office it is to deliver it to the poft-mafter: the box is faftened on the courier's fhoulders with ftraps, and is decorated at the bottom with a number of fmall bells, which being fhaken by the motion of the horfe, make a loud gingling noife, that announces the approach of the poft. The poft-man is efcorted by five light-horfemen to guard him from robbery or interruption. The fwifteft horfes are alfo employed on the occafion, which are renewed at every ftage; fo that the pofts of China may vie in expedition with the Englifh mail.

1793.
October.
Thurfday 24.

The fucceffion of populous and large towns was fo continual, that it would be tedious to mention them but as a general characteriftic of the country; unlefs fome particular circumftance, from its novelty or intereft, fhould juftify defcription.

Friday 25.

When I rofe this morning, I was furprifed to find the junk fleet at anchor in the heart of a very large city, through the center of which the canal paffes: it is here croffed by a continual fucceffion of bridges, which are connected with a circular breaft-work on each fide, guarded by foldiers, who fuffer no veffels to pafs till they have been infpected by mandarins who prefide over that department. The fleet was favoured here with the ufual falute of three guns, and a very large body of foldiers was drawn up on both fides of the canal: they were completely armed, and wore large helmets, which gave them a very military appearance, while their ranks were enlivened with feveral ftands of colours.

At fix o'clock the fleet left this city, and at ten paffed through another, which, as far as we could judge from our paffage, was of equal dimenfions and population. Its name is Kord-cheeaung.

To

1793.
October.

To the left of the canal, and in the center of the city, we faw a very magnificent and lofty pagoda; it rofe to the height of ten ftories, each of which is furrounded with an elegant gallery, and projecting canopies, fupported by pillars.

The chief mandarin of the place has an handfome palace guarded by a fort, whofe garrifon came forth to falute the Ambaffador, as the veffels paffed by it.

In the fubfequent progrefs of this day's voyage we paffed four other cities, of equal magnitude with thofe which have been already mentioned ; and about nine o'clock at night anchored in the city of Lee-yaungoa, which was illuminated to do honour to the diftinguifhed perfons on board the fleet ; nor were any of thofe marks of refpect omitted which had been demonftrated in all the places, according to their rank, through which we had paffed.

A very large body of troops, confifting at leaft of a thoufand men, were drawn up on the banks of the canal ; and each man held a pole, with a coloured paper lanthern hanging from it, which, when the troops halt, is ftuck in the ground ; the whole forming a very fingular and pleafing fpectacle.

Saturday 26.

The air was this morning extremely cold ; the thermometer having funk fo low as forty degrees. At feven o'clock we paffed a lock, whofe current bore us into the city of Kaunghoo, which, from the great number of junks laying there, muft be a place of immenfe trade. Indeed, the water was fo entirely covered with them, that our fleet was obliged to come to anchor, in order to give time for a paffage to be made between them. The canal took a winding courfe through this place, which is elevated above it, and its banks fall in beautiful flopes to the water.

The

The weather was moderate and agreeable: and the prospect was varied with meadows of the richest verdure, and covered with flocks of sheep and herds of cattle. We passed also several large fields of paddy and millet, and the eye ranged over a vast extent of flat and fertile country.

The voyage of this day furnished no variety—unless a great number of flour-mills may be supposed to vary the scene.

The growing wealth of cultivation we had seen every hour as we proceeded on our voyage, and not a spot appeared, which towns and villages did not occupy, but proved the skill and labour of the husbandman. This morning, however, gave us a prospect of that labour, for we passed several extensive fields where the peasants were busy with their ploughs; these machines, so essential in agriculture, were drawn by oxen, and though of a very clumsy form, when compared with those of our own country, perform their office with good effect, as the ground appeared to be got into a very promising state of tillage.

We saw a fleet of junks laden with tea for the Canton market; nor was it an unnatural, or uninteresting observation, that in the chance of commerce, some of their cargoes might ultimately be consigned to our own country, and arrive there before us.

The prospects of this day were enlivened by pagodas, and country seats; some of which were adorned with beautiful gardens, and others surrounded with the finest orchards I ever beheld.

This morning the fleet passed through a walled city named Hoong-loafoo. This is another of those places where the vast number of junks which covered its canal, justify the opinion of its extensive commerce. In its neighbourhood there are large plantations of tea, extensive fields of tobacco, and a great number of large flour-mills.

I

We

We had feen frequent and large plantations of rice; but the fields of cotton, which this morning prefented themfelves to our attention, formed a curious and pleafing novelty. I obferved that the cotton was of the nankeen colour, and is plucked from the top of a fhort ftalk.

Of cities, towns, locks, and bridges, we have feen and faid fo much, that the reader and the writer would be equally fatigued with the daily enumeration of them.

CHAP.

C H A P. XVII.

Various circumstances of the voyage. Enter the Yellow River. Pass several towns, lakes, &c. Ceremonies at the city of Kiangsou. Enter a beautiful lake; description of it. Enter another river; circumstances of it. Pass several cities, &c. Dock-yards for building junks. Arrive at the city of Mee-you-mee-azong—beautiful country. Further account of the Chinese troops. A mandarin's palace and pagoda described.

THE canal appeared now to have assumed the form of a considerable river, and brought us to a very large city, where we came to an anchor at six o'clock in the morning, having passed a fort at the entrance, by which the fleet had been saluted.

When I mention the situation and circumstances of this city, it would be needless to describe it as a place of great trade, or speak of the inconceivable number of junks which were moored at its quays and wharfs, it will be sufficient to say, that it is washed by large canals, and that, on the south side of it, there is an extensive bay which communicates with the Yellow river, to give some notion of its commercial character.

Here the fleet remained at anchor about an hour; when it unmoored, and soon entered the bay, with an alarming rapidity, through a large lock, constructed with rushes, curiously matted together, and secured with logs of wood.

This bay is of great extent, and would contain the proudest fleets of Europe, while its shores offer an amphitheatre of landscape

C c

beauty.

1793.
November.

beauty. The hills are verdant to their very fummits, which are fome-times crowned with pagodas; and the lower parts are enriched with houfes and gardens, and that variety of cultivation which diftinguifhes this extraordinary country.

On entering this bay, it was difcovered that there were a variety of currents running with great violence, and in oppofite directions, at not lefs than feven miles an hour; and the fkill of navigating it confifts in being able to get into that individual current which runs towards the place of the veffel's particular deftination.

In this fituation we fhould have been glad, if it had been confiftent with the courfe of the voyage, to have caft anchor, and enjoyed, at leifure, the contemplation of its beauties; but the fleet immediately fteered towards a large river, which it foon entered, and whofe ftream foon bore us, as it were, into the bofom of a rich and beautiful country.

At the mouth of this river there is a large town, with the palace of a mandarin of the firft clafs, furrounded by a ftrong ftone wall: it is a very large edifice, crowned with turrets, richly gilt and ornamented after the fafhion of the country. The front looks towards the bay, of which it commands an extenfive and enchanting profpect.

Town now fucceeded to town; the country offered the moft beau-tiful views, of which no adequate idea can be given by written defcrip-tion. And when I mention the country as one fcene of varied cultiva-tion, divided by well-planted enclofures, peopled with farms that are furrounded by orchards, enriched with villas, and their ornamental gardens, a very inadequate picture is given of the expanfive fcenery on either fide of the navigation which bore us through it.

At two o'clock, and as we were preparing for dinner, the junks arrived at a very large town, through which the river took a courfe of at leaft three miles. This place is formed on a more regular plan than any which we had feen in China. The houfes were uniformly built of brick, varied with an intermixture of blue ftone, and feldom deviated from the height of two ftories.

1791.
November.

The ufual honours of forts and military guards were received here, as through every place we paffed, of whatever fize or diftinction it might be: the walled city, and the village, were equally attentive to this act of official civility, according to their refpective capacities. It may, indeed, be here obferved, that through the whole of our travels in this country, whether by land, or by water, and not excepting Tartary, the villages, as well as the cities, have their mandarin, and his guards proportioned to the magnitude and confequence of the place where they are cantoned; and that the interior parts of the kingdom are equally fecured by troops, as the frontiers, or fea coaft: we may, therefore, be faid to pafs, almoft, between a continued line of foldiers, on each fide of the canals, or rivers; where the intervals are fo fmall between thofe villages and great towns, which form a chain of military cantonments.

In the latter part of the afternoon we anchored, for fome time, at another confiderable town, where the junks ftopped to take in a fupply of China wine. It is fituated on the fide of a large lake, which, in fome places, was divided only by a bank from the river on which we failed. As I could not difcover any land in the diftant part of this large body of water, I was difpofed to confider it as an inlet of the Yellow fea.

The country now began to wear a fwampy appearance, and, of courfe, did not altogether retain thofe beautiful features, which I have faintly reprefented it to poffefs, during the more recent parts of our voyage. This circumftance naturally arifes from the great number of rivers, canals, and lakes, that aid the navigation of this part of the

country;

1793.
November.

country; which being subject to occasional inundations from them, is frequently in the situation that I have described.

In the evening we saw a very fine palace belonging to the mandarin of a town, through which we afterwards passed in the night, and neither knew its form or character: nor should we have even discerned the grandeur of the mandarin's residence, if he had not illuminated it in honour of the Ambassador and his brethren on board the junks; and ordered out his guard, consisting of at least five hundred men, to enlighten with their paper lanterns the banks of the river.

Sunday 3.

This morning was very keen and frosty. The fleet anchored opposite to a large lake, which appeared to communicate with several considerable rivers. The country continues its flat and swampy appearance. I have this day been informed that the river on which we are proceeding is called the Yellow river, which may probably be owing to the communications it may have with the Yellow sea. There is a considerable town situated between the lake and this river.

The junks remained at anchor no longer than was necessary to receive the usual supply of provisions and wine. In a short time we passed another lake; and, without enumerating the canals, with their stone and wooden bridges, as well as the villages and towns that claimed our transient attention, I shall come at once to another lake that appeared to be much larger than any of those which have been already mentioned. A great number of junks were sailing across it in different directions, and several hundred fishing-boats were employed on it in their necessary occupations. It is said to abound in fish; those we procured were small, of the size of a sprat, but in taste and shape resembling an haddock. Nor was our river deficient in its produce, as plenty of fine trout were taken in it.

At some distance from the river, on the side opposite to the lake, is a very large, and, as far as we could judge, magnificent city, surrounded

by

by a wall, named Chun-foong. The suburbs which extend towards
the water, are also very confiderable, and the houfes of which they
confift are built of a dark ftone, roofed with tiles of the fame colour.
They are only of one ftory, and their windows are circular and grated
with iron, which give them a very difagreeable appearance. The wall
of this town is not fo high as thofe we have hitherto feen, and, as far
as I could judge by the telefcope, does not rife above fourteen or fifteen
feet. The part of it which we paffed could not be lefs than two miles
in extent; which may lead us to the plaufible conjecture that the city itfelf is at leaft eight miles in circumference. From its general appearance and acceffary circumftances, no doubt could be entertained of its
extenfive commerce; and, from the drefs and manners of its inhabitants,
a fimilar opinion might be entertained of their urbanity and opulence.

At four o'clock the fleet anchored at the extremity of the wall of
this city, and received a frefh fupply of wine and provifions: thefe,
indeed, were now provided in fuch plenty, that the poor people who
navigated the junks found themfelves in a ftate of unexpected and
unexampled luxury, from the fuperabundance of them.

Several of the gentlemen from the other junks did us the honour to
pay us a vifit, which produced an evening of great mirth and feftivity.

The weather was extremely cold. We paffed two large lakes,
which, by their refpective branches, unite with the river. At noon we
failed through a confiderable town, and beyond it, faw feveral fmall
canals on either fide of the river, with many boats on them employed
in fifhing. The country is flat and marfhy, and wherever the road on
the fide of the river paffes over fwampy dips or vallies, wooden plat-
forms are erected to preferve the level, and avoid the inconvenience of
finking into them.

A large walled city, whofe name is Kiangfou, next claimed our
attention. At the entrance of it a mandarin and his guards appeared

on

on the water-fide in martial figure, to give the cuftomary falutes. At each end of the line of troops there was a temporary arch erected, with a connected platform, about three feet from the ground, guarded by railing, and projecting into the river: thefe temporary ftructures were covered with beautiful matting, the rails were bound with filk of various colours, and ornamented with knots and feftoons: the arches were decorated in fimilar tafte, and the whole was erected for the convenience of the Ambaffador, if it had fuited his convenience to ftop, and vifit the mandarin.

At a fmall diftance, and on an elevated fituation, was an encampment of the mandarin's guards. The tents were pitched clofe to each other, in a circular form, with a fmall vacant fpace as an entrance to the mandarin's pavilion, which occupied the center: it was decorated in a very elegant manner with ribbons and filken ftreamers: the front of it was open, and difplayed its interior ornaments; it contained a table covered with a collation, and furrounded with fine chairs, with a canopy over one of them. The mandarin's attendants appeared to be in waiting, and a centinel was on duty on each fide of the pavilion.

This regale was prepared with great politenefs and hofpitality in honour of the Ambaffador and the mandarins on board the junks, if the order of the voyage would have permitted them to have delayed its progrefs for a fhort time, to have acknowledged thefe refpectful attentions.

Each tent had a flag of green filk, ornamented with golden figures and Chinefe characters, flying on the top of it, fo that this encampment was a very pretty and picturefque object.

At a fmall diftance from it, there was a large town, the houfes of which being built of ftone gave it a very fuperior appearance, and the inhabitants poffeffed all the exterior of an opulent and polifhed people.

Here

Here we stopped for a short time in order to receive a supply of provisions, as well as to be furnished with a body of those men whose
employment it is to tow the junks. They wore a kind of uniform,
and had red caps on their heads, by which their laborious profession
is known and distinguished. Our eyes were very much gratified at
this place by the sight of a considerable number of women, who
appeared to us not only to possess fine features, but fair complex-
ions.

At five o'clock we came to the suburbs of a very large city, and
passed at least a mile along the suburbs before we reached the wall of
it. From such a view as my situation would admit, and the best
information I could obtain, this place is at least nine miles in circumference. Several hundred junks were moored along its wharfs, some
of which were of very large dimensions. The wall is at least forty
feet in height, and has a very ancient appearance. The redoubts which
support the gates are such as I had not seen in China, being in the
form of an half-moon. The troops were drawn out, as in other
places, on our arrival, and a very brilliant illumination, exhibited by
the mandarin, did not fail to dissipate the gloom of the evening.

This morning the fleet entered a large lake, adorned with a great
number of beautiful islands. The most considerable of them is on
the south-west side of the lake; its length is about three quarters of a
mile, but not of equal breadth. It contains a mandarin's palace,
with several summer houses fancifully scattered about it; the whole
shaded with the finest trees, and presenting to us, as we sailed by it,
a most inviting scene of rural elegance. But beauty was not the
only circumstance which allured our attention to this charming
island; a considerable rock, an object of comparative grandeur, also
rose from the midst of its groves, and was crowned with a stately
pagoda.

We

We had no sooner passed this delightful spot, possessing so much beauty in itself, and commanding so large a portion of fine prospect around it, than we entered another river, the mouth of which is surrounded with high lands, offering the most picturesque scenery that can be imagined: thick woods, stately edifices, lofty pagodas, and mountainous shapes, with the river and the lake, all blended together in one picture, may exercise the imagination of those who read this work, but far transcends the descriptive powers of the writer of it. It may not also be unworthy of remark, that all the houses which occupy the heights surrounding this bay, are ornamented with gilt pyramids or pinnacles, which rise from the roof, and give some of the buildings the appearance of Gothic architecture.

This river, as might be expected, soon brought us to a town, where the soldiers, which were drawn up on either side of the water to salute the fleet, were different from those we had already seen, by the variety of their dress and the colour of their standards; which were now multiplied into white, scarlet, orange, light and dark blue and green.

A mandarin's palace, very finely ornamented with painting, gilding, and silken streamers, a river crowded with junks, and a charming country on either side of it, were the only objects that presented themselves to us, till we arrived before the city of Mee-you-mee-awng. The walls are of great height, and guarded by towers; while a kind of glacis slopes down from the foot of it to a meadow, agreeably planted with trees that stretch along the side of the river, and add very much to the beauty of the place.

Here the fleet anchored for a short time to take in the usual supply of provisions; and, from the general appearance of the city, as well as of the adjacent country, they seemed to have been formed by the hand of Commerce itself for the purposes of navigation.

Beauty

Beauty of fituation might alfo be added to the abundance of its productions; for the banks of the river that paffed before its walls, when
they rofe into height, were covered with hanging woods and gardens,
which gave a charming variety to the tranfient fcene.

1793
November.

To thefe pleafing objects fucceeded one of a very different nature,
and, by its contraft, acquired an additional importance. It was no
lefs than a large body of foldiers drawn up on an efplanade; the line
of which, extending near a mile, divided into companies diftinguifhed
by the variety of their uniforms, and enlivened by the number, as well
as colour of their ftandards, offered a very beautiful fpectacle.

No other object for fome time attracted our notice, except a fmall dock
yard for building junks, enclofed in a fine grove, which formed
a pretty, picturefque fcene. The river now appeared to be proceeding boldly on into a rich, fertile country, but of more unequal furface
than any we had yet feen; when, by an unexpected meander, it
brought us back to the city of Mee-you-mee-awng, to aftonifh us
with the extent of it. Here we paffed through another large bridge,
and near a circular baftion which commanded, by its battery, every
direction of the river.

On another turn of the ftream, a very fine hill rofe up, as it were,
before us, whofe fummit is crowned with a magnificent pagoda,
and whofe declivities have all the decoration that could be conferred on
them by beautiful gardens and elegant buildings. At the foot of this
elevated fpot are two ftone arches, or gateways, which open to a
walk that winds gradually up the hill to the pagoda.

The palace of the mandarin, of whofe garden this hill appeared to
form a part, is fituated on the banks of the river, from whence a broad
flight of fteps afcends to the gate of the outer court. This edifice is
perfectly fuited, both in its fize and appearance, to the dignity of its pof-
feffor. Like other buildings of the fame kind and character in China,

it is perfectly uniform in all its parts. The body of the house rises to three stories, and the wings are diminished to two. A paved court occupies a large space in the front; and the whole is enclosed by a wall, including a large garden, that extends to the beautiful hill, of which a very inadequate sketch has been already given.

The country continues to make great advances in landscape beauty: fields full of fertility, with their thick and shady enclosures; farms embosomed in orchards; villas, and their gardens, we have long continued to see: but now the mountain rises before us, not rugged and barren, but verdant to its very top; while innumerable herds of cattle, and flocks of sheep, hang down its sloping pastures.

Another town soon succeeded; and to that a lake, surrounded by hills of the same kind, and covered with the same inhabitants as those which have just been mentioned. From this enchanting spot our fleet passed through a lock, and between a draw-bridge, into a canal, that divides another large commercial town. Here we saw a brick-kiln, and a great pile of bricks just made: they appear to be composed of a kind of sand, mixed up with the mud of the river. The kiln itself is built of the materials which it makes, and is in the form of a sugar loaf.

In the evening we passed a large walled city, containing all the circumstances of the various places of that description which have been already enumerated. Several pagodas were illuminated on the occasion, and had a very pretty appearance amid the gloom of night.

C H A P.

C H A P. XVIII.

The voyage continued. A succession of various objects. The elegant attentions of a mandarin to the embassy. Captains of the junks punished for embezzling the provisions supplied for the use of the Ambassador and his suite. Husbandry of the Chinese. Preparations for sending the heavy baggage belonging to the embassy to Chusan: several persons of the suite ordered to accompany it. Arrive at Hoang-tchew. Captain Mackintosh, and the other gentlemen, set off for Chusan.

1793.
November.
Wednes-
day 6.

A TOWN, which we entered this morning, had a very dismal appearance, from the colour of the houses, which are all built of a black brick. They were, however, much more lofty than any we had yet seen in China; some of them rising to four stories; and there were very few indeed that had less than two.

We passed beneath a very handsome stone bridge of three arches, that appeared to be of recent erection. It was built in the manner of our bridges in England; the center arch occupying a much larger span, and rising to an higher elevation than the lateral ones. On the parapet, over the former, were fix round small stones, by way of ornament, with Chinese characters engraven on them.

The mandarin's palace, a very singular structure, immediately attracts the attention on passing the bridge near which it stands. On each side of the principal gate are two lofty walls, painted of a red colour, to prevent the building from being seen but in a front view of it. The gateway is very much enriched with sculpture, and the usual accompanyments of Chinese characters: it is of stone, and

D d 2

supports

1793.
November.

supports an apartment. The houfe itfelf is painted of different colours, with a ftone gallery in front, and covered with a roof of the fame material.

The mandarin, who refided here, had given to his hofpitality the moft elegant appearance. He had caufed a temporary ftage, or platform to be erected, from the palace to the fide of the river, in cafe the Ambaffador, and the mandarins, fhould find it convenient to land. The roof of this building was covered with filk of every colour; a great number of lamps were fufpended from it, fancifully adorned with gauze and ribbons, and the floor was covered with a fine, variegated matting. But this was not the whole of the elegant attentions which were exerted by the mandarin on the occafion; as he had caufed a large fcreen, or curtain, of this matting, to be fixed on the oppofite fide of the water, in order to hide fome ruinous buildings, that would otherwife have difgraced the gay picture he had contrived, by their deformity.

The foldiers, under the command of this mandarin, were of a different appearance from any we had feen. They wore red hats, with a very high and pointed crown; on the fide of which was a brafs plate, that appeared to be faftened with yellow ribbons.

Towns, locks, bridges, and pagodas ftill continued to appear in an hafty and aftonifhing fucceffion. In the afternoon, a very large country refidence was feen at fome diftance, with a very lofty pagoda rifing, as it perfpectively appeared, from the center of it. The tower terminated in a cupola, with a fpiral ornament rifing from the top, crowned with a ball, from each fide of which a chain hung down till it touched the upper ftory of the building.

Soon after we had paffed this ftructure, the banks of the river were, for a confiderable diftance, fo high, as to obfcure all view of the adjacent country.

When

When the fleet came to anchor, the grand mandarin vifited all the junks, in confequence of a complaint that had been made againft fome of the captains of them, for embezzling the provifions which were daily fupplied for the ufe of the embaffy. After a fevere examination into this bufinefs, the mandarin was fo convinced of the truth of the charge, that the perfons accufed were immediately fentenced to be bambooed : they were accordingly ftretched on the ground, and being held down by two foldiers, were ftruck, in a very violent manner, acrofs the hips, till the judge gave a fignal for the punifhment to ceafe.

It had been a very foggy night, and the weather continued to be hazy till ten o'clock, when the fog cleared away, and a fine day fucceeded, which unfolded to the view a charming and fertile country, bounded by hills, whofe fummits were crowned with pagodas.

I, this day, caught a tranfient view of the practical hufbandry of the country; as the different operations of digging, manuring, and ploughing were going forwards in fields on the river's fide. And though the Chinefe farmers certainly produce as fine crops of grain as any I have ever feen in Europe, this circumftance muft arife from the fole efforts of perfevering labour, as their agricultural utenfils are of a very clumfy form and inconvenient mechanifm.

In the courfe of this day we paffed through a noble arch, and entered a very large town, whofe houfes, which are, many of them, fo lofty as to reach to three ftories, are covered with plaifter, and univerfally painted black. After a courfe of at leaft two miles through this town, we paffed beneath another arch of dimenfions equal to that, through which we had entered it.

Another town, of the fame fize and appearance, foon fucceeded; where, as a part of the houfes, on the fide of the river, projected a

fmall.

1793.
November.

Tuefday 7.

1793.
November.

fmall fpace over it, the men who towed us could be of no fervice, and the junks were dragged forwards very flowly by boats.

The continual interfection of canals, with the fucceffion of lakes and rivers, may be fuppofed to have perplexed a more keen obfervation than mine; and, in the extraordinary fucceffion of objects, I may not have always been correct as to the exact character of the water on which we failed: the rivers may have fometimes affumed the form of canals, and the canals have fometimes expanded into the appearance of rivers; but if I fhould, at any time, have miftaken the one for the other, either from inaccuracy of obfervation, or the hurry of the moment when I wrote thofe remarks from whence this volume is formed, fuch an accidental circumftance will not operate as to the more particular and important information of it. I fhall not, however, hefitate to confider it as a very noble river, which brought us beneath the walls of the city of Chaunopaung, that were crowded with its inhabitants to fee us pafs: and as the ftream foon bore us from it, there was no opportunity to obferve whether it had any circumftance of novelty worthy of record.

Friday 8.

At noon the junks came to an anchor in the country. When his Excellency fent for feveral perfons of his fuite, to inform them of the regulations which would take place on their arrival at Hoang-tchew, that they might make the neceffary arrangements. They were as follows:

All the heavy baggage was intended to be forwarded from Hoang-tchew to Chufan, in order to be put on board the Hindoftan, and conveyed by fea to Canton. It was accordingly ordered, that no perfon fhould retain any thing but what might be neceffary for prefent ufe, as the junks, which would fhortly receive us, were not fufficiently large to carry heavy cargoes.

It was alſo ſettled, that Lieutenant-Colonel Benſon, Docter Dinwid- dic, and Mr. Alexander, were to accompany Captain Mackintoſh to Chuſan : four ſervants, and two mechanics, to take care of the ſtores, were alſo to attend upon thoſe gentlemen. The reſt of the ſuite were to accompany his Excellency over land, and I was of that number.

1793.
November.

The country ſtill continued to be as we have for ſome time deſcribed it. As we proceeded, and the country became more unequal, the pagodas, which are almoſt always placed on heights, ſeemed to mul- tiply ; and there were few of them that did not reach to ſeven or eight ſtories. As for towns and villages we never ceaſed to ſee a con- tinual ſucceſſion of them ; and when they did not cover the banks of our river, they appeared at a diſtance, where we might ſuppoſe them to be reflected by ſome other water.

Saturday 9.

At three o'clock in the afternoon, the fleet was ordered to anchor in the open country, near the ſhore, when the grand mandarin, Choo- Tadge-In, came round to each junk, the owners of which he ordered into his preſence, and, after a ſhort examination, commanded every one of them to be bambooed: though I could never learn the offence which produced this example of ſummary juſtice.

This morning the air was extremely cold and piercing. We paſſed ſeveral plantations of tallow-trees, and arrived at Hoang-tchew in the afternoon, when the whole fleet came to anchor in the principal part of the city.

Sunday 10.

The junks were now faſtened together, and orders were iſſued to forbid any perſon belonging to the ſuite to go on ſhore. Indeed, as it appeared, to prevent any attempt of that kind, a body of Chineſe ſol- diers pitched their tents in the ſtreet oppoſite the junks, and formed a little camp there, to do duty over the embaſſy.

In

1793.
November.
In the fame ftreet there were alfo feveral erections like triumphal arches, where the mandarins ufed to come every day, to fit in ftate; and, as we were informed, to confult on the affairs of the city.

Monday 11.
No circumftance of any moment happened from this time, till the Thurfday following, which was the day of our departure; and the bufinefs of arranging and dividing the baggage, according to the orders iffued for that purpofe, did not allow us much leifure for obfervation, if any thing had occurred worthy of attention: but, the truth is, nothing did occur, but the never-ceafing uproar of the inhabitants of the city, who were continually flocking to the junks to take a view of us.

On Wednefday night the attendant mandarin paffed through all the junks, and requefted that the different articles of the baggage fhould have the refpective names of Chufan, or Canton, written upon them, according to their refpective deftination; which was no fooner completed, than thofe configned to the former place were fent off by coolies to the depot appointed to receive them.

The Ambaffador ordered ten dollars to be given to the owners of each junk, for their refpective crews.

Thurfday 14.
Lieutenant-Colonel Benfon, Doctor Dinwiddie, Mr. Alexander, with the fervants and mechanics already mentioned, fet off this morning, to proceed with Captain Mackintofh, to join the Hindoftan at Chufan.

CHAP.

C H A P. XIX.

The Ambaffador, with his fuite, proceed through the city of Hoang-tchew to the Green River, where they embark. Formalities on the occafion. Circumftances of the voyage. Defcription of the country. Refpect paid to the Ambaffador. Leave the junks, and proceed by land. Mode of conveyance. Return to the junks. The voyage continued.

THE Ambaffador, after having received the farewell vifit of the mandarin of Hoang-tchew, fet off, with his whole retinue, for the Green river, where they were to embark in junks of a leffer burthen. His Excellency was carried in a palanquin, and the reft of the fuite in a kind of fedan chair. The guards, commanded by Lieutenants Parifh and Crewe, preceded the cavalcade.

On paffing through the city gates, the embaffy was faluted with three guns. The diftance between the two rivers could not be lefs than feven miles, the whole of which was covered by the city and fuburbs of Hoang-tchew. The ftreets were lined, on either fide, with foldiers, or it would have been impoffible to have paffed, from the prodigious crowds of people, whom curiofity had collected on the occafion.

The ftreets of this city are very narrow, but well paved; and the houfes, which are two and three ftories high, being uniformly built of brick, have a very neat appearance. The warehoufes of the merchants exceed any I ever faw, both for fplendor and magnitude; while the fhops are fitted up, both within and without, in a ftyle of the greateft elegance. Their goods, whether inclofed in packages, or difplayed to view, were difpofed in the moft pleafing and attractive

mode

mode of arrangement. Hoang-tchew is a very magnificent, populous, and opulent city, maintaining by its commerce the immenfe number of its inhabitants; and is the capital of a province to which it gives a name.

At noon his Excellency arrived at the Green river, on whofe banks a very large body of troops, all armed with helmets, and accompanied with a large corps of artillery, were drawn up in regular order: the whole confifting, as it appeared, of feveral thoufand men; the grandeur of whofe appearance was enlivened by a great number of gaudy ftandards and enfigns. The artillery troops were dreffed in blue, and had figures of the ordnance embroidered on their cloaths, by way of diftinction. They confifted of feveral companies, and were ftationed in the center, and on the flanks of the lines. Their cannon were by much the largeft we had feen in China : and as the Britifh cavalcade paffed through two very elegant triumphal arches, it was faluted by a difcharge of artillery.

The river being very fhallow towards the fhore, the junks lay at the diftance of fifty yards from it, and were ranged in a line clofe to each other. A platform was erected from the triumphal arch to the junk appointed to receive the Ambaffador, which confifted of a great number of carts faftened together, with fplit bamboos laid acrofs them.

The multitudes of people affembled to fee the embarkation were fo great, that I fhould hazard credibility were I to exprefs my opinion of them. Befides the crowds which were on foot, great numbers were mounted on buffaloes, or drawn in carts by the fame animals, who were tame and docile as our oxen. Some of them had three or four perfons on their backs at the fame time, whom they bore with great eafe, and were fubmiffive to their riders. The buffalo is very much ufed in this country in every kind of draught labour, and particularly in the occupations of hufbandry.

On.

On entering thefe junks, they were found, though of fmall dimenfions, to be fitted up with great neatnefs and peculiar accommodation.
At five o'clock in the afternoon the whole fleet was unmoored, and
proceeded on its voyage.

I went on board the ftore junk, where I faw the mandarin, Van-
Tadge-In, examining one of the people belonging to it, concerning
fome mifdemeanour he had committed. The poor culprit was ordered
to be punifhed with a baftinado, and he accordingly received two
dozen ftrokes from a bamboo acrofs the thighs.

The greater part of this day's voyage was between ranges of mountainous country, offering a great variety of romantic and picturefque
fcenes. The intervening vallies were covered with the tallow and
mulberry trees; from the former of which the Chinefe make their
candles, which are of a fuperior quality. This tree is here called
the latchoo, and is remarkable for the beauty of its appearance; it is
the fize of an apple tree, having fcarlet leaves edged with yellow, and
bloffoms of a pale purple. The mulberry tree is cultivated in China
with great care, for the produce of filk, which is a principal article of
Chinefe commerce.

We this day paffed feveral fmall villages, and a walled city, named
Syountong: it is fituated about three quarters of a mile from the river,
and near a large foreft that fhades the country about it.

This part of the river, though very broad, is feldom more than
two or three feet in depth, and in no place more than four. The
water has a green hue, and the bottom gravel. The beach, however,
is a mixture of fand and ftones.

In the evening of this day we were very much delighted with a view
of the city of Zauguoa in a ftate of magnificent illumination. The
troops were alfo drawn up on the banks, as we perceived by their

1793.

November.

Friday 15.

E e 2

lanterns;

lanterns; and from the number of them, as well as the brilliant appearance of the place, there was every reafon to confider it as in the
firft rank of Chinefe cities. The Ambaffador was faluted here as he
had been by a great number of forts in the courfe of the day.

Saturday 16. The weather was exceeding cold, accompanied with rain.

We paffed feveral ftone pagodas of a greater height than any we
had yet feen, fome of them reaching to nine ftories. The environs
of the river ftill continued to be mountainous and full of picturefque
beauty, heightened by the fancy and fingular genius of the inhabitants,
both as to cultivation and ornament. Large plantations of the tallow
and mulberry tree occafionally appear, to vary and enliven the fucceffion
of delightful views which unfolded themfelves as the ftream bore us
along.

The falutes of artillery were now become fo frequent, that they were
tirefome; as the banks of the river are, in a great meafure, lined with
forts, which expended their gun-powder in doing honour to the embaffy. It may, indeed, be faid, with a ftrict regard to truth, that in
our long journey through this kingdom, we had never proceeded a
fingle mile without receiving the falute of fome fort or military cantonment: nor were thefe military honours altogether confined to the fides
of the river; for this evening the fleet was an object of refpect from
a body of troops at a confiderable diftance, as we could judge from
their illumination; which had a very pleafing effect.

Sunday 17. About three o'clock in the morning I was awakened by a very
heavy difcharge of artillery; and inftantly quitting my bed, I perceived, by the number of lanterns, that a very large body of men were
drawn up on the fhore: but this was not all; for a lighted torch was
fixed to the carriage of every gun, and the bearer of each ftand of
colours was alfo diftinguifhed by a flambeau, which gave new brilliance and effect to the military illumination.

In

In an early part of the afternoon the fleet came to an anchor oppofite to a fmall, but very pretty town, on the banks of the river; and in a fhort time the conducting mandarin vifited the junks, to convey to the whole of the ambaffador's train, according to their rank, prefents of perfumes, fans, Imperial tea, and nankeen.

1793.
November.

We now feemed to have quitted the mountainous country for an extenfive plain, covered with plantations of the tallow and mulberry tree, intermixed with villages, and the ornamented habitations of mandarins; fome of which were faced with a lead-coloured plaifter, bordered with white;—an arrangement of colours not uncommon in our own country, whether applied to the furniture of houfes, or the drefs of ladies.

Monday 18.

The provifions which we now received, though by no means deficient in quantity, were far inferior, indeed, in quality to thofe we received in the former part of our journey; which we were made to underftand arofe from the nature of the country, rather than from any inattention to the comfort and convenience of the embaffy. Indeed, there could be no reafon to fuppofe that the Emperor had not even been anxious to render our departure from his kingdom as agreeable as refpect and exterior honour could make it. In fhort, from Tartary to Canton, it was a chain of falutes, which were fo frequent, as I have before obferved, that it might be compared almoft to a train of wild-fire laid from one end of the empire to the other.

I faw a groupe of water-mills, confifting of ten or twelve of them, all turned by a fmall cut from the river, which made a circuit round a meadow where they were erected: they bore an exact refemblance to our flour-mills in England, and appeared to be worked on the fame principle: they were now, however, become very common objects. Thofe, which I have now mentioned, were, as I underftood, employed in threfhing rice. Among the various circumftances

common.

1793.
November.

common to the country, we this day saw a pagoda that rose to the height of eleven stories.

The fleet anchored at night before the gates of the city of Tooatchou.

Tuesday 19.

The country in some degree resumed its former appearance; the plains on each side being backed by a long range of mountains rising in the horizon.

The fleet anchored this morning before a very considerable village, to wait for the junks of Lord Macartney and Sir George Staunton, which had fallen considerably astern.

Wednesday 20.

Soon after dinner the whole fleet was moored opposite to a large town, a spot which offered such a display of beautiful and contrasted objects, as I never remember to have seen. The river was, of course, the central object of the picture: on one side of it was a town with all its peculiar circumstances; and before it a military encampment with all its gay and gaudy decorations. On the other side was a range of lofty, perpendicular mountains.

The rest of this day was passed in making preparations for proceeding a short way by land; in order to embark in other junks.

Thursday 21.

At an early hour the Ambassador and his whole train disembarked, and proceeded in palanquins, sedans, and bamboo chairs, or on horse-back, as they severally chose: for, in all our expeditions by land, the mandarin Van-Tadge-In always consulted the suite as to the mode of travelling which they preferred, and never failed in accommodating them according to their respective inclinations.

The cavalcade proceeded but a short way, before we entered a walled city of considerable extent, and with very large suburbs, called

I

Chan-

Chanfoiyeng. It is fituated in a valley formed by two large hills, and about a quarter of a mile from the river. On the fummit of one of thefe eminences is a pagoda of a very ancient conftruction, and flat at the top, inftead of being crowned with a turret, or rifing to a point, like thofe which every moment prefented themfelves to our view. On paffing through the gates of this city, both as he entered and paffed out of it, the Ambaffador was honoured, as ufual, with a difcharge of artillery. The ftreets were very narrow and lined with fhops, fitted up with that interior arrangement and difplay of commodities, as well as exterior decoration, which has diftinguifhed fo many of the towns which we had vifited. ·

After paffing another walled city, and feven villages, which were alfo furrounded with walls, we arrived at one o'clock at the city of Sooeping, wheré dinner was already prepared. The remainder of our journey was along a good road, through a fertile country varied by hills; till, after paffing, and furprifing by our appearance, a fucceffion of villages, we arrived at five o'clock at the city of Youfaun, and were introduced to the houfe of a mandarin, oppofite to the wharf where the junks lay at anchor, in which we were to continue our voyage. The baggage of the embaffy had arrived before us, and was diftributed in the feveral courts of the building. After being refrefhed with tea, every one was bufy in feeing their baggage properly ftowed on board their refpective junks; and, in the evening, the Ambaffador and his whole retinue were fafely embarked, and not only ready, but anxious, to proceed on their voyage.

The rain was without remiffion through the whole of this day, fo that the junks were prevented from quitting their fituation; a circumftance that did not fail to exercife the patience of the paffengers of every rank, who had not yet learned to prefer the accommodations, however well contrived, on board a junk moored to a wharf, to the comforts of an houfe on the fhore..

C H A P.

1793.
November.

Friday 22.

C H A P. XX.

The voyage continued. Curious circumstances of the banks of the river. The embassy leaves the junks for vessels of a larger size. Circumstances of the voyage. Appearance of the country. Presents from the mandarin of Tyaung-shi-senna. Brief account of tombs and sepulchres. Pass the town of Saunt y Tawn, and a cluster of three cities. Arrive at Chinga-foo.

1793.
November.
Sunday 24.

THE fleet had sailed in the night, and anchored early in the morning before a large city called Mammenoa.

The river now flowed between a range of huge unconnected masses of stone, which, as they did not appear to be rooted in the earth, cannot be called rocks or crags; but had all the appearance of having been disjointed and thrown about by some strange convulsion of nature. In the interstices between them there were veins of earth of different appearances, but not in regular strata: some of these were of a deep brown or black colour, others were yellow; and they were occasionally intermixed with sand and gravel. In some parts I observed people cutting the stone into the shape of bricks, and in others, there were large heaps of them, which were of a deep red. Several of these huge stones had been excavated with great labour, and formed a sort of dwelling, many of whose inhabitants came forth to see our fleet pass along before them. Some of the intervals between these stones were of sufficient extent to admit of gardens with their buildings and pagodas, which produced very picturesque, romantic, and delightful pictures. When the country, which is in the highest state of cultivation, was let in through the open spaces between these stones, it produced a curious and pleasing perspective. This very singular

and

and stupendous scenery continued, for a length of several miles, with
little change, but what arose from the lesser or greater magnitude of the
objects, and the occasional decorations of art in building and ornamented gardens.

In the afternoon the fleet anchored before the city of Hoa-quoo,
where we were agreeably surprised to receive orders for the removal of
the embassy into larger junks, in which we should find a very pleasing
change in our accommodations and comforts. These junks were
hauled up along-side those which we then occupied; and, in a very
short time, the whole of the baggage was shifted into them.

Here the grand mandarin of Hoa-quoo sent to each junk, except
that which contained the soldiers, two cases of various fruits, and as
many boxes of sweet cakes and confectionary.

The rain which had continued almost without ceasing for the last two
days, abated, and the weather became moderate. The city of Quiol-
shee-sheng, where the fleet anchored for some time, has nothing remarkable but its wall, which is built of the red bricks that I mentioned yesterday.

The appearance of the country was as beautiful as cultivation could
make it; with a few rocks of a red stone occasionally breaking the
level of it. Near to some of them there appeared to be quarries where
the people where hewing the large stones into smaller pieces, of the
same size and figure of those already described.

The river had this day a more busy appearance than it had yet assumed, from the great number of rice mills which were at work on
this part of it.

The fog of this morning so far obscured the country, as to render
the distant parts altogether imperceptible. At noon, however, the

F f

atmosphere

1793.
November.

atmofphere became clear, and the eye ranged over a flat, but as ufual, fertile range of country, which, as far as I could diftinguifh, abounded in fields of rice: but the broadeft and moft uninterrupted level never prefented a dull or uninterefting profpect in any part of China through which we had paffed; as the feats of the mandarins and their gardens, with the farm-houfes embofomed in the trees, and the long line of thickets that frequently form the enclofures of the fields, compofe a picture which, though it may not be altogether fuited to the canvas, is very pleafing to the eye in its natural appearance.

The provifions with which the junks had been for fome time fup-plied, were of fo bad a quality that we frequently gave them to the poor people who conducted the veffels. This day, however, brought us the hope of better fare, by an improvement in the quality of the various articles which were now fent on board: but our table funk again, on the fucceeding day, to that ftate of mediocrity to which we had been habituated fince our departure from Houang-tchew.

Wednef-
day 27.

The morning was very cold and hazy:—the thermometer funk to forty-fix degrees.

I faw feveral fields where the farmers were bufy in ploughing: they ufe buffaloes for that purpofe. We were furprifed alfo with a very unufual fight, which was a village of mud houfes or huts, where the appearance of the inhabitants was as wretched as their dwellings. This circumftance I was not able to reconcile to the ge-neral induftry of the inhabitants; and, particularly, in that abundant part of the country, where it appeared, to me at leaft, that induftry could always find a comfortable fupport.

The fuite this day received from the mandarin a prefent of caddies of tea to every perfon who compofed it.

From the breadth of the river, the ftrength of the current, and
boifterous wind, the waves run high, with a violent furf. Here the
aftonifhing navigation of the river was varied by a fleet of fifhing-
boats, confifting of at leaft an hundred fail; and, during the whole of
this day's voyage, we continually encountered little fquadrons of
them.

In the afternoon we paffed the city of Tyaung-fhi-fennau, which
is not only one of the largeft places we had feen, but the moft commodioufly fituated for commerce, being near the conflux of feveral
rivers; nor can I be accufed, with juftice, of the leaft exaggeration,
when I affert, that there were not lefs than a thoufand junks at anchor
before it.

Almoft oppofite to this city, but fituated on another branch of the
river, is a large town in an elevated pofition, but not furrounded with
a wall, which is called Tfua-feenga. Nor can I refift making the obfervation, that, however I might be amufed with the variety of profpects, and novelty of objects which continually folicited and rewarded
my attention, I never felt an interval of aftonifhment at the villages,
towns, and cities, with which, if I may ufe the expreffion, the banks
of this river were thronged; as well as the myriads of people that they
poured forth as we paffed by, or anchored near, them.

The grand mandarin of Tyaung-fhi-fenna, came on board the
Ambaffador's junk, with a numerous train of attendants, to vifit his
Excellency. This ceremonial was accompanied with prefents of
filks, pieces of fine fcarlet cotton, various coloured ftuffs, elegant fmel-
ling bottles, pieces of porcelain, and caddies of the fineft tea.

A village, whofe houfes are all built with a blue brick, and roofed
with pantiles of the fame colour, was the only object in this day's
voyage that poffeffed any circumftance of novelty. The cities, mandarins palaces, and pagodas, did not differ, as far as we could judge,

F f 2

from

1793.
November.

from thofe which the reader may think, perhaps, have been too often defcribed. The profpect of the country was fometimes interrupted by banks of fand, which continued for many miles on each fide of the river.

We paffed two brick kilns, with a fmall village around them, built for the accommodation of the workmen employed in the manufactory. We could form fome judgment of the trade of the place by the large quantities of bricks formed in regular piles; both of thofe which were burned, and fuch as were ready for the kiln. This place is called Yu-was, which fignifies, as I was informed, a furnace for making bricks.

Saturday 30.

A city, at the diftance of two miles from the river, furrounded with meadows and orchards, and a very pretty fmall town, with feveral detached villages fcattered about it, were the only objects which gratified our attention in the early part of this day. As we proceeded, the profpect was more delightful than the imagination can conceive; not merely from the beauty of the objects, but their contraft to each other. On one fide of the river a verdant plain of vaft extent, covered with herds of cattle, and flocks of fheep, ftretched on to a range of lofty mountains that rofe boldly in the horizon: while the whole country, on the oppofite fide of the river, was fhaded with forefts, in whofe openings we could diftinguifh the humble cottage of the peafant, and the painted palace of the mandarin.

Cities and towns, as ufual, continually appeared on each bank of the river; and having paffed a fmall lake, we came to a village furrounded with trees, and diftinguifhed by the ruins of a pagoda. The part that remained, confifted of three ftories, and that which had fallen, lay in fragments about it.

The river, which was very unequal in its fize, as well as depth, now expanded into great breadth; and, as the wind blew frefh, the

current

current fwelled into what might almoſt be called a rough fea. The waves were fo violent, that the junk in which I failed, was in great danger of being overſet.

1793.
December.

The thermometer was funk fo low as forty degrees, and the fields were covered with froſt. The country was, for fome time, bounded on either fide by beautiful mountains, which funk at length into one un-varying level; where fields of rice, and flouriſhing orchards, were thofe branches of cultivation which we could beſt diſtinguiſh.

Sunday 1.

I mentioned, on a former occaſion, that there were no public cemeteries, or places of burial, but in the vicinity of large towns and cities; and that, at a diſtance from them, the fpot where a perfon dies always affords him a grave. Hence it is that the whole country may be confidered as a place of burial; and we could never turn our eyes to either bank of the river, but fome trophy of death appeared, of rude conſtruction, or more elegant form, according to the rank and opu-lence of the victim. Nay, it is not uncommon among the Chinefe, to erect, during their lives, thofe fad repofitories which are to contain their remains, when they are no longer numbered among the living. A greater number than ufual of thefe folemn objects, and of more diſtinguiſhed form than are generally feen, attracted our attention in this part of our voyage, and fuggeſted the preceding obfervations.

The town of Taung-fong-au, by which we now failed, has no-thing to diſtinguiſh it from thofe which every hour prefents to us, but the pleafing circumſtance, which is not common to all of them, of its being furrounded with meadows, groves, and gardens.

The town of Saunt-yo-tawn, containing feveral elegant pa-godas, which were feen above the groves that furrounded it, was a very pleafing and picturefque object. A fucceſſion of timber yards covered the banks of the river, and a large quantity of timber was foaking in the water before them, which I underſtood to be in a ſtate

of

of preparation for building junks ; a principal bufinefs of the place. It muft, indeed, be a principal bufinefs of the country at large ; for when the internal commerce of China is confidered, and that almoft the whole of it is carried on in thefe veffels, on the numerous rivers and canals which every where interfect, and form a communication through the greateft part of this extenfive kingdom ; the quantity of timber ufed, and the number of artificers employed, in the conftruction of them, muft render any attempt at calculation an idle prefumption in a perfon under fuch confined circumftances as myfelf.

The quantity of gunpowder, expended in paying military refpect to the diplomatic fleet, has, I fear, been already repeated ; but I cannot omit that the Ambaffador received, this day, more than ufual honour from the artillery of May-taungo, a very confiderable fortrefs on the bank of the river.

On the other fide of the water is a very ftately pagoda, built on an elevated fpot, with a fmall village fcattered about it. It may be fuppofed to belong to the mandarin, whofe country refidence is at a fmall diftance from it.

Art and nature have equally combined to form the fcenery of this charming place ; but the moft diftinguifhing circumftance of it is its contiguity to a clufter of three cities, which are not feparated by the interval of a quarter of a mile from each other. Their names are, Loo Dichean, Morrinn Dow, and Chic-a-foo. The latter is built on a large fand bank in the middle of the river, but they are, all of them, more remarkable for their fituation than their extent ; or, as it appeared, their commercial importance. Of brick-kilns, indeed, there were plenty about them ; and at a fmall diftance I faw vaft columns of fmoke, which rofe, as I was informed, from the furnace of a Porcelain manufactory.

In

In the evening we arrived at the city of Chinga-foo, where, from the crowd of people, the buftle made by the attendants of the mandarin, with the difcharge of artillery, and the firing of rockets, fuch a fcene of noife and confufion took place, as would have alarmed the whole Britifh embaffy on its firft arrival in this country.

Several temporary buildings were erected on purpofe, as it appeared, to difplay a complimentary illumination of great magnificence, which was formed by a profufion of lamps, candles, and flambeaux.

A prefent of fruit and confectionary concluded the attentions which were received during our anchorage before this city.

CHAP. XXI.

The voyage continued; various circumstances of it. Pass the ruins of an ancient building. Peculiar modes of fishing in China. Extra-ordinary custom of employing birds in catching fish. Pass several cities, towns, &c. Arrive at Yoo-jenn-au; its beautiful situation. The junks anchor before Kaung-jou-foo. The reception of the Ambassador.

_{1793.}
December.
Monday 2.

THOUGH this country abounds in a succession of never-ceasing variety to the traveller, it will not, I fear, possess that pleasing appearance in the opinion of the reader; as it is impossible to convey, by words, that diversifying character to the page of a printed book, which is seen in every leaf of the volume of Nature.

The slightest bend of the river presents a new prospect, or a new view of what has been already seen. Every city differs from the last; no two villages have the same form; and a multiplicity of circumstances occur, which occasion decided differences in the landscape figure of similar objects, that are incommunicable by any art of verbal description. Thus, I fear, it will prove, that, while the writer is receiving pleasure from the variety of objects that occur to his memory, he is preparing dullness for the reader by an enumeration of them.

The weather continued to be cold.—The river, for several miles, was flanked on each side by a range of hills; but the open country again appeared with its usual accompanyments of villages, towns, and cities. These, however, were now relieved by the contrasted appearance of a magnificent wood, or forest, that spread over a great extent of country.

The

The feafon of the year was now unfavourable for rural profpects, but ftill the country, almoft every hour, prefented fcenes that would appear on the canvas with great advantage, if reprefented there by the pencil of a mafter. Though the frequency of pagodas may, fometimes, produce too much uniformity in the profpects of China, there are certain fituations which receive a very great addition, taken in a picturefque view, from that kind of building.

1793.
December.

The city of Fie-cho-jennau was fo obfcured by the plantations of trees about it, that we could not altogether judge of its extent ; though we had now been long enough in China to have other criterions, by which we could determine on the fize, or commerce of any place, befides a perfonal examination of it. The number of junks which were anchored near it, told the general ftate of its trade, while the crowd of fpectators who came to gaze at us, or the number of foldiers who were drawn up to falute us, were fufficient indications of its extent and population. Of Fie-cho-jennau, we had no other means to form an opinion, but they were fufficient to fatisfy us that it was in the firft clafs of Chinefe cities.

We, this morning, paffed by the ruins of an ancient building ; but to what purpofe it had been originally applied, whether as a temple, erected by fome great mandarin for his private worfhip, or a banqueting houfe for his private pleafure, I fhall not pretend to determine ; though the opinion of thofe I could confult, was in favour of the former fuggeftion. It had once been a confiderable edifice, and the apartments that ftill remained were ornamented with fhell-work. The dilapidated part of the building formed a large heap of ftones and rubbifh. It was called by the people on board the junks, Wha-zaun.

Tuefday

It is altogether unneceffary when we enter upon an hilly or mountainous country, to mention the addition of pagodas, which never fail to accompany it, as that command of profpect which is poffeffed by elevated fituation, forms the delight of thefe buildings, as the loftinefs of

G g

them

them marks the dignity or wealth of thofe to whom they belong.

Situation is an object of univerfal attention among the Chinefe in erecting their places of refidence, or of pleafure. Nor do I recollect feeing any houfe, or palace of a mandarin, which was not in the heart of a city, that had not been erected with a palpable view to the local circumftances about it. Sometimes they are feen in vallies, on the declivities of hills, and on the banks of rivers; while their gardens never fail to have fomething of a romantic character given to them by artificial rocks, or ruins, and the introduction of grotefque forms of art or nature.

In the afternoon we faw a great number of fifhermen, who had changed their nets for rods and lines, and were bufily employed in their neceffary bufinefs. The modes of catching fifh in the lakes, rivers, and canals of China, are various, and fome of them peculiar to that country.

In the lakes and large rivers they frequently ufe the kind of baited lines, which are employed on board fhips to catch fifh in the fea. In other parts they ufe nets of the fame kind, and in the fame manner as the fifhermen in Europe. In fome places they erect tall bamboo ftalks in the water, on which they fpread a curtain of ftrong gauze, which they extend acrofs certain channels of the rivers; and fometimes, where there is an opportunity, acrofs the rivers themfelves : this contrivance effectually intercepts the paffage of the fifh, which, from the baits thrown in, or attached to the gauze, are brought there in fhoals; great numbers of boats then refort to thefe places, and the fifhermen are feen to employ their nets with great fuccefs.

It appeared, however, on inquiry, that the rights of fifhery are as ftrenuoufly exerted in China, as in our own country : for we were in-

4

formed,

formed, that none of thefe arts to get fifh were employed but for the mandarin who poffeffed the fhores of that part of the river, or by thofe who paid a rent for that privilege.

The fifh caught in the rivers which we have navigated, confift chiefly of a kind of whiting, and very fine trout, of an excellent quality and flavour; and they are fo abundant, that though the fifhermen are fo numerous, and the demand fo great from the junks, the former gain a very good livelihood, and the latter are well fupplied with a food, which the crews of them are faid to prefer.

But the moft extraordinary mode of fifhing in this country, and which, I believe, is peculiar to it, is by birds trained for that purpofe. Nor are hawks, when employed in the air, or hounds, when following a fcent on the earth, more fagacious in the purfuit of their prey, or more certain in obtaining it, than thefe birds in another element. They are called Looau, and are to be found, as I am informed, in no other country than that in which we faw them. They are about the fize of a goofe, with grey plumage, webbed feet, and have a long and very flender bill, that is crooked at the point. This extraordinary aquatic fowl, when in its wild ftate, has nothing uncommon in its appearance, nor does it differ from other birds whom nature has appointed to live on the water. It makes its neft among the reeds of the fhore, or in the hollows of crags, or where an ifland offers its fhelter and protection. Its faculty of diving, or remaining under water, is not more extraordinary than many other fowl that prey upon fifh: but the moft wonderful circumftance, and I feel as if I were almoft rifquing my credibility while I relate it, is the docility of thefe birds in employing their natural inftinctive powers, at the command of the fifhermen who poffefs them, in the fame manner as the hound, the fpaniel, or the pointer, fubmit their refpective fagacity to the huntfman, or the gunner.

The

1793.
December.

The number of thefe birds in a boat are proportioned to the fize of it. At a certain fignal they rufh into the water, and dive after the fifh; and the moment they have feized the prey, they fly with it to their boat; and though there are an hundred of thefe veffels in the fleet, thefe fagacious birds always return to their own mafters, and amidft the throng of fifhing junks which are fometimes affembled on thefe occafions, they never fail to diftinguifh that to which they belong. When the fifh are in great plenty, thefe aftonifhing and induftrious purveyors will foon fill a boat with them: and will fometimes be feen flying along with a fifh of fuch fize, as to make the beholder, who is unaccuftomed to thefe fights, fufpect his organs of vifion: nay, it has been fo repeatedly afferted to me as to prevent any doubt of the information, that, from their extraordinary docility and fagacity, when one of them happens to have taken a fifh which is too bulky for the management of a fingle fowl, the reft will immediately afford their affiftance. But while they are thus labouring for their mafters, they are prevented from paying any attention to them-felves, by a ring which is paffed round their necks; and is fo con-trived as to fruftrate any attempt to fwallow the leaft morfel of what they take.

We alfo faw another fifhing party, which, though it had more of ridicule than curiofity in it, I cannot forbear to defcribe. It confifted of at leaft thirty fifhermen feated like fo many taylors on a wide board, fupported by props in the river, where they were angling. There was another groupe of thefe people near the fhore, who had embanked a part of the river with fand, where, by raking the bottom with a kind of fhovel, they caught large quantities of fhrimps and other fhell fifh.

At an early hour in the afternoon we arrived before the city of Vang-on-chean, where the junks anchored for two hours, and the Ambaf-fador received a vifit from the grand mandarin. This place is of
confiderable

confiderable extent, and covers the whole flat that lies between the river and a range of high mountains.

1795.
December.

The river was for fome diftance enlivened by a fucceffion of villages on each fide of it. We then paffed fome confiderable towns, which were fucceeded by a double range of fteep and craggy hills, with groves and thickets hanging down them; and wherever there was any flat or level fpot, whether it was towards the bottom of thefe cliffs, or midway, or on their fummits, an houfe was erected, which formed the moft delightful and romantic fcenery that can be conceived. Wednefday 4.

I have already obferved, that, in this part of our travels through China, the villages were not only populous, but in general of a pleafing appearance, and that a clufter of cottages, whofe exterior form betrayed internal wretchednefs, is by no means a common object. This morning, however, prefented us with one of them, where the habitations were, in a great meafure, formed of logs of wood; but the eye had not leifure to give them more than a glance of commiferation, fo very alluring were the charms of the furrounding country; where, not only the refidences of perfons of diftinction, but the village and the farm houfe, are placed in the moft romantic fituations, and individually difplay the moft pleafing pictures, or together, compofe the magnificence of landfcape.

The weather was become moderate and pleafant; but the river was fo fhoaly in fome places, and fuch a rocky bottom in others, that it was confidered as dangerous to proceed after fun-fet. Thurfday 5.

The pencil of a mafter might here communicate fome general idea of the peculiar beauties of the country through which we paffed, and the continual variation of it; but it is not in the power of language to convey any correct image even of the individual objects, much lefs of

the

1793.
December.

the picture formed by the combination of them. When I mention that I have seen forests and gardens, mountains and vallies, the palace and the cottage, the city and the village, the pagoda and the mill, with a variety of subordinate, but heightening circumstances, in one view, I certainly inform my readers of the constituent parts of the prospect; but to give them the least notion of their actual arrangement and relative situation, of their proportions and contrast, of their general distance from the eye, and comparative distance from each other, is beyond any exertion of verbal description.

At a large town, called Yoo-jenn-au, which is situated at the foot of a very high mountain, the river on which we had sailed so long communicates with another equally capacious with itself. The situation of this place may be in some measure conceived, when we consider its position at the influx of two large rivers, both pouring their streams from mountainous and rocky chasms, whose declivities are enriched with woods of various trees, and adorned, where they are capable of receiving ornament from the hand of art, with airy buildings and hanging gardens.

My curiosity led me to examine several houses which were building at this place, when I observed that the scaffolding before them was constructed according to the principles which the builders and bricklayers of our own country employ in similar erections.

We passed an island which divided the river into two equal channels, and which some mandarin had made the place of occasional retirement. It contained an elegant house, with groves and gardens, and formed a charming contrast to the shores of rock and sand, on either side of the water that surrounded it.

It

It will be fufficient to add, that the country never appeared in a more beautiful or romantic drefs, by day, fince we entered it; and the city of Kaung-joo-foo prefented the moft brilliant illumination we had feen by night.

1795.
December.

A prefent of fruit, cakes, and confectionary, concluded the many complimentary attentions which the embaffy received at this place.

CHAP.

C H A P. XXII.

*The voyage continued. The manner in which the Chinese water their
fields. Sepulchres. Change in the appearance of the country. Leave
the river at the city of Naung-aum-foo to travel over land. Circumstances of the journey. Arrive at the city of Naung-chin-oa. Some
account of it. The Ambaffador re-imbarks to continue the voyage
down another river.*

1793.
December.
Friday 6.

IN this part of the river we faw a great number of the machines at
work with which the Chinese water their grounds. They confift of
a wheel made of bamboo, which is turned by the ftream, and throws
the water into large refervoirs, from whence it is let off by fluices into
channels that interfect the fields.

The pretty village of Shaiboo, fituated on an high bank of the
river, is the only object that recalls the eye from wandering over the
general beauty of the country; till, at the turn of the ftream, the attention is folicited by the pagoda of Tau-ay, an ancient and very lofty
building, whofe upper ftory being fallen, gives it a more picturefque
appearance, and is, on that account, emblematical of the little cemetery beneath it, which contains feveral fepulchres and other memorials
of the dead. But whether this fpot fo appropriated belongs to any
city or town, which we could not perceive, or is the burying place of
any particular family of diftinction, I could not learn. But though
the ground at the foot of this pagoda is affigned to the dead, the
upper part of the building is fo fituated as to delight the living by the
view it affords of the furrounding country, and the windings of the
river, for a very confiderable diftance, in both directions of it.

I cannot

I cannot omit mentioning the town of Whan-ting-taun, not merely because its environs are divided between woods and rice fields, but, as it is the only place of any importance which we have seen in our voyage of this day. Villages were, as ufual, in frequent fucceffion; and among many of them which wore the appearance of induftry and comfort, we were again diffatisfied with a collection of huts, that did not appear to be capable of preferving their inhabitants from the inclemency of winter, or the heat of fummer.

This was the moft extraordinary day which we had yet known in China, as we faw neither city, town, or village, in the courfe of it. A few farm houfes, with their orchards, were the only habitations that we faw in the extent of beautiful country through which we paffed: nor could I, by any inquiries, in my power to make, difcover whether it arofe from accident, or any local circumftances, that the banks of the river, which had fo long teemed with cities, towns, and villages, with palaces and pagodas, fhould at once become fo barren of them.

But though we were, for fome time, deprived of the wonders of population, a very fingular and curious object accompanied a confiderable part of this day's voyage, to continue, in fome degree, the exercife of our aftonifhment.

It was a very lofty, perpendicular, natural mound of red earth, that embanked one fide of the river, whofe naked furface was marked in a very extraordinary manner by horizontal veins or ftripes of ftone, in a direction as perfectly rectilinear, as if they had been made with the line or the rule; and which continued without any apparent deviation, from this wonderful regularity, during a courfe of feveral miles.

The river was now become fo fhallow, that it was neceffary to change feveral of the large junks for fuch as would draw lefs water, a circumftance which occafioned fome delay; and it was not till eight

1790
December.

o'clock that we paffed the only inhabited place of this day's voyage ; and which might now have efcaped our notice, if the foldiers of the cantonment had not exhibited their paper lanterns, and difcharged a few vollies of refpect towards us.

Sunday 3.

The weather has, for fome time, been temperate and pleafant : the country alfo has gradually loft its fertile appearance, and is now become mountainous and barren : fome of the mountains, indeed, are covered with wood, but the furface of the earth has here loft all that richnefs which had fo long cloathed it. The population of the country may be fuppofed to have fuffered a proportionate diminution ; but the villages, though they are more thinly fcattered than they have hitherto been, become more picturefque objects both from their form and fituation.

The high grounds near the river, in many places, lofe their abrupt and rugged appearance beneath the verdure of dwarf-trees of various kinds, among which the camphire tree is faid to predominate.

But though the profpect was now become a mere fucceffion of rude mountain and barren valley, it was fometimes enlivened by a pagoda in the diftance, while the village ftill continued to animate the banks of the river.

We now obferved feveral fepulchres or funeral monuments that had been erected in various parts of the mountains, with excavations in the rocks beneath them to receive the dead. That an amiable fuperftition might wifh to confign the remains of the parent or the child, the friend or the relation, to fuch a fepulchral retreat, elevated as it were above the world, and, as it might be thought by the Pagan mythology, nearer to that heaven, where their fpirits were deftined to wing, or had already taken flight, is not inconfiftent with the beft feelings of nature and religion. But fome of thefe places facred to the dead appeared to

us,

us, at leaft, to be in fuch fituations, as to render the attempt to gain
accefs to them, a circumftance of no fmall hazard to the living.

About fun-fet we paffed a large town called Syn-cham-au, which is fituated on a fmall plain between the river and fome high mountains covered with wood ; nor is this romantic appearance leffened by a large pyramidical rock, with a very lofty pagoda on the top of it.

Two confiderable towns and feveral villages, with their junks, were the principal objects of this day's voyage ; till we arrived in the evening at the city of Naung-aum-foo. As the embaffy was to make a journey of one day over land from this place, preparations were made accordingly under the ufual directions of the attendant mandarin.

The Ambaffador ordered four dollars to be given to the crews of the refpective junks ; and, after an hafty breakfaft, the fuite followed the baggage, which was already fent on fhore.

The landing-place was adorned with a grand triumphal arch, decorated with filk and ftreamers of various colours. Here I was prefented with a ticket, the meaning of which I did not comprehend. I then proceeded along a kind of platform, covered with fine matting ; its roof and railing were ornamented with ribbons and filk, in the fame manner as the triumphal arch, and a range of lamps were fufpended in a very elegant form on each fide of it.

This platform led to a circular court, furrounded by a fcreen of filk, which contained, as well as I could calculate from the view of them, between two and three hundred horfes, attended by their owners, and from which every perfon in the Ambaffador's retinue was at liberty to chufe a beaft for the journey of the day ; as from the badnefs of the roads, and the length of the way, it was ordered that the whole fuite, except the Ambaffador, Sir George Staunton, and

H h 2

Mr.

1793.
December.

Mr. Plumb, should proceed on horseback. I accordingly chose an horse, for which I was obliged to deliver the ticket already mentioned. It was a very wild and mettlesome steed, which, on my first mounting him, was so restive and unmanageable, that I wished to make an exchange; but I had delivered my ticket, and was obliged to abide by my choice, such as it was.

When all the arrangements were settled, the horses selected, and the whole suite transformed into a body of cavalry, his Excellency, with Sir George Staunton, and Mr. Plumb, came from the junk to their palanquins, and the cavalcade commenced, attended by a considerable body of Chinese soldiers.

Naung-aum-foo is a walled city of considerable extent, built on a rising ground above the river, and is commanded, both behind, and on the opposite side of the water, by lofty hills; on one of which is seen a solitary pagoda. Its suburbs are large, and, from the number of small junks, suited to the shallowness of the stream that washes its banks, it may be esteemed a place of some commercial character.

In about half an hour we had got clear of the city, when every exterior object was lost in attending to the peculiarities of our own appearance. Such a troop of equestrians are not often seen in China, or any other part of the world. The gentlemen of the suite, with the mechanics, soldiers, and servants, were all on horseback; many of whom were but indifferent riders, and some of them now found themselves obliged to ride for the first time. The horses themselves, on setting out, were also very frolicksome and ungovernable; so that the ridicule which attached itself to our general appearance, and the diversion which successively occurred from the cries of alarm, the awkwardness of attitude, and the various other circumstances, which the reader, without having been in China, may very readily conceive, served to

amuse

amufe the tedioufnefs of travelling through a mountainous and unpro-
ductive country.

At noon we came to the foot of a mountain, which was fo fteep as
to make it neceffary for us to difmount, and lead our horfes over it,
being an afcent of two miles, which required an hour to mafter it.
We paffed feveral villages, and dined at the town of Lee-cou-au,
where a confiderable body of foldiers, in armour, lined the road as
we paffed; and both on entering, as well as quitting the lines, the
Ambaffador was faluted with the difcharge of three pieces of artillery.
This military parade, with the variety of colours, which never failed
to accompany the leaft appearance of foldiery, had a very pretty
effect.

The women, in this part of our journey, were either educated with
lefs referve, or allowed a greater fhare of liberty, than in the country through which we had lately paffed, as we frequently faw them
indulging their curiofity in obferving fuch a new and extraordinary
fight as we muft exhibit.

I have already mentioned that we had, for fome time, exchanged a
fertile for an unprofitable foil; and all the fplendor of cultivation, for
the barren mountain. The eye was, however, fometimes relieved by
large patches of camphire, and other medicinal, trees; at leaft, as I was
informed by thofe who might be fuppofed to be able to inftruct me.

The fun had fet, when we arrived at the gates of the city of Naung-
chin-oa. It ftands in a plain, furrounded on three fides by mountains;
on the fourth and to the fouth, flows the river on which we were to
continue our voyage. It is a place of fome extent and confiderable
commerce. The ftreets, like thofe of almoft all the towns we have
feen in China, are very narrow, but they have the advantage of being
well paved, and well kept in the material article of cleanlinefs. The
houfes are chiefly of wood, and their general height is two ftories.

Though

1793.
December.

Though elegance, either interior or exterior, is not the peculiar character of this place, some of the shops were gilt and varnished in a manner that might bring them within that denomination. At every door in the streets, after sun-set, a large paper lamp is hung up, and forms a very pretty illumination. These lamps display the name of the person who lives in the house, his trade, and the articles in which he traffics. The palaces of the mandarins are also ornamented with lamps, according to the dimensions of the building, or the rank of their inhabitants.

The streets were lined with soldiers to repress the curiosity of the people, which would, otherwise, have impeded our passage; and it was near seven o'clock when we arrived at the palace of the grand mandarin of the city. It is a very noble residence, composed of various courts, and several ranges of apartments. In spacious open galleries, on each side of the first court, tables were plentifully spread with tea, meats, of various kinds, and fruits, for the refreshment of the inferior orders of the suite; while other galleries, that opened on the interior courts, were magnificently illuminated, and prepared for the higher department of it. In short, throughout the palace, there was such a profusion of lamps and other lights, as, in my unexaggerated opinion, would serve the palace of an European sovereign for a month. But without this observation, which, I believe to be founded in fact, it must have already appeared, in the course of this Narrative, that illumination is a very principal feature of Chinese magnificence.

The Ambassador and Sir George Staunton preferred going to the junks instead of passing a night in the palace; and, accordingly, after having taken the refreshment prepared on their arrival, they repaired to them. The rest of the embassy remained on shore, and apartments were assigned them for their repose.

The baggage which was brought all the way from Naung-aum-foo on mens shoulders, arrived by degrees; but the whole of it had not

reached

reached its destination till nine o'clock; when all the mandarin's principal servants assisted in depositing it in a long gallery, where it was arranged with the utmost regularity; each package having a ticket pasted on it, corresponding with the junk to which it was to be removed on the following day.

CHAP.

C H A P. XXIII.

*The fuite embarks on board the junks; the voyage renewed; circum-
stances of it. A curious pagoda. Defcription of fepulchres. Vaft
rafts of timber. Embark in larger junks. Pafs fome curious mountains; a defcription of them. Extraordinary illumination.*

1793.
December.
Wednef-
day 11.

AT an early hour of the morning the baggage was put on board the
junks, with a regularity, as well as difpatch, that cannot well be defcribed. There was a fufficient depth of water in this river to bring
the junks clofe to the quay; fo that the coolies, of which there were a
great number, acting under the orders of the mandarin and his fervants, and guarded by foldiers, foon transferred every article that belonged to the embaffy on board the veffels to which it was fpecifically
affigned.

The junks, to which we were now removed, were of lefs dimenfions
than thofe we had left; in conformity to the navigable ftate of the
river, which only admitted veffels of fmall burthen.

About eleven o'clock the fuite were all on board, and the whole fleet
ready for failing. We accordingly renewed our voyage, and began
it by paffing under a wooden bridge of feven arches, or rather, if accuracy of expreffion fhould be confidered as indifpenfable, of feven
intervals. Thefe intervals are formed by ftrong ftone pillars, built
in the water, and overlaid with planks, guarded by a double railing. This ftructure ftretches acrofs the river, to form a communication between thofe parts of the fuburbs of Naung-chin-oa, which are
divided by it. Forts garrifoned with troops, and well fupplied with
artillery, guarded either end of it; nor was the fleet unnoticed by

2

them; as in paffing the bridge it was honoured by the parade of the one, and the difcharge of the other. The city itfelf is alfo well de- 1796. December. fended by walls, which are, at leaft, thirty feet in height, towards the river, with ramparts that take the whole circuit of the place, and fquare towers which are not confined to the gates, but appear to rife above the walls in other advantageous fituations.

At a fmall diftance from the bridge the river divides into two branches, that take almoft oppofite directions: on that whofe ftream bore us along, we faw a large quantity of fmall timber in rafts.

In the afternoon we paffed a pagoda, fituated on a bank of the river, which was of a more fingular appearance than any of the great num-ber of that kind of edifice which we had feen in our travels through the country. It confifted of five ftories, which terminated in a flat roof, with trees growing on it. The body of the building, from many parts of which alfo fhrubs appeared to fprout forth, was covered with a white plaifter, and decorated with red paint in its angles and inter-ftices.

The country ftill remained barren and mountainous; nor was its rude and dreary afpect enlivened by any appearance of cultivation. A confiderable town called Chang-fang, was the only place we paffed in the fhort voyage of this day.

The natural face of the country was ftill dreary; and its artificial Thurfday 12. circumftances did not enliven it by their character. The mountains, as we paffed by them, exhibited a great number of thofe fepulchres of which fome defcription has been already given. Thefe, as the former, were in fituations not eafily acceffible, and varied in their appearance, as may be fuppofed, according to the wealth or dignity of the perfon whofe remains they already contained, or were, hereafter, deftined to inclofe.

I i

When

When we mentioned thefe folemn repofitories in a former page, the thought fuggefted itfelf, that fuperftition might carry the dead to thofe high places, on the fame principle that idolatry has raifed its altars there; but, when it is confidered that the dreary, uncultivated mountain is better fuited to the character of the fepulchre; and that there is, perhaps, fomething confolatory in the idea of that fecurity which belongs to thefe awful, and almoft inacceffible folitudes; we may probably approach nearer to the real motives of configning the dead to thefe elevated tombs.

The general conftruction of them appears to be the fame: it confifts of an excavation in the mountain, chifelled out in the form of a large niche, which is then paved, and concealed by a wall with an ornamented door. Some of thefe places are covered with domes; from others pyramidical forms fpring up, and the façades of them were, as far as I could diftinguifh, painted of a lead colour, with a white border.

Thefe receptacles of the dead were fucceeded by few habitations of the living that have any claim to particular notice or obfervation, till we came to the large and populous village of Ty-ang-koa. Here we faw a vaft length of timber in rafts floating down the river, with feveral bamboo huts erected on it, and the families belonging to them. Great numbers of people were alfo employed in bringing timber to the water fide, either on their fhoulders, or in waggons; while others were occupied in forming rafts.

The country ftill retains its barren afpect, though a pagoda was occafionally feen to grace the fummits of the mountains.

We this day paffed a confiderable town called Tya-waung, part of which was in ruins; and, a little further down the river, we came to the city of Shaw-choo; the fuburbs of which extend to the water fide, and where the houfes are built in fuch a manner as to be in con-

tinual

tinual danger of falling on the heads of their inhabitants, and in-volving them in one common deſtruction. A wooden frame work reſting ſometimes upon a foundation of clay or ſtone, with a few ſlender uprights, are the only ſupports of thoſe habitations that ranged along the ſhore; where frequent ruins manifeſted the folly as well as the frailty of ſuch architecture.

1794.

December.

The fleet came to an anchor at the extremity of the city, before the palace of the grand mandarin, which was finely decorated with triumphal arches: a platform was alſo erected from the banks of the river to the houſe, to accommodate the Ambaſſador, if his Excellency had found it convenient to go on ſhore. The ſoldiers belonging to the mandarin were alſo drawn up in due form, and gave the uſual ſalute.

At this place large junks were prepared to receive the embaſſy; and, in a very ſhort time, the whole ſuite and the baggage was removed on board them. Our accommodations were accordingly increaſed in proportion to the ſuperior dimenſions of the veſſels that now contained us.

In the evening the grand mandarin ſent the ſuite a very handſome preſent of China, together with a large ſupply of proviſions; we alſo received, at a later hour of the evening, a large parcel of tobacco, ſome ducks cured in the manner of hams, of a very delicate flavour, together with a conſiderable quantity of dried fiſh.

The voyage was this day agreeably varied by an occaſional, though not very frequent patch of cultivated ground, which was now become, in ſhape, ſize, or ſituation, a cheering object.

The weather was moderate and pleaſant; and, though there appeared a very ſmall proportion of cultivated land, the mountains were ſometimes clothed with wood. The village of Shoong-koang, ſituated

Saturday 14,

on

on a plain, with the river before, and an amphitheatre of mountains behind, it, drew our attention, as a very pleafing object, and furprifed us with the number of inhabitants which it poured forth, to fee the ftrangers pafs.

I have already mentioned that fmall portions of cultivated ground now began, though very rarely, to make their appearance : this circumftance, however, had no influence on our fupplies ; as the provifion-boats of to-day brought us the fame indifferent eatables which we had, for fome time, been accuftomed to receive.

In the evening, the hills gradually approached the river, till, at length, they clofed upon it, and formed a rude and lofty barrier, which, at once, confined and obfcured its channel. This fcenery continued for a confiderable diftance, as it were, on purpofe to lead the eye to a mountain of fuch ftupendous magnitude, as the defcription which I am about to give, will not be able to convey, I fear, to the mind of my readers. It was fo late as feven o'clock at night before we arrived at the commencement of it ; but the moon fhone in all her fplendour, and enabled the eye to trace every part of this enormous object with lefs diftinctnefs, perhaps, as to minute parts, but with better effect as to its magnificent outline.

This mountain rifes from the river to the perpendicular height of at leaft three hundred yards. The face it prefents towards the water is divided between bare rock and fhaggy foliage : the upper part appeared, in fome places, to project over the river, and offer a moft tremendous fhape to the voyagers who fail beneath it : when, therefore, to fuch an elevation of folid rocky mountain, with its rugged bafe, and craggy fummits, is added the extent of near two miles of lengthening precipice, fome faint notion may be entertained of this ftupendous object.

Its

Its termination is equally abrupt with its beginning; and all its
parts fupport the favage grandeur of the whole. On the extreme
point, as we paffed down the river, a pyramidical rock appeared to
fpring up to a confiderable height above the edge of the precipice, and
finifhed in a peak.

This immenfe fhape is feparated by an intervening plain, that extends to the foot of diftant mountains, from another enormous rock;
which, though of different form, and lefs extent, poffeffes the fame
awful and majeftic character. It rifes with a fteep but gradual afcent
from the river to a certain height; when it fhoots up, as it were, in a
bold, unvarying, perpendicular elevation, to the clouds, affording
another vaft example of the fublime in nature.

As a range of hills may be faid to conduct us along the river to
thefe ftupendous objects, a fucceffive boundary of the fame kind continued during a courfe of feveral miles after we had left them. But
it was the peculiar office of this extraordinary night to awaken our
aftonifhment by the grand exertions of art, as well as by the enormous
works of nature; for, at the conclufion of this chain of hills, that
had fo long excluded any view into the country, we were furprized
with a line of light that extended for feveral miles over mountains
and vallies, at fome diftance from the river, and formed one uninterrupted, blazing outline, as they rofe or funk in the horizon.

In fome parts of this brilliant, undulating line, it was varied or
thickened, as it appeared, by large bands or groups of torches; and,
on the moft confpicuous heights immenfe bonfires threw their flames
towards the clouds. Nor was this all, for the lights did not only
give the outline of the mountain, but fometimes ferpentifed up it,
and connected, by a fpiral ftream of light, a large fire at the bottom,
with that which reddened the fummit.

The

1793.
December.

The number of lanterns, lamps, or torches employed on this occa_fion, muſt have been beyond all calculation, as the two extremities of the illuminated ſpace, taken in a ſtrait line, and without eſtimating the ſinkings of the vallies, or the inequality of the mountain tops, could not exclude a leſs diſtance from each other than three miles. Whether theſe lights were held by an army of ſoldiers, and a very large one would have been neceſſary on the occaſion, or were fixed in the ground, I could not learn; but it was certainly the moſt magnifi_cent illumination ever ſeen by the European traveller, and the moſt ſplendid compliment ever paid to the public dignity of an European Ambaſſador. Not only a vaſt range of country, but the courſe of the river, for ſeveral miles, received the light of day from this artificial blaze. Succeſſive diſcharges of artillery were, at regular diſtances, ad_ded to the honour of this amazing and moſt ſuperb ſpectacle.

C H A P.

C H A P. XXIV.

The voyage continued. Description of a curious mountain. Various circumstances of the river. Arrive at the city of Tuyng-yan-yean. Pass numerous villages, towns, &c. Anchor before the city of Tsyn-tian. Arrive at Canton. Formalities on the occasion, &c.

AT seven o'clock this morning the whole fleet came to an anchor beneath a mountain, which is considered by the Chinese, in respect to its elevation, figure, and extent, as one of the natural wonders of their country. It is called Koan-yeng-naum.

The grand mandarin, who had the care of conducting the embassy, with that attention which distinguished every part of his official duty, had ordered the fleet to stop in this place, in order to give the Ambassador, and his retinue, an opportunity of indulging their curiosity, by taking a view of this extraordinary mountain.

It rises perpendicularly from the water to an amazing height, and terminates in a peak. Vast pieces of the rock project from the face of it in such a manner, as to have a most tremendous and threatening aspect; nor is it easy to persuade oneself, on looking up, that they will not instantly fall and fill up the channel of the river beneath them.

Several large caverns are among the curious circumstances of this mountain. The principal of them is about forty feet above the river, and the passage to it consists of a flight of fifty steps cut out of the rock, and guarded by a rail, which are over-shadowed by a projection of the mountain. A door, prettily ornamented with painting, opens into a handsome room of about forty feet in circumference, and nine

feet

1793.
December
Sunday 15.

1792.
December.

feet in height, which contains a sacred image, to whom the Chinese, on their entrance, pay their adorations. There is also a window, chisseled through the stone, with a balcony before it, from whence there is a delightful prospect of the river. From this chamber we ascended, by an artificial staircase, to two other apartments of the same size with the former, and fitted up in a manner suited to the character of the place.

These rooms were excavated at the expense of the mandarin to whom the mountain belongs, and must have been a work of incredible labour. At the foot of the steps, an arch had been erected, with the usual decoration of silk and ribbons, of various colours.

Though the country still continued to be rude and uncultivated, it was, occasionally, varied by large woods, that hung down the steeps, or thickened in the vallies. The ranges of mountains also, that branch off from Koan-yeng-naum, take such different directions, as to form a variety of grand, and even sublime, pictures of nature.

At noon the fleet anchored, for a short time, before the city of Shizing-ta-heng; situated on the upper part of an inclined plain, that advances with a scarce perceptible ascent from a large sandy beach of the river, to the foot of the mountains that rise behind it. This plain is also adorned with the most beautiful trees, so that the view may be sup-posed to consist of a river in the fore-part of it, a fine plain, covered with plantations, stretching away from the banks, and a large city be-yond it, backed by a bold, unequal range of mountains. When to these circumstances are added, the woods on the opposite side of the river, and the magnificent pagoda which rises before them; the beauty of the landscape may be conceived without any very uncommon stretch of the imagination.

The river, in a very winding course, now afforded but little variety. The same lofty barriers continued to confine its course; and where a

casual

casual opening suffered the eye to advance beyond them, it looked towards nothing more than similar objects, with no other circumstances
of variation but such as might be supposed to arise from the peculiarities of light and shadow, and the diminution of distance.

We not only observed, but also heard the labours, of large bodies of
people, who were employed in blowing up certain parts of the rocks, to
obtain that stone with which the Chinese form their pavements, whether for their houses, courts, or public ways.

Beneath one of these mountains was a large village, which had a
very mean appearance; and, as I afterwards learned, was entirely inhabited by the people employed in blowing up rocks, and working
quarries, that were in the neighbourhood of it.

Several spires of smoke, ascending from the mountains, attracted
our attention; when, on making inquiry concerning the fires that
occasioned them, we found that it was a process preparatory to agriculture; by burning the heath on certain parts of these elevated situations, in order to commence the experiment of cultivation.

The evening of this day was also cheered by an illumination of the
distant hills; and though it did not, in any degree, equal, either in extent or splendor, that which had so lately excited our astonishment, it
had a very singular effect, and exhibited a very pleasing appearance.

Rugged and steep rocks, some of which were covered with
wood, still continued to inclose, on either side, the channel of the
river. Among them there rose a large mountain, shaded by an hanging
forest, which was not only a very grand object in itself, but was also
accompanied with circumstances that enlivened and adorned it. At
the foot of it a road had been cut out of the solid rock, and to communicate with it a large arch of stone stretches across a deep chasm. In
the center of the wood, there is the palace of a mandarin, surrounded

K k

with

1793.
December.

with detached offices, and at some small distance a temple, which belongs to it, and contains the image which is the usual object of religious worship. There are several burying places in different parts of the wood, which are the mausoleums of the mandarin's family to whom the palace belongs. It is called Tre-liod-zau.

This magnificent object, which, on a particular turn of the river, presented itself in charming perspective, is very much heightened by a contrasted succession of bare and barren mountains.

This rude and rugged scenery, at length, began to subside; when a rich, fertile level opened again upon us; and after we had been accustomed for seven days, to the bleak and barren appearances of nature, the tranquil scenes of cultivation afforded a most refreshing prospect.

We now passed the city of Tsing-yan-yenn, a place of great extent and commerce. It is surrounded by a wall, whose gates are flanked by strong towers, and which extends near three miles along the river; but of its breadth we were prevented from forming any accurate judgment, by the intervening groves, which appear before, and rise above, the walls. The suburbs had a mean appearance; and the houses projected over the water in the same insecure and alarming manner, as I have already described: a mode of building, common to all towns, and lesser places, which are situated on the banks of rivers. The great number of junks which were here at anchor announced the commercial state of the city; and the succession of timber yards, all stored with great quantities of planks, and wood for every kind of construction, marked a principal article of its trade. Several regiments of soldiers were drawn up on the beach, with a train of artillery: they were accompanied with triumphal arches, decorated in the same pretty and fanciful manner as has already been told of other complimentary erections of the same kind.

From

From this place the river takes its courſe in a ſtrait, undeviating direction for three miles, between a very fertile and highly cultivated country, in which rice fields appeared to abound. The mountains, which ſo lately roſe on the banks, ſeemed now to have retired, as it were, into the diſtance, and ranged along the horizon.

1793.
December.

In this afternoon a very ſerious accident happened, which might have produced the moſt fatal conſequences: it was no leſs than a fire in one of the inferior junks; and, if great exertions had not been made, the veſſel would have been very ſoon conſumed. It was ſuppoſed to have been occaſioned by a ſpark falling unobſerved from a tobacco pipe, which, trifling as it was, threatened the junk with irreſiſtible conflagration.

The whole fleet experienced the good effects of the rich and fertile country which we now entered, by the improvement that was experienced in every article of our daily ſupplies. We this day received a large quantity of excellent proviſions, with a jar of a very pleaſant liquor, which is extracted from the ſugar cane, and reſembles in flavour the rum ſhrub, ſo well known in our own country.

The ruins of a pagoda, and ſome of thoſe ſepulchres which I have already mentioned, gave a pic, appearance to the ſpot where they had been erected, and were the concluding objects of this day's voyage.

The weather was warm and pleaſant, and the country in a fine ſtate of cultivation; while the river increaſed in breadth, and admitted junks of a larger ſize than we had yet ſeen.

Tueſday 17.

At eleven o'clock this morning we paſſed the large village of Ouzchouaa, with a crowd of manufactories in its neighbourhood: whether they were in the porcelain or iron ſervice, I could not diſ-

cover;

1793.
December.

cover; but the fmoke of their furnaces told us that fire was a principal operator in them.

As we proceeded, the country increafed in beauty on both fides of the river, and foon became a continued chain of pretty villages, fruitful fields, and handfome houfes.

In the afternoon the provifion junks ftill improved in their cargoes, and brought us an abundant fupply of excellent provifions and fruits, with a quantity of Samptchoo, a liquor which has been already mentioned.

At eight o'clock in the evening the fleet anchored before a very large and commercial city, called Sangs-wee-yenno, when the Ambaffador was faluted with an amazing difcharge of artillery from all quarters of it. This mark of refpect was accompanied by every other demonftration of regard that could be fhewn on the occafion : triumphal arches appeared with all their gaudy decorations ; temporary pagodas were erected to heighten the artificial fcenery ; and a platform, fuch as has been already defcribed in former parts of our voyage, was prepared to accommodate his Excellency, if it fhould be his wifh to vifit the grand mandarin : to thefe circumftances may be added all that illumination could do, in a country where that fpecies of fplendor is fo well underftood and in fuch continual practice ; fo that fome notion may be formed of the manner in which the fleet was received by this city.

Wednef-
day 18.

In the courfe of this morning we paffed feveral very large and commercial towns ; and, if any judgment could be formed from the unceafing difcharge of artillery, it might be fuppofed that a chain of forts lined the fhore : if we are alfo juftified in drawing a conclufion from the numbers of people on the banks of the river, and in veffels on the water, we might believe that, from the time we failed, which was at fo early an hour as two o'clock, the fleet was paffing for upwards

of

of two hours through the middle of an immenſe city, which had poured forth all its inhabitants to catch ſuch an imperfect view of us, as the early part of the morning would allow.

At the dawn of day, we came to the city of Tayn-tſyn-tau, a place of great importance and immenſe trade. Several thouſand ſoldiers were drawn up along the beach, with a proportionate train of artillery, which thundered out a ſalute as we paſſed.

This city, or, perhaps, to ſpeak more correctly, the ſuburbs of it, are built on each ſide of the river; which, for many miles, was covered with junks laden with merchandiſe, or preparing to receive it; and ſome of them were of very large dimenſions.

We continued ſailing before, or rather through, this place till ſeven o'clock, and, from the rate of our paſſage, I have no doubt but it is eight miles in length: of its breadth, no judgment could be formed on board the fleet; but, from the general appearance of the city, and the houſes of the reſident merchants, with other commercial circumſtances, its trade muſt be immenſe, and its opulence in proportion: it appeared, indeed, to be only inferior to the cities of Pekin and Canton.

The river continued to be covered with a crowd of junks; ſo that it was with ſome difficulty the fleet proceeded on its voyage, which at length approached its termination; for, about noon, it came to anchor within a mile of the city of Canton, and but two miles diſtant from the Engliſh factory.

In conſequence of an expreſs diſpatched by the conducting mandarin to Canton, to notify the arrival of the Ambaſſador, ſeveral mandarins, in the different departments of government, came to viſit his Excellency. They were ſoon followed by the Britiſh commiſſioners, the Company's ſupercargoes, and Colonel Benſon, a very welcome
viſitor,

vifitor, for he not only brought the public difpatches for Lord Ma-cartney, but a large packet of private letters from England, and all the news-papers which had arrived by the laft fhips from Europe.

Orders were iffued by the Ambaffador for the whole fuite to difem-bark on the following day.

 The embaffy was removed into larger junks, which had been pre-vioufly fitted up to go down the river.

In paffing down this fpacious river it is impoffible to defcribe the magnificence of its navigation; for we faw, without exaggeration, feveral thoufands of trading junks; nor were the veffels which were crowded with people to fee us pafs inferior in number; while the banks on either fide were covered with houfes, built very much in the ftyle of European architecture.

There are alfo a fucceffion of forts well fupplied with men and ar-tillery; and their refpective garrifons were drawn out in military array on the beach before them, with their colours, mufic, and all the enfigns of war. Thefe forts faluted the fleet by a fucceffive difcharge of artillery, and indeed the air refounded for near an hour with the repeated firing of great guns from every quarter.

There were alfo feveral thoufand foldiers in military junks, who added the compliment of their mufquetry. It was a very large army both on land and water, and the whole of them funk down on their knees, as a manœuvre of military refpect, till the Ambaffador had paffed.

At one o'clock we arrived oppofite the Englifh and Dutch fac-tories; when both of them faluted his Excellency with a difcharge of artillery, and inftantly hoifted the ftandards of their refpective nations.

4

Here

Here we faw great numbers of boats, containing all kinds of provifions, fruits and merchandize, for fale. They rowed backwards
and forwards, announcing, at the fame time, their various commodities, with very violent vociferation, as is feen and heard among the
owners of provifion wherries on the Thames.

It appeared very fingular to us, that moft of the boats which we had
feen for feveral days, were rowed and fteered by women. It is not,
indeed, by any means, uncommon to fee a woman, with a child tied
by a linen bandage to her back, and another fuckling at her breaft,
while the mother herfelf is employed in handling the oar, or guiding the
helm. I have alfo continually obferved women on fhore engaged in the
moft laborious employments, with an infant faftened to their breaft.
Such unpleafing, and it may be added to the feeling mind, fuch an
affecting fpectacle, is never feen in any of thofe parts of Tartary
through which the embaffy paffed; for the women there, as well as
in the northern provinces of China, have their feet crippled from
their infancy, fo that they can never fubmit to fuch fatiguing occupations. I was permitted to take the meafure of a lady's foot, who was
twenty years of age, which meafured no more in length than five
inches and an half. Of this compreffion of the feet, it may, indeed,
be faid to be a partial practice.

Lord Macartney, and the whole fuite, went afhore, and took pof-
feffion of the refidence which the Eaft India Company's fupercargoes
had provided for the ufe of the embaffy, during its ftay at Canton.
This temporary habitation, both in refpect to accommodation and
extent, was far fuperior to any we had feen in our long journey through
this country. Nor was it among the leaft agreeable circumftances
of our prefent fituation, that we faw, once again, a domeftic arrangement which partook of the habitual comforts of our native foil.

C H A P.

C H A P. XXV.

Some account of Canton. Proceed from thence to Wampoa, and Ma-
coa; brief account of them. Circumstances relative to the residence
of the embassy at the latter place. Sail for England.

CANTON, or Quanton, is situated on the south side of the river, to
which it gives a name, and lies in about one hundred and twelve degrees
east longitude, and twenty-four degrees south latitude. It is surrounded
by a wall, near thirty feet in height, built of stone, and defended in every
direction, particularly towards the river, by very strong forts, mounted
with heavy artillery, and garrisoned with numerous troops. It is impossible, however, to form an accurate judgment of its extent, as it is
built on a plain; the surrounding country being one continued
level, except towards the south, where strangers are never permitted
to go.

The streets of the city are, in general, from fifteen to twenty feet in
breadth, and paved with broad stones. The houses seldom rise above
one story, and are built of wood and brick. The shops have their
fronts fancifully ornamented, with a balcony, that rises from the pent-
house roof over the door, and is adorned with gilding and colours.

The dress of the inhabitants does not differ from those which have
been already described. It is, however, a very remarkable circumstance,
that notwithstanding this city is so much to the southward of Pekin,
the winter should be so severe as to induce the inhabitants to wear
furs: and that such cloathing is not altogether considered as a matter of
luxury, or confined to the higher order of the people, is evident from
the

the great numbers of furrier's fhops which I faw, and, as it appeared, ftocked with large quantities of fur cloathing. It confifted of the fkins of leopards, foxes, bears, and fheep. The fkins were well dreffed, made up in the form of jackets, and are worn with the rough fide towards the fkin.

The Viceroy's palace at Canton, in form, dimenfions, and ornaments, is the counterpart of that which the Ambaffador occupied at Pekin : any defcription of it would, therefore, be fuperfluous. Of public buildings there are none, unlefs triumphal arches, and gateways, which are very numerous, may be included under that denomination.

The number of inhabitants in this city is eftimated at a million : and its large and extenfive fuburbs may, without exaggeration, be faid to contain half that number. Indeed, if the perfons are included, who navigate, and live on board, the very numerous junks and fampans, or fifhing boats, with which the Canton river is covered, my calculation will be confiderably exceeded.

This river, as it approaches the city, is equal in breadth to the Thames, in its wideft part. It abounds alfo in various kinds of fine fifh ; but the water is very unwholefome for ftrangers, till it has ftood long enough for a very confiderable fediment to fubfide : the people, however, who live in the junks, ufe it, as I am informed, for every purpofe, and without any inconvenience that I could learn.

When we were on the river that flows by Tong-tchew, an experiment was made refpecting the water, and, in a fingle gallon of it, there remained, on ftraining it, half a pint of yellow fand ; yet in this ftate the people of the country univerfally ufe it, and have no idea of purifying it by filtration. We had no opportunity of becoming acquainted with the common maladies of the people who live on the banks of that river—but water fo charged as this appears to be, muft have

L l

fome

fome prejudicial effect on the conftitutions of thofe who continually ufe it.

Though this is the only port in the empire of China, where Europeans are fuffered to trade, all commercial bufinefs is tranfacted in the fuburbs, which are about a mile from the city. They are very extenfive, and without any pretenfions to grandeur or elegance. The ftreets are, in general, very narrow, and always thronged with people. The houfes are of wood, confifting only of a ground floor and upper ftory. They all contain fhops, and are fitted up within after the Englifh manner, to which the inhabitants appear to have a decided partiality. Indeed, it was not uncommon to fee their names written on the figns, in Englifh characters, and adapted to Englifh orthography. The porcelain warehoufes which I faw here, are faid, and I believe with great truth, to exceed any fimilar repofitories in the world, for extent, grandeur, and ftock in trade. The warehoufes of the tea merchants are alfo filled with extenfive ranges of chefts, which contain an article, now become almoft a neceffary of life in our country, and of increafing ufe in every other part of Europe.

The factories of the feveral European companies, who trade to this part of the eaftern world, are formed in the ftyle of that quarter of the globe to which they belong. The buildings are conftructed of ftone and brick, on a very fubftantial plan; they fo far conform to the architectural defigns of the country, which I believe to be the beft, that they inclofe large courts, where there are apartments for the fupercargoes and writers, as well as for the captain and mates of fhips, during the time they are loading their fhips.

There is a range of thefe factories along the river, but without the leaft communication with each other; and their general diftinction is the flag, or ftandard of their refpective countries, which are feen flying during the day on fome confpicuous part of each factory.

The

The feveral nations whofe trading companies have factories here, are England, Holland, France, Sweden, Denmark, Portugal, Spain, and America. But the Englifh, both from the extent of their buildings, and the number of their fhips, appear to engrofs almoft the whole of the China trade to themfelves.

The refidence of Lord Macartney was on the oppofite fide of the river; and, as a mere place of temporary accommodation, was contrived with great judgment, and arranged with uncommon attention to the convenience of the upper order of the embaffy : the reft of the fuite occupied fome of the company's ftore-rooms, which were fitted up in a very neat and commodious manner for the occafion.

For feveral days after his Excellency's arrival at this place, he was entertained during dinner by a Chinefe play, on a ftage erected before the windows of his apartment ; and with extraordinary feats of legerdemain, which always accompany their public entertainments of this country.

The Viceroy of Canton paid the Britifh Ambaffador only one vifit during his ftay here, which was followed by large prefents of fugar-candy, porcelain and nankeen, to the whole retinue of the embaffy.

The gentlemen of the Britifh factory entertained Lord Macartney and the whole fuite with great elegance and hofpitality, on Chriftmas day, 1793, and the firft day of January 1794. They alfo made a requifition to engage the band of mufic that had accompanied the embaffy, from whofe fervice it was accordingly difcharged, and entered into that of the Englifh factory ; a very valuable acquifition in a country and fituation, where fo little exterior amufement of any kind is to be obtained.

Nor can I, in this place, where I am to take leave of Canton, avoid expreffing a regret, that the inhabitants of it are very different

in

in point of honesty, from the people of every other part of China where we had been; at least, as far as my means of observation would enable me to judge. Nor is it with less concern that I attribute this local character, which is knavish in the extreme, to their being the inhabitants of the only place where there is any communication with the natives of other countries.

On the eighth of January, 1794, Lord Macartney set off with his whole retinue, in boats, for the Lion man of war, then lying at Wampoa. At the same time, Mr. Maxwell and Mr. Barrow, with certain attendants, were ordered to proceed to Macao, to make preparations for the reception of his Excellency at that place. They went in junks by another river, which flows from Canton to Macao, and passing by that place, empties itself into the sea.

The country on each side of the river, between Canton and Wampoa, is rich, fertile, and full of variety; several lofty pagodas successively enlivened the distant parts of the progressive prospects.

Wampoa is the place where all ships come to an anchor, being universally prohibited to proceed further up the river.

It is a very beautiful and populous village, at the distance of about eighteen miles from Canton. The houses are built of a lead-coloured brick, with numbers of fine trees interspersed among them. The adjacent country is a continued level; but the opposite side of the river, which is not so wide here as at Canton, wears a different and more irregular appearance. At no great distance from this place there is a sand-bank or bar, which cannot be passed by large vessels but at high water. There are also two necks of land that project on either side of the river, which form the passage called the Bocca Tygris. Here are strong forts on each side with batteries and troops; and as the Lion passed she received a salute of three guns, from each of them.

Previous to the departure of Lord Macartney from Wampoa, he received the farewel vifit of the attendant mandarin Van-Tadge-In. Of this diftinguifhed perfonage and amiable man, it is impoffible to ufe expreffions beyond the merit he difplayed in his care of, and attention to, every perfon attached to the Britifh embaffy. He was appointed by the Emperor of China to attend and conduct it; and, from the time we landed on the fhore of the Yellow fea, to our arrival at Wampoa, he never quitted it for a moment. In all this long and various journey, he never neglected for an inftant the duties of his office, nor omitted any opportunity of executing them in a manner the moft agreeable to thofe who were entrufted to his care and direction: it was a talk of no common trouble and difficulty; but he was not feen on any occafion or at any time to fpare himfelf in performing it. He was amiable in his manners, affable in his demeanour, ready in his communication, active in his arrangements, and folicitous in the extreme not only to procure all poffible accommodations, but to fuit them, as far as the circumftances of the country would allow, to European habits and cuftoms. He was a mandarin of the firft clafs, and held a very high, if not the higheft rank, in the army of China: but neither fituation or dignity had elevated his mind above the difcharge of duties, whatever they might be, or the fuggeftions of kindnefs, to whatever objects it might be directed. Nor was this all: in the true fpirit of benevolence, he acquired a friendfhip for thofe in whofe fervice it had been fo continually employed; and his laft adieu to the Ambaffador and the fuite was accompanied with the tears of affection.

The mandarin Van-Tadge-In, we well know, is high in the confidence of his fovereign; and, from his virtues, there can be little doubt that he bears a very diftinguifhed character in the fphere of private life and public duty. But though the teftimony of refpect which is recorded on this page cannot add to his fame, it will prove, at leaft, a fincere admiration of fuperior merit, and a grateful fenfe of condefcending favour, in the writer of it.

The

1794.
January.

The Canton river is fo well known, that it would be not only fuperfluous, but impertinent in me, to add another defcription to the many which have been already given of it.

Wednef-
day 14.

Lord Macartney landed at Macao, and was received to dinner at the houfe of the Governor. In the afternoon he went to the refidence of Mr. Drummond, one of the fupercargoes of the Eaft India Company, where his Lordfhip refided during his ftay at this place. Here the gentlemen of the feveral European factories have their feparate houfes, as they are not fuffered to remain at Canton beyond the time neceffary to prepare cargoes for the fhips of their refpective nations.

Macao is fituated in 110 degrees of eaft longitude, and about 22 degrees of fouth latitude. It is a place of fome extent, and built on a rock. The houfes are of ftone, and conftructed on the plan of European architecture, but without exterior elegance : the ftreets are very narrow and irregular, as they take the unequal furface of the fpot on which they are erected. The public buildings confift of churches, convents, and the fenate-houfe, which terminate the only fpacious and level ftreet in the town. The Governor's houfe is fituated on the beach, oppofite the landing place, and commands a beautiful profpect, but is not remarkable for external elegance or interior accommodation. Contiguous to it is the Englifh factory, a plain, commodious building ; the other factories are in the fame ftyle, and all of them furrounded with gardens. The upper parts of Macao command very extenfive views of the fea and adjacent country. The harbour is very commodious, and fheltered from the winds, but will not admit fhips of large burden. The town is defended, in all directions, by ftrong forts mounted with heavy cannon, and garrifoned with Portuguefe troops. The fea runs into the harbour, through a narrow channel between the Ladrone iflands and the town, and forms a fine bay behind it, extending at leaft four miles, when it is bounded by a neck of land that feparates it from a large river. Here the Chinefe

have

have a fort that looks towards the Portuguese territory, and it is the principal duty of the garrison to prevent strangers from passing the limits of it. No one is suffered to walk on the neck of land, nor is any boat permitted to approach that side of the shore. There is a small, pretty island, in the middle of the bay, which contains the habitation of a mandarin, who frequently resides there, but seldom visits the town.

Macao is generally supposed to be situated on an island; but the fact is otherwise; nor is there any natural barrier which separates it from the Chinese territory. The whole extent of the Portuguese possessions does not exceed four miles in length, and one mile and an half in breadth: the limits of which are accurately determined, and cannot be passed without danger.

This place is divided in its jurisdiction between the Portuguese and Chinese over their respective people. The latter, however, exact very heavy duties on all goods landed, or shipped, on account of the European factories. There is a Governor, and a Judge, appointed by the court of Lisbon, who have an arbitrary power vested in them, to the extent of their jurisdiction. There is also a Portuguese custom-house and quay, on the south side of the town, where all ships coming into the bay are obliged to pay a duty. There are not more than two hundred and fifty European soldiers for the defence of the place, who are well clothed, and whose pay is very much advanced on their arrival there.

The residence of Lord Macartney was one of the most beautiful spots that the imagination can conceive. It was small, but built in the English manner, and surrounded with pleasure grounds of considerable extent, beautifully disposed and planted for prospect and for shade. The view which it commands combines a most delightful picture of river and sea, of cultivated island, and mountainous shore.

The

The Chinefe, who refide in this place, retain their own cuftoms with a rigid preference; nor has the long intercourfe they have here had with Europeans of different nations, induced them to deviate in the leaft article from the long-eftablifhed, and, as it appears, invariable ufages of their country.

Macao was originally fortified by a wall, a great part of which ftill remains, to the eaftward of the town, where it paffes between two hills, and connects itfelf with a fort, and a convent, that appear on their fummits.

Without this wall is the common burying-ground of the place, where I faw the memorials of feveral of my countrymen, whofe afhes repofe at fuch a diftance from their friends and native land. This cemetery, however, is exclufively occupied by the Chinefe, and fuch Europeans who are not of the Roman Catholic perfuafion; as the papifts have particular places of interment for thofe who depart this life in the faith of their church.

At this place Mr. Plumb quitted the fervice of the embaffy. He was very amiable and obliging in his conduct to every one engaged in the fame fervice with himfelf. He was offered a fuitable provifion, if he would return to England; but, though he appeared to part from his European friends with a fenfible regret, he very naturally preferred to return to the bofom of his family and friends, from whom he had been fo long feparated, and to pafs the remainder of his days in the country that gave him birth.

Lord Macartney remained at Macao till the eighth day of March, 1794, when his Lordfhip, and the whole retinue, embarked from the Governor's houfe. The troops were all drawn out on the beach on the occafion, with fix brafs field-pieces, from which they fired a falute of nineteen guns, which was anfwered by feveral forts.

The

The Lion received Lord Macartney with a falute of fifteen guns, and every other mark of refpect ; as did alfo the King Charles, from Spain, and the Bon Jefus, from Portugal, with three country fhips belonging to the Englifh Eaft India Company.

In the afternoon the fleet of homeward-bound Eaft Indiamen anchored off Macao roads, to proceed under convoy of the Lion to England, when they, feverally, faluted the Commodore with nineteen guns as they fucceffively came to anchor. The companions of our outwardbound voyage, the Jackall and Clarence brigs, as the embaffy was concluded, were fold; the former to Capt. Proctor, in the marine fervice of the Eaft India Company, while the latter found a purchafer at Macao.

Early this morning the fignal was made for the fleet to weigh: and at feven the Lion got under fail, in company with the following fhips :

Lord Thurlow,	Lord Walfingham,
Glatton,	Triton,
Abergavenny,	Henry Dundas,
Exeter,	Ceres,
Hindoftan,	Ofterley, and
Royal Charlotte,	The Jackall, the Company's marine brig.
Hawke,	
Warley,	

To thefe homeward-bound Englifh fhips may be added,

> The King Charles, Spaniard ;
> Bon Jefus, Portugeufe ;
> General Wafhington, American.

At eleven the fignal was made to form the order of failing, and the whole fleet ftood to fea.

M m

No

No occurrence happened, of any kind, worth relating, till three o'clock in the afternoon of this day, when the Henry Dundas made the fignal for feeing fix ftrange fail, eaft-fouth-eaft. A fail to the north-eaft proved to be the Nancy grab, of Bengal. At four, the Hindoflan and Exeter received a fignal to chafe. At five, fhewed our colours to a brig and feveral prows.

The brig was commanded by a Moorifh captain, and well armed: the prows were alfo mounted with cannon, as one of them returned, with a fingle fhot, the fire of the Englifh fhips, to bring them too. Thefe prows had upwards of fifty Malays in each veffel, and frequently do a great deal of mifchief on the coaft of Sumatra, where we now were, as well as in other parts of thefe feas.

Saw two ftrange fail, in confequence of which all the guns were fhotted, and the fhip was cleared for action. They were, however, foon difcovered to be Englifh; and inftead of the fharp returns of enemies, we interchanged the falutes of friendfhip.

We anchored at Angara Point; where we were employed in wooding and watering till Saturday the nineteenth; when the whole fleet

fet fail, and continued its courfe for England, except the Jackall brig, which now feparated from us.

Nothing occurred between Angara Point and Saint Helena, except feveral very heavy gales of wind, particularly in doubling the Cape of Good Hope.

We this day anchored at Saint Helena; his Majefty's fhips the Sampfon of fixty-four guns, Captain Montague, and the Argo, Captain Clarke, of forty-four, &c. had arrived that morning.

Lord Macartney and his retinue went on fhore, where they remained till the firft day of July, when they returned on board, and the

the fleet set sail for England, with the addition of the following ships which we found at anchor here on our arrival : (the two men of war excepted)

1794.
July.
Tuesday 1.

       The Sampson, 64 guns,
       The Argo,   44 ditto.

And the following East-Indiamen :

       General Coote,
       Fitzwilliam,
       Belvidere,
       Fort-William,
       Marquis of Lansdown, with
       The South Sea Whaler, Lucas of London.

We parted company with the General Washington, who saluted the Commodore with nine guns, which were returned in the usual manner.

Thursday 3.

This morning the Sampson fired a gun, and made the signal for a fleet. After some hours of suspense, and having made every preparation for an engagement, it proved the outward bound fleet of East-Indiamen, under convoy of his Majesty's ship Assistance, Captain Brunton ; which now parted company with his convoy, and joined our fleet.

Monday 21.

Nothing occurred during the remainder of our passage, that would justify my adding a line to this page, till the third of September, when at three A. M. we were seriously alarmed with running foul of a fleet, off Portland Roads ; which was soon discovered to be the grand fleet, under the command of Earl Howe, coming up the Channel. This strange accident was attended, however, with no other inconvenience than the damage which was received by the Royal Charlotte, Triton, and Osterley Indiamen.

September.
Wednesday 3.

M m 2

At

At five o'clock P. M. we anchored fafe, after a long and curious voyage, at Spithead; and foon felt the inexpreffible fatisfaction of once more treading the terra firma of our native country.

SUPPLE-

SUPPLEMENTARY CHAPTER.

Brief account of the passage from Hoang-tchew to Chusan, by Captain Mackintosh, &c. Various customs of the Chinese, &c. Miscellaneous articles, &c.

OF this short account of the passage of Hoang-tchew to Chusan, by Captain Mackintosh, and the gentlemen who separated from the embassy at the former place, to join the ships at the latter, I speak on the authority of others; and, therefore, give it a place among the miscellaneous matter, which I could not introduce elsewhere, without breaking the chain of narration, which the nature of the work appears to require.

The river which took this detachment of the suite to Chusan, differed very little, as I was informed, in exterior appearance from those that have been already described. A succession of mountains and rocks, and cultivated plains, formed the natural scenery of its banks, while the pagoda and the palace, the village and the city, were the artificial objects that enlivened or ennobled the prospect which the stream offered to the voyagers on it.

But this river met with interruptions that we never experienced in those on which we passed; and its course was occasionally broken by cataracts of a deep fall and formidable appearance. Such circumstances would necessarily impede the navigation of the rivers where they present themselves, if the unparalleled industry, perseverance, and, I may surely add, the ingenuity of the Chinese, had not surmounted this obstacle; and in a manner, which it requires some confidence in those who informed me of it, to relate.

To

To accelerate the paſſage of veſſels at thoſe places where the difference of levels forbids any further progreſs on the ſurface of the water, the powers of mechaniſm are applied to let the veſſel down into a lower ſtream, or lift it up into an higher one, in the following manner. In the firſt place, two ſtrong ſtentions are fixed in the center of the river, from which two large beams are made to project in a ſtate of ſuſpenſion over the other water : to theſe, ſtrong blocks are attached, with ropes of ſufficient ſtrength; ſo that when a junk arrives at the place, ſhe is well ſecured afore and aft, to preſerve an equilibrium; when the perſons, who are always ſtationed at theſe places for the purpoſe, and are accuſtomed to the buſineſs, hoiſt the junk, with its paſſengers and contents, from one river into the other, over every intermediate obſtruction. So certain is this extraordinary operation, that it occupies but a few minutes in its execution, and is not conſidered by thoſe who navigate theſe rivers as attended with greater danger, or more liable to accident, than many other frequent contingencies which are inſeparable from the voyages on them.

Captain Mackintoſh and his party were treated by the mandarins, of the different cities and towns through which they paſſed, with a degree of attention and hoſpitality equal to that which the embaſſy itſelf received. They were ten days in their paſſage from Hoang-tchew to Chuſan.

I ſhall now proceed to give ſome detached accounts of the manners and cuſtoms of the Chineſe, as they came beneath my obſervation.

To give an accurate deſcription of the marriage ceremony in China, is to do little more than to reply to the Abbé Groſier, whoſe account of the Chineſe nuptials, as well as of many other of their cuſtoms, is, altogether, erroneous. The Abbé ſays, " On the day appointed for the ceremony, the bride is firſt placed in an encloſed chair, or palanquin, when all the articles that compoſe

her

her portion are borne before and behind her by different perfons of both fexes, while others furround her, carrying flambeaux, even in the middle of the day." The marriage ceremony, which I faw at Macao, had little in common with this defcription, but the palanquin. The bride, feated in that machine, was preceded by mufic, and enfigns of various colours were borne by men both before and in the rear of the proceffion, which confifted principally of the relatives of the bride and bridegroom, who efcort her to the houfe of her hufband, where a feaft is prepared, and the day is paffed in mirth and feftivity. Nor is the evening concluded with thofe abfurd ceremonies, with which the Abbé Grofier, and other authors, have ridiculoufly encumbered the confummation of a Chinefe wedding.

The idea which he and others have propagated of the rigid confinement of the Chinefe women, is equally void of truth. In different parts of that extenfive country, different cuftoms may prevail; and the power of hufbands over their wives may be fuch as to render them mafters of their liberty, which they may exercife, with feverity, if circumftances fhould, at any time, fuggeft the neceffity of fuch a meafure, or caprice fancy it : but I do not hefitate to affert, that women, in general, have a reafonable liberty in China; and that there is the fame communication and focial intercourfe with women, which, in Europe, is confidered as a principal charm of focial life.

The Abbé has alfo afferted, with equal ignorance of the country, whofe hiftorian he pretends to be, that mafters are defirous of promoting marriage among their flaves, in order to increafe the number of them, as the children are born to inherit the lot of their parents. This is a mere fable, as there are no fuch clafs of people as flaves in the Chinefe empire. They cannot import flaves in their own veffels, which are never employed but in their domeftic commerce; and he muft be afflicted with the moft credulous ignorance, who believes that they import them in foreign bottoms. If, therefore, there are any flaves in

China,

China, they muſt be natives of the country; and among them, it is well known, that there is no claſs of people who are in that degrading ſituation.

Certain claſſes of criminals are puniſhed with ſervitude for a ſtated period, or for life, according to the nature of their offences; and they are employed in the more laborious parts of public works. But if this is ſlavery, the unhappy convicts, who heave ballaſt on the Thames, are ſlaves. There is a cuſtom, indeed, in China, reſpecting this claſs of criminals, that does not prevail in England, which is, their being hired for any ſervice they are capable of performing: and this frequently happens, as theſe convicts may be had at a cheaper rate than ordinary labourers. This regulation, however, has one good effect, that it exonerates government from the expenſe of maintaining ſuch unhappy perſons without leſſening the rigor or diſgrace of the puniſhment. But I re-aſſert that ſlavery by which I mean the power which one man obtains over another, by purchaſe, or inheritance, as in our Weſt India iſlands, is not known in China. Indeed, ſome of the Chineſe in the interior parts of the country, were, with difficulty, made to comprehend the nature of ſuch a character as a ſlave; and when I illuſtrated the matter, by explaining the ſituation of a negro boy, called Benjamin, whom Sir George Staunton had purchaſed at Batavia, they expreſſed the ſtrongeſt marks of diſguſt and abhorrence. This converſation took place at Jehol, in Tartary. But at Canton, where the communication with Europeans gives the merchants a knowledge of what is paſſing in our quarter of the globe, poor Benjamin was the cauſe of ſome obſervations on his condition, that aſtoniſhed me when I heard, and will, I believe, ſurpriſe the reader when he peruſes them. The boy being in a ſhop with me in the ſuburbs of Canton, ſome people who had never before ſeen a black, were very curious in making inquiries concerning him; when the merchant, to whom the warehouſe belonged, expreſſed his ſurpriſe, in broken Engliſh, that the Britiſh nation ſhould ſuffer a traffic ſo diſgraceful to that humanity which they were ſo ready to profeſs: and on my in-

forming

forming him that our parliament intended to abolish it, he furprifed me with the following extraordinary anfwer, which I give in his own words:—" Aye, aye, black man, in Englifh country, have got one " firft chop, good mandarin Willforce, that have done much good " for allau blackie man, much long time: allau man makie chin, " chin, hee, becaufe he have got more firft chop tink, than " much Englifh merchant-men; becaufe he merchant-man tinkee " for catch money, no tinkee for poor blackie man: Jofh, no " like fo fafhion." The meaning of thefe expreffions is as follows : " Aye, in England, the black men have got an advocate and friend, " (Mr. Wilberforce) who has, for a confiderable time, been doing " them fervice; and all good people, as well as the blacks, adore the cha- " racter of a gentleman, whofe thoughts have been directed to meliorate " the condition of thofe men; and not like our Weft India planters, " or merchants, who, for the love of gain, would prolong the mifery " of fo large a portion of his fellow-creatures as the African flaves. " But God cannot approve of fuch a practice."

That fome general knowledge of the politics of Europe may be obtained by the mandarins and merchants in the port of Canton, might be naturally expected, from their continual communication with the natives of almoft every European country; and as many of them underftand the European languages, they may, perhaps, fometimes read the Gazettes that are publifhed in our quarter of the globe. But that the queftion of the flave trade, as agitated in the Britifh Parlia- ment, fhould be known in the fuburbs of Canton, may furprife fome of my readers as it aftonifhed me. Nor will it be unpleafing to Mr. Wilberforce to be informed, that, for the active zeal which he difplayed in behalf of the nations of Africa, in the fenate of the firft city of Europe, he fhould receive the eulogium of a Chinefe mer- chant beneath the walls of an Afiatic city.

There are frequent feftivals in China, and we faw at Macao, the principal of them which celebrates the beginning of the New-Year.

N n

According

According to the Chinese calendar, it commences on the second day of
our month of February, and is obferved with great joy and gladnefs
throughout the whole empire, and by an entire fufpenfion of all bufinefs. Of any religious ceremonies that ufher in the dawn of the year, I
cannot fpeak, as all the diftinctions of the feafon which appeared to us,
confifted of feafting by day, and fireworks by night. This feftival is
prolonged, by thofe who can afford it, for feveral days: and they,
whofe circumftances confine their joy to one day, take fo much of it,
that they generally feel its effects on the next.

Of the manner in which they keep or obferve their ordinary holidays,
I fhall give the following account :

In the firft place they purchafe provifions according to their fituation
and capacity, which are dreffed, and placed before a fmall idol, fixed
on an altar, with a curtain before it: and fuch an altar, in fome
form or other, every Chinefe has in his habitation, whether it be
on the land, or on the water, in an houfe, or a junk. This repaft, with
bread and fruit, and three fmall cups of wine, fpirits, and vinegar, are,
after a threefold obeifance from the people of the houfe to the idol,
carried to the front of their dwelling : they there kneel and pray, with
great fervour, for feveral minutes ; and, after frequently beating their
heads on the ground, they rife, and throw the contents of the three cups
to the right and left of them. They then take a bundle of fmall pieces
of gilt paper, which they fet on fire, and hold over the meat. That
is fucceeded by ftrings of fmall crackers, hanging to the end of a cane,
which are lighted and made to crack over the meat. The repaft
is then placed before the idol, or Jofh, as it is called, (a term which
means a deity) and after a repetition of obeifances, they conclude
with a joyous dinner, exhilarated by plenty of fpirits, which are
always boiled in fmall pewter or copper veffels before they are taken.

On the firft of March it is ufual, according to ancient cuftom, for
dramatic pieces to be performed on ftages in the principal ftreet of
3   the

the different towns throughout the empire, for the amufement of the
poor people, who are not able to purchafe thofe pleafures. This beneficent act continues for a fucceffion of feveral days, at the expenfe of
the Emperor; fo that every morning and evening, during this period,
the lower claffes of his fubjects enjoy a favourite pleafure without
coft, and blefs the hand that beftows it on them.

Of the knowledge of medicine among the Chinefe I can fay no
more, than that I was witnefs, in one inftance, to a fkilful application
of it, in the cafe of John Stewart, a fervant of Capt. Mackintofh,
who, on our return from Jehol, had been feized with the dyfentery,
which increafed fo much on the road, that at Waunchoyeng, there
were no hopes entertained of his being able to leave that place.
Whether it arofe from the defire of the patient, or was fuggefted by
any perfon in the fuite, I know not, but a Chinefe phyfician was
called to his affiftance; when the man's cafe was explained to
him by Mr. Plumb, in the prefence of Sir George Staunton.
The phyfician remained a confiderable time with his patient, and
fent him a medicine, which removed the complaint, and reftored
him to health.

The people are, in general, of an healthy appearance: it is very
rare, indeed, to fee perfons marked with the fmall-pox; and, except
in the fea-ports of Macao and Canton, feveral of the diforders unfortunately fo frequent in Europe, are not known in China.

The caxee is the only current coin in China: any other fpecies of money is abfolutely forbidden, and is made of a white
metal of about the fize of our farthing, with a fmall fquare hole
driven through the middle, for the purpofe of running them on
a ftring to be compofed into candereens and maces: but although
the terms candereen and mace are employed to certify a certain
quantity of caxees, there are no coins in the country which bear

that

that fpecific value ; fo that, in fact, they are only imaginary denomi-
nations, like our pounds, &c.

The comparative eftimation of the caxee with Britifh money cannot
be afcertained with any degree of accuracy, as it bears no fterling value
even in that country; every province having its particular caxee,
which is not current in any other. In the province of Pekin a
Spanifh dollar will produce, in exchange, from five hundred to
five hundred and eighty caxees, according to the weight of the dollar,
which the Chinefe prove by a fmall fteel-yard like ours in England; though they fometimes employ fcales. In the province of
Hoang-tchew the dollar obtains from feven hundred to feven hundred and fifty caxees; in other places it will find a ftill more various
exchange.

I cannot conclude this volume without paying a tribute of refpectful veneration to the great and illuftrious, the wife and beneficent
Sovereign of China ; who, in a long reign of near fixty years, has,
by the general voice of his people, never ceafed to watch over and
increafe their happinefs and profperity. Of the manner in which he
adminifters juftice, and gives protection to the meaneft of his fubjects,
the following anecdote, which I heard frequently in the country, is
an affecting example :

A merchant of the city of Nankin had, with equal induftry and
integrity, acquired a confiderable fortune, which awakened the rapa-
cious fpirit of the vice-roy of that province : on the pretence, therefore, of its being too rapidly accumulated, he gave fome intimations
of his defign to make a feifure of it. The merchant, who had a numerous family, hoped to baffle the oppreffive avarice that menaced
him, by dividing his poffeffions among his children, and depending
upon them for fupport.

I

But

But the fpirit of injuftice, when ftrengthened by power, is not eafily thwarted in its defigns; the vice-roy, therefore, fent the children to the army, feized on their property, and left the father to beg his bread. His tears and humble petitions were fruitlefs; the tyrannical officer, this vile vicegerent of a beneficent fovereign, difdained to beftow the fmalleft relief on the man he had reduced to ruin; fo that, exafperated by the oppreffion of the minifter, the merchant, at length, determined to throw himfelf at the feet of the fovereign, to obtain redrefs, or die in his prefence.

With this defign he begged his way to Pekin; and, having furmounted all the difficulties of a long and painful journey, he at length arrived at the Imperial refidence; and, having prepared a petition that contained a faithful ftatement of his injuries, he waited with patience in an outer court till the Emperor fhould pafs to attend the council. But the poverty of his appearance had almoft fruftrated his hopes; and the attendant mandarins were about to chaftife his intrufion, when the attention of the Emperor was attracted by the buftle which the poor man's refiftance occafioned: at this moment he held forth a paper, which his Imperial Majefty ordered to be brought to his palanquin; and, having perufed its contents, commanded the petitioner to follow him.

It fo happened, that the vice-roy of Nankin was attending his annual duty in the council: the Emperor, therefore, charged him with the crime ftated in the poor man's petition, and commanded him to make his defence: but, confcious of his guilt, and amazed at the unexpected difcovery, his agitations, his looks, and his filence, condemned him. The Emperor then addreffed the affembled council on the fubject of the vice-roy's crime, and concluded his harangue with ordering the head of his tyrannical officer to be inftantly brought him on the point of a fabre. The command was obeyed; and while the poor old man was wondering on his knees at the extraordinary event of the

moment,

moment, the Emperor addreſſed him in the following manner: Look, ſaid he, on the awful and bleeding example before you, and as I now appoint you his ſucceſſor, and name you vice-roy of the province of Nankin, let his fate inſtruct you to fulfil the duties of your high and important office with juſtice and moderation.

A P P E N D I X:

CONTAINING AN

ACCOUNT OF THE TRANSACTIONS

OF THE

S Q U A D R O N

DURING THE ABSENCE OF THE

E M B A S S Y,

Till their Return on Board his Majesty's Ship the Lion, at Wampoa.

A P P E N D I X.

Remarks on Board his Majesty's Ship the Lion, in the Yellow Sea.

MODERATE and cloudy. A. M. killed a bullock, weight 341lbs. got all the baggage into the junks, with foldiers, mechanics, fervants, botanifts, &c. At half-paft eight the Ambaffador went on board the brigantine Clarence, manned the fhip, and faluted him with 19 guns, and three cheers, as did the Hindoftan.

Ditto weather. Adam Bradfhaw, a light dragoon, departed this life, and his body committed to the deep. A. M. wafhed the lower and orlop decks, fumigated the fhip with devils, wafhed the fides and beams with vinegar.

Light breezes and cloudy. People employed occafionally. A. M. killed a bullock, weight 282lbs. fail-makers repairing main-top-fail.

Ditto weather. At 9 P. M. the Clarence anchored, and brought the Jackall's men on board. At half-paft four weighed and made fail, founded in 7 and 9 fathoms water. At noon killed a bullock, weight 301lbs. Hindoftan and Clarence in company.

Moderate and cloudy. P. M. ferved tobacco, founded from 15 to 17 fathoms water, obferved feveral fmall meteors in the air. At 6 A. M. faw a junk fteering S. E. killed a bullock, weight 323lbs. faw the land bearing fouth-caft.

Light breezes and clear. P. M. at fun fet, extremes of Meatow iflands from S. E. to E. by N. 5 or 6 leagues diftant. A. M. killed 2 bullocks, weighed 400lbs. At 8 the high land of Tangangfoe N. E. by E. 3 or 4 leagues. At noon came to with the coafting anchor in 10 fathoms water—foft mud.

O o

Moderate

Marginal dates:

1793.
August.
Monday 5.

Tuefday 6.

Wednefday 7.

Thurfday 8.

Friday 9.

Saturday 10.
At anchor off the high land of Tangang-foe.

1793.
Auguft.
Sunday 11.

Moderate and hazy. At half-paft noon the Hindoftan came to. At 6 weighed: at 9 made the anchoring fignal with a gun, and came to with the coafting anchor in 9 fathoms water, Meatow iflands from N. E. by E. to eaft: killed a bullock, weight 290lbs. At 5 A. M. weighed and made fail. At 7 fhoaled our water from 9 to ½ 7. ¼ 7. and ¼ 4 fathoms water. At 8 came to in 7 fathoms water, Meatow ifland from N. by W. to E. by N. At half-paft 9 weighed.

Monday 12.

Light airs and fqually. At half-paft 3 P. M. came to with the coafting anchor in 21 fathoms water, Tangangfoe town, S. by W. ¼ W. killed a bullock, weight 287lbs. A. M. received a prefent of provifions and vegetables. Sailed the Clarence.

Tuefday 13.
Off the high land of Tangangfoe.

Light breezes and cloudy. P. M. received feveral hogs, fheep, &c. At 7 weighed founded from 21 to 16 fathoms water, tacked occafionally, wafhed the lower and orlop decks, and the fick birth with vinegar. At noon the Hindoftan in company.

Wednefday 14.
Cape Cheatow.
S. E. by E.
37° 40′ N.

Light airs, inclinable to calm. P. M. 5 made fail. At 7 fhortened fail and came to in 11 fathoms water with the coafting anchor, eaftermoft of Meatow iflands. North, a low rocky point S. S. E. 3 or 4 miles. At 7 weighed and made fail. At noon the Clarence joined us.

Thurfday 15.

Light breezes and cloudy. P. M. tacked occafionally. At half-paft 6 fhortened fail and came to with the coafting anchor in 9 fathoms water, cape Cheatow E. by S. Departed this life Philip Payne, feaman. At 5 A. M. committed his body to the deep, weighed and tacked occafionally.

Friday 16.
Coon Coon Ifland.
37° 33′ N.

Moderate and cloudy. P. M. at 2 came to with the coafting anchor in 7 fathoms water, cape Cheatow N. ¼ E. A. M. at 7 the Clarence weighed and made fail to found. At 9 we weighed, foundings from ¼ 4 to ½ 5 fathoms water, cape Cheatow N. by W. Employed occafionally.

Saturday 17.

Light airs. P. M. tacked occafionally. At half-paft 6 the weftermoft point of the land E. N. E.—the eaftermoft of Coon Coon Sheen iflands N. W. by N. tacked every 2 hours. A. M. hove to and
hoifted

hoisted in the launch, killed a bullock, weight 289lbs. Hindostan and Clarence in company.

Light airs. At 4 P. M. in 1st reef top-sails extremes of the land to the easterward S. E. by E.   A. M. sounded from 13 to 16 fathoms water. At 7 tacked, sounded in 16 fathoms water. Hindostan and Clarence in company.

Light breezes and cloudy. P. M. sent the yawl to sound to what appeared to us shoal, but proved to be the reflections of the clouds. At 6 extremes of the land from S. E. by E. to W. by S. distant 3 leagues, tacked occasionally, and sounded in 30 fathoms water. A. M. killed a bullock, weight 280lbs. washed lower and orlop decks. Hindostan and Clarence in company.

Ditto weather, with a south-east swell. P. M. at 3 squally. At 5 light airs, saw the land from S. by W. to S. W. by W. 6 or 7 leagues. At midnight calm. At 4 A. M. light airs, with a S. E. swell. At 6 cape Chanton, S. S. W. 19 fathoms water. Employed occasionally.

Light airs, with a south-east swell. P. M. at three squally. At 4 cape Chanton N. W. ¼ N. sounded in 16 fathoms water. At midnight clear. A. M. employed occasionally.

Moderate and clear. P. M. saw a whale, and at half-past 9 an eclipse of the moon, which continued to half-past 12, never being more than two-thirds eclipsed, by which we calculated our longitude to be 122 deg. 41 min. east of Greenwich. *

Light breezes and clear. P. M. at 2 sounded in 22 fathoms water. At midnight sounded in 20 fathoms water. At 4 A. M. sounded in 19 fathoms water. At 6 made sail, and at 8 sounded in 20 fathoms water.

---

* It appears evident from this observation, that those historians who have treated of China were very imperfect in their geographical estimates; as Pekin, which is considerably to the east-ward of that coast where the observation was taken, is only stated at 116 degrees of east longitude; so that the difference is almost 7 degrees; a cogent proof of their ignorance relative to the interior history of this empire.

          Light

1793. Auguſt. Saturday 24.	Light breezes and clear. Tried the current and found it ſet N. ¼ E. 2 miles; at 8 cloudy, at midnight no bottom, at 3 A. M. made ſail, waſhed the lower and orlop decks, Hindoſtan and Clarence in company.
Sunday 25.	Moderate and clear. P. M. Made ſail; at midnight departed this life Robert Chambers, cooper, at 2 A. M. committed the body to the deep. At 6 ſaw the land bearing from S. by E. to S. S. W. at 7 ſqually, at 9 Clarence iſland 6 or 7 miles bearing S. by E. at noon ſounded in 20 fathoms.
Monday 26. Whelps S. S. W. Buffaloe's Noſe N. W.	Moderate and cloudy. At 5 P. M. extremes of Jackall's iſland from weſt to W. N. W. At 6 departed this life Wm. Bell, ſeaman; at 9 committed the body to the deep. Lion iſland W. Blunt Peak iſland W. by S. in 7 fathoms water.
Tueſday 27. Off Tree-a- top iſland.	Freſh breezes with rain. At 1 P. M. came to with the coaſting anchor in 5½ fathoms. Buffaloe's Noſe S. S. E. Truman's iſland S. ½ E. At 5 out launch, at 6 the cutter with Mr. Whitman went on an embaſſy to Chuſan. A. M. Frequent guſts of wind.
Wedneſ- day 28.	Freſh breezes and ſqually, with rain. People employed occaſionally.
Thurſday 29.	Squally, with rain. Departed this life Mr. Wm. Cox, 4th Lieutenant, ſent the body on ſhore to be buried. A. M. Arrived the Clarence.
Friday 30. At anchor off Kitto's point.	Ditto weather. At 2 P. M. weighed, turning through Goff's Paſſage; at 7 anchored in 11 fathoms, Kitto N. E. ¼ N. At 5 A. M. weighed, at half paſt 7 anchored in 10 fathoms, Kitto Point N. ¼ E. Read Mr. Omanny's commiſſion as 4th Lieutenant, and Mr. Warren's as acting to the ſhip's company.
Saturday 31.	Ditto weather. Employed occaſionally; ſent the cutter to found, and waſhed the decks.
September. Sunday 1.	Moderate and cloudy. A. M. Half-paſt 4 weighed, working into Chuſan harbour, at 11 came to with the coaſting anchor in 9 fathoms; carried out a kedge with 4 hawſers to warp the ſhip into the anchoring place; at half-paſt 11 weighed. Employed warping.

Freſh

Fresh breezes and squally, with rain at times. Employed warping
to the kedge; at 2 came to with the best bower in 6 fathoms,
moored ship a cable each way, best bower to the N. N. E. small
bower S. S. W. center of the hill at the east end of Chusan town
N. E. by E. ¾ mile. A. M. Light breezes and fair; loosed sails
to dry. Employed rounding the small bower cable.

Light breezes and cloudy. P. M. Sent down royal masts and rigging: unbent the sails, and unrove the running rigging. A. M. Sent
down top-gallant masts. Received water.

Light breezes and fair. Employed overhauling the rigging; at 6
A. M. sent the sick on shore; struck yards and top-masts, shipped
fore and main top-masts.

Light breezes and cloudy. Employed over-hauling the top-mast
rigging; received a bullock on board.

Ditto weather, with lightning in the S. W. People fitting the rigging afresh. A. M. Launch watering, killed a bullock 201 lbs.
Departed this life Richard Welsh, seaman; committed his body
to the deep.

Moderate and cloudy. Employed about the top-mast rigging; received 2 bullocks and 105 pumpkins. A. M. Employed as before; killed a bullock 204lbs. washed lower and orlop decks.

Moderate and fair. Employed about the rigging; killed a bullock
236lbs. A. M. Yawl watering; received a bullock and 4 goats.
Punished John Francis, seaman, with 12 lashes, for theft.

Light breezes and cloudy. A. M. Received water per launch; rig-
ged the top-mast, killed a bullock and 4 goats, 291lbs. received
water per launch and 2 bullocks.

Moderate and cloudy, with heavy rain. A. M. Light winds and
fair. People about the rigging and blacking the yards, caulking
over the side, launch watering; killed 2 bullocks 393lbs.

Light airs and cloudy. Employed overhauling the rigging. A. M.
Roused up the best bower cable and stowed staves under it. Departed this life Stephen Pounce, seaman; interred the body.

Moderate and cloudy, with heavy rain. Employed as necessary.
A. M. Launch and yawls watering.

Moderate

1793.
September.
Friday 13.

Moderate breezes with rain. Employed as before, launch and yawls watering. A. M. Employed clearing the after-hold and rattling the top-maft rigging. Saluted a mandarin with 3 guns.

Saturday 14. Ditto weather. P. M. Employed in the after-hold; saluted a mandarin with 3 guns, and a superior one with 7. A. M. Punished Henry Morris, seaman, with 12 lashes, for drunkenness.

Sunday 15. Light breezes and cloudy. Arrived the Endeavour brig. A. M. The Endeavour saluted with 7 guns, returned 5; received water, employed starting it; swayed up the lower yards, fidded top-gallant and royal masts, rattled the lower rigging, received bread from the Hindostan.

Monday 16. Moderate breezes. Employed watering.

Tuesday 17. Light winds and cloudy. P. M. Received bread from the Hindostan. A. M. Sent the launch to the Jackall's assistance, she being on shore without the harbour. Employed shifting the coals and rattling the rigging. Fired 21 lower-deck guns being the Emperor of China's birth-day; killed a bullock and 4 goats.

Wednesday 18. Moderate and cloudy. Launch assisting the Jackall; at midnight fresh breezes and squally, with violent peals of thunder and fierce flashes of lightning; struck the royal masts, secured the pumps and magazines. A. M. Yawls watering.

Thursday 19. Ditto weather. Yawls watering; got royal masts upon deck, struck yards, top-masts and top-gallant masts. A. M. People employed occasionally, received from the Hindostan beef and pork.

Friday 20. Light breezes and clear. Employed in the after-hold; caulkers on the larboard side; received on board beef from the Hindostan, and water per launch.

Saturday 21. Ditto weather. Employed stowing the after-hold; launch and yawls watering, received from the Hindostan beef and pork. A. M. Received from ditto beef, oatmeal, and flour; cooper repairing the heads of the casks. Scraped the larboard side.

Sunday 22. Light breezes and cloudy. Employed stowing away provisions, coopers as before. A. M. Cleared hause, launch watering.

4

Light

1793.
September.

Monday 23. Light breezes and cloudy. Caulkers as before. A. M. Punished Jeremiah Harrington, seaman, with 12 lashes for insolence. Coopers and caulkers as before; launch and yawls watering. Received bread from the Hindostan.

Tuesday 24. Ditto weather. Caulkers on the larboard side; received peas from the Hindostan; received water. Painters about the stern. A M. Received pork, beef, oatmeal, and flour, from the Hindostan.

Wednesday 25. Fresh gales and squally. People and painters as before. A. M. Employed scraping the sides; received 4 bullocks, killed 2, weight 426lbs.

Thursday 26. Ditto weather. People and painters as before. A. M. Received rum from the Hindostan; received water on board.

Friday 27. Moderate and fair. Received beef and pork from the Hindostan, painters about the sides, caulkers and sail-makers employed, people in the hold, received a bullock, killed 2, weight 432lbs. A. M. Received from the Hindostan beef, pork, suet, and vinegar. Launch and yawls watering.

Saturday 28. Ditto weather. Painters as before; sail makers repairing the Clarence's sails; received pease, oatmeal, and flour from the Hindostan. A. M. Received vinegar, beef, and pork from the Hindostan, and water per yawls.

Sunday 29. Fresh breezes and cloudy. P. M. Completed the holds; received 3 bullocks, killed 2, weight 371lbs. received from the Hindostan beef, pork, suet, and vinegar. A. M. Yawls watering.

Monday 30. Ditto weather. Gunners painting the guns. A. M. Carpenters repairing the launch on shore, people pointing the ends of the cables, received bread from the Hindostan, served vinegar to the people.

October.

Tuesday 1. Moderate and fair. Gunners as before, carpenters repairing the launch; killed 2 bullocks, 311 lbs. set up the fore and main rigging. A. M. Sail-makers as before.

Wednesday 2. Moderate and cloudy, with rain. Received 8 bullocks, 16 goats, and 700 bundles of wood, saluted a mandarin with 7 guns, received

wood

1793. October.	wood from the Hindostan. A. M. Coopers shaking empty casks ; yawls watering ; killed 2 bullocks, 367lbs.
Thursday 3.	Ditto weather. Carpenters repairing the launch ; killed 2 bullocks 305lbs. coopers as before. A. M. Received 2 bullocks, scraped lower gun-deck, yawls watering.
Friday 4.	Fresh breezes and cloudy. Carpenters lining the lower deck ports and repairing the launch, cleared hause, received water, killed 2 bullocks weight 307lbs.
Saturday 5.	Weather as before. Employed working up junk, carpenters as before, caulkers caulking the launch's bottom. A. M. Rain. Employed working up junk ; killed 2 bullocks, 300lbs. received water per yawls.
Sunday 6.	Ditto weather. Carpenters, caulkers, and sail-makers as before ; received water per yawls, killed a bullock, 241lbs. A. M. Received on board a bullock ; cleared hause.
Monday 7.	Moderate and fair. Caulkers on lower-gun deck ; received 4 bullocks. A. M. received water per yawls ; washed and smoked lower gun-deck, carpenters repairing the launch, sail-makers repairing the foresail, caulkers on board the Clarence, killed 2 bullocks, 431lbs.
Tuesday 8.	Ditto weather. Caulkers and sail-makers as before ; received 2 bullocks, killed 1, weight 273lbs. A. M. Employed watering, surveyed the gunner's stores, the sick returned on board.
Wednesday 9.	Light breezes and fair. Carpenters lining lower deck ports. A. M. Swayed up top-masts, lower yards, and top-gallant masts. Sail-makers as before ; killed a bullock, 228lbs.
Thursday 10.	Weather as before. Employed setting up the top-mast rigging, coopers repairing banacoes, received water per yawls. A. M. Cleared hause ; killed 2 bullocks, 240lbs.
Friday 11.	Ditto weather. P. M. Sent a party to bring off the launch. A. M. Rove the running rigging and bent the sails ; sail-makers making hammocks, received wood, killed a bullock 215lbs. yawls watering.

Moderate

1763.
October.

Saturday 12. Moderate and fair. P. M. Received 2 bullocks and 4 goats; killed 2 bullocks, 479lbs. The grand mandarin paid us a visit; saluted him with 7 guns on his coming on board and leaving the ship: manned ship at his passing. A. M. Employed getting ready for sea.

Sunday 13. Ditto weather. Received 4 bullocks and 8 goats. A. M. unmoored ship; employed watering; at 11 weighed the small bower, and shifted 2 cables length further down, and came to in 6 fathoms: received 2 bullocks, and killed one of them, weight 228lbs. Sailed the Endeavour and Jackall.

Monday 14. Light breezes and cloudy. Received wood and 2 bullocks, killed 1, weight 293lbs. sail-makers as before: departed this life Thomas Addison, seaman; interred the body.

Tuesday 15. Moderate and cloudy. Caulkers on the main deck. A. M. killed a bullock, weight 234lbs.

Wednesday 16. Light breezes and fair. Sent 10 invalids on board the Hindostan. A. M. Punished Thomas Lock, seaman, with 12 lashes, for riotous behaviour.

Thursday 17. Moderate and clear. Saluted a mandarin with 7 guns, returned the Hindostan's salute with 9; at 5 weighed, found the anchor stock gone; half-past 5 came to with the coasting anchor in 19 fathoms, Deer Island N. by W. A. M. Half-past 9 weighed, turning towards Kitto point; carpenters employed making an anchor stock.

Friday 18. Moderate and clear. P. M. At 3 running through Goff's Passage; at 4 saluted a mandarin with 4 guns on his leaving the ship; half-past 5 came to with the coasting anchor in 7 fathoms, Buffaloe's Nose S. W. by W. hoisted in the launch, killed 2 bullocks 462lbs. A. M. At half-past 6 weighed and made sail, Clarence in company; at noon Patchacock island N. W. ¼ N. 7 or 8 miles.

Saturday 19. Fresh breezes and cloudy. Half-past noon extremes of Hesan islands from S. W. by W. to S. W. by S. at 6 in 2d reefs, at 10 in 3d reefs; at noon the Clarence in company.

P p

Fresh

1793. October. Sunday 20.	Fresh breezes and cloudy. P. M. At 2 out 3d and 2d reefs; strong breezes, at 9 in 3d reefs. A. M. Killed a bullock, 224lbs. at 9 lowered the top-sails to keep the Clarence a-head; sail-makers making a covering for the pinnace: at noon Clarence in company.
Monday 21.	Fresh breezes. P. M. At 2 hoisted the top-sails, at 6 spoke the Clarence, at 5 A. M. out 3d reefs, at 10 saw 6 junks, at noon several junks in sight; carpenters stocking the best bower anchor, Clarence in company.
Tuesday 22.	Fresh breezes and cloudy. P. M. At 5 out 2d reefs. A. M. At 6 saw Pedro Blanco N. by E. ¼ E. at noon the west end of the great Lama N. by W. east end N. E. by N. armourers at the forge.
Wednesday 23. At anchor off Macao, among the Ladrones.	Ditto weather. P. M. At 4 the body of the island of Tarlow Chow N. N. W. shortened sail, and came to with the coasting anchor in 6¼; sent the Clarence to Macao. A. M. At 9 weighed and made sail; at noon came to with the coasting anchor in 8 fathoms, Tarlow Chow N. by E. ¼ E. Macao town W. N. W. 7 or 8 miles.
Thursday 24.	Ditto weather. Yawls watering. A. M. Gunners stretching breeching stuff, coopers repairing banacoes.
Friday 25.	Ditto weather. Yawls watering. A. M. Squally; coopers as before.
Saturday 26.	Fresh breezes and cloudy. Yawls watering, sail-makers making coats for the masts. A. M. Yawls as before, shewed our colours to a ship in the offing, cleared the boatswain's store-room.
Sunday 27.	Fresh breezes and fair. Yawls watering. A. M. Employed occasionally.
Monday 28.	Light breezes and pleasant weather. P. M. The Clarence anchored close to us; passed us the Washington, American ship. A. M. Sail-makers covering man-ropes, and other jobs.
Tuesday 29.	Ditto weather. Yawls watering; at 8 sailed the Clarence for Macao. A. M. At 6 weighed, found the stock of the coasting anchor gone, made sail, half-past 9 shortened sail and came to with the best bower in 10 fathoms, Tarlow Chow N. W. by W. ¼ W. Sam Coke N. W.

1793.
October.

N. W. ½ N. carpenters fitting a new anchor stock, a swell, E. S. E. At noon weighed and made sail, sail-makers as before.

Wednesday 30.
Off Macao, among the Ladrones.

Light breezes and pleasant weather. Half-past 12 found the fore-top-mast, sprung down top-gallant-yard and mast upon deck, shortened sail. At 4 came to with the best bower in 10 fathoms water, Tarlow Chow E. N. E. down fore-top-mast, sent the pinnace and yawl on service, carpenters fishing the fore-top-mast, and cutting another fid hole, washed lower gun-deck.

Thursday 31.

Fresh breezes and foggy. Carpenters as before, swayed the fore-top-mast and end, and flatted the top-mast rigging. A. M. Fidded the top-mast, and set up the rigging, carpenters making a coasting anchor stock, the boats returned on board, anchored a schooner with hands for us.

November.
Friday 1.

Ditto weather. Swayed up the fore-yard. A. M. Swayed up top-gallant-masts, carpenters as before, sail-makers repairing the main-sail.

Saturday 2.

Moderate and fair. P. M. At 4 arrived a ship from the N. N. E. which shewed French colours, sent the boats after her, cut the best bower cable, and made sail, fired a shot to bring her to. At 6 she run into the Typer, hauled our wind to port, tacked occasionally: at half-past 7 came to with the coasting anchor in 5 fathoms water, Macao town W. by N. 3 miles, Tarlow Chow S. E. 7 or 8 miles: at 9 the boats returned. A. M. At 5 sent an officer to Macao. Departed this life Stephen Smart, quarter-master: at 8 committed the body to the deep: half-past 9 weighed and made sail, turning towards the buoy of the best bower, coopers packing empty staves.

Sunday 3.

Moderate and fair. P. M. At half-past noon shortened sail and came to with the coasting anchor in our old birth ; employed creeping for the end of the best bower cable, and getting it entered hove short on it. A. M. hove up the best bower. Half-past 8 weighed the coasting anchor and made sail ; washed lower and orlop decks. At noon the body of Tarlow Chow, E. by S. 6 miles.

P p 2

Light

1793. November. Monday 4.	Light airs and cloudy. At 5 asses ears S. ¼ W. 6 miles. A. M. At 9 fresh breezes and cloudy: split the fore-sail, clewed it up to repair, rove double sheets and proper tacks.
Tuesday 5.	Ditto weather. At 6 Pedro Blanco, N. N. E. 5 leagues. A. M. At 3 in 2d reefs. At 9 split the main-top-sail, clewed it up to repair. Half-past 7 tacked down top-gallant-yards, carried away the mizen-top-sail-yards, unbent the sail, sheeted home main-top-sail. At noon got up a jury mizen-top-sail-yard, and set the sail. Carpenters making a mizen-top-sail-yard.
Wednesday 6.	Moderate and cloudy. P. M. unbent the fore-sail, and bent another; sounded in 23 fathoms water. At midnight in 3d reefs, and furled mizen-top-sail. At 3 A. M. set the mizen-top-sail; sail-makers making a new main-top-sail out of two sprit-sail courses. Half-past 10 tacked out 3d reefs. At noon got up a proper mizen-top-sail-yard. Pedro Blanco, E. S. E. 7 miles.
Thursday 7.	Ditto weather. P. M. unbent the mizen to repair, sail-makers as before, and repairing the fore-sail. A. M. tacked occasionally.
Friday 8.	Fresh breezes and cloudy. P. M. At 8 more moderate, out 2d reefs. At midnight tacked. A. M. carried away the jib-stay and hall-yards, spliced them: carpenters making a machine to make rope with.
Saturday 9.	Ditto weather. P. M. At 4 unbent the new fore-sail, and bent the old one. At 2 A. M. carried away the jib-tack, repaired ditto. At 5 carried away the main-top-gallant-sheet, spliced ditto, employed making rope.
Sunday 10.	Ditto weather. P. M. At 6 in 2d reefs: at 7 found the fore-top-mast sprung 5 feet above the cap, in 3d reef fore-top-sail, down fore-top-gallant-yard and mast. A. M. strong gales, down main and mizen-top-gallant-yards: at 4 in 4th reef fore-top-sail: at noon squally, furled the mizen-top-sail.
Monday 11.	Fresh gales and cloudy. P. M. At 4 wore ship: at 6 strong gales and hazy, with a heavy sea, handed fore-top-sail: at 8 heavy gales, handed main-top-sail, split the main-sail, set main-stay-sail, and handed part of the main-sail, the remainder having blown from the

yard:

yard: at 9 set main-top-sail: at half-past 9 set mizen-top-sail: at A. M. split main-top-sail, furled it, balanced and set mizen: at 3 set storm, fore and mizen-stay-sail: at 6 split main-stay-sail, hauled it down to repair: at half-past 8 set fore-top-sail, close reefed, unbent main-top-sail, and sent it down: at noon a heavy sea.

Fresh gales and cloudy. P. M. At 2 unbent the remainder of the main-sail, bent another main-top-sail, and set it close reefed. At 6 furled the fore-sail, bent another main-sail, and furled it. A. M. At 5 out 4th and 3d reefs fore-top-sail, and 3d reef main-top-sail, set mizen-top-sail, saw the land N. W. by W. loosed courses. At 8 found the main-top-mast sprung in the cap, out 2d reef mizen-top-sail. At noon the east end of the Great Lama, E. N. E. Asses Ears W. S. W. swayed up fore-top-gallant-mast.

Light breezes and fair. P. M. At 4 out all reefs: at 7 shortened sail and came to with the coasting anchor in 16 fathoms water, Cockerpow N. W. by W. A. M. At 9 weighed and made sail: at 11 in 2 reefs, tacked ship. At noon the Grand Ladrone, W. by E. a heavy swell.

Fresh breezes and clear. At 1 came to with the coasting anchor in 13 fathoms water, the Grand Lama, W. S. W. A. M. At 6 weighed and made sail: at 10 shortened sail and came to with the coasting anchor in 7½ fathoms water, Tarlow Chow, N. N. E.

Ditto weather. P. M. At 4 weighed and made sail; at half-past 4 came to with the coasting anchor in 7 fathoms water, Sam Coke, E. ½ S. A. M. Half-past 6 weighed and stood into Sam Coke. At 7 came to with the coasting anchor in 6 ¼ fathoms water, Sam Coke, E. S. E. 1 mile, got fore and main-top-gallant-masts upon decks: yawls watering.

Fresh breezes and hazy with rain. Sent the main-top-mast down, and another up; carpenters making a fore-top-mast out of the old main one, sent down the fore-top-mast, and cut it up, it being unserviceable in its proper use. A. M. Fiddled main-top-mast, and swayed up the yard: employed making rope.

Fresh

1793.
November.
Sunday 17. Fresh breezes with rain. Carpenters converting the main-top-mast into a fore one. A. M. Arrived the Clarence.

Monday 18. Moderate and cloudy. Dried fails, yawls watering, swayed up top-gallant-mafts, and fet up the rigging : yawls watering.

Tuesday 19. Moderate and hazy. P. M. Yawls as before, carpenters repairing the Clarence boat, fail-makers repairing the fore-fail, people making rope, failed the Clarence. A. M. Rove new fore and main-top-fail-braces : yawls watering.

Wednesday 20. Fresh breezes and fair. P. M. At 5 loofed and hoifted top-fails, fired 4 fhot to bring to a veffel in fhore, fhe fhewed Englifh colours, fent a boat on board her. A. M. Muftered at quarters, found the fhip driving, dropt the beft bower, carpenters repairing the yawl.

Thursday 21. Fresh breezes and cloudy. P. M. At 1 fired a fhot and brought to a brig under American colours, fent an officer to examine her papers, and found fhe belonged to the ifle of France, named the Emilla, Dumift and Roufell, merchants on the faid ifland, laft from the N. W. coaft of America, with 271 fur fkins on board ; detained her as a prize, fent a petty officer and 7 men to take charge of her. At half-paft 1 weighed the beft bower. A. M. At 5 the prize fired 3 mufquets, fent a boat on board her, found her driving, fecured her with hawfers, &c. At 8 found our fhip driving, dropt our beft bower ; the yawl that was aftern of the prize was loft, the officer brought her ftern on board.

Friday 22. Fresh breezes. P. M. At 4 hove up the beft bower, employed making rope. A. M. Found the fhip driving, dropt the beft bower. Half-paft 7 ftruck top-gallant-mafts, made the hawfer, the prize was riding by faft to the fhip through the gun-room-port forward.

Saturday 23. Fresh gales and cloudy. P. M. Employed working up junk : at 5 anchored the Clarence. A. M. The Clarence drove, with 3 anchors, a-head : fail-makers repairing the fore-fail.

Sunday 24. Fresh breezes and clear. Sail-makers repairing the main-fail ; the Clarence weighed her anchors, fent her under the lee of Tarlow Chow for fhelter. A. M. Muftered at quarters.

Fresh

Fresh breezes and clear. People employed occasionally. A. M. Weighed the best bower, and parted the coasting cable, let go the small bower, yawl, and pinnace creeping for the end of the cable. Cast off the Prize.

1793.
November.
Monday 25.

Moderate and clear. Received 9 seamen and a boy from the Clarence; yawl and pinnace as before; sail-makers repairing courses. Departed this life Thomas Steward, seaman. A. M. Committed the body of the deceased to the deep.

Tuesday 26.

Ditto weather. P. M. Yawls and pinnace as before, creeping for the end of the cable, which they got; employed securing it. A. M. Sailed the Prize brig for the Typer, to land the prisoners at Macao.

Wednesday 27.

Light breezes and fair. P. M. At 5 hove up the best bower, and warped the ship to the coasting anchor, got the end of the cable on board, and weighed the anchor, made sail. At half-past 5 came to with the best bower in 7 ¼ fathoms water, Sam Coke, E. by S. 2 miles. A. M. Yawls watering, bent the coasting cable, the inner end to the anchor, washed below. Arrived the Emilla.

Thursday 28.

Moderate and cloudy. P. M. At 3 weighed and stood in for the watering island, but falling little wind came to again with the best bower in 5 fathoms water, Sam Coke, E. by S. sail-makers repairing the courses. A. M. Yawls watering.

Friday 29.

Fresh breezes and cloudy. P. M. At 3 weighed and stood nearer to Sam Coke. At 4 came to with the best bower in 6 fathoms water, body of Sam Coke, E. by S. 1 mile. A. M. Stayed the masts, and set up the rigging.

Saturday 30.

Fresh breezes and cloudy. Small boats watering, sail-makers repairing courses. A. M. Caulkers about the water ways.

December.
Sunday 1.

Ditto weather. Employed occasionally. A. M. Employed knotting yarns and making rope, sail-makers repairing main-top-sail. People employed occasionally.

Monday 2.

Fresh breezes and cloudy. Small boats watering the Clarence. A. M. Hoisted out the launch, sent a kedge anchor and hawser on board the Prize; carpenters repairing the pinnace.

Tuesday 3.

Moderate

1795.
December.
Wednesday 4.

Moderate breezes. Employed making rope, sailed the Prize from the Typer. A. M. Fresh gales and hazy. Sail-makers repairing the main-top-sail. Sailed the Clarence.

Thursday 5.

Moderate and hazy. Employed as before. A. M. Small rain, swayed up top-gallant-masts. At 11 the Clarence arrived from the Typer, with some English seamen from the Emilla Prize, sent the boat on board and took them out.

Friday 6.

Light breezes and thick foggy weather. Launch watering, carpenters repairing the boats. A. M. Half-past 8 weighed and made sail, tacked occasionally: passed by 3 Dutch ships.

Saturday 7.

Moderate breezes and pleasant weather. P. M. At 2 tacked: half-past 3 came to with the best bower in 14 fathoms water, the north end of Linton island, N. by W. south end E. N. E. anchored the Clarence. A. M. Washed decks: sailed the Clarence.

Sunday 8.

Light airs and clear. Launch watering, received 3 bullocks. A. M. killed them, weight 513lbs. launch watering.

Monday 9.

Light airs and cloudy. P. M. Received 11 bullocks, killed 4, weight 689lbs. A. M. Struck main-top-gallant-mast, and lowered the the main-yard, lifted the main rigging, to splice one of the shrowds, it being stranded in the wake of the service; sent the yawl on board the Warley Indiaman in the Offing.

Tuesday 10.

Moderate and hazy. Employed fitting the main shrowds. A. M. Passed by the Warley for Canton, employed staying the main-mast and setting up the rigging, anchored the Clarence. A. M. Swayed up the main-yard and rattled the rigging.

Wednesday 11.

Light breezes and clear. P. M. Sail-makers making skreens for the fore hatchway, sailed the Clarence. A. M. Received water per launch, carpenters repairing the cutter.

Thursday 12.

Ditto weather. P. M. Received wood and 6 bullocks. A. M. Launch watering, swayed up royal masts, people making nippers and rope, painters employed painting the cabin and cutter; arrived the Clarence.

Friday 13.

Light airs and fine. P. M. Received water. A. M. At 6 weighed and made sail, as did the Clarence, running towards the Bocca Tigris. Half-past 9 inclinable to calm, shortened sail, and came to

with

with the best bower in 6 fathoms water, veered ½ a cable the entrance of Bocca Tigris, N. N. W.

Fine weather.   At 3 P. M. weighed and made sail, tacked occasionally. *Saturday 14.* At 7 in tacking touched the ground, run the after guns forward, hoisted out the boats to tow, sent a boat to sound round the ship. Half-past 7 the Clarence anchored on our larboard bow, carried out a hawser to her, and hove on it, but finding her anchors came home, sent down royal and top-gallant-yards and royal masts on decks, struck top-gallant-masts, furled the sails, barred the ports in fore and aft, stocked the coasting anchor, and bent the stream cable to it, when a-ground the body of Langute, S. W. ¾ west, the north easter-most of Sama Chow islands, N. by W. the south westermost W. S. W. at dead low water having 15 feet the ship healed to port. A. M. Employed starting water, carried out the coasting anchor to the S. E. and hove a strain, but could not move her; started more water.   Half-past 11 the Clarence weighed and anchored on our larboard, killed 5 bullocks, weight 640lbs.

Light breezes and pleasant weather.   P. M. The Clarence hauled *Sunday 15.* alongside and received our small bower anchor and 2 cables, slipt the end from the hawse, and took it in at the larboard stern port.   Half-past 3 the Clarence hauled off and laid the anchor to the eastward, hove taut: at ¼ flood slipt the stream, and hove off to the eastward in 6 fathoms water.   A. M. Fidded top-gallant and royal masts, swayed up the yards, Clarence weighing the coasting anchor.

Light breezes and fine weather.   Hauled the Clarence alongside and *Monday 16.* took the coasting anchor from her.   A. M. At 7 weighed and made sail, half-past came to with the best bower in 5 fathoms water, moored ship, the north fort at the entrance of Bocca Tigris, N. south fort N. W. by N. a small rocky island at the entrance, N. N. W. received 1733lbs. of beef.

Ditto weather.   Punished Francis Otto, seaman, with 12 lashes, for *Tuesday 17.* theft; exercised great guns, sail-makers making a quarter-deck awning.

Q q

Light

1793.
December.
Wednesday 18.

Light breezes. Received water. A. M. Sail-makers as before; gunners thumming a screen for the magazine; saluted a mandarin of the first order with 3 guns on his coming on board.

Thursday 19. Weather as yesterday. Saluted a mandarin with 3 guns on his leaving the ship; passed by a ship under English colours. A. M. Arrived 4 ships bound to Canton, viz. Ceres, Abergavenny, Osterley, and Lord Thurlow; sent a boat on board them.

Friday 20. Light breezes and clear. People making stoppers; sail-makers repairing the Clarence's fore-top-sail: exercised the guns.

Saturday 21. Moderate and cloudy. Got the guns out of the cabbin, completed 6 on the quarter deck and 2 on the fore-castle. A. M. Half-past 9 weighed with a pilot on board to take us up the river; received 1053lbs. fresh beef.

Sunday 22. Light breezes and cloudy. Employed working through the Bocca Tigris; 2 forts saluted us with 3 guns each, we returned equal number, they likewise displayed the colours over the guns and drew themselves up in ranks: at 5 shortened sail, and came to with the small bower in 5 fathoms water, veered ¾ of a cable, the north point of Sketop island N. N. W. a pagoda on the said island N. W. A. M. Sail-makers making a poop awning; people making stoppers.

Monday 23. Light breezes and clear. P. M. Weighed and made sail, half-past 2 anchored with the small bower in 6½ fathoms: veered ¼ of a cable, the north point of Sketop island N. N. W. ½ W. A. M. At

At anchor in Wampoa river.

3 weighed, out all boats to tow, which were assisted by 19 Chinese boats with another tow-rope; half-past 3 crossed the bar between 2 lines of boats full of lights; half-past 7 came to with the small bower in 6 fathoms; veered away and moored ship S. W. by S. and N. E. by N. a cable on the small bower to the ebb and ½ a cable to the flood, a square pagoda S. E. off shore 1½ cable, Wampoa town W. S. W. 2 miles; found here the Hindostan, Royal Charlotte, Osterley, Ceres, Earl of Abergavenny, and Lord Thurlow, English Indiamen; Jackall, Company's marine, and 2 Americans; received on board wood.

Light

Light breezes and clear. P. M. Employed occasionally. A. M. Read Mr. Ommancy's commissiom from the Lords of the Admiralty as 5th Lieutenant, but as Lieut. Cox's commission was vacant, Capt. Gower ordered him to act as 4th; read the order, and Mr. Tippet's acting order as 5th, likewise Mr. Warren's as 6th, also the articles of war, and Capt. Gower's orders to the ship's company: washed decks, arrived the Glatton.

Weather as before. People employed occasionally. A. M. Received 715lbs. of fresh beef: at noon part of the soldiers that attended the Ambassador to Pekin returned on board.

Ditto weather. P. M. and A. M. Carpenters fixing spare cabbins under the half deck.

Light breezes and hazy. P. M. Employed occasionally. A. M. People making rope; came along-side several country boats with the Ambassador's baggage, and 13 chests of presents for the ship's company from the Emperor of China.

Moderate and cloudy. P. M. Received water; employed stowing the Ambassador's wine; punished Peter Ashton and Richard Gur, seamen, with 12 lashes each, for disobedience of orders; Richard Manning, Wm. Tipple, Robert Edwards, and John Hogan, seamen, with 12 lashes each, for disobedience and drunkenness.

Light breezes and hazy. Employed stowing the after-hold. A. M. Received 595lbs. fresh beef.

Ditto weather. P. M. Manned ship for his Excellency Viscount Macartney, as did the Hindostan and Clarence: his Excellency was cheered by all the ships as he passed; at 2 he came on board, at 5 he left the ship. A. M. Employed fleeting the rigging: punished James Hervey and John Evans, seamen, with 12 lashes each, for disobedience of orders.

Light breezes and fair. Employed setting up rigging, and in the after-hold: cleared hause; sent 13 casks of beef and 7 of pork on board the Hindostan. A. M. Arrived the Lord Walsingham from England: sent 30 casks of beef and 25 of pork on board the Warley: employed in the hold.

1793.
December.
Tuesday 24.

Wednesday 25.

Thursday 26.

Friday 27.

Saturday 28.

Sunday 29.

Monday 30.

Tuesday 31.

Q q 2

Light

1794. January. Light breezes and fair. Employed in the hold: sent 13 casks of beef and 7 of Pork on board the Hindostan.

Thursday 2. Moderate and cloudy. P. M. Employed as before. A. M. Carpenters nailing battin in the hold to stow staves over: coopers setting up casks.

Friday 3. Fresh breezes and fair. P. M. Employed in the holds: fell overboard and was drowned Alexander Ramsey, seaman. A. M. Employed in the hold.

Saturday 4. Light airs and clear. Arrived the Hawke and Exeter from England. A. M. People employed occasionally; arrived the Henry Dundas from England.

Sunday 5. Ditto weather. People as necessary; received a boat load of water, arrived a Spanish ship, received a top-mast from the Ceres Indiaman. A. M. Employed in the after-hold, washed lower gun-deck.

Monday 6. Light breezes and fair. Employed in the after-hold: coopers repairing banacoes: punished Ralph Pilkinton, dragoon, with 12 lashes, for disobedience of orders, riotous behaviour, and drunkenness.

Tuesday 7. Moderate and cloudy. Received 3064lbs. of bread and some of the Ambassador's baggage. A. M. Bent sails, punished Henry Nicholls and John Smith, seamen, with 12 lashes each, for theft, and Benjamin Addison, marine, with 12 lashes, for insolence.

Wednesday 8. Ditto weather. Employed as necessary. A. M. Employed getting the baggage belonging to the Ambassador and suite on board: received on board wood.

Thursday 9. Light breezes and fair. Manned ship and saluted Lord Macartney with 15 guns on his coming on board, his suite likewise embarked; employed getting in the baggage. A. M. Cleared hause, and unmoored ship; at 11 weighed the small bower, and dropt a little lower down the river, and came to with the small bower; received 1600lbs. of fresh beef.

GLOSSARY.

GLOSSARY

OF

CHINESE WORDS.

CHINESE.	ENGLISH.
Tongau - - - - - - - -	Sugar.
Pytong - - - - - - - -	Ditto, moist.
Pyntong - - - - - - -	Sugar-candy.
Swee - - - - - - - - -	Water.
Lyangfwee - - - - - -	Ditto, cold.
Kiefwee - - - - - - -	Ditto, hot.
Pynfwee - - - - - - -	Ditto, ice.
Man-toa - - - - - - -	Bread.
Tchau - - - - - - - -	Tea.
Ttchau-woo - - - - -	Tea-pot.
Tchee-tanna (*in the northern pro-vinces*) - - - - - - -	} Eggs.
Kee-tanna (*in the southern pro-vinces*) - - - - - - -	} Ditto.
Yien - - - - - - - - -	Tobacco.
Yien-die - - - - - - -	Tobacco-pipe.
Jee-au - - - - - - - -	Fowls.
Yaut-zau - - - - - - -	Ducks.
Ly-fau (*in the northern provinces*)	Rice.

Faun-na

Rice.

CHINESE.	ENGLISH.
Faun-na (*in thofe about Hontchew province*) - - - - - - -	} Rice.
Mee (*fouthern provinces*) - - -	Ditto.
Joo-au - - - - - - - - -	Wine.
Samtchoo, *or* Sowtchoo - - -	Spirits.
Yeu-oa - - - - - - - -	Fifh.
Loa-boo - - - - , - - -	Turnips.
Chutz-yau - - - - - - -	Pepper.
Jifhimau - - - - - - -	To afk the name of a thing or place.
Chou-au - - - - - - - -	Good.
Boo-chou - - - - - - -	Bad.
Yinna - - - - - - - -	Salt.
Poit-zic - - - - - - -	General term for greens.
Tannau - - - - - - - -	Coals.
Yoong - - - - - - - -	A hawk.
Pyeng - - - - - - - -	Soldier.
Pyng - - - - - - - - -	Ice.
Quoitzau - - - - - - -	Chop-fticks for eating with.
Laatchoo - - - - - - -	Candle.
Tchooa - - - - - - -	Light.
Tzou-fhia - - - - - - -	Shoes, *in general.*
Chow-chow - - - - - -	Victuals *or* meat.
Chee-fanna - - - - - - -	To eat meats.
Kowaa - - - - - - - -	To broil.
Mann, Mann - - - - - -	Stop *or* wait.
Lobb, Lobb - - - - - -	Joining *or* coition.
Tziu - - - - - - - - -	Paper.
Jofh - - - - - - - - -	God *or* Deity.
Chinchin - - - - - - -	To fupplicate *or* pray.
Youwafs - - - - - - -	Furnace.
Too-paa - - - - - - -	A pagoda.
Tong-joo - - - - - - -	A fweet fpirit like rum-fhrub.

Chop-

CHINESE.	ENGLISH.
Chop-chop	To make haſte.
Foockee	Man.
Foockee-lou	Good-morrow, Sir.
Niodzaa	Milk.
Hoong	Cheeſe.
Toudzaa	Knife.
Ickoochop	Very beſt.
Icko	One.
Liaungko	Two.
Suangko	Three.
Soocko	Four.
Oocko	Five.
Leowcko	Six.
Shicko	Seven.
Packo	Eight.
Jowcko	Nine.
Sheego	Ten.
Sooee	Sleep.
Hongjoo	Red wine.
Tchau-wanna	A tea-cup.
Jeebau	2¼ cubits, *or* 1 yard.
Tyſhauſuee	Bed.
Mecoulaa	Have not *or* cannot.

FINIS.

www.ingramcontent.com/pod-product-compliance
Lightning Source LLC
Chambersburg PA
CBHW031152120726
47905CB00006B/1915